SUGAR
LAND
TEXAS

SUGAR LAND TEXAS

RIO DE LOS BRAZOS DE DIOS

George W. Barclay Jr.

iUniverse, Inc.
Bloomington

SUGAR LAND TEXAS
RIO DE LOS BRAZOS DE DIOS

iUniverse books may be ordered through booksellers or by contacting:

iUniverse
1663 Liberty Drive
Bloomington, IN 47403
www.iuniverse.com
1-800-Authors (1-800-288-4677)

ISBN: 978-1-4620-4230-2 (pbk)
ISBN: 978-1-4620-3902-9 (ebk)

Printed in the United States of America

iUniverse rev. date: 07/21/2011

═ LIST OF MAJOR CHARACTERS ═

SANDRA LERNER
Houston Criminal Defense Lawyer—Main Character Zoloft for bad dreams

DR. AUSTIN HALE
Forensic Pathologist—Sandra's Fiancé—ranch at Brazoria with oil

BOB BURRELL
Field Geologist for SROCO

SHERRY DEAGIO
Lawyer—Legal Department of SROCO

JACK DANIELS
SROCO helicopter pilot

MARIA TANTALIA
The boss—Granddaughter of Mafia Don. POB of USN and SROCO

PRINCE KAHLI
Co-owner of SROCO with Maria

WALLACE DEREK
(Dirk) STRONG Private Detective—Had Bypass—takes aspirin

HEIDI
Guide, Benedictine Monastery, Einsiedeln

BROTHER THOMAS TANTALIA
Monk, Benedictine Monastery

MIRIAM TRAVITAS (BAUTISTA)
Heir to Cuban gold

FREIDA ALLEGROMANDE
Drug widow—owns Pancho's Automotive

EVITA GARZA
Drug Queen—wife of General Emil Fernandez—good with knife

HE LI WU, PhD
Postdoctoral student USN

GENERAL HE WU
Commander China's PLA

GENERAL EMIL FERNANDEZ	*Colombian Rebel*
COLONEL WANG HOI	*Bodyguard of He Li*
HO CHI, PhD	*Professor of China Studies USN*
CHRISTY ISAAC PhD	*Professor of Arab Studies USN*
LI LE	*Houston Jade dealer at the Laughing Buddha Temple in Briar Forest*
JERRY BILLINGS	*Captain DPS—undercover narcotics*
PETER ROCKFORD PhD.	*Academic Geologist at USN—Most loved Professor 1993*
ILYSA STROMBOLI	*Agent CIA*
DR. JOY BURRELL M.D. PhD	*Psychiatrist, Bob's wife*
LEVITRA BATTENBERG PhD	*Professor of Asia Studies*
TISHA LAFEMME	*Private Detective at USN—has 3 ex-husbands. Loves "Peter" Rockford*
MISTY TANTALIA	*President of El Cyuga Bank—Maria's youngest sister*
DONALD TANTALIA	*Mafia Don retired to Sicily, Maria's father, calls every night*
SAM DEAGIO SR.	*Mafia capo retired to Costa Rica, Jerry's grandfather*
BILL RILEY DA	*Likes high yellow—married to Bette Tantalia—runs loose ship*
BOOKER WASHINGTON	*Sergeant—Top Cop Homicide—hired Cealis out of Texas Southern*
DEVINE SPARKS	*Criminal Law—Sandra's Associate—Miss Jamaica of 1986—long on brains*

OPAL HONY	*Chief ADA—Peaches and Cream with dirty mouth—drives yellow Ferrari*
RUTH SANCHEZ	*Nurse ER Del Arroyo—Divorced—Sandra's sister*
DR. TAMARA LEWINE	*Sandra's gynecologist*
DR. ROBERTA ALLEN DDS	*Sandra's dentist*
DR. REUBEN SANCHEZ	*Cardiovascular Surgeon at Del Arroyo*
DR. OII NU	*City-County Coroner and Forensic Pathologist*
ANGELLE EMANUEL, RN	*Supervisor, Del Arroyo*
DR. CHESTER FELL	*ER physician at Del Arroyo*
DR. GUADALUPE ALVAREZ	*Deceased Surgeon at Del Arroyo*
KAY BERKELEY	*Newspaper reporter, English, divorced from Winston*
JUANITA ALVAREZ	*Widow of Guadalupe*
NEVA BRAUN	*Sergeant Homicide North Patrol, many male friends*
OLINDA STARR	*Sergeant Homicide Northwest Patrol, spit and polish*
REGINALD DEWBERRY	*Sergeant Willow Bend Patrol—Head of HPD SWAT*
HERNAN COSTELLO	*Lieutenant Homicide Southeast Patrol—went to Milby High, football star*
SHEILA MELLONS	*Sergeant Vice, Exotic dancer and fashion model*
MIGUEL MONTALBAN	*Sergeant Vice, family man, pumps iron, body builder*

MICHAEL (Mickey) FINN

Deputy Sergeant—born to lose—property clerk—recycles drugs

ELTON (Happy) EARLY

Sergeant Homicide—Northeast Patrol—friend of Micky, bad news

JAMES (Jim) BEAM

Sergeant DPS helicopter pilot

JUDGE LOIS MORRISON

56ᵗʰ Criminal District Court

JUDGE EVA PETRARCELLI

104ᵗʰ Criminal District Court

CHRISTY ISAAC Ph.D.

Academic Archaeologist at USN—Holy Land Expert

MAMBO NIGERA Ph.D.

Head Department of Anthropology at USN, Comparative Religion

AMY OMIKAMI Ph.D.

Astrophysics and Cosmology at USN, Consultant at NASA

WINSTON BLOOD Ph.D.

Professor of History at USN—Sandra's ballroom dance partner

SYLVIA PASTEUR Ph.D.

Professor Biology at USN

ARISTOTLE PLOTINUS Ph.D.

Professor of Metaphysics at USN

EROS ZENOVENUSETTI Ph.D.

Professor of Epistemology at USN

MORTON SALTER Ph.D.

Professor of Engineering at USN

DR. FATIMA HUSSAIN MD, Ph.D.

Forensic Pathologist and Molecular Biologist at USN

HO CHI Ph.D.

Professor of China Studies at USN

MAGDALENA

(Maggie) de MUERTA Ph.D. Professor of South American History at USN

BOB WALLER

Deceased ADA—from Big Spring

RENE' DESCARTE

Inspector of Homicide HPD

GENERAL TUFFAN MEAN *CO*	*of 44th Armored Infantry Division, US Army*
GENERAL TRUDY GRITS *CO*	*of First Armored Infantry Brigade*
EVON GALBREAUX	*Drug widow—owns Claud's Automotive*
REX (0009	*DEA agent Guadalajara—has blood hound*
BETTE RILEY	*Bill's wife and sister of Maria—into competitive ballroom*
JEANANNE RUSSELL	*Sexy black exotic dancer and Teller at El Cyuga Bank*
LI CHEN	*Exotic dancer—undercover narcotics DPS*
DORIS RUSSELL	*Belly dancer—undercover narcotics DPS*
ELOISE JOHNSON	*Bill Riley's personal legal secretary*
AUGUSTUS GALBREAUX	*CPA*
JÉSUS POSADAS	*Deceased—former drug king SE Houston*
PRESIDENTE RAUL PORTAPOTILLO	*Deceased President of Mexico*
GENERAL RUIZ PORTAPOTILLO	*Deceased owner of the Mexicana Norte Luxury Hotel in Houston*
GENERAL LUPE LOPEZ	*Commandante—Mexican Judicial Police, deceased*
RENE' LOPEZ	*Lupe's widow*
WANDA TOWNSEND	*Escort Service—high class Madam*
RUBY REDMON	*Owns Ruby's Bar out by the docks*
RAFAEL CARO QUINTERO	*Mexican Drug Lord and Bandito*
ANGEL CARO QUINTERO	*Rafael's brother*

FATHER VILLA — *Deceased Mexican Priest and drug trafficker*

FATHER CERVANTES — *Cuban Bishop into drugs big time*

FATHER ESCOBAR — *Colombian Priest and drug trafficker*

TINA QUINTERAS DEAGIO — *Business Manager of the Water Mellon Man Club, Caesar's wife*

CAESAR DEAGIO — *Runs Deagio Bail Bonds*

DESI CARTENEGRO — *Owner of Water Mellon Man Club—Cuban Mafia*

RICO CARBELLO — *Now deceased—Pistolero for Desi Cartenegro, Cuban Mafia*

MARCI GALBREAUX — *ADA—Maria's daughter*

ROXANNE STRONG — *Bombshell Stripper-Dirk's ex-wife—would cost an arm and leg*

JULIE STRONG — *Dirk's unmarried pregnant daughter—University senior and Exotic dancer*

REVEREND JESUS MUHAMMAD — *Lady Mullah of Shiite Baptist Church*

DR. AL-MEHDI — *Physician—runs Quick Doc. Immam of Shiite Baptist Church*

DR. VLADIMER PUSSKE' — *World famous Transplant Surgeon*

DR. RICHARD LANGLEY — *Deceased ER physician of Bayou Den Hospital*

LYNETTE DEMATEREZ — *Deceased Secretary of Juan Baptista*

JUDGE WILLIAM LOWMAN — *Justice of Peace—slow but sure*

JUDGE XAVIER VARGUS — *Justice of Peace, in State pen*

JUDGE BUZZ ALLRED	*Justice of Peace—Always rules suicide*
JESSIE WHITE	*Constable Houston Heights—into drugs, sex slaves*
JOSEPH STALIN	*Johan Milkozavitch back from the grave*
SAM PABLO HUSTON	*Councilman—Houston Heights—takes bribes*
JUAN BAPTISTA	*Deceased Mexican lawyer*
CARL BRIBEY	*Lieutenant Detective—North Patrol—half crook*
DR. JACK STRONGBACH	*Transplant surgeon—agreed to pay Julie's child support*
AL HAWALLA	*Air Service picks up contraband off the Cuban Submarine*
NATADA KLODYASKA	*Syracuza's Abattoir—Russian Mafia*
CARMALETA POSADAS	*Rich widow of Jésus*
ELIZABETH BORDEN	*Deceased senior ADA from Muleshoe*
VACA CABEZ de VACA	*Wife of deceased President of North State Bank*
DR. RAUL CAPISTRANO	*Administrator Del Arroyo, money launderer for Cuban Mafia*
JOTTE' JALOPENA	*Abbey Lane look-alike. Great singer at the Water Mellon Man Club*
DR. SIGMOID FREID	*Austrian-American Psychiatrist—Sees Sandra monthly for nightmares*
DR. HELGA SCHMIDT	*Resident Psychiatrist at Del Arroyo-wears Butch*

CEALIS PARKS — *Rene' Descarte's legal secretary & the hostess with the mostest*

ELLA WYATTS — *Sergeant HPD CSI—tells secrets*

SCARLET SWYZE — *Sergeant DPS undercover narcotics, Rita Hayworth look-alike*

PENELOPE (Penny) BROWNRIG — *Freelance Australian Photographer and reporter—talks outback*

DR. HARVEY CUSHING — *Chief of Neurosurgery at Del Arroyo, hypomanic*

UZI KALASHNIKOV — *Owner of Golden Apple—Russian Mafia*

CISSY BURGER — *Secretary—Israeli Intelligence*

PATSY REDMON RN — *Supervisor—West Mean MASH*

DR. JENNIFER JAUREZ — *Forensic Psychiatrist*

LIEUTENANT SHIRLEY BLOOM — *Male detective at NE Patrol—hates Shirley*

GENERAL LI SHAN — *Burmese War Lord in Shan Hill country*

ANTHONY PARIGELLO — *Sandra's law associate*

TONTO — *Nehautl Indian trail guide with 12 wives and burros*

GENERAL JOANN JOHNSON — *USAFR, Ellington Field (former test pilot and Astronaut at NASA)*

SAM DEAGIO JR. — *Owner Sam's Gym and Ball Room*

OZMA BEN LADIN — *Bodyguard of Prince Kahli*

AE-IOU — *Hey you—Bodyguard of Prince Kahli*

A. FULLER BOTTLE — *Trial Lawyer, suing Sandra for malpractice*

BETTY	*Sandra's Legal Secretary*
QUETZALCOATL	*Lives on Venus, Aztec Messiah, feathered serpent god*
NASA	*National Aeronautics and Space Administration (Houston)*
USN	*University of Saint Nicholas*
SROCO	*Saudi Royal Oil Company*
POB	*President of the Board of Directors, Maria*

FORWARD

Houston Heights, Texas
8 A.M., Saturday, December 14, 1993
Fair, no storm clouds
Temperature 75/44°

Captain Jerry Billings DPS had been married in the remote past and preferred separate apartments to living as a couple. Two really couldn't live cheaper than one, if one were an impulse buyer. All men when they reached a magic age thought owning a $40,000 BASS RIG was a rite of passage to middle age, and it was so in East Texas. They watched professional football religiously, and wouldn't go to church or spare a pence for Saint Peter.

Jerry was Catholic and divorced. If she got married again, that would be adultery in the eyes of the Catholic Church. The Pope, John Paul himself, would excommunicate her, forbade her the sacraments, and spoil her chance for Purgatory and Paradise in the hereafter. Paradise was Persian for walled garden.

When she was happy, she never thought about a hereafter, but when she was depressed or worried, she pictured herself shoveling coal in hell and a red devil with a forked tail and pitchfork standing behind her. She surmised every divorced Catholic felt the same. Protestants didn't believe in Purgatory, and Atheist didn't believe in hell. WOW! Every Italian (Sicilian) she knew was Catholic. Italy and Mexico were the two most Catholic nations in the world. At least the Mexican illegals selling us dope, crossing our borders, and taking our lower paid jobs were Catholics. You couldn't talk any sense with an Islamic Jihadist. Paradise was a walled off oasis with 70 virgins.

*　　*　　*

When Dirk didn't come home last evening, Jerry checked with his answering service, and his cell phone and beeper were out of range. The lady at the answering service unsolicitedly dropped a hint that Dr. Joy Burrell, Psychiatrist, was at the same place as Dirk, and she couldn't be reached either. Dirk's bass boat and SUV were gone from the garage. So she deducted that Dirk and Joy went bass fishing and decided to spend the night.

She called the county dispatcher in Brazoria County who gave her the home phone number of Warden James Tharp who didn't get in until 9 P.M. and told her that Dirk and some blond stuck his SUV in a marsh. He heard him racing his motor and spinning his wheels. He figured Dirk and the lady would spend the night in an old house place and call a tow truck the next morning. Jerry thanked Warden Tharp and explained she was inordinately concerned about their "daughter", but Dirk being a policeman and all could take care of himself. Actually, she did feel better that Dirk was all right, but of Dr. Joy Burrell, she was suspicious.

Jerry ate breakfast, put on denim, attached 0.32 Cal. back and leg guns, brushed her hair and teeth, fixed her face, and drove her red Mitsubishi sports car over to Sandra's apartment to see Devine' about Sandra, the courthouse, and Dr. Joy Burrell, the Psychiatrist. Normally, she would drive her patrol car with siren and flasher on and show off, but she was concerned about how the world was turning.

Jerry had a U.S. Army Colt 45 given her by her ex-husband before he joined the U-2 pilots. It held a loaded clip and an empty chamber, so she had to chamber a round before firing. Unlike the Glock and Beretta, it had a thumb safety when it was chambered and ready to fire. You didn't have to chamber a round with a revolver, and a man good with a knife was faster than either at 20 feet. Dirk carried a balanced throwing knife strapped to his leg, but she didn't. She was on the Olympic pistol team in law school and DPS Lady Champion.

*   *   *

"Come in, it's unlocked," yelled Devine' before Jerry could go for her key. Only Deviné, Jerry, and Austin Hale had keys to Sandra's apartment.

She found Devine' lying flat on her back with both legs up on three pillows reading *Mutiny on the Bounty*. Her briefcase and legal briefs lay nearby, and pop top cans of Diet Pepsi and Slim Fast were on the lamp stand by the head of her bed. A tennis ball can and rolled toilet tissue were under the foot of the bed.

"Deviné, did you hurt your back, for goodness sake?" asked Jerry.

Deviné, embarrassed, smiled and whispered, "don't tell anybody. I'm trying to get pregnant."

Jerry, who had never enjoyed the pregnancy experience, laughed. "If you're not on the pill and ovulate and there are sperm swimming around, you'll get pregnant. Sperm swim upstream. Every male ejaculate has a million all fighting to get that little egg."

"I'm giving them a gravity advantage," replied Deviné, proudly. She hadn't been out of bed for 24 hours.

"You can't feel it when you ovulate? Boy! I can. If it's on the right, I think I have appendicitis."

"I've never felt ovulation, and I was too early to have a positive urine."

"Who's the lucky guy? You don't have any black male friends."

"The guy wasn't black, and I loved all three, but I had my favorite, and he died trying. He wanted a son badly to carry on his work."

Jerry didn't have to think. She went to Donald Tantalia's funeral. Nobody mentioned he died in the saddle. Devine' was not present at his Rosary. She was *persona non grata*. "You might as well tell me the other two. Did Don lay you on the sea wall at Galveston?"

"They are secrets. Why did you ask about the Galveston Sea Wall? Misty said it was a joke," asked Deviné. As long as she didn't admit it,

Jerry wouldn't know for sure. Any lawyer knew that. That was the reason for the Miranda warning.

Lie to your lawyer. Lie to the court. Lie to your fellow convicts and parole board. Texas had 20,000 recidivist prisoners in the State Penitentiary at Huntsville, and all lied. Just ordinary people in their daily conversations lie 95% of the time, and everybody lies under oath. It's okay for lawyers and preachers to lie. They get paid for lying.

Society would fall apart if people went around telling truth.

*　　*　　*

Jerry went to Sandra's windows and looked out over northwest Houston, the loop, and uptown Galleria shopping area with multiple high-rises and hotels, etc. She could see River Oaks and Buffalo Bayou. Even though it was Saturday, cars and shoppers were crowding up the place. She turned back to Deviné.

"You're not going anywhere at all?"

"That's right. I'm trying to get pregnant," replied Devine' adamantly.

"Devine' tell me about Dr. Joy Burrell, the Psychiatrist. I don't keep up with what's going on at the University," suggested Jerry.

*　　*　　*

Dirk worried about Jerry and wondered whether truth or lie was best. He'd tell the truth and leave out Dr. Joy Burrell. She'd feel sorry, but if she knew Joy was along, wow, she'd get angry. Women all felt insecurity and didn't trust other women with their man of the moment. Except for drunk driving, love triangles accounted for most traumatic deaths in modern civilized societies. The two most dangerous calls a policeman made were traffic stops and late night domestic quarrels between husband and wife. By nature, men had more extramarital affairs and were apt to be intoxicated. Rule Number One: never leave a loaded gun around the house where the wife can find it and never never leave it in the bedroom.

Dirk left Joy off at the Braeswood LUX without making another date. She knew about Jerry and understood.

CHAPTER 1

Houston, Texas
December 12, 1993

"Jésus is back," explained Carmaleta Posadas, trembling. She had just moved in 806 at the Granada high-rise next to Evita and Frieda.

Both women, confused, sat speechless.

Carmaleta continued, "He's sitting in the living room of our old house on Dewberry, drinking a beer, and watching sports on **ESPN**."

Evita, skeptical, asked, "Are you sure? Maybe you dreamed it."

"I know it's crazy, but I'm sure. It's been ten years since I saw him, and he's been dead eight months. They buried him under concrete in seven iron caskets at Saint Monica's."

"What did he say?" asked Frieda.

"Just, 'hello Carm, remember me?'"

"I'm going to call your brother, Hernan. He'll know," replied Frieda.

"No! I'm going down there next. Jésus and Hernan were close. Jésus and I were cousins, and we married outside the church. That's a family secret. His mother and my mother were sisters. I can't go back home. I bought Juan Baptista's home from his estate. That's the first place Jésus would go. Juan was his lawyer and best friend. They flew together."

*   *   *

Brazoria County Court
Angleton, Texas
8 A.M., Thursday, December 12, 1993
Warm, few clouds

"Next case."

"Wallace Derek Strong. Charges: Shooting at running deer while standing on highway. Public intoxication. No previous offense."

Dirk was dressed and ready to leave. If you pleaded guilty and paid your fine in cash, they'd not enter it on a rap sheet and close the case with a warning. He saw nobody around when he drew down on the deer, and he drank three swallows of Old Taylor after unloading his service revolver at the fleeing deer.

"How does the defendant plea?"

"Guilty, your honor," spoke up Dirk's lawyer, Freeman Jackson.

*   *   *

Dirk knew he wasn't supposed to shoot at a deer from the road.

When he and Mr. Jackson arrived at Hale's gate on Hale Road, the doe decoy was still in the same place. The game warden was somewhere out in the bush watching.

"This road is closed at the river because the bridge collapsed. There's a few black settlements back in the woods on the left, maybe an African Baptist Church, and an abandoned fish and recreation club on the left at the river. That's where Captain Billings DPS and lawyer Sandra Lerner found the mutilated body of Sergeant Bobby Crawford from Houston and shot at an alligator that tore off his leg," said Mr. Jackson, as a matter of fact.

"Yeah, I'm into that investigation. He along with his patrol car were dumped down here," replied Dirk, ho! hum!

"That barbed wire on our right goes completely around Hale's property. It starts back there and runs five miles north to the back fence which goes down to the river. It's probably down in places. The easiest thing to do is hire a fencing crew to run the line. Since the oil wells were switched off and they stop running cows, nobody's been back there to check. Absentee landlords don't keep up a place. County and school taxes eat 'em up. If you go to the tax appraiser's office, that old house is valued at $50,000. They put a cap on the percent they could levy, and the appraisers upped the value, and the taxes got higher not less. Now, they are trying to cap punitive damages in civil cases. Small town juries love to soak the corporations and rich people, like doctors, etc." commented Mr. Jackson.

A crushed shell road, now overgrown, started at the gate and ran off passed a dilapidated farm house and headed northeast into the woods, mostly cypress and ancient huge gnarled oak covered by Spanish Moss. **Swamp!** thought Dirk. There were a few pine, sweet gum and holly, but to set out Superior Loblolly he'd have to have it clear cut and bulldozed which would cost too much up front to make it profitable. You couldn't hire people to bulldoze a swamp, too many water moccasins, mosquitoes, and alligators. There was a lock on the front door of the farm house and a rusted tractor under a collapsed barn in back.

"I don't plan to drive any further. I'll give you the keys, and you can come back in a jeep with a wench. I'd bring a buddy. You get bogged down in there, and you'll have to wench out. The rest is swamp, has all sorts of game, and about a dozen old strippers that were shut down years ago when oil went down to $10 a barrel. All the wells around here are over salt domes about five or six thousand feet. They claim 60% of the oil and 80% of the gas is still down there, but as long as the Arabs keep it cheap, the majors won't touch it, and the independents went broke. The only people making any money now are the Mexican illegals. They plant marijuana in patches and camp out all up and down this river. They travel by boat at night. Somebody reported they have a homemade submarine that looks like a big alligator." Mr. Jackson chuckled and continued.

"This place was one of the old Austin 300, and they had slaves and raised sugarcane. I've never gone back there, but you can see pilings of a previous steam boat dock and slave cabins. Every plantation owner had a kiln, and they made their own bricks. All that has *GONE WITH THE WIND*. You close your eyes, and you can see Howard Keel and

Ava Gardner, and that old black dude singing *OLD MAN RIVER*. That's what it was like until June 16, 1865 when they freed the slaves. There's still a bunch around here living in the woods. Sometimes you got time drive out White Oak Road to the White Oak Baptist Church. It's the oldest church in Texas and goes back to 1836. Before that everything was Catholic."

CHAPTER 2

After sharing the blanket with Devine' two nights, Austin announced he had bought a house in Sugar Land and was moving his household belongings from New Orleans so he could keep an eye on his new clinic under construction and line up some super specialist to join him, clinical research types with academic backgrounds who would take patient referrals, lecture to faculties and students, and conduct ongoing funded research programs in multiple specialties. Academics that were comfortable with juggling three balls at once.

He thanked her for her hospitality and great sex and would invite her out as soon as he got his new house straightened and telephone installed. He bought a new Compac Presario and recommend she do the same.

"You need any help?" asked Deviné, eagerly.

"Oh, I'm sorry. I've already accepted Dr. Joy Burrell's kind offer. Thanks just the same. Has Cealis already left for work? I'd like to thank her too."

"Sorry! Cealis left early to buy Dunkin' Doughnuts and make coffee for conference at the courthouse. I'll tell her. Please call. Sandra should be back in another week. They're stuck in Dubai."

*   *   *

Devine' was early to Bill Riley's morning skull session. Cealis was doing her thing. Devine' took Sandra's seat on Mr. Riley's right and studied Sandra's list.

Cealis giggled and asked, "Is it true that Pathologist are into necrophilia?"

5

Devine' was offended. After two nights of unprotected sex with Austin, she had become fond of him and hated to see him leave, but knew it was inevitable. She could see what Sandra liked about Austin. He was a stud, tall, and handsome. She smiled and answered, "That's what they say. There is an afterlife."

"Austin licks pussy," commented Cealis, giggling. "After you went to sleep, he crawled in bed with me."

"You're lying. Where were you?"

"In Sandra's extra bedroom."

Sheila Mellons and Miguel Montalban came in and sat at the end of the table, then Judges' Eva Petrarcelli and Lois Morrison, Sergeant Booker Washington, Inspector Rene' Descarte and lastly Bill Riley DA took a seat at the head.

"Look whose here, Deviné," said Bill Riley DA, cheerfully.

"I have a doctor's appointment," replied Deviné, sarcastically. By now everybody knew she had a passionate affair until Bill's father-in-law, Donald Tantalia. Devine' was off the pill and was carrying the sperm of three potent males, Bill, Donald, and Austin. It was too early for a pregnancy test, but Bill got the message. "May we discuss my cases first?" Devine' glanced at Sandra's list.

Bill could dismiss any he wished. He was responsible only to the voting public. It's better to let ten guilty men go free than convict one innocent.

"May I interrupt," asked Sergeant Sheila Mellons.

Devine' frowned, but Bill said, "Surely, you got something new?"

"Carmaleta Posadas moved in the Granada high-rise and said Jésus is back and staying at their old home on Dewberry."

Everybody knew of Jésus Posadas. He was infamous. They'd buried him in 7 steel caskets and poured concrete on top three months ago.

"He's an E.T.," commented Rene' Descarte. "We need to put a tail on him. We'll have to stake his heart next time."

There was silence. "Maybe old Jésus pulled a switch, and Lupe shot the wrong guy. I smell a conspiracy. Jésus was killed right after Archbishop

Jésus Llano was assassinated in a drug shootout on the airport tarmac in Guadalajara. Where's Opal? She's never missed work."

Nobody knew Jésus, and Opal had taken a day off without calling Bill. She'd called in to Eloise and said she was shopping for a house in Sugar Land with an old flame, Dr. Austin Hale, who she knew from before in Brazoria.

Bill said, "Sheila, I'm assigning Jésus to you and Miguel. It's best you work as a pair. Jésus is a legend around these parts. It seems everybody's heard of him, but no one has seen him alive. Follow him wherever he goes and keep Booker posted. Put a bug on your car, so the dispatcher can track you. Carmaleta and Jésus were separated years before his murder. Juan Baptista, deceased, was his lawyer, and Lieutenant Hernan Costello was his cousin. Also lawyers Percy Lovett and Frank Bagetti, 3800 Main, owe Jésus $5,000,000 in cash plus interest. A Mrs. Cecile Black is secretary to Mr. Bagetti, and Barbara Quick is Percy Lovett's law partner. Before his untimely death Jésus was crime boss of southeast Houston." Bill turned to Deviné, "Please make it brief. I'm due in court in ten minutes."

Devine' was surprised. "Anything I have will take longer than ten minutes."

"Why don't you just put off Sandra's cases until Opal shows up. I can't remember all that stuff. Lists can be subpoenaed. They are prompt notes, remember Oliver North? Fiction becomes fact to a jury, if they are placed in evidence. Take my advice. Don't make notes. Civil trial lawyers love them. They will subpoena any and all notes when they sue you. Don't shred notes, ever. Look at Arthur Anderson. Obstruction of justice! It's best just to file notes away in the waste basket of memory and concentrate on the police record at the trial. Every policeman on the case files a signed record. That's what the jury wants to know, just the facts."

CHAPTER 3

Sugar Land, Texas was close to number one and offered proximity to downtown Houston in an all white neighborhood in a country club setting. Homes were $250,000 and up and were typically two story, four bedroom, five baths, LDK, study and double and triple garages with swimming pool option. All additions had golf course, lake, park, jogging and cycling paths. Most schools were in walking distance, and there were extensions of five major universities and all the Texas Medical Center hospitals. Except for diverse professionals it was lilly white. It was a place where everybody would like to live, but most couldn't afford. They were the real producers, movers, and shakers of the American upper middle class, and deserved the best teachers, schools, hospitals, community universities, and gracious living. For all but the exceptional few (upper 3%) it was the American Dream. It was a city of the "Almost rich."

Pearland across the county line, however, was not as new, rich and exclusive and had minorities and Mexicans, but like Friendswood, Richmond and Katy it was less expensive, and crime was less than in Houston US 610 loop (inner city).

*   *   *

Dr. Austin Hale, Chief of Medicine and Pathology at Charity in New Orleans, remembered Opal who was special state's attorney at his brother's, Jerry, trial. She was bright, intelligent, peaches and cream, and had nice teats and ass. Like Ty Ty Walden in *God's Little Acre*, she made him want to get on his hands and knees and lick something. After they picked out a nice house, he was going to fuck her.

Unknown to Opal, he'd promised Dr. Joy Burrell, who, like he, needed a library and work space. Dr. Burrell was a well known Academic in Psychiatry and would add value and prestige to his Sugar Land clinic now under construction.

Dr. Tamara Lewine, an Obstetrician and Gynecologist in South Houston, was a Jewish *Magna Cum Laude* from Harvard that did her Internship and Residency at Charity in OBGYN. She was a star in her own right, but took charity seriously and opened her practice in an all black neighborhood in Houston. He had sent her a note of his intentions, but had not received an answer. Knowing Tamara he knew she was thinking about his invitation. At New Orleans she was into same sex, but definitely was not gay. She had a mystique and loved fishing as a hobby.

CHAPTER 4

Barclay Theater
University of Saint Nicholas
12 noon, Thursday, December 12, 1993

Dr. Mambo Nigera was at the lectern.

"I consulted with Sheriff Herra in Brazoria County about the Karankawa Indians who were massacred at Jones Creek by the Austin Colony, and if any were still alive. He said the only Indian he knew about was old Bezoar about a mile north of the Brazoria Nuclear Power Plant back in the woods only approachable by water. He thought Bezoar was a Pentecostal because he spoke in tongues.

"I'll be ready to show my Brazos River camp house a week after this coming Saturday, $50,000 for the house and $300,000 for 100 acres. You get full mineral rights, and it has never been drilled for gas and oil. Cash, please! You can negotiate terms with your friendly loan officer.

"Today, we'll have four lectures. That will give us 15 minutes each. Dr. Battenberg is back from New Delhi and will lecture on Great Britain. Dr. Blood will continue with the Russians. Dr. Peter Rockford will begin a series on pre-historic Europe, and Amy will keep us abreast of the Cosmos, Uncertainty, Complexity, and Chaos."

"Levitra."

Dr. Levitra Battenberg wrote on the green board. **TARA, WHITE MARE, HUMAN SACRIFICES, CELTS, DRUIDS, BOGS, LONDINIUM, HADIAN'S WALL, CONSTANTINE I, ANGLES, SAXONS, SAINT COLOMBO, WHISKEY, AND LOCH NESS**.

"The Druid priests forbade writing to protect their secrets. Any prehistory before the Romans had to be word of mouth and legend. The same over Europe. We get our prehistory from Archeologists, so I'll leave prehistory to Peter. There's one I have to tell. The Irish Celts had their king have sex with a white mare, and they butchered the mare and made stew. The capital was Tara, like *Gone With the Wind*.

"The priests selected the strongest, tallest, and most athletic male, bound and blindfolded him, knocked him in the head and pushed him in the bog. On Halloween they sacrificed a virgin (young female).

"Ireland and Russia sell and burn peat for fuel. It's about 60% carbon, but you have to dry it first. It's cheaper than wood, coal, and natural gas. Many of the farmers until this day don't have windows, and their houses are whitewashed stucco with thatched roofs. They burn the peat in the center of the room, and it smokes up the place. There are about 60-70 million Irish in the United States and Canada. Ronald Reagan and Bill Clinton are Irish. Senator Ted Kennedy is Irish. There're probably more Irish than Scots, English, and Germans all put together.

"The Welch, Irish and Scots are Celts while the English are a potpourri of Angeles, Saxons, Vikings, and Normans. The Romans ran England 300 years, and left us London, York, Chester, and Hadrian's Wall where 15 generations of Romans lived and spread Latin and the Roman Catholic Church. In fact, Constantine I (the Great) was elected Emperor at York while fighting the Scots at 18 when his father was killed in battle.

"There's no way Maria can fly our tour group west without changing planes at Heathrow. Heathrow buses their standbys to a nearby Hilton Hotel surrounded by London's largest Cricket stadium, Islamic Mosque, and Commons (public park). The taxis are two English Pounds ($US4) to downtown, Buckingham Palace, Harrods's, KFC, and McDonald's. A dinner for one in London is about twenty pounds, and you pay extra for water. Tea comes with the meal. In Paris it's $US 70, and they give you a whole bottle of great French wine. Everywhere in Europe you pay extra for water, and if you want ice, WOW! They stick it to you. The alternative is Mexico and South America. You get the shits down there, if you drink their water and eat their ice. There are no free public toilets in Europe except at ESSO, McDonalds, and KFC.

"The most important thing is that English drive on the left. So do the Indians, Japanese, and all former English colonies except Burma, United States, and Canada. Please don't step off the curb while waiting to cross the street. You go to SEA where they drive on the right, and the steering wheel is on the right, you can bet they bought it second hand from Japan. Japanese cars get low mileage, and they last forever.

"You've heard the English expression, 'Rob Peter to pay Paul' and 'Give a pence to Saint Peter.' They were referring to Saint Peter's Cathedral in Rome. This was after King Henry the VIII excommunicated the Pope, seized all Catholic properties, and ran off the priests. Catholic priests were like roaches. You couldn't keep them out.

"I had a lawyer next door that drove to Mass at 7 AM every morning, and I'd whisper, 'thank God for Henry the VIII.'

"The English got civilized by the Romans, and the Scots and Irish did not. Their greatest legacies were coins, baths, and laws. The Romans invented property law, private property, marriage to one woman, divorce, and inheritance. That's civilized! Like all other large cities, London had plagues, fires, and war. London is the largest and arguably the greatest city in Europe.

"Londinium was garrisoned as a fortified port in (50 c.e.-410 c.e.) by the Roman Empire. England had no riches to exploit, and it was not essential to the defense of Rome. They were easily tamed and furnished manpower for the Roman Legions. When the Roman's left in 410 a.c.e., the Catholic Church was established, and the priest could read and speak Latin.

"Romans planned and built Londinium like Rome. They chose an east-west river narrow at one point for a north-west bridge. The Thames was deep enough for ocean going ships.

"The Celts retaliated. In 60 c.e. a warrior Queen Boudicca leading 100,000 warriors, many in chariots, slaughtered 80,000 Romans from Chester (Colchester) to London (Londinium) and burned Londinium to the ground. Responding, the Romans crossed over three legions and killed 80,000 Celts and Boudicca.

"By 200 c.e., Londinium had a population of 100,000 and was capital of Roman Britain. It elected its own officials and council by free-born males in annual assembly. Hence, the Romans gave them democracy and public voice. That's civilized. London's temples became churches, and it became a religious center. The Romans built roads over much of Britain leading to Londinium. They built a wall around London, just like Rome.

"When things got great, Germanic tribes invaded the whole Roman Empire. Rome withdrew her troops from England. The Angeles from Sweden and Saxons from Germany invaded and established permanent colonies. They weren't interested in trade. Londinium shrunk to 10,000 and from 500-600 c.e. there was no historical or archeological proof that Londinium existed. Adios!

"I'll stop here, and tomorrow we'll fast forward to the Vikings. According to Thomas Malthus and Charles Darwin, populations outgrow their resources, and, only the fittest survive.

"Just an item of minutiae. Saint Paul's Cathedral was established by King Ethelbert of Kent in 604 c.e.

"Cheerio! Winston."

Dr. Winston Blood wrote on the green board. **TSAR, GOD, VODKA, ABSOLUT RULE, MILITARY EXPANSION, TOP 3%, BLACK ROBE, SERFS, PUSKIN, WESTERNIZERS, SLAVOPHILES, AND INTELLIGENTLY**.

"The Tsars chose Christianity over Islam because they loved vodka and pork. Also, they believed in monogamy. The Tsar was head of the church and had power of arbitrary capital punishment. He bound the serfs to the land on which they were born. Nobility served at the Tsar's pleasure, and the military served for life. Russia under the Tsars was the most religious country in Europe. Russia, has always had a highly intelligent, educated, sophisticated elite, the upper 3% that our Democrats love to tax, and a large loyal military. To a man with a hammer everything looks like a tack. They expanded in all directions, coveted a deep water port on the black sea, and wanted a piece of Poland who were Roman Catholics and not to be trusted. They refused to accept the Original Sin, Predestination, etc. as Augustinian foolishness and thought the Roman Catholic Pope was the Great Satan.

"The Tzar was God's Vicar and let the priests marry. Once they made Bishop, they divorced their wife, and celibacy was a joke. The Tzar drank vodka, and the priests drank wine.

"From the Roman Catholic view, the Orthodox Church were all excommunicated, heretics, blasphemous and bound for hell.

"In 1964, they met on friendly terms, lifted the excommunication, kissed each other on the cheek, and agreed to **DISAGREE** on church doctrine and remain friends. Pope John Paul was Polish.

"The Roman Church offered to revoke excommunication to the Lutherans, Anglicans, Episcopals, and Methodist if they reverted to Roman Catholism. They did not invite the Pentecostals who John Wesley excommunicated from the Methodist Church for 'tongues'.

"Yesterday, we discussed Nicholas I, the terminator, and the December 14, 1825 rebellion of the young aristocrats whom Tsar Nicholas hung or exiled. They were young liberal aristocrats and army officers, future leaders of Russian society, the *crème-de-crème*. What were they after?"

Dr. Blood wrote on the green board.

1. *Human rights and citizenship*
2. *Freedom of speech, press, religion, assembly, and rights to bear arms.*
3. *Abolition of serfdom*
4. *Education for the masses*
5. *Individual freedom, personal dignity and self-fulfillment*
6. *Russia respected in the world, not feared and hated with contempt by most Europeans.*

"Since the fall of the USSR the former Soviet KGB and Mafia have immigrated to Israel, the USA, and anywhere accepted, and are the most ruthless assassins ever organized. Things didn't change under Communism.

"Their newly elected Tsar, Prime Minister Putin, former head of the KGB is fondly referred to by his friends as Vladimir II. Lenin was Vladimir the I after the revolution.

"Alexander Pushkin, a black aristocrat, grandson of Hannibal the Great and reared by Peter and Catherine the Great, was shot in a dual defending his wife's honor and became Russia's National Poet.

"He had the largest funeral before Vladimir Lenin. He became a symbol of all that is great in Russia. Hang on to literary names. After I get past WWI and the Communist Revolution, I'm going to discuss Russian Literature.

"Pushkin has a national monument in Moscow. Dostoevsky spoke at its unveiling and declared Pushkin a uniquely Russian and a 'universal' man. Actually, Pushkin was a drunk, ran up huge gambling debts, and committed adultery with about every nobleman's wife in the Saint Petersburg's social circle. He was drunk when he called out the Dutch Ambassador's son and Army officer who was expert with a pistol to fight a dual in the snow. A black man, Pushkin felt free to have sex with every pretty woman he met, but became passionately angry when his own wife offered her charms to the young Dutch Calvary officer.

"The Russians have a ten month winter and prefer long books. Tolstoy re-wrote *War and Peace* eighteen times in pencil before he got it short enough to publish.

"As people became more informed the noble elite became 'Westernizers and Slovophiles.' Lumped together they were called 'Intelligently'.

"Tomorrow, I will fast forward to the Crimean War, Alexander II, Emancipation of the Serfs, and the Conquest of Central Asia. Somewhere in there Leo Tolstoy published *War and Peace* and *Anna Karenina*. The former took place during the Battle of Borodino, the burning of Moscow and the French retreat (1812). The setting of *Anna Karenina* was the eve of the Crimean War (1853-1856)."

"Thank you. Peter!"

Dr. Peter Rockford wrote on the green board. **APES, HOMO, NEANDERTAL, HUMANS, DNA, CAVEMEN, PALO, MESO, NEOLITHIC, WINDMILL, AVEBURY, STONEHENGE, BEAKER PEOPLE, CELTS, DRUIDS, AND ROMANS**.

"Looking back at newspaper articles recently, in Germany they found a skull which resembled a combined Neandertal and Cromagnon. In Burma, French Archeologist reported finding a jaw that was intermediate between a great ape and Homo species. DNA taken from scientifically identified Neandertal revealed they were red headed, freckled, and had blue eyes. In Spain, they found ape like humans that walked upright and claimed Homo originated in Spain and not Sudan which was where the oldest skeleton of Homo erectus was found and dated back seven million years.

"China has reported villages that date back 100,000 years and Australia 40,000. By DNA, the Homo sapien species dates back 200,000 years using female ribosomal DNA. WOW!

"The Neandertals were scattered all over Europe at least 300,000 years ago and disappeared 35-40,000 years ago. Humans (Homo sapiens) got there about 125,000 years ago and had a gene mutation for speech and art about 40,000 years ago. Religion went back to the early cave paintings. You guessed it. They drew the bull with big testicles first worshipped in Egypt, Greece, Anatolia, Persia, and India etc. The first religions were fertility rights. Semites circumcised their male infants as sacrifices to the fertility god in cavemen days.

"Prehistoric humans in Europe built their houses on stilts out over lakes first discovered in Switzerland when they drained a lake. Recently ruins of prehistoric houses around a lake in northwest England with thatched roofs, piers and dugout canoes that dated back to 8000 bce. There are caves in France and northern Italy with wall paintings and frescos. The earth is 4.5 billion years old, life started 4.0 billion years ago. The great Ice Age started 1.6 million years ago and started thawing 10-12,000 years ago depending how far you were from the Equator or North Pole. What happened? The axis of the earth shifted a fraction of a degree closer to the sun, and we had global warming. What else? At present time we are in a 10-20 thousand year interglacial period which by applying previous data should last only 10,000 years and back to the deep freeze and another long ice age. Should we be worried? You bet! During the time of the dinosaurs, the temperature was 120°, the continents were at the equator, and there was no ice anywhere.

"Cow flatus and burning fossil fuels are not going to cause global warming, but that little bit of extra CO_2 might cause the trees and vegetation to grow better.

"Climate change came in Western Europe in 8000 b.c.e. Agriculture began in the fertile triangle, Egypt, and spread to western Europe. Domestication of animals and pastoral types evolved simultaneously.

"The Windmill Culture developed in southern Britain at Avebury in the County of Wiltshire. The stones and ruins are still there. They erected massive stone monuments called 'Megaliths.'

"Next came the Beaker People (beer mugs). They brought their mugs, beer, bronze metallurgy, horses and carts. They brought the end of the Stone Age. Octoberfest celebrated in Munich Germany and Bavaria antedated the Romans. I'd guess the Beaker People were from southern Germany.

"Stonehenge was begun in 3000 b.c.e. and finished in 1350 b.c.e. by the Windmill People and their descendents.

"The Neoliths and early bronze age cultures, evolved through many generations and passed on general knowledge, pastoral and agricultural skills, habits, arts, science, and religious attitudes that are with us today.

"If you go on a guided tour of England, you see Avebury and Stonehenge. The stones are planted in the ground and huge. They'll take you before daylight to watch the sun come up in Stonehenge. It was a religious burial site.

"What's more intriguing to me are the stone fences that go all way back to Neolithic times. All farms have work dogs that round up the sheep and cows. They improved on their clay pots in shape and design from generation to generation which allows you to arrange them chronologically.

"Stone fences along with underground stone dugouts, bunkers, and houses are on the Atlantic side of Ireland and in northern Scotland and adjacent islands. They buried their dead under the bed and in the corner of their lodges.

"Neolithic societies were ruled by theocracies, ruling priests, who were war-leaders and communicated with the spirit world. They became God-Kings and assumed power by heredity. The warrior leader who collected the most women and most cattle was usually chief. Polygamy was a privilege of the ruling class.

"The British Isles separated from the European continent in 600 b.c.e. Avebury and Stonehenge are 18 miles apart. A henge is an earthwork of circular canal and a bank surrounding a sacred place. Neoliths practiced excarnation and buried the bones under their floor.

"Tomorrow, I will take up the Celts, Romans, Angeles, Saxons and Norman. Thank you."

"Amy."

Dr. Amy Omikami wrote on the green board. **CHAOS, COMPLEXITY, RANDOMNESS, UNCERTAINTY, NON LINEAR, DETERMINISTIC, STRANG ATTRACTOR, ITERATION, BUTTERFLY EFFECT, AND SHIT HAPPENS**.

"Random is unpredictable, unplanned, and shit happens. We live with uncertainty from cradle to grave. Complexity is the world in which we live. Charlie Brown said he loved mankind. It was people he couldn't stand.

"In modern science and mathematics you may program high speed computers to estimate the result when a project or idea, called an emergence, is acted on by networks of associated factors and fed both positive and negative feedback and determine the end results.

18

Complexity is non linear, non deterministic, and the end product unpredictable. This happens every second in downtown traffic and on the New York Stock Exchange. Your brain is complex when you are asleep. Chaos wakes you and maintains consciousness.

"Everybody starts out with a goal in mind, ambition, or a project. It finally emerges with no fixed point, is acted on by networks of known and unknown agents. It speeds up with robust positive feedback and slows with negative feedback. What you end with may not be what you planned and may cost 3 times as much. That's complexity! It's used to help planning.

"Chaos may come as a complete surprise and thought to be random. Many occurrences thought to be random are actually chaotic and in retrospect solved by turning knobs on especially program high speed computers back to the origin which is located at a fixed point with only a tiny difference in its beginning. You can start with the beginning and predict the end. It's deterministic, and that's how it's different from complexity. Both are non linear.

"What I just described is the computer mathematics science of the twenty-first century. No formula to memorize. It's like Carnation milk a hundred years ago. No teats to pull, and no hay to pitch. Just punch a hole in the son-of-a-bitch.

"Our time is up. Tomorrow, I'm going to start with your brain. Chaos wakes you from sleep, and that's when you get your best ideas. Eureka! I have found it. Hasta La Vista. Chaos separates genius from the dummy. Knowing how to plan from the beginning by simulation on a computer may result in success rather than chaos and cost a lot less money. The best example I know is the BP well explosion and oil gusher in the Gulf. Had they used a Chaos Computer, they would have used more mud and cement and a stronger automatic blowout preventer.

"Chaos and Complexity Computations will change the way we plan new projects in the 21st century. The Three Gorges Dam in China is a perfect example which I'll discuss tomorrow. Shit really does happen, and it will stop up a dam. That's Chaos! I'm going to add Complexity and Chaos to my Predictions for the 21st century. You can predict Chaos and make it your friend. Look at Bill, Monica, and **NAYPYIDAW**. The key was the **STRANG ATTRACTOR**. Three Gorges has a fecal impaction, and BP discovered the greatest oil field in history.

CHAPTER 5

Devine' kept her gynecology appointment with Dr. Tamara Lewine on the corner of South Queen (MLK Blvd.) and South Mean. She had difficulty finding her way in that neighborhood. It was a white oasis in a sea of blacks with bars on everything. Streetwalkers plied their trade, and eyes of the tiger peered from barred windows. Cur dogs on chains growled at strangers.

Tamara was upstairs over the KGB Insurance, next door to the Golden Apple, across the street from the Vista Ole Motor Hotel, and one block from Pancho's Automotive all owned and operated by Uzi Kalashnikov, the recognized head of the local Russian Mafia.

Since the City Crematory broke, and the Pauper's graveyard washed away, Uzi had contract with the city to collect and cremate the unclaimed street dead and funeral home rejects and dispose of them discreetly at Syracuza's Abattoir. Donald Tantalia had deed to most of the swamp land behind Syracuza's extending from Brakes Bayou all way to Clear Creek. It wasn't good for anything except mineral rights.

Oil companies wouldn't drill unless all owners signed a lease, and then they didn't validate a check on a lease for 15 days. If the price of gas or oil dropped they didn't validate at all. Royalties were calculated on a daily basis. Lease holders could check the newspaper and calculate their royalties minus taxes.

It wasn't manna from heaven. The oil company paid a 40% corporate tax, stockholders paid a dividend tax, and everybody paid tax at the pump.

The state and federal governments taxed the hell out of oil products at the pump, and Jimmy Carter put on an obscene profits tax to punish the oil companies during the Arab embargo when gasoline jumped from

21 to 75 cents a gallon and everybody got in line. John D. Rockefeller said, "the whole world runs on oil." Many countries nationalized their oil companies, kept the profits, and set the prices at the pump.

*   *   *

"Both your vaginal and cervical smears show viable wriggling sperm. There were no dead or defective sperm I could see," reported Tamara. "Your hymen was torn and stretched, and your cervix is small and nulliparous. The balance of your physical exam is normal. How long have you been off oral contraceptives?" asked Tamara.

"One month! Bill and I had intercourse on Saturday and Sunday three weeks ago when we saw A&M play Arkansas in the Cotton Bowl. Thanksgiving we saw the Dallas Cowboys and stayed at the Anatolia on Stimmons Thursday, Friday and Saturday nights. We drove to College Station and watched the Aggies play the Long Horns on Friday. The last time we had intercourse was Sunday morning before we checked out of the Anatolia and drove back to Houston.

"Monday after Thanksgiving, his wife flew in from Turkey, and his father-in-law flew in from Sicily, and that was the end of our brief but passionate affair. I've been sleeping with my feet propped up. Donald Tantalia and I spent the night in the Holiday Inn-Galveston, and he died while I slept after our third successful sexual intercourse and a fourth by him masturbating into a handkerchief which I hid and had frozen under my name at a private sperm bank." Devine' stopped talking. She was exposed on Tamara's examining table with her feet in the stirrups, knees bent, pushing down while Tamara was performing a pelvic exam and pushing forward.

Tamara did a bimanual of her uterus and both ovaries, lubricated her index finger and repeated the examination with her thumb and forefinger in her vagina and her index finger up her rectum. Devine' was sore from having sex with Austin Hale two nights in a row.

Tamara put her right foot on the stool, pressed her elbow against her knee and said, "I'll push as hard as I can, and you push down against me, and I'll feel your ovaries between both hands, and we'll be through. Now, push down as hard as you can while taking a deep breath and holding it."

Devine' gripped both sides of the table, took a deep breath and pushed down against Tamara's two hands with a finger up her rear and expelled some colonic gas in the process. She lay back, relaxed and panted when Tamara was through. She remembered seeing a show woman have sex with a donkey when she was a little girl back in Jamaica.

"Why don't you play music?" asked Deviné.

"Too much trouble. My patients don't scream. A pelvic is not supposed to hurt. Colonoscopists do because they pump in air and distend the colon. I don't want to contaminate my gloves on the radio. There's nothing sterile about a colonoscopy," replied Tamara.

Tamara made a wet slide of Deviné's vaginal secretions and checked her stool for parasites and blood. "I don't see Trichomonas, but there was a third guy. You didn't tell all. You had sex last night. Don't tell me, I'd rather not know, if it is a secret. But I'll be frank, they look like Austin Hale's."

"It's a secret, for God's sake! You mean you can look at sperm and identify the donor. A machine can't do that, and DNA is not 100% accurate. You're putting me on.

"Somebody told you. I'd like to see your appointment schedule. Sandra will hate me if she finds out. She'll want me to be bride's maid at her wedding, and I can't look her in the eye," replied Deviné, upset.

"Speaking of Dr. Hale, I'm keeping this office as a satellite clinic and moving to Sugar Land to see more affluent patients. They have gynecological problems too. President Clinton is putting all my welfare mothers to work, and they'll not get Medicaid. I might sell this practice or give it away."

* * *

When Devine' got back to Sandra's office, there were three clients with appointments: Carmaleta Posadas, Patsy Redmon, and Frank Bagetti of the law firm of Love, Quick, Bagetti and Quinteras. It was 3 P.M., Thursday, December 12, only 13 more days to Christmas.

*   *   *

"I hadn't seen Jésus in 10 years. We were separated, and I lived in Matamoros where I was employed as a clerk typist in the Cuban Consulate and worked undercover for our DEA. I worked for both sides. I was aware Jésus was into crime here in Houston, but that was after we decided to go our separate ways and stay married. We were Catholic. It's easier just to live with somebody else than to get a divorce. Jésus has been dead eight months now, and no ex-girlfriend has come forth. He and my brother, Hernan Costello, and Juan Baptista, were close friends and played sports at Milby High. I'd begun to believe Jésus was just a legend until I walked in our old house on Dewberry, and he was drinking beer and watching sports on TV.

"I'm having the house refurbished and painted. Those old Victorians with gables, balconies, and wrap around porches sell for a premium. I had the garages and garage apartment torn down. People would never pay a premium if they knew a gorilla ripped a woman to pieces and stuffed her in a washing machine drier on Sunday morning in broad daylight. That story gets worse every time it's repeated.

"What would you like for me to do? Sandra won't be back until after Christmas."

"Warn lawyer Percy Lovett that Jésus is back and will be coming after his money, the $5 million Jésus asked him to keep. Also please ask Detective Derek Strong to see me at his earliest convenience. He knows Cecile Black who stole the money. I'm in 806 at the Granada high-rise, temporarily I hope."

*   *   *

"Hernan Costello called and warned me that Jésus Posadas has returned, and will be looking for his five million that lawyer Percy Lovett put in our office safe," explained Lawyer Frank Bagetti.

"And?" asked Deviné.

"You remember? Cecile Black had it carried out in cardboard boxes and stored in her husband's appliance store on South Main where it disappeared never to be seen again."

"Did you tell Percy Lovett?"

"He's in jail for murdering Jésus Navarre. No jury would convict him. Jésus Navarre needed to be killed. I might have done it myself," replied Frank, chuckling.

"Does Cecile still work for you?" asked Deviné.

"No! Her husband offered her more than I could afford, and she's back managing his Appliance and Parts store on South Main. He fired all his blacks, hired cheap Mexican help, and is branching out to all points of the compass. He put in a new store in Sugar Land. I believe he's into dope and plans to take Black's public. I know you don't solicit advice, but I'd put Dirk on it. He bought out Blackie White's Appliances and Icon. Dirk knows most of them and doesn't need warrants like the cops."

*   *   *

Patsy Redmon RN smoked and offered Devine' a Lucky Strike which had clearly lost share in the U.S.A. They lit up, inhaled, leaned back and blew little smoke rings.

"Luckies taste good like a cigarette should," sang Deviné.

"More physicians smoke Luckies," stated Patsy, cheerfully.

"You had sex with Don Tantalia down on the sea wall, and you woke and found him dead?" asked Patsy.

"My goodness! How did you find out? That's shocking! Nobody was supposed to know. I can't admit to something as shameful as that. He was a sweet old man, like a Teddy Bear," replied Deviné, taken back.

Patsy leaned forward. "The Israeli Intelligence keep up with everything going on around NASA. That sweet old Teddy Bear was a Mafia Don. He sold the Chinese the Russian bomb used on Naypyidaw. Have you met Cissy Burger, Mrs. Joe Cain, that's secretary to James Fry Jr. at Blue Bird Hospital in Pasadena, Texas?" asked Patsy.

"Yes, I met her under very unusual circumstances. Baby Jane put everybody in a trance like the Manchurian Candidate, and I didn't get to question Mr. James Fry Jr.'s secretary. Everybody called her Cissy," replied Deviné, perplexed.

'Hah! Hah!" Patsy laughed. "Baby Jane is my granddaughter. Her stepmother was a witch. Tamar is my daughter by James Fry Sr., and I gave her up for adoption when she was six weeks old. James Jr. and Tamar Fry had the same father. James Fry Sr. was shot by my first husband in front of the Blue Bird Clinic with Joe Cain's deer rifle in 1968. The case was never solved. Two unsolved murders were committed with that deer rifle, and Cissy Burger's husband, Joe Cain, was the third shot by a sniper the same way. That priest that gave Joe last rites was my first husband. You've seen him. Didn't you attend the Rosary of Dr. John R. Brinkley at Savemore in Pasadena?" asked Patsy, proudly.

"Yes, I did. Sandra and I watched the audience and didn't notice the priest. He had pale skin almost like a ghost," replied Devine' in thought.

"That was Father Bernard, my first husband. His skin was pale because he cut off his balls with a rusty pocket knife in a state of manic psychosis and almost bled to death. Even after castration, he's subject to those spells of rage, especially when he gets off his Lithium.

"Sandra knows all about that. She defended Joe in the murder trial. All I can tell you is my Billy popped out from nowhere and gave Joe last rites. I'd send my detective or wait until Sandra gets back. I go by and see Billy from time-to-time. He has a free standing Mexican Mission in South Pasadena and masquerades as a non affiliated Catholic Priest. When I fell in love with him, he was a self ordained Pentecostal Evangelical and had the biggest Cathedral in Pasadena and his own radio and TV Gospel hours. The Savemore Mortuary has him on contract to perform prepaid funerals."

CHAPTER 6

When Dirk picked up his car in Angleton he had hours before he met Devine' at Park Shops across from the Houston convention center and Enron Stadium. Business was slow, and he decided to drive around Brazoria County, look at the Brazoria P&L Nuclear Plant, and visit Mambo Nigeria at her place on the Brazos River. It was too early for lunch, so he passed up the chance to eat "home cooking" in the Courthouse Buffet (Cafeteria). Pearland (pop. 90,000) was the largest town and across Texas 6 from Sugar Land on Texas 35 to Alvin. He decided to see it last since it was a straight shot up Tex 35 from Alvin through Pearland to the Park Shops and downtown Houston.

He took a right at the main traffic light in Angleton and west on Texas 35 toward Bailey's Prairie, East Columbia, Varner's Creek and the Brazos River which was once the Capital of the Republic of Texas, now just a Historical Marker, an occasional pumping oil well, a few cows and a bunch of minorities and illegals "hanging out" and smoking marijuana.

Where had the jobs gone? Mexico, China, Taiwan, Argentina and Saudi Arabia, wherever there were cheap labor and cheap oil. Like Liberty, Texas, there was nothing sadder than an abandoned oil field town. That 60% still down there was like pussy on a fat woman, nobody cared.

*   *   *

Captain Jerry Billings driving her DPS patrol car with flasher and siren was able to get around the roadblock and detours at Saint Colombo Cemetery and Cathedral which was a hundred years old and not a big loss. It was near the beginning of Cavalcade next to a railroad about two blocks over. Down the street was a playground, city park and the Congo Jungle which had been in her family since the "roaring twenties."

Caesar Deagio, her father, Tina Deagio, her stepmother, and two stepsisters La Quinta Quinteras and Elizabeth Quinteras were hyper excited about the prospects of untold riches from the "Colombo Gusher."

Her grandfather, Sam Deagio, was flying up from San Jose Costa Rico to check on the deeds. Jerry didn't know the details.

The relief well was completed and was closed off for now. The wasted oil was sucked by vacuum tanker trucks and carted off to a local refinery. Oil workers were cleaning up Saint Colombo cemetery, and a construction crew was leveling and repairing Saint Colombo.

CHAPTER 7

Dirk arriving 30 minutes ahead of Devine' was met by the work day traffic fleeing downtown Houston. Not a multilane freeway Tex 35 ran right through an all Mexican neighborhood that resembled Matamoras with graffiti, iron bars, street peddlers, tattooed cutthroats, and prostitutes that lined both sides of Texas 35 under the overpasses that encircled Houston. You could purchase marijuana on every corner along with hot tamales, barbequed canine, tortillas, boiled roast ears on a stick, frijoles patties, and visit a Cantina and view Spanish TV while drinking real Mexican beer, Tequila, and Mescal with a live worm in the glass. There were "no blacks" and "no gringos" signs over their doors.

There was no way that Dirk would take Tex 35 under the overpasses entering and leaving Houston at night. He took a left and followed the access road around the convention center and Enron Field. The Park across from Park Shops was gone, and a new Hilton Hotel was under construction.

Only two weeks to Christmas, the traffic was impossible, and there was no place to park. It occurred to Dirk that Luby's on Live Oak two blocks from the Galleria where Live Oak intersected Westheimer would be worse. Live Oak and Westheimer were called "Uptown" and the Criminal District Court and Jones Convention Center were called "Downtown."

The tunnel that ran under Houston connecting all the big commercial buildings and hotels was just called "The Tunnel." All streets Downtown were one way except Main Street which extended south as South Main and north as North Main had the only metered parking. The one way streets were changed from day-to-day, and you could pass by your destination several times before giving up and parking six blocks away.

San Jacinto was always one way east and ran passed the Criminal District Court, a pay per hour or day commercial parking, and the County Jail. Directly across were the District Civil Court and the Juvenile and Family Courts. They were connected by separate underground tunnels guarded by County Deputies from courts to jails.

Fannin which paralleled Main Street and San Jacinto was always one way west and passed south of Herman Park Zoo and took you directly to the Texas Medical Center, Medical Towers, Diagnostic Clinic, Methodist Hospital, and Baylor Medical School, etc.

Saint Joseph Hospital was a couple of blocks from Enron Park and "Downtown."

Dirk put his flasher on top, jumped the curb at the courthouse, found a place in the police parking space, left an official POLICE sign inside his windshield, locked his car, and walked six long city blocks to Park Shops, entered on the street side, and took the escalator up to Fast Food Heaven which was packed with early shoppers and got in line behind Devine' who had arrived by taxi for **BEANS AND RICE**. It would have been closer to park at the Greyhound Bus Station, but the chance of vandalism and tow away were prohibitively high.

They had to wait for a booth to be vacated. "We have to stop meeting like this," remarked Dirk, chuckling.

They found a place to lean up against the wall and eat, but it wasn't leisurely or private.

"Where are you parked, Dirk?"

"Down by the courthouse. It's six blocks. You got any suggestions?"

Devine' unfolded Sandra's list and held it where Dirk could see it. She had to speak above the crowd.

1. R. Capistrano & J. Alvarez—GRD JY NO BILLED—CHARGES DROPPED—FBI
2. Dr. G. Jekyl—Murd I—11/27/93—JY Marci & Eliz—pick jury—Castroil

3. Hosea Gomer—Murd. I—11/28/93—JY Devine' picks jury—Dutch Royal

4. R. Capistrano, S. Fox, B. Redmon, Wilbur Everett—Bench Warrant 11/23/93—Trafficking cocaine—Cuban Mafia

5. D. Cartenegro, S. Pablo Huston, Carl Bribey—Bench Warrant 11/23/93—drug, bribes, pushing dope

6. S. Bloom, E. Early, Michael Finn—Key to warehouse—Bench Warrant 11/23/93

7. P. Lovett, Murder I, Grand Jury True Billed—Arraignment 11/24/93

8. T. Lovett—MI—Hosp. Hysteria, Depression—Lockup—Psycho. Dr. Helga Schmidt

9. Muhammad Abdullah Hussain—Murd I Jail—Crazy Shiite Muslim

10. Jessie Dan White—Shoot Lib. Open 3D Bench Warrant—11/23/93

11. Jotte   Jalopena—MI—Charges Dropped—11/23/93—Bench VACA de VACA

12. Kenneth Clark Kent—ADA 11/23 Single, no kids, Big Student Loan, Marci—DA's niece—Yale Law—Neva Braun—Day court —

13. Rafael and Angel Quintero—Jail awaiting Deportation or Fed Wit. Program.

14. Knockers Motorcycle Club—Tillie Lovett, Neva, Warehouse, H.H.

15. Elvis Jones—Six Pack Jones—All American—Pr. View—Kansas City Chiefs Special T. beat Dallas in Super Bowl—will flip to save skin

16. Horace   Greely—Elvis—KNOCKERS—SEX TRAFFICKING, PIMP, CRACK—Off duty Res. Deputies —

17. James Fry Jr.—MI, 11/24/93, Deer Rifle—shot Dr. Joe Cain MASH, Patrolwomen Haley and Budd.

"I'm going to skip a lot. Bill asked me not to try any of Sandra's cases until she got back.

"Mambo Nigera wants to sell her camp house and hundred acres with full mineral rights. She and her husband are moving to a place with a swimming pool and golf course in Sugar Land.

"Carmaleta Posadas came in to see Sandra. Jésus is back and wants to see Percy Lovett and Frank Bagetti about the five million they lost of his.

"I'll go see her. She still living in Juan Baptista's house?" asked Dirk.

"806 in the Granada high-rise."

"Patsy Redmon saw the priest that said last rites on Dr. Joe Cain. Said his name was Father Bernard and runs a mission in Pasadena. That's all I can think of just this minute. If I think of anything else, I'll give you a call. Would you like to meet me at the Red Flounder at 5 P.M. tomorrow night in Sugar Land? It's in the new mall at the corner of Texas 6 and U.S. 59S, just 15 minutes from Downtown Houston."

"Red Flounder at 5 P.M. repeated Dirk. "I have to be going. Julie, my daughter, dances at the Water Mellon Man at 10 P.M. I want to make sure she doesn't have any stalkers following her home."

"Dirk, if Julie's old enough to pull her clothes off in public, she has to be able to look after herself. You'd be the stalker," commented Deviné, giggling. "She's had a baby and an adult affair with Dr. Strongbach. What makes you think she won't seduce you?"

"It's her drive home to Atascocita that bothers me. After you get off Texas 1960, it's a half mile along Lake Houston that's scary. I wish I didn't agree to let her stay in my apartment."

"Which cop patrols out there?" asked Deviné.

"Neva, I think. They don't patrol everywhere past Humble. They respond to 911 calls. It's too much. It's an old oil field town."

"Why don't you ask Jerry to let her go through the Police Academy, learn how to shoot, and buy her a gun. Under Texas law she's allowed to carry a gun. I carry one every time I go out and have a pull down gun under the dash of my car. I won't leave home without it," replied Deviné.

"I still see a little girl. I can't imagine her carrying a gun and stripping in public. That's beyond my comprehension," replied Dirk, tenderly.

Devine' grew impatient. "Fuck her Dirk. She's on the pill. You'll grow up in a hurry. It's you, not Julie that needs to grow up. Then you'll quit worrying like a father. You never worried when your wife stripped in public and drove herself home. How old was Roxanne when you married her?"

"Probably 19 or 20, women never tell their right age," replied Dirk.

"Was she a virgin?" asked Deviné, giggling.

"No! No! The thought of other men never occurred to me."

"Grow up, Dirk. You see a pretty woman. She's got a man somewhere, and he's usually big, hairy, and mean. Better you than him. He may slap her around and give her Herpes, gonorrhea, or something worse."

CHAPTER 8

Barcelona Spain
8 A.M., Friday, December 13, 1993
Cool, clear, and cloudless
Sunny, Temp 79/60°

The USN Anthropology tour thought they had died and gone to heaven. Barcelona effects everyone the same. If you were rich, had a penchant for the arts and gracious living, then Barcelona was where "it was at."

Except for the occasional poor and lower middle class, most spoke and understood Spanish, French, and English. Compared with the rich in Dubai and Bahrain, Barcelonans were laid back and really enjoyed life.

Sandra didn't see any nude women, but plenty wore short shorts, string halters and bikinis. In contrast to the Arabs, Barcelonans ate roasted day old suckling pigs and drank rich red wine. It was Grande, like Mexico City without the Mexicans. It was nice to get rid of the Bourqas and walk down the street without worrying about getting raped by the Shariah patrol or your head chopped off. Catholics knew how to live it up. Barcelona was an old Roman town before the Spanish. They were civilized. Last year they hosted the 1992 Summer Olympics.

Maria had no difficulty locating the downtown Best Western, and there were KFC and McDonalds with clean rest rooms all over town.

After a buffet breakfast they were pretty much given a free reign and free condoms in case of emergency. There were plenty of handsome Latin lovers eager to speak English with rich American girls.

Every tourist attraction had a local guide who was university trained and spoke several languages well. Christy Isaacs had spent an undergraduate year and three summers in Barcelona and had volunteered to lead a leisurely walking tour of the major tourist's attractions. Barcelona had an excellent subway and a 160 mph bullet train to Madrid and Granada which came as a packaged deal.

"Other than covering their head and not wearing a bikini in a Mosque or Catholic Cathedral, there were no restrictions on women. Sandra saw one young woman kissing her boyfriend on a park bench and giving him a hand job through his jeans. She would have been stoned to death in Dubai. People passed by and paid no mind in Barcelona. Barcelona was the favorite of young Holiday Trekkers and foreign students from Europe and the Americas. Most were from affluent families and could afford a liberal education.

The main Piazza in the center of the old city was octagon shaped and had eight straight boulevards coming together like the spokes on a wheel. The traffic was not heavy like Rome and most big cities. The weather was invigorating, and many walked.

Sandra read:

U.S. DEPARTMENT OF STATE

Bureau of European and Eurasian Affairs
Kingdom of Spain: Background Notes: 1993.

Population:	**Spain 47 million**
	Madrid Capital 5.5 million
	Barcelona 4.9 million
	Seville 1.8 million
Size:	**Arizona and Utah**
Terrain:	**High Plateau, Mountainous, and coastal plains**
Climate:	**Temperate**
Time Zone:	**1 hour ahead of Greenwich**

Nationality:	Spaniards
Ethnic:	Basques, Catalans, Galicians
Religion:	Catholic, Islamic, Protestant
Literacy:	97.6%
Work:	Services and Tourism 70%, Construction, 13%, Agriculture 4%, Industry 16%, Fishing 5%
Government:	King Juan Carlos Constitutional Monarchy
Education:	Catholic and Public (1-12) Universities and Postgraduate
People:	

Spain's population density, lower than that of most European countries, is roughly equivalent to New England's. In recent years, following a longstanding pattern in the rest of Europe, rural populations are moving to cities. Urban areas are also experiencing a significant increase in immigrant populations, chiefly from North

Africa, South America, and Eastern Europe.

Spain has no official religion. The constitution of 1978 disestablished the Roman

Catholic Church as the official state religion, while recognizing the role it plays in

Spanish society. According to the National Institute of Statistics 74.7% of the population are Catholic, 2.3% belong to another religion, 13.8% are agnostic, and 6.9% are atheists.

HISTORY:

The Iberian Peninsula has been settled for millennia. Some of Europe's most impressive Paleolithic sites are located in Spain, including the famous caves at

Altamira that contain spectacular paintings dating from about 15,000 to 25,000 years ago. Beginning in the ninth century BC, Phoenicians, Greeks, Carthaginians, and Celts entered the Iberian Peninsula. The Romans followed in the second century BC and laid the groundwork for Spain's present language, religion, and laws. Although the Visigoths arrived in the fifth century AD, the last Roman strongholds along the southern coast did not fall until the seventh century AD. In

711, North African Moors sailed across the straits, swept into Andalusia, and within a few years, pushed the Visigoths up the peninsula to the Cantabrian

Mountains. The Reconquest-efforts to drive out the Moors-lasted until 1492. By

1512, the unification of present-day Spain was complete.

During the 16th century, Spain became the most powerful nation in Europe, due to the immense wealth derived from its presence in the Americas. But a series of long, costly wars and revolts, capped by the English defeat of the "Invincible Armada" in

1588, began a steady decline of Spanish power in Europe. Controversy over succession to the throne consumed the country during the 18th century, leading to an occupation by France during the Napoleonic era in the early 1800s and a series of armed conflicts throughout much of the 19th century.

The 19th century saw the revolt and independence of most of Spain's colonies in the

Western Hemisphere; three wars over the succession issue; the brief ousting of the monarchy and establishment of the First Republic (1873-74); and, finally, the

Spanish-American War (1898), in which Spain lost Cuba, Puerto Rico, and the

Philippines to the United States. A period of dictatorial rule (1923-31) ended with the establishment of the Second Republic. It was dominated by increasing political polarization, culminating in the leftist Popular Front electoral victory in 1936.

Pressures from all sides, coupled with growing and unchecked violence led to the outbreak of the Spanish Civil War in July 1936.

Following the victory of his nationalist force in 1939, General Francisco Franco ruled a nation exhausted politically and economically. Spain was officially neutral during World War II but followed a pro-Axis policy. The country signed the

Mutual Defense Assistance Agreement with the U.S. on September 26, 1953 and joined the United Nations in 1955. In 1959, under an International Monetary Fund stabilization plan, the country began liberalizing trade and capital flows, particularly foreign direct investment.

Despite the success of economic liberalization, Spain remained for years the most closed economy in Western Europe-judged by the small measure of foreign trade to economic activity—and the pace of reform slackened during the 1960s as the state remained committed to "guiding the economy. Nevertheless, in the 1960s and

1970s, Spain was transformed into a modern industrial economy with a thriving tourism sector. Its economic expansion led to improved income distribution and helped develop a large middle class. Social changes brought about by economic prosperity and the inflow of new ideas helped set the stage for Spain's transition to democracy during the latter half of the 1970s.

Upon the death of General Franco in November 1975, Franco's personally—designated heir Prince Juan Carlos de Borbon y Borbon assumed the titles of king and chief of state. Dissatisfied with the slow pace of post-Franco liberalization, he replaced Franco's last Prime Minister with Adolfo Suarez in July 1976. Suarez entered office promising that elections would be held within one year, and his government moved to enact a series of laws to liberalize the new regime. Spain's first elections since 1936 to the Cortes (Parliament) were held on June 15, 1977. Prime Minister Suarez's Union of the Democratic Center (UCD), a moderate center-right coalition, won 34% of the vote and the largest bloc of seats in the
Cortes.

Under Suarez, the new Cortes set about drafting a democratic constitution that was overwhelmingly approved by voters in a national referendum in December 1978.

GOVERNMENT AND POLITICAL CONDITIONS

Parliamentary democracy was restored following the 1975 death of General Franco, who had ruled since the end of the civil war in 1939. The 1978 constitution established Spain as a parliamentary monarchy, with the prime minister responsible to the bicameral Corte (Congress of Deputies and Senate) elected every
4 years. On February 23, 1981, rebel elements among the security forces seized the
Corte and tried to impose a military-backed government. However, the great majority of the military forces remained loyal to King Juan Carlos, who used his personal authority to put down the bloodless coup attempt.

In October 1982, the Spanish Socialist Workers Party (PSOE), led by Felipe
Gonzalez, swept both the Congress of Deputies and Senate, winning an absolute majority. Gonzalez and the PSOE ruled for the next 13 years. During that period,
Spain joined the North Atlantic Treaty Organization (NATO) and the European
Community.

Terrorism

The Government of Spain is involved in a long-running campaign against Basque
Fatherland and Liberty (ETA), a terrorist organization founded in 1959 and dedicated to promoting Basque independence. ETA targets Spanish security forces, military personnel, Spanish Government officials, politicians of the Popular Party
(PSOE), and business people and civilian institutions that do not support ETA. The group has carried out numerous bombings against Spanish Government facilities and economic targets, including a car bomb assassination attempt on then—opposition leader Aznar in which his armored car was destroyed but he was unhurt. The Spanish Government attributes over 800 deaths to ETA terrorism since its campaign of violence began. In recent years, the government has had more success in controlling ETA, due in part to increased security cooperation with
French authorities.

Al Qaeda is known to operate cells in Spain. 10 bombs were detonated on crowded commuter trains during rush hour. Three were deactivated by security forces and one was found unexploded. Evidence quickly surfaced that jihadist terrorists with possible ties to the Al Qaeda network were responsible for the attack that killed 191 people. Spanish investigative services and the judicial system have aggressively sought to arrest and prosecute suspected Al Qaeda members and actively cooperate with foreign governments to diminish the transnational terrorist threat. A Spanish court convicted 18 individuals for their role in supporting Al Qaeda, and Spanish police disrupted numerous Islamist extremist cells operating in the country. The trial against 29 people for their alleged participation. The prosecutor asked for sentences as high as 30,000 years of jail for some of them. Three of the suspects were convicted of murder for their roles and received over 42,000 years in prison.

Overall, 21 of 28 defendants were found guilty of some offense for their role in the bombings.

Spanish authorities in Barcelona arrested 14 people believed to be connected to a

Pakistani terrorist cell allegedly sympathetic to Al Qaeda. The group, potentially linked to Islamic terrorist activities, was believed to be on the verge of a terrorist bombing campaign against Barcelona's transportation network and possibly other targets in Europe. An informant working for the French intelligence services notified Spanish authorities of the pending attack.

Spain has maintained its special identification with Latin America. Its policy emphasizes the concept of Hispanidad, a mixture of linguistic, religious, ethnic, cultural, and historical ties binding Spanish-speaking America to Spain. Spain has been an effective example of transition from authoritarianism to democracy, as shown in the many trips that Spain's King and Prime Ministers have made to the region. Spain maintains economic and technical cooperation programs and cultural

exchanges with Latin America, both bilaterally and within the EU.

Spain also continues to focus attention on North Africa, especially on Morocco, a source of much of Spain's large influx of legal and illegal immigrants over the past 10 years. This concern is dictated by geographic proximity and long historical contacts and more recently by immigration trends, as well as by the two Spanish enclave cities of Ceuta and Melilla on the northern coast of Africa. When Spain's departure from its former colony of Western Sahara ended direct Spanish participation in Morocco, it maintains an interest in peaceful resolution of the conflict brought about there by decolonization.

*   *   *

Sandra had not seen Al Qaeda in print before. Maybe they made a mistake and meant EL instead of AL. Everything AL was the in Arabic. Everything EL meant the in Spanish.

"Maria, what's El Qaeda?" asked Sandra. She was at the vanity brushing her hair, and Maria was taking a shower.

"Never heard of it. How is it used?"

"It's some sort of terrorist organization in Spain and Morocco. The Basques are the big deal in Spain. I thought Símońe Bolivar was a Basque."

"Bolivar's father was a Basque. Símońe was a bastard," replied Maria, giggling. "Isn't Barcelona out of this world? They've got so much to see. Everybody is either a tourist with a lot of cash, or somebody working in the tourist trade. We're not going by bus. They have the best subways and bullet train in the world (160 mph). After Iran and the United Arab Emirates Barcelona is like dying and going to heaven."

*   *   *

Once the greatest empire in the world under Charles V and Phillip II who fought the Reformation, Counterreformation, defeated to Ottomon fleet, killed one million Jews and seven million Germans, colonized the Americas and robbed Mexico and Peru of their silver and gold while conducting the Spanish Inquisition and rid the Roman Catholic of its heretics, present day Spain was just a pussy cat. The conquistadors lived on in the Mestezos and half breeds of Mexico, South America, Caribbean, and the Philippines etc.

Barcelona, home of the 1992 Olympic Games, was the number one tourist destination in Europe. Why? It had a fantastic past history, plenty of old statues and Gothic Cathedrals. Not to mention beautiful women, bikinis, sand, sex, and sun. Europe had a two thousand year's head start on the Americas at perfecting the simple pleasures of life, metabolism and reproduction.

*   *   *

Barcelona, was in Catalonia, where their heritage was an amalgam of Spanish and French. They said Sant Pau, the Portuguese Sao Paulo, the Spanish San Pablo, and the English Saint Paul. Sandra didn't know what the French and Germans said. It was the fourth most visited city in Europe after London, Paris, and Rome, had 5 million tourists a year, and its ultramodern airport handled 30 million passengers a year. If you have the money, they got the time, etc.

It was named after its founder Hamidcar Barca, the father of Hannibal the Great. The Romans designed the Gothic Quarter (Old Town). It was conquered by the Visigoths, Moors, Charlemagne's son, Aragon, and Isabella of Castile. The latter by love not war when she married King Ferdinand of Aragon in 1469 and established Madrid as the capital of Spain. Then there was the Plague of 1649-52 which killed off half the people and Napoleon in 1807. Franco killed 50,000 in the

Spanish Civil War. It was 100 miles south of the Pyrenees, skiing and the border of France.

What do you get when you cross a Spaniard with a Frenchman? A Catalonian, of course. They can go either way. Barcelona's Convention Center, Financial District and Grandest Luxury Hotels were near the waterfront. It was ideal for entertainment festivals, Sicilian Mafia, Arab Sheiks, Revolutionaries, International Terrorists (Al Qaeda), and the celebrity jet set. Next to Tel Aviv, the Russian Jewish Mafia and ex-KGB liked it best.

Like other cities in Spain, Barcelona had an illegal immigrant problem from Latin America, Africa, and Asia. It was like the *Field of Dreams*. You build it, and they will come. Much like Texas and Mexico. They were seeing the end product of 2000 years of culture, and to the victor goes the "spoils."

*   *   *

Maria gave them a free day to follow Christy Isaac to the Gothic Quarters or sit in the shade of an outdoor café and flirt with the many handsome young would be Don Juan's all over. There was almost no way they could get lost with 10,000 taxi cabs and the best public transportation in Europe.

After a Buffet Dinner in the Best Western, Christy Isaac addressed their group.

"Tomorrow morning I want you down in the lobby with passport, money belt, bag, and baggage, and dressed to go. We'll take a bus to the airport, and as a group go through customs and whatever and sit as a group in coach on Swiss Air to Zurich. You can eat breakfast and nap on the plane. It's a two hour flight. Go to the bathroom and check your room before you leave.

"We've been lucky, so far. We're going to sit on our bags in Zurich International and catch the next flight available to Heathrow in London where they'll put us up in the Hilton until we can catch a flight home.

From here on out we'll be fighting the Christmas rush, and you'll meet plenty of college students coming and going both ways just like you. If we get caught in a blizzard, we may not make it home until after New Year's.

"Maria!

"When Hernan Cortez stepped ashore in Mexico and claimed all the Americas, he read a proclamation to the natives. I Hernan Cortez acting in behalf of God, the Pope, and the King and Queen of Spain do hereby seize all your land and wealth and will treat you as master to a vassal and do mean things to you if you disobey. If anybody objects, I will have him beheaded, or words to that effect.

"Approximately one month ago, our group was present and stood aside as the Israeli Secret Service rolled out the red carpet and escorted King Juan Carlos of Spain in and out of the Church of the Holy Sepulcher where he lit a candle at the altar, kneeled, and visited Jesus' tomb.

"King Carlos had just addressed the Israeli Knesset and asked their forgiveness for King Ferdinand's and Queen Isabella's killing or running all the Jews out of Spain in 1492.

"Pope John Paul, a Pole by birth, came to Israel to pray at the Wailing Wall and asked forgiveness for Pope Pius XII and the entire Vatican for looking the other way while Adolph Hitler gassed 6 million Jews during WWII.

"Tonight, we'll have only one lecture. You can't leave Europe without a formal lecture on the Reformation.

"Dr. Aristotle Plotinus please."

Dr. Aristotle Plotinus wrote on the green board. **GRECO-ROMAN CULTURE, AMERICA, ROMAN CATHOLIC CHURCH, REFORMATION, SPANISH INQUISITION, PROTESTANTISM, DANTE, SCHOOL OF ATHENS, ICE CREAM, PASTA, PIZZA, AND SOPHIA LOREN**.

"The Catholic Rosary was presented to Saint Dominic of Castile by the Holy Virgin mother who appeared before him in the summer of 1206 ce. Mary insisted he read it 150 times to produce miracles.

"Pope Innocent appointed Saint Dominic leader of the First Christian Crusade against Christian Spain to annihilate the Albigensian heresy spread to southern France. Saint Dominic organized the Dominis Canis, hounds of the Lord, and the Dominican Order who conducted the Spanish Inquisition in Spain, Europe, and New Spain (Mexico).

"The Reformation and Counter Reformation were from 1500 ce to 1700 ce. The Catholics burned thousands at the stake from 1400 ce to 1700 ce for specific religious reasons, exorcism, and purification by fire. After the great Bubonic plagues there were a lot of unattractive, elderly, and cranky old ladies around, so they accused them of having intercourse with the devil and burned them as witches.

"During the thirty year religious war in Germany seven million were killed. That wasn't topped until Adolph Hitler, a Catholic, gassed six million Jews during the last two years of WWII. Then Stalin and Mao executed their millions and ten millions to establish Communism. Anybody that resisted got executed.

"When most of the pillage, burning, rapine, and killing of humans and the decapitation of statues were over in Europe and Great Britain, the Roman Catholics and multiple Protestant denominations shared at least six things in common. They were: COSMIC SIN, SAINT PAUL MYSTICISM, HEAVEN, HELL, TITHE, and HOLY BIBLE.

"They disagreed on the infallibility of the Pope and the interpretation of the Holy Bible. People learned to read. The printing press was invented, and Bibles became available to the masses.

"Actually, the Catholic Church expanded, and, what they lost in Europe, they more than made up with the natives of South America and a very ambitious foreign missionary program. The Pope was still infallible, and the Roman Catholic Church was still the most powerful religion in the world.

"Millions were killed during the two hundred years of the Protestant reformation. Seven million combatants from all over Europe were slaughtered in Germany during the Thirty Years War. That's not counting the German peasants during Martin Luther's time, and the French Huguenots. A million Jews were killed during the Crusades and the Spanish Inquisition, and six million Jews were gassed in the holocaust of more recent times. GRACE does not come cheaply. Everybody was fighting for GRACE, glory in the sight of God.

"Jesus was an itinerant Jewish Rabbi, who was circumcised as an infant and lived by the 613 laws of Moses in the Hebrew Torah. He spoke Aramaic in a Greek speaking world ruled by the Roman empire. Nobody remembered his real name. He was condemned for heresy by the highest Hebrew court and crucified by the Romans.

"Much later the Roman Catholic Church under the Emperor Constantine banned crucifixion and adopted burning heretics alive and naked at the stake.

"The English chopped off the heads of royalty and hung, disemboweled, quartered and drew the mutilated carcasses of criminals and dissidents and burned witches at the stake during the seventeenth century.

"The Spanish tortured and burned thousands at the stake during the Catholic Inquisition in Europe and South America. It goes on and on. They all wanted GRACE, favor and glory in the sight of God.

"GRACE is a hard word to define. It's abstract. GRACE, like beauty, is in the eyes of the beholder. It doesn't hang on a tree, and you can't buy it in a store. Your mother, grandmother, or Santa Claus can't put it in your stocking.

"Plato called it piety, something for which all philosophers and good citizens of Athens should strive. The Greek author of the Book of James wrote 'faith without works is dead.'

"Saint Paul Mysticism achieves favor in the sight of God which Paul called GRACE. GRACE through faith in the resurrection of Jesus Christ and baptism for the cleansing of sins.

"Saint Paul was a Hebrew Apocalyptic Rabbi who taught the world was coming to an end during his lifetime, any minute, and recommended to the Gentiles they substitute baptism for circumcision and belief in Jesus' resurrection for the 613 Jewish laws of the TORAH. We call it Saint Paul Mysticism, because nobody knew, but Paul, why such a miraculous transaction would occur.

"Four hundred years later, Saint Augustine invented Cosmic Sin and recommended infant baptism to cleanse the sin of tainted sperm from Adam in the Hebrew scriptures. Saint Augustine established GRACE as a predestined and preordained gift from God. You couldn't earn GRACE by works (613 Jewish laws) or buy it with money. You were either born with GRACE or you burned in hell for an eternity and God knew from the beginning of creation who was going to be born with GRACE. Saint Augustine agreed with Saint Paul that belief is acquired through faith, but added the COSMIC SIN for all humankind.

"You can thank Saint Augustine for the original sin, predestination, and belief through faith. Saint Augustine wrote 'Faith is the love you give to God, and GRACE is the love God gives you in return'.

"Martin Luther took the Book of James out of his Lutheran Bible and proclaimed to Europe that 'By faith alone you are saved and stand beside Jesus to achieve favor in the sight of God'. By faith alone and baptism started the Protestant Reformation.

"Saint Thomas Aquinas, doctor of the Catholic Church, who lived around 1200 ac, eight hundred years after Augustine and four hundred years before Luther, wrote that salvation may come natural (e.g. Noah and Abraham) outside the church or more commonly within the Catholic Church through the Holy Sacraments. He wrote that infant baptism, frequent communion through the Eucharist, and extreme unction would achieve everlasting GRACE before God and salvation from original sin. Thomas Aquinas believed in transubstantiation by consecration of the wafer and wine into the flesh of Jesus Christ which imparted healing salvation on a regular basis following confession, repentance, absolution, and penance.

"The Catholic Church agreed with Saint Thomas and Saint Augustine and ex-communicated and damned to hell Martin Luther and all Protestants. They burned heretic Catholic priests and chopped poor Father Zwingli of Zurich into little pieces, barbequed him over a spit, and spread his ashes over Zurich. Father Zwingli married a widow in a civil ceremony against the Pope's wishes and proclaimed, 'if it's not in the Bible, it's not law!' The Pope disagreed.

"Later at the Council of Trent the Bishops passed a law that all Catholic Church Doctrine was divinely revealed truth same as the Bible. They declared the Pope was God's vicar on earth, and his words were God's wishes and commands. Anybody who disagreed with the Pope would be declared a heretic, offered a chance to recant, and, if no recantation, burned alive and naked at the stake.

"A generation after Zwingli and Luther, John Calvin resigned his Catholic priesthood and became the pastor of the largest Protestant church in Geneva, Switzerland.

"A fiery evangelist and strict Christian teacher, Calvin became the greatest teacher in Protestantism.

"Calvin tossed out all Catholic sacraments except Baptism and the Communion which he demoted to a symbolic ritual to be performed as a church formality once a year in honor of Jesus' wishes at his last supper. He declared that the Catholic Eucharist was superstition. Priests could not pray and change wine and bread into Jesus' blood and flesh, and the whole ritual was a pagan holdover from cannibalism and blood sacrifices. Calvin abolished confession, penance, absolution, purgatory, indulgences, celibacy, most of the Catholic holidays, all the Saints, and condemned Maryology and Patron saints as heretical and nonsense. He declared that the Holy Bible was 100% true from cover to cover in all things and raised the scripturally inspired sermon to the status of the Catholic Eucharist.

"It was Calvin's opinion that an hour's hellfire and brimstone once a week did more to achieve salvation than a wafer and a sip of wine, and ordinary people could speak directly to God, not to some statue, patron saint, or Virgin Mary. Protestants would deal directly with God, not some priest confessor or Pope.

"There's always a downside, however. Calvin was a lawyer as well as a religious fanatic. He believed in enforcing the church's laws by the same death sentence used by the Catholic Church, burning live at the stake.

"Calvin kept Incarnate Word, Holy Trinity, Predestination, and Elective Grace. He had two Spanish Catholic priests burned at the stake when they confessed that they believed Yahweh was God, and Jesus was the son, and they couldn't understand how you could get three persons into one.

"Calvin, being fair, offered them a chance to recant, and, when they refused, Calvin lit their bonfires himself.

"Calvin said GRACE was a gift from God, and you could not earn it or buy it. If you accepted Calvinism and were truly saved, you'd know GRACE.

"The big mystery in the Christian religion is Saint Paul Mysticism. Why should it work? Why should Adam's tainted sperm be passed down through millions of generations?

"The only answers are faith. If you don't have faith, you don't have religion. If you don't accept Saint Paul mysticism, you are not a Christian.

"GRACE was what they were all fighting about. Grace doesn't come cheap. After GRACE, it's all downhill.

"I personally believe that you cannot understand Protestantism and Christianity unless you know the Reformation and Counterreformation. Hotheads were slaughtered on both sides. It was the biggest destruction of property and murder of innocent women and children until the two World Wars.

"We saw Dante's statue in Napoli. Dante wrote *Comedia* which established *Paradisio*, *Purgatorio*, and *Inferno* in the imagination of Europeans. He was the greatest poet ever and influenced religion even to this day.

"We saw Vesuvius and the excavated ruins of Pompeii and Herculaneum and how the upper middle class lived in 79 ce. Public toilets that could accommodate 50 people at once. A statue of young Jesus wearing a golden fig leaf. A 25 feet young David in the nude getting ready to fight Goliath. The port of Ostium, where Saint Augustine and his mother, Saint Monica, saw the light from heaven and felt God. We ate pasta brought back from China by Marco Polo, pizza invented in Napoli out of scraps for the homeless and starving, and ice cream invented in 6 ce by the poet Ovid during the reign of Augustus. Trevi Fountain, where Audrey Hepburn and Gregory Peck enjoyed a Roman Holiday. The Basilica of Saint Francis, where Francis stripped naked, walked around preaching to the birds and squirrels, and panicked Europe who thought Jesus had returned, and the world was at end. The brilliant painting by Rafael in the Vatican Library of the *School of Athens* showing Plato, Aristotle, Euclid, Hippocrates, and all the classic Greek Thinkers whose ideas have been handed down to us today.

"I hope you realize that everything we know today, and all our academic disciplines started in Greece and spread to the Romans and down through generations until North America is the end products of Greco-Roman culture and knowledge."

Dr. Aristotle Plotinus erased and wrote on the green board. **METAPHYSICS, GREEK CLASSICS, MYTHOLOGY, CULTURE, CREATION STORY, ILIAD, BURNT SACRIFICES, AJAX, CASSANDRA, ATHENA, SOUL, HEAVEN, AND HEMLOCK**.

"How would you like to go to a medical lab, get a blood test and find out just how religious you really are? It would separate the true believers from the hypocrites and tell us who the criminals, car salesmen, and politicians will be. When the human genome studies are complete, you will be able to do just that.

"Geneticist have long known that humans pass on a religion gene. It is a dominant, non-sex linked gene, passed by both parents to each offspring. If the offspring receives a double dose, he's highly religious. You might find double dosers in priests, nuns, etc. Single dosers are your poor churchgoers, backsliders, and most of us, since single dosers make up seventy percent of the population. No dosers would probably end up in jail. It is very important to select your parents carefully!

"The Neandertals went back three hundred thousand years. They ranged in packs, lived in caves, thought their shadow was a soul, and worshiped animals, bears, spirits and just about everything and anything. Most of you saw the movies Cave Bear, Ada, etc. Hollywood gave a very good depiction of early prehistoric humans. The Cro Magnum evolved at least one hundred thousand years ago, and their caves have been found all over Europe, the Middle East, Africa, China, Australia, etc. They buried their dead with their weapons and utensils, put flowers on their graves, and painted animals on the walls of their caves.

"Recorded history goes back five thousand years or earlier. The Sumerians developed cuneiform, the Egyptians hieroglyphics, and the Chinese characters.

"Gilgamesh, an epic poem written in cuneiform, was recorded two thousand years before Genesis was penned in ancient Phoenician. Gilgamesh set out to find immortality. He interviews an ancient couple that were the only survivors of a great flood. They tell Gilgamesh about the plant of eternal life which he subsequently dives and retrieves from the bottom of a great sea only to have the serpent eat the plant of life while he is changing into dry clothes. So the serpent achieved immortality and sheds his skin every year, and Gilgamesh went back to rule Ur and die a natural death like all mortals.

"The thought of death and nothingness is incompatible with human mentality. People just won't accept a nothing hereafter. The one big exception is Buddhism where Nirvana in the here and now and escape from the cycle of birth, suffering, death, and rebirth is their goal, but most are destined to come back again.

"Socrates, around 400 bce, was first to conceive of heaven, soul, and rebirth. Both Zoroaster of Persia, and priests of Ancient Egypt developed the concept of afterlife and judgment at least a thousand years before the Hebrews started their westward migration. The Hebrews developed the concept of a single living God, final resurrection, and judgment. Isis resurrected Osiris from the Nile long before Jesus was resurrected from the grave.

Religion is a cultural phenomena. When you travel at the speed of light, distances shorten, time slows down, space time curves, triangles have more than one hundred and eighty degrees, and history seems quaint. The future is youth, and the present is old age.

In space, religion is even more of a regional cultural phenomena. You can't understand a civilization or its people without knowing their superstitions and religious beliefs. Most of you have watched enough Star Trek to understand that. You people are thinking about going to Mars. Your children will think about our galaxy, and your children's children will think about our universe.

"Before the end of the ice age, the beaker people occupied the British Isles, and the Cro magnum were scattered over Eurasia and Africa. 30,000 years ago the Aborigines migrated from southeast Asia to Australia, and the Japanese migrated across from Korea. 20,000 years ago the isolated voyages, and the long migrations began to the Americas. 12,000 years ago the glaciers melted, and our present interglacial period began and should last another 10,000 years. The Siberian migrations covered both North and South America. At the beginning of the BRONZE AGE, the Egyptians were flourishing along the Nile, the Sumerians in Mesopotamia, the Hittites in Asia Minor, the Mycenaean's in Greece, the Minoans on Crete, the Etruscans in Italy, the Phoenicians along the Mediterranean, the Babylonians, the Persians, the Hindus, the Germanic tribes around Denmark, the Celts around Salzburg and Austria, the Vietnamese, Koreans, Mongolians, Chinese, the Polynesians, island hopping eastward across the Pacific, the Lap Landers inside the arctic circle, the Eskimos and on and on. Most practiced human sacrifice and cannibalism as a religious ritual. Early on, Isis resurrected Osiris from the Nile and gave birth to the Egyptian gods. Each migration had its own gods and goddesses adapted to fit their needs and culture. With the onset of the IRON AGE, weapons and tools got better, and conquests got serious. The great religions that survived were: Islam, Christianity, Hinduism, Buddhism, Shintoism, and Judaism.

"Every tribe, every island, every nation, every civilization had its own creation story, deity, and religious customs. Each tribe had their own set of beliefs and their own revealed truths. Religion is hereditary in humans, and instead of being classified Homo Sapiens we should have been called Homo Religiosus. Only humans have a soul and an afterlife. All the other animals do not, and that includes Charlemagne's horse and your dog. My dog is human, and he'll be there when the roll is called up yonder.

"Today I will discuss the human soul. The concept of the human soul is totally abstract. No one has ever seen a soul. Cicero described it as a spark that enters an infant at birth when he takes his first breath, others say at the time of conception. All have agreed that the soul leaves the body at death. Soul was a Greek idea. Plato was first to write it down.

"Master of abstract thought and logic, Plato first described the Tripartite Mind: reason, spirit, and desire. Sigmund Freud called the Tripartite Mind: superego, ego, and id. Plato thought conflicts could be settled by reason over desire, but Sigmund Freud invented the subconscious which controls us all. Freud said that all human action is irrational, the ego is weak, and either the id or the superego is always in charge.

Plato's heaven was conceptualized along with the Divine mind, the soul, and the tripartite human mind around 400 bce in Athens, Greece.

"Augustine, Greco-Roman scholar, Professor of Rhetoric, and Catholic priest, performed a tremendous work in combining the metaphysics of Plato with the fundamental beliefs of the Judeo-Christian church.

"It has been said that all philosophy and metaphysics is but a footnote to Plato, and it can equally be said that all Christian church doctrine is a footnote to Augustine, Bishop of Hippo, 400 AD, who gave us silent reading, the mind's eye, the inner self, the religious experience, grace, predestination, providence, fall of Adam and the original sin, infant baptism for erasure of the original sin, free will, and on and on. Augustine was a Platonist Christian, Catholic church father, and Saint.

"Augustine wrote that the mind's eye and the inner self are the soul. When they look upward and connect with the Divine Mind, a person experiences a religious conversion. Faith is the love the inner self gives the Divine Mind, and Grace is the love it receives in return. Augustine described it as like falling in love. Like walking out of a dark cave into the light. Like: Ah hah! Now I see it.

"Cicero, the great first century Greco-Roman scholar and orator was right. He wrote that a human's soul leaves the body at death and ascends upward to take its place among the stars.

"Physicists today would say the soul rises as a photon of light to become suspended in a black hole and converted to an electron which is stored in a giant computer for eternity.

"Pericles, Socrates, Plato, Pythagoras, Hippocrates, Sophocles, etc. lived during the time of classical Greece which died with Socrates. Most of the Greek myths were at least a thousand years old and were inked on papyrus with the same alphabet we use today during the period 600-800 bce. The masses in Greece believed in the gods of the Iliad and built magnificent temples and burnt offerings to them. The scholars were into philosophy and logic. Athena didn't save Cassandra from rape and murder by Ajax, and fifty percent of Athenians and Pericles and his family died during the plague of 450 bce. Neither the Greeks nor the Romans required a citizen to 'believe' the mythology. In fact, they told them for amusement, but by law they worshipped and made sacrifice at the temples on state holidays or they were condemned of 'impiety' and were put to death like Socrates whom they accused of starting a new religion, which of course he did.

"Socrates came up with 'soul and heaven'. It was myth about the underworld, Hades, and three headed dog. The Greek temples and theaters were closed down by Emperor Theodosius in 394 AD in Greece, and Christianity was made Official Religion of the Roman Empire.

"Since, Antigone had a long run on Broadway starring Vivian Leigh in the title role. Media was made an opera, and Greek Theaters are active again in Sicily and Greece where people understand and speak Greek.

"I'll stop here. Thank you."

CHAPTER 9

Houston, Texas
10 P.M., Thursday, December 12, 1993

The best made plans of mice and men oft go awry. Tisha LaFemme and Le Li (Shan) disembarked Continental Air from LAX, and nobody met them at baggage claim except porters and taxi cab drivers. When Bangladesh declared war on Myanmar (Burma), no one anticipated it. Bob and Elvis put them on the next plane home and took off to parts unknown. It was a secret. Elvis was on orders from the CIA, and Bob was Geologist for SROCO exploring for gas and oil in SEA.

* * *

Kuala Lumpur Malaysia
8 A.M., Friday, December 13, 1993
Hot, Humid, Equatorial

"My phallus is bigger than your phallus," remarked Elvis Pressly CIA (Lt. Col. US Army, Retired) to Bob Burrell, Geologist from SROCO, as they looked up at the PETRONAS NOC twin towers with adjoining walkway in the center of Kuala Lumpur. Before the Burj Khalifa in Dubai, they were the tallest buildings in the world. Growing from a small holding company twenty years ago, the National Oil Company of Malaysia, PETRONAS, had become one of the "Seven Sisters of Big Oil." Now rich, it would take on risks, and, like the other big intergrateds, would drill anywhere in the world if the profits were "right."

Citizens spoke English as a first language in Malaysia whose population was 50% Malay, 40% Chinese, and 10% Indian (Hindu). Malays were Muslims, and if you wanted to eat lunch during RAMADAN, you found a Chinese Restaurant or KFC and McDonald's. Women wore bourqas by choice, but the Mullahs didn't broadcast calls to prayer all over town. There were no overt signs of hostility since Hindus made up only 10% of the population. The Chinese were richest and owned all the banks. There was a saying that a Malay kept his store open 8 hours, the Hindu 12 hours, and the Chinese stayed open 24 hours a day (Wall Street Journal). Chinese, by habit, saved 40% and ended up owning the banks by default. The Cufan prohibited loaning money at interest.

Passing up the classiest and most expensive hotels and restaurants in Malaysia, Bob and Elvis checked into the Holiday Inn-Downtown which guaranteed no surprises, since they were mostly the same all over the world. MasterCard and Visa were better than money in Kuala Lumpur but identified you as American to casual observers. They went through the buffet, carried their trays out on a patio surrounding a swimming pool beside which was an outdoor bar at the water's edge selling mixed alcoholic drinks and beverages. Water and ice were safe and free, and if you avoided the Indian spices, you would be reasonably safe from not coming down with "Delhi belly" which in Texas we called "tourista" or the Mexican shits.

There was a slender freckled young lady who followed them out to their table for four, smiled, and set her tray down in front of the empty chair between them.

"May I join you two gents? I have to get my stuff from the lobby before it's stolen. I'll be right back." Her breakfast was two slices of toast and black coffee.

"Her voice identified her as Australian, and her outback hat, boots, and denim made her look like Crocodile Dundee with curves and busts. She returned from the lobby with a photographer's bag hanging from one shoulder, a carry on, and luggage. She'd come from the airport, sat in the lobby, and chose them amongst many for whatever reason. Maybe they were old enough to be her father and looked "safe." To an attractive young woman in a foreign country alone, safe was a relative term to say the least.

She introduced herself as Penny Brownrig, a freelance journalist and photographer on assignment from Perth Australia and wanted to know if they were planning to go all the way.

"All the way where?" asked Elvis, amused.

"Good question!" exclaimed Penny. "I figured you two gents were American CIA taking the Oriental Express to Chang Mai, the end of the line. We could get a car for four with sleepers and have our meals brought to us with almost complete privacy except when we change trains at Bangkok," explained Penny, smiling.

Elvis hesitated. "This is a Muslim country. I don't think they'd let a woman and two men travel together, especially if they weren't married." He looked worried.

"I forgot to tell you. I'm on a very tight budget. One of you gents will have to go to the Hotel Admission clerk and sign me on as your wife. Same on the train. It's done all the time. Why don't you flip a coin and choose head or tail."

* * *

When they came down for dinner, Penny was in a cocktail dress, heels, her hair was down, her eyes sparkled, and she radiated sex. Elvis guessed head, and Bob got tail. Bob signed on Penny as his wife.

They found a table for four in the same buffet restaurant, and a middle aged balding Sicilian walked in and chose the empty chair across from Penny. He put down his bag and baggage, and asked, "May I join. I'm Don Tantalia from Houston. I'll pay."

CHAPTER 10

After dinner Don lit a Cuban cigar, leaned back and smiled at the three, Penny, Bob, and Elvis.

"Did you kids see the movie where Clint Eastwood took a bath with Meryl Streep?"

"Yes," gasp Penny. "Romantic! I hope it comes out on a VCR, so I can watch it again and again. *Bridges of Madison County*. He was photographing the wooden bridge for National Geographic."

"Would you call that art or porno?"

"Art, my God! Porno turns me off. That was a wonderful movie."

Don smiled, approvingly. He was leading them down a path. "Would you agree that acting and actors are the differences between art and porno?"

"Yes! I want you to see my Elvis Presley act. I have these college age beer drinkers get in a too small cage and hook up by any means possible while I play my guitar and sing *Hound Dog* and *Heartbreak Hotel*. All they have to do is get off." I run an "Elvis Lives" mission in Tachilek Myanmar at the bridge to Chang Rae in the heart of the Golden Triangle.

"If the authorities question us I'll show them our National Geographic credentials and Penny will have photographs and photography equipment. We'll fly to Haiphong-Hanoi, take a chartered boat to KaLong, fly back to Saigon (Ho Chi Min city) where we'll take a helicopter and search the southern coast of Vietnam, Cambodia, Thailand and Malaysia and end up in Singapore. Depending on how the war goes in Myanmar and Bay of Bengal. We've only committed SROCO to drill the You River basin in Quanxi and have not spent one nickel on Myanmar and Cambodia.

"Besides signs of oil and gas, for what are we looking?" asked Bob.

"Negritos," replied Don. "They are little black people who hide in rain forests, hunt monkeys, eat humans, and gather maggots off leaves and dead carcasses. They use poison darts and arrows to kill their prey.

"Negritos migrated along the southern coast of Africa, Arabia, and India between 40,000-50,000 years ago, and DNA studies show they are cousins to the Pygmies of Zaire. The Japanese killed about 200,000 during their occupation of Borneo in WWII. The last living tribe are in the rain forests of the Andaman Islands off the west coast of Myanmar in the Bay of Bengal. There are about a thousand islands, and the Chinese have a submarine base there guarding the Straits of Malacca.

"The political hot spots now, because of their known gas and oil potential, are the Spratly Islands in the South China Sea. Vietnam and China have already fought a naval battle over the Spratlies and every country bordering on the South China Seas in staking a claim. The United States, Vietnam, Taiwan, and the Philippines are trying to block China from hogging it all," explained Donald Tantalia.

They nodded. Elvis quipped, "I thought Negritos were salted corn snacks sold in Brazil."

CHAPTER 11

Zurich, Switzerland
1 P.M., Saturday, December 14, 1993
Temp 26°F, Snow

It was snowing heavily when they claimed their baggage in Zurich and headed for Immigration and Customs. Their passport was sufficient and no visa was necessary since they were just passing through. All the rooms were taken at the Inn, so Maria rented them a conference room for the night. The ticket counter opened at 4 A.M. for early morning flights. They got breakfast, free coffee, and an *USA Today* on the plane.

*   *   *

Before formal lectures Maria took the microphone and smiled.

"Swiss Air has never had an accident or a delayed flight. They don't let Brahman cows or sheep on the runways. I want you all lined up at the ticket counter downstairs at 4 A.M. We'll have coffee and breakfast of cheeses and chocolates on the plane and land at Heathrow at 8 A.M.

"It is not snowing in London. They get our Gulf Stream to keep them warm. It will drizzle and rain so carry your umbrella and raincoat and hat overhead with your carry-on.

"In London, we will stay in the downtown Hilton next to the largest Cricket Stadium and Islamic Mosque. Past the Mosque, there's a commons (public park) where you can jog, ride a bike, make a speech, and rent a dog to walk as a great conversation piece. Red double decker buses stop at the corners and their destinations are listed under a map with **YOU ARE HERE**. London has a "tube" underground railroad which we call a subway that'll take you anywhere and half England. Their taxis are characteristically tall and stubby and painted with yellow checkers. They are unionized, and the set fee is two English Pounds one way fare.

"Paris has six Poodles for every tree and 6000 full time "pooper scoopers" riding on bicycles as a lifetime career which have a very well organized union and early retirement. London has two taxis for every pedestrian, and they all speak English and wear uniforms.

"We will have a week to wait to catch our plane to New York, Washington D.C., or Atlanta to go through Immigration and Customs. If we get Atlanta or Washington D.C., we'll fly standby to Houston. If New York, LaGuardia or Kennedy, we'll fly to Chicago, O'Hare, and then to Houston.

"We now have eleven days until Christmas. Like Henry Kissinger, we'll be home by Christmas. Like Ross Peron, I got you out of Iran safely.

"I will not risk losing anybody in London. Backpackers and college students will be everywhere. I'll charter a local one day tour to Avebury and Stonehenge, have lectures that night, and board a chartered bus to York, Hadrian's Wall, Scotland with overnight stays at Edinburg and Glasgow, and a brief stop at Loch Loma. From Glasgow we'll fly to Dublin, visit Trinity University, and take a ferry and bus back through Wales.

"If anybody is interested we might detour to Blarney Castle, climb an outside winding stairway to the top and hang by our heels and kiss the blarney stone. The last time I was at Blarney Castle it was raining, so I found a nice warm pub. Oh yes! You'll find the Scots cold and formal, but the Irish invented whiskey (water of life), and I have never met a true native Irishman that wasn't full of Blarney. They all kissed the Blarney Stone. Remember, the Scots are proud, and the Irish are friendly, at least to women.

"Zurich more than any other place was the home of the Catholic Reformation. Unfortunately, Ulbricht Zwingli, ended up being roasted on a spit and his ashes scattered.

"Tonight, Dr. Christi Isaac will discuss London. Dr. Aristotle Plotinus will discuss the Roman Catholic Reformation and Counter-Reformation. I personally don't believe you can understand the Christian religion in the western world without studying the Reformation. We have heard it over and over again, but, if you confess to Roman Catholicism as I, then you should never tire of hearing it. They don't even mention it in Protestant (reformed Catholic) churches. Americans are functional illiterates when it comes to the theological basis of religion.

"Lastly, Dr. Eros Zenovenusetti, will tell us about our hero, Ulbricht Zwingli, whose greatest wrong was falling in love and marrying a rich widow. By the way, to put things in perspective, when John Calvin was pastor of the largest church, the population of Geneva Switzerland was only 5000 and most were Catholics. Calvin wrote the Protestant Bible while Martin Luther wrote the Lutheran Bible. King James chained his Theologians to their desks until they translated and composed the King James, Original, in 16th Century vernacular English which became the vocabulary of the common folk in the English speaking world for the next 200 years."

CHAPTER 12

After spending a leisurely afternoon in the world's most modern aeroport in the world's richest and most expensive city, they took an underground tunnel and an escalator up to the world's most modern shopping mall that was equal to Osaka, Tel Aviv, and Ankara. Most took a nap on the floor using their bag and baggage as pillows and were alert and elated at lectures that night. They felt safe in Christendom with no mullahs calling them to prayer five times a day.

Maria Tantalia wrote on the blackboard. **CATHERINE OF ARAGON, HENRY VIII, MARTIN LUTHER, ZWINGLI, CALVIN, CELEBACY, DOMINIC, POPE INNOCENT, AND HAIL MARY**.

Maria began, "all this started when King Henry VIII wanted to divorce Catherine of Aragon and marry Anne Boleyn, and Martin Luther, Ulbricht Zwingli, and John Calvin, all Catholic priests, wanted to shed the stigma of adultery and take on the bonds of matrimony. They'd preach against adultery in the pulpit and go home to a common law wife.

"There's nowhere in the Bible where it says a priest can't get married, or divorced for that matter. Catherine of Aragon was King Ferdinand of Spain's sister and King Charles of Spain's aunt. Not only did the Pope say no, but the King of Spain who was the Emperor of the Holy Roman Empire, was personally insulted. Pope Innocent I got uptight about the Manicheans and Albigenseans on the Spanish-French border who published their own Bible and were seeking coverts among the Roman Catholics. The Virgin Mary paid a earthly visit to Saint Dominic of Castile and recited the Catholic Rosary 150 times. Pope Innocent I declared a Christian crusade against heretics and appointed Dominic the leader of the Domini Canis, Hounds of the Lord, Head Brother of the Dominican Order, and founder of the Spanish Inquisition against Catholic heretics. To be a heretic you had to be a Catholic first. Orthodox Jews and Muslims who did not convert to Catholicism were not heretics. The Catholic Reformation lasted 200 years, and the Spanish Inquisition lasted 400 years and ended up in Monterrey Mexico where they serve Kosher on request today. The same at Chihuahua which was settled by former Muslim Conversos who ate Halal dogs.

"Tonight I've asked Dr. Eros Zenovenusetti to take Zwingli, and Dr. Aristotle Plotinus will take Martin Luther and John Calvin. We'll save Henry VIII until we get to England.

"I've asked Christy to finish up with a quick lecture on Zurich. We're sleeping in the airport of the richest city in the world, and all we'll see is snow.

"When she gets through, I'll tell you about my father's uncle, and the oldest continuously occupied Benedictine monastery where Jesus Christ himself appeared alive and in person at its inauguration back in 800 c.e. If you don't believe me, look it up. It's in *WORLD BOOK.* The Virgin Mary gave Dominic the Catholic Rosary alive and in person. It's in *HAIL MARY.*

Dr. Eros Zenovenusetti wrote on the blackboard. **CHARLEMAGNE'S HORSE, GROSSMUNSTER, HILDEGARD, FRAU-MUNSTER, ULRICH ZWINGLI, REFORMATION, BAR-B-Q, LUTHER, CALVIN, AND HOLY MATRIMONY**.

"Father Ulrich Zwingli, a Catholic priest, lived on the premises of the Grossmunster Cathedral in Zurich for 47 years, but met his death leading a Protestant Army against a Catholic Army and was horribly murdered, chopped up in little pieces, burned over a barbeque pit, and his ashes scattered over Lake Zurich.

"At the time Zurich had a population of only 3000, and rural folks took religion very seriously. When John Calvin was the pastor of the largest Protestant Church in Geneva it only had a metropolitan population of 5000. By today's standards, we're talking about a town the size of Liberty or Vidor, Texas.

"Both Zwingli and Calvin got involved in town politics, like to run things, and had an eye for the fair sex (young women). When Pandora opened her magic box, all the evils that afflict mankind flew out, and both preachers, loud in the pulpit, had a secret sin, sex. In defiance of the Pope, they got married in a civil ceremony outside the Catholic Church. Luther was ex-communicated before he and the brothers all married local nuns.

"Now, you may think those antics humorous, but back in those days ex-communication was a capital offense, and any local lawman had orders from the King to strip you naked on the spot and burn you alive at the stake, and the crown would confiscate and seize your property for the King's treasure.

"Most of the Reformed Catholics weren't called Protestants unless they refused to recant and were ex-communicated and damned to hell, no question. That goes for the so-called Protestant sects and Orthodox and Russian Christians prior to 1964. Pope John Paul is trying to persuade the Methodist, Episcopalians, Anglicans, and Lutherans back under the protective umbrella of Roman Catholicism by offering to lift their ex-communication as bait (reward). There's no hope for the Calvinists, pagans, Mormons, Jehovah Witnesses, and non-Catholic Jesus cults which spring up in every big city.

"I'm going to stop, since I'm Greek Orthodox, love Greek Mythology, and wasn't indoctrinated early on in Augustine Christianity. Dr. Plotinus keeps all those names and dates written on his sleeve like an NFL quarterback."

"Aristotle, please."

Eros erased the blackboard and Dr. Aristotle Plotinus wrote on the blackboard. **LOUIS THE GERMAN, FRAUMUNSTER, HOLY ROMAN EMPIRE, BENEDICTINE MONASTERY, EINSIEDELN, JESUS CHRIST IN PERSON, CHOCOLATE AND CHEESES, REFORMATION, COUNCIL OF TRENT, COUNTER-REFORMATION, IGNATIUS LOYOLA, AND SPANISH INQUISITION.**

"Fraumunster Abbey (853 c.e.) was built by Lewis the German, the grandson of Charlemagne, for is daughter Hildegard, and the Grossmunster (820 c.e.) was built by Charlemagne in memory of his war horse who died of old age. Grossmunster means great minister, and it was declared Charlemagne's Imperial Church after he was crowned the first King of the Holy Roman Empire. Later the Russ took the name Czar (Tsar), and the Prussians Kaizer after Caesar August. Julius Caesar was crowned the first Pontius Maximus from which we got Pope, the Bishop of Rome.

"The Benedictine Monastery at Einsiedeln just 30 miles south of here up in the alps was Charlemagne's favorite summer retreat. They don't need cars up there, and they have a nine month winter. It was visited by Jesus after its opening back in 780 a.c. Maria visited a great uncle there and can describe it in more detail.

"The Grossmunster, Fraumunster, and the Benedictine Monastery at Einsiedeln in the Swiss Alps are "must sees" on any summer and autumn Christian tour. There's a hotel across from the monastery built like a rustic medieval Inn, and chocolate and cheese stores in the village along narrow cobblestone streets. You can gaze down at the clouds and across the mountains at alpine villages dotted with cows and haystacks and hear horns and milkmaids singing.

"I'll confess. I've been there, stayed at the Inn, tasted the homemade cheeses and chocolates, and thought I was in heaven until I found out the Catholic Elementary School run by the brothers costs a kid $26,000 a year in tuition alone.

"It was like Santa Barbara, California. Any place where I'd really like to live, cost much more than I can afford. If you can afford to spend $120,000 on your kid's grammar school and live on cheese and chocolates, then Einsiedeln is the place for you. There's no business there except tourism about three months a year. The rest of the time you are snowed in.

"We covered Martin Luther, the Ana-Baptists, Huldrich Zwingli and John Calvin in great detail back home plus all the bloodshed over many things we don't take seriously now. The counter reformation, Council of Trent, Ignatius Loyola and the Brotherhood of Jesus, and the Spanish Inquisition, etc., etc. and on and on. Oddly enough the war and all the riches you see in the Catholic Churches today were paid for with Mexican and Peruvian silver and gold. Spain created the greatest empire on earth until the Spanish Armada was defeated by the British in 1588, and that was the beginning of the end of Spanish greatness. The Philippines were named for King Phillip II.

"Zurich is where the Reformation started."

"Christy."

Dr. Christy Isaac wrote on the blackboard. **STREETS OF GOLD, EUROPE'S CLEANEST AND BEST, ZWINGLI, REFORMATION, PRIDE OF ROMAN EMPIRE, GROSSMUNSTER, FRAUMUNSTER, AND CHARLEMAGNE'S HORSE**.

"It occurred to me as I listened to Eros and Aristotle that we don't have a historian on board. We went on a Holy Land Anthropology Tour, and we're back in western civilization and modernity. Dr. Winston Blood where are you now when we need you?

"Zurich is simply the biggest and best and the richest city in Switzerland. Its stock exchange is 150 years old. All the Swiss Banks are headquartered here, and every major corporation in Europe and the Americas has an office building or an affiliate here. It has been named the city with the best quality of life, best research and education, and the best universities with over 60,000 students in residency.

"Settlements of Neolithic and bronze age people dating back 7000 years lived around Lake Zurich. The Romans established it as an outpost in 15 b.c.e. Celts were here before the Romans. An inscribed tombstone dates back to 2 c.e. A Carolingian Castle was built by Charlemagne's grandson, Louis, in 835. A city wall dates back to 1230 c.e.

"The Grossmunster was finished in 823 c.e. and Ulrich Zwingli was its senior priest and minister from 1484 to his horrible death in 1531. Martin Luther came to Zurich to confer with Zwingli, and they agreed on everything but the presence of Jesus in person at the

Eucharist. Zwingli said communion was symbolic of Jesus' wishes at the Last Supper, but Luther wouldn't budge on Jesus' presence in person. In fact, Martin Luther admitted publically that Zwingli was crazy. Martin was hung up on faith alone and left the Book of James out of his Bible while Zwingli said, 'if it's not in the Bible you don't have to do it'. The Pope disagreed with both.

"Zwingli died fighting, and Martin Luther hid out a year in a rich widow's castle translating a Latin version of Erasmus of Rotterdam's Bible into German. Zwingli wrote a Zurich Bible. Anybody can write a Bible and several did, but back in those days it was a capital offense, and you were burned at the stake. Bloody Mary had Tyndale's body exhumed and burned at the stake.

"John Calvin rewrote, embellished, and edited Tyndale's Bible and called it the Geneva Bible which became the Bible of the Calvinist Protestant Reformation. A lot of additions, subtractions, and changes were made before the movable printing press and King James' version. The experts, in good faith, couldn't agree with each other. That's why we have 900 (+) Protestant sects today. It fits the Chaos Theory perfectly, slight changes can lead to Chaos.

"Down on the lake passed the Grossmunster is Saint Peter's which has the largest clock in the world. Albert Einstein while on his honeymoon drove passed and wondered what would happen to time as he approached the speed of light. Many expert pathologist examined Albert Einstein's brain and concluded he had a normal amount of neurons like everybody else. A lady pathologist counted his glial cells and demonstrated he had more than normal between short memory and long memory neurons, and they transmitted electrical impulses just like neurons. We were taught that glial cells provided connective tissue covering of the brain and had no neuronal properties. WOW!

"They built a wall around Zurich in 1624 and avoided the bloody 30-year's religious war in Germany. The Zurich stock exchange was founded in 1877. Switzerland stayed out of both WWI and WWII, and both sides stored wealth in Zurich banks.

"Its mean temperature is 31°F in the winter and 67° in July-August. Zurich Airport has its own underground railway connected to Zurich and most major cities. Its population is 360,000 inside city limits with a metropolitan population of 1.7 million. 80% speak German. It has 30% Catholics, 17% Atheist, and the rest are Protestants, Muslims and Jews. 3% are unemployed and 4% or on welfare.

"Zurich has the world's biggest gold exchange. If you cross the bridge at Lake Zurich and visit the clean and prosperous old business district, you'll think you died and went to heaven. The cobblestone streets were paved with gold.

"I'm going to turn down the lights so you can nap. We'll go as a group down to the ticket counter at 4 A.M. Go to the rest room, don't forget your passport, pocketbook, money belt, top coat, bag and baggage. It's only a couple of hours to London. Hasta La Vista."

CHAPTER 13

Houston, Texas
Friday, December 13, 1933
Temp 67/45°
Sunny, Partly cloudy

Murder yes, ghosts no! So Jésus liked haunting his old house on Dewberry. It needed to be haunted. If Lynnette showed up, Dirk would get interested. He thought of Lynette's stinking malodorous body with a thousand slashes stuffed in her clothes dryer and blood all over the house. Flies and maggots in the wounds! Buzzards were perched on the roof and in the trees.

Dirk developed an immediate dislike of Lieutenant Shelby Fox when they first met. Lieutenant Costello was being investigated as suspect in Dr. Guadalupe Alvarez's murder. All evidence led to Rico Carbello who was murdered before they could get an admission. Fathers Villa and Cervantes were murdered, and terrorist backed a truck through the wall and carted off 4 tons of recycled cocaine from Father Villa's room and stashed it at Pancho's Automotive.

Dirk, Miguel, and Sheila assisted by Sergeant Reginald Dewberry and HPD SWAT caught Shelby and Ivry Cost in the act of loading the dope, all 4 tons, on a Renta Truck.

Dirk was out of the country when the initial drug bust was made back in June.

Lieutenant Fox and Ivry Cost were arrested with the contraband and charged with possession with intent to distribute. Sergeants Wilbur Everett and Patrolman Brice Redmon were also arrested. They pled not guilty and claimed they were on duty and performing their own drug bust.

Dirk couldn't remember how the trial turned out. Houston experienced a record breaking freeze from August 15 to October 15. He was called to active military duty and made several trips to Mexico. Someway, they must have gotten a plea bargain, because Fox was terminated. Wilbur Everett was demoted to patrol, and Brice Redmon was transferred to the sanitation department.

He first saw Lieutenant Fox sitting at the table beside Father Villa and listening to Dr. Capistrano and Rico Carbello arguing over money at 4 A.M. the morning of Dr. Guadalupe Alvarez's murder. He didn't know him then.

Debra Crawford admitted she and Jésus Muhammad saw Shelby murder Sergeant Bobby Crawford and heard him order Happy Early and Mickey Finn to dispose of the body and make it look like a drug deal gone sour.

Ivry Cost using a Claud's Renta Truck drove for Shelby the night of the original pickup and arrest and delivered it from the Private Waste Disposal on the Brazos River to Father Villa's room at Saint Colombo.

* * *

Detours and barricades were still up around Saint Colombo Cathedral and cemetery, but the cops and firemen were gone. A portable drilling rig was over the open grave, and the gusher had been capped. Dirk looked for a sign to identify the driller but saw none.

Home leveling crews were working around the base of the cathedral, and work crews were cleaning the oil soaked graveyard. Bacteria were supposed to clean up the rest.

Dirk parked across the barricaded area and walked to the front door and through the auditorium to the bachelor quarters in back. He found Archbishop (retired) Joseph Galbreaux, Father Eusebius, and a younger priest, about 45, sharing a quart of Old Crow in front of the TV in the priest's lounge.

Dirk was friends with the retired Padres, and they stood, offered Dirk a drink, and introduced a new colleague, Father Jésus Posadas, transferred from Guadalajara to take over Father Villa's duties as parish priest. Father Posadas spoke English well.

*   *   *

Driving his SUV and towing his recently acquired 17 feet fiberglass fish and ski, Dirk picked up Dr. Joy Burrell, Psychiatrist, at her apartment at the Braeswood LUX. Joy liked to fish and was still new in Houston and not overloaded with work in her chosen field, Hysteria and Functional Sexual problems of females. She was a recognized International authority in Cognitive Therapy and was addressed as Lady Burrell in England. Dirk knew of her latest husband, Bob Burrell, Geologist with SROCO on site in China at Quanxi basin which Dirk had visited with Maria several months ago.

Joy had a research grant to study the longitudinal effects of incest and was signing up couples for a five year pilot study. One of the principal goals of Cognitive Therapy was channeling in treatment of cultural taboos. She needed 100 couples among academics, professionals, and clergy for obvious reasons. Just plain ordinary folks lie 95% of the time and 100% lie under oath on the witness stand. Dirk chuckled. He didn't qualify and neither did Dentists and Veterinarians. She wanted medical doctors and lawyers who by selection and training broke out with hives if they deliberately told a lie. Experts who questioned everything.

The U.S. Department of Health, Education, and Welfare gave Joy a blank check and were all for it. Incest was an excellent way to prohibit the spread of infectious venereal diseases and AIDS and combat overpopulation in the twenty-first century when we ran out of precious non renewable resources.

CHAPTER 14

Devine' was off the pill and carrying the semen of three men, Bill Riley DA, Donald Tantalia, and Dr. Austin Hale. She propped her feet up on pillows while in bed hoping to get pregnant. She hadn't any of the early signs: nausea, weight gain, fluid retention, food cravings and etc., and her urine pregnancy test was too early to tell. Sperm live a long time in a woman's vagina, reproductive tract, and abdomen, WOW! They don't live in her stomach because of the gastric juices. She decided to stay in bed and keep her feet propped up on three pillows so nothing drained out.

Devine' took Sandra's list and studied. Bill put Shelby Fox and Ivry Cost on Lois Morrison's docket Monday at 8 A.M. She had Sandra's notes and autopsy reports from the office. Charges were murder, possession, and trafficking cocaine.

*   *   *

1. R. Capistrano & J. Alvarez—GRD JY NO BILLED—CHARGES DROPPED—FBI
2. Dr. G. Jekyl—Murd I—11/27/93—JY Marci & Eliz—pick jury—Castroil
3. Hosea Gomer—Murd. I—11/28/93—JY Devine' picks jury—Dutch Royal
4. R. Capistrano, S. Fox, B. Redmon, Wilbur Everett—Bench Warrant 11/23/93—Trafficking cocaine—Cuban Mafia
5. D. Cartenegro, S. Pablo Huston, Carl Bribey—Bench Warrant 11/23/93—drug, bribes, pushing dope

6. S. Bloom, E. Early, Michael Finn—Key to warehouse—Bench Warrant 11/23/93

7. P. Lovett, Murder I, Grand Jury True Billed—Arraignment 11/24/93

8. T. Lovett—MI—Hosp. Hysteria, Depression—Lockup—Psycho. Dr. Helga Schmidt

9. Muhammad Abdullah Hussain—Murd I Jail—Crazy Shiite Muslim

10. Jessie Dan White—Shoot Lib. Open 3D Bench Warrant—11/23/93

11. Jotte Jalopena—MI—CJ Charges Dropped—11/23/93—Bench VACA de VACA

12. Kenneth Clark Kent—ADA 11/23 Single, no kids, Big Student Loan, Marci—DA's niece—Yale Law—Neva Braun—Day court —

13. Rafael and Angel Quintero—Jail awaiting Deportation or Fed Wit. Program.

14. Knockers Motorcycle Club—Tillie Lovett, Neva, Warehouse, H.H.

15. Elvis Jones—Six Pack Jones—All American—Pr. View—Kansas City Chiefs Special T. beat Dallas in Super Bowl—will flip to save skin

16. Horace Greely—Elvis—KNOCKERS—SEX TRAFFICKING, PIMP, CRACK—Off duty Res. Deputies —

17. James Fry Jr.—MI, 11/24/93, Deer Rifle—shot Dr. Joe Cain MASH, Patrolwomen Haley and Budd.

After statements of new evidence by Ivry Cost and Debra Crawford, the State (Opal
Hony) dismissed the jury and dropped charges on Bloom and Early for the murders of Sergeant Robert Crawford and Father Villa. They

were going to choose a new jury and try Dr. Capistrano, Lieutenant Shelby Fox and Brice Redmon. That was *déjà vu* all over again.

She studied the list. Number 1: The charges of the murder of Theresa Capistrano by Dr. Capistrano and Juanita Alvarez was no billed by the Grand Jury when the FBI failed to produce incriminating films which they apparently lost or erased. Number 2: Charges were dropped against Dr. George Jekyl for the murder of nurse Janis Cotton after the FBI located the platinum reactor smuggled out in nurse Cotton's car trunk and arrested the real murderers. Number 3: Hosea Gomer proved to have a solid alibi, and an eyewitness reported seeing Mrs. John Brinkley club Angella and store her in a deep freeze for two months before Mrs. Brinkley and her daughter took her out in the bay and dumped her frozen body. Angella's skeleton washed in on West Beach with a fractured skull and mummified hands and feet after crabs and fish ate everything else. The eyewitness produced Angella's bloody nightstick used by Mrs. Brinkley as the murder weapon. When Angella's body was identified, Dr. Brinkley committed suicide by swallowing a bottle of sleeping pills and getting in the same deep freeze in which Angella died. They left a bastard child who was entitled to half the estate.

Number 4: Dr. Raul Capistrano, Shelby Fox, and Brice Redmon would appear as defendants Monday and answer to the charges of murders of Sergeant Bobby Crawford and Father Villa, possessing and trafficking bulk cocaine with intent to distribute. Charges had been reduced on Ivry Cost and Everett Wilbur for turning state's evidence and agreeing to witness for the state. Deborah Crawford and Jésus Muhammad witnessed Shelby shoot Bobby Crawford and Happy Early saw Shelby crucify Father Villa and Father Escobar castrate Father Villa after the fact. Angel and Rafael would identify Shelby as the assassin of General Lupe Lopez and killer of the jailhouse clerk and deputies. It went on and on. Devine' wasn't about to defend Brice Redmon, Shelby, and Dr. Capistrano without Sandra. WOW!

She took Sandra's Gideon Bible off the nightstand. Jesus smiles every time somebody steals a Gideon Bible. She turned to the story of

Rachael and Jacob in the Hebrew Old Testament. She turned to page 36, Genesis 31.

> **34. Now Rachael had taken the images, and put them in the camels furniture, and sat upon them. And Laban searched all the tent but found them not.**
>
> **35. And she said to her father. Let it not displease my lord that I cannot rise up before thee: for the custom of women is upon me. And he search, but found not the images.**

Devine dialed Bill Riley DA's office at the courthouse. Eloise Johnson, his private legal secretary answered.

"This is lawyer Sparks. May I speak to Mr. Riley please?"

"This is Eloise. He be at Booker's meeting, Opal too. I'll take the message. That's my job. Where are you? They held the business," replied Eloise.

"I'm indisposed. I'm coming down with the 'flu'. Would you ask him to change the docket on the Shelby Fox case until after New Year's?" pleaded Deviné, lying.

"I'll take care of it right now. Nobody wants to work Christmas. You can't get a jury, half the cleaning people will call in sick, and they'll close the coffee shop in the basement," replied Eloise.

"Please get Bill's permission. That's a big case. Sandra has been ordered by Governor Ann Richards to defend those guys. Bill needs to notify the State Attorney and Governor Richards," replied Deviné, coughing.

"It's as good as done. It's my job. Bill never crosses me. I don't want to work either."

*   *   *

The power of suggestion was miraculous. Devine' developed a scratchy throat, runny nose, itching eyes, and dry cough. She put out a box of Kleenex beside her and looked at the list.

Bill had dropped charges on 5, 6, 7, and 8. Muhammad was still in jail with no hope of discharge. It was either a life sentence or execution. He deliberately ran and backed over Principal Hank Greenberg 3-4 times with the whole neighborhood watching. He knew what he was doing and demanded a Mullah, Shariah, and martyrdom to get his due reward of virgins in paradise. Muslims were the only religion Devine' knew that guaranteed sex in heaven. She was always taught that souls didn't have gonads (testicles).

Jessie Dan White, Jotte Jalopeno, and Tillie Lovett were all released without charges. That left Rafael and Angel Quinteros who would identify Shelby as the jailbreak shooter. Elvis and Horace were waiting on the Grand Jury, and number 17 was waiting on Sandra.

*　　*　　*

Devine' looked at the autopsy reports on Sergeant Robert (Bobbie) Crawford and Father Villa.

Actually, Lieutenant Shirley Bloom, Sergeant Happy Early, and Sergeant Michael (Micky) Finn had been tried for these same murders a month ago, but new evidence cast a significant doubt on their guilt and charges were dismissed. Dirk, Sheila Mullins, and Miguel Montalban accompanied by Reginald Dewberry and Houston SWAT caught Shelby Fox and Ivry Cost loading up 4 tons of recycled cocaine into a Renta Truck in back of Pancho's Automotive. They were arrested, booked, and jailed by Sheila and Miguel after they had gotten a call from Evon at Claud's Automotive that Ivry had rented one of her trucks.

Using dynamic persuasion, Sergeant Booker Washington was able to get a full confession from Ivry Cost and viable eyewitness accounts incriminating former Internal Affairs Lieutenant Shelby Fox of multiple murders of which Bobby Crawford and Father Villa were only two. Mr.

Riley decided to try only the two because the evidence wasn't as good on the others. Most people enjoyed only one lifetime without parole for first degree murder. Dr. Raul Capistrano was the principal smuggler of the cocaine, suspected head of the Cuban Mafia, and brother-in-law of Shelby Fox who was taking orders from Dr. Capistrano (the buck stops here). A rumor started by Debra Crawford, undercover IRS, was that Dr. Capistrano's credentials were all faked. He wasn't a Dermatologist, and he was *persona nongrata* with the IRS. She and Sandra were saddled with defending those "clowns." WOW!

Dr. Nu had explained the autopsy reports, *ad nauseum*, to the previous jury.

Sergeant Bobbie Crawford was a 35 year old black police officer who was murdered allegedly by Lieutenant Shelby Fox near the railroad tracks behind the Shiite Baptist Mosque as witnessed by several with gunshot to the chest and heart resulting in instant death. On orders of Lieutenant Fox, he was mutilated by his fellow officers and dumped along with his city patrol car near an abandoned crack house on the bank of the Brazos River in Brazoria County. The crime scene was investigated by Captain Ira Johnson, Brazoria County Sheriff's Department, after which his body and patrol car were transported back to Harris County for criminal investigation. He arrived headless with hands and feet chopped off and a missing left leg to above the knee torn off by an alligator. He was malodorous with no signs of rigor mortis. He was dead three days when Captain Jerry Billings DPS and lawyer Sandra Lerner shot at the alligator with the severed leg and scared the buzzards out of the crack house. They correctly called the local law. Later, Detective Derek Strong wrestled Bobbie's head, feet and hands away from the buzzards in a side tracked boxcar out where the murder occurred and while fighting the buzzards locked the remaining parts in Sergeant Sheila Mellons patrol car. She forgot and turned in her squad car, and the buzzards took away the head from Sergeant Reginald Dewberry in the motor pool leaving the hands, feet, and scalp which he turned into Evidence, and Booker showed at trial. WOW! Sergeant

Crawford was a known diabetic, and his body was covered with piss ants, and his urine was sweet. A butcher knife was found in the trunk of Desi Cartenegro's Corvette which was thought to be the knife used to mutilate Sergeant Crawford and demasculate Father Villla. Also found along with the knife was a kilogram of recycled cocaine stamped HPD in red with Lieutenant Shelby Fox's thumbprint. WOW!

*   *   *

Father Francis Villa, 45, Mexican citizen on expired green card visa, was parish priest at Saint Colombo. He was a known homosexual and had close intimate relationships with Blackie White, deceased, Rico Carbello, deceased, and Father Escobar, deceased and his esteemed colleague. The manager of Blackie Whites' Appliances in North Park admitted she saw Father Villa with his black frock up leaning over the counter in the back of their warehouse and submitting to receptive anal intercourse by Blackie White while engaging in tongue kissing in a passionate affectionate way. Rico went to confession every morning where he engaged in anal intercourse as penitence. Father Escobar and Villa were each others confessors. It was Father Escobar that emasculated Father Villa after he died on the cross from exhaustion and asphyxia. Ivry Cost would testify he watched Silvestor Fox, Brice Redmon, and Father Escobar crucify Father Villa, and after he was dead, Father Escobar took a butcher knife, sliced off Father Villa's genitalia and stuffed them in Father Villa's mouth.

Dr. Nu's diagnosis were: Acute asphyxia, crucifixation, mutilation of genitalia, and retrograde ejaculation. He had sperm in his bladder urine at autopsy.

CHAPTER 15

Opal slept late after spending the entire night with Dr. Austin Hale in the Holiday Inn in Pearland. He'd bought a nice two story house on a golf course with swimming pool in Sugar Land, and Austin rose early to catch Delta back to New Orleans for Christmas and retire from his position as Chief of Medicine and Pathology at Charity Hospital and Tulane Medical School. Austin had two married daughters with children and a son who was surgery resident at Harvard University Hospital in Cambridge, Massachusetts.

He left a key for Dr. Joy Burrell who was to move in upstairs where she would pay rent and share utilities and miscellaneous expenses. After his kids left, he planned to put his New Orleans mansion up for sale and move his furniture and stuff to Sugar Land. He asked Joy not to buy furniture or fixtures. A widower, Austin had the same arrangements with Dr. Fatima Hussain when she was his chief Fellow and assistant at Charity.

Opal was too late to make it to Bill's meeting on time. It was worth it. Casual sex was much more fun than routine sex with the same partner. She hated to see him go back to New Orleans. Apparently, he fucked Devine' and Cealis the two nights he stayed over at Sandra's.

Tex 35 ran straight north through Pearland, under Texas 6, and under US 610 Loop plus multiple overpasses that resembled something out of the Jetson. Just before the Loop was a Mexican ghetto that had sprung up and expanded which looked like the poor section of Matamoras, Nuevo Laredo, or any cutthroat border town. She rolled up her windows and locked her doors. She always carried a 0.32 cal. revolver in her purse or strapped to her thigh. For emergencies she had a 0.45 Cal. U.S. Army Colt automatic pull down under her dash. She routinely traveled IH-45 and would never take Tex 35 from Pearland under the Loop at night.

There was heavy construction of hotels and high-rises in the space where the Parks had been between the Convention Center, Enron Field and Park Shops spoiling a wonderful view from the restaurants on the ground floor Fast Food Heaven at Park Shoppes. Cones, barriers, and detours were up. She got on San Jacinto, drove passed the Criminal Court Building and into the Cops' and Lawyers' parking lot. A blue Buick LaSabre was in her parking space. It looked like Liz Borden's, but that couldn't be. Liz was buried in Muleshoe a month ago. The lot was full. *What the hell!*

She got back out on San Jacinto, parked in public parking, paid for one hour ($1.25) and refused to consider paying $10 for a whole day, although the hourly rate was the same. She planned on excusing herself at 11:00 A.M. to attend seminar in Barclay Theater at Saint Nicholas University. With all the construction and Christmas coming on, it was chaos everywhere, to say the least.

She went to the x-ray rest room (crowded), brushed her hair, made her face, and blotted her lipstick with a Kleenex from her purse. She'd forgotten to slip on her *Victoria Secrets*. She didn't want semen draining down her leg.

Opal smiled in the mirror. She had dimples, blue eyes that sparkled, peaches and cream complexion, and kissable lips. She believed she looked even prettier and sexier after a night in the sack with a stud like Austin. She knew what Sandra saw in Austin Hale and all that money, ranches, and oil. WOW!

She was an hour late, and Bill was at the blackboard lecturing. Elizabeth Borden was sitting in her chair, and Bob Waller from Big Spring was sitting in Sandra's. Sheila, Miguel, and Rene' Descarte were gone, but Booker, Ella Watts, and Judges Morrison and Petracelli were present. Bill nodded to Opal and pointed toward a chair at the end of the table by Cealis who grinned. Cealis guessed she spent the night with Austin Hale. Cealis jumped up and put hot coffee and two Dunkin Donuts in front of Opal. Opal ate three while Bill was talking. She'd missed work yesterday and drug in late today. She didn't feel guilty. Had it do over, she'd do the same thing. Austin was a once in a lifetime kind of guy.

*   *   *

"It's my opinion that California will legalize marijuana. How that will affect us in Texas, depends on how it plays out in the Federal Courts. We have plenty of homegrown around here. Hispanics, both illegals and legals, are growing it in hard to reach concealed areas. It takes lots of sunshine, flood lamps, and running water.

"Like the Japanese in WWII, they are using miniature submarines with periscopes and quiet engines to transport bulk cocaine.

"They are 100 feet long, camouflaged, and carry 3 or 4 men and 15 tons of cocaine. They are manufactured in Cuba, air conditioned, and carry enough oxygen to submerge 10 hours. In the past airplanes flew out to the continental shelf and loaded off contraband and illegals from the Cuban Submarine. Maybe that's still going on, and they are bringing them in on life rafts at night. Could be!

"Things have been pretty quiet since Al Hawalla moved his crop dusting outfit to Alaska. These miniature subs can't carry near the tonnage that a big sub can, but they can navigate in bays, shallow water, and up and down rivers. They could come right up the ship channel like the Japanese did at Pearl Harbor. They can hide them in our swamps. 100 feet is about 30 yards which is too big to hide in your back yard.

"I'd like to welcome back Bob Waller and Elizabeth Borden to their old jobs. Opal is our official Chief ADA. We've put off the Bobby Crawford and Father Francis Villa trials to the first week in January. Devine' has the influenza, and Sandra will be home by Christmas. Let's meet tomorrow at 8:00 A.M. sharp, please. We'll take up any problem cases, and I'd like to discuss in some detail what I detect as a shift in the type crimes we are seeing, a shift in paradigm. Dismissed!

"Opal Hony, may I see you in my office at your earliest convenience, please."

CHAPTER 16

They were having a housing boom in Sugar Land. Just make a right at the lights at the intersection of freeways US 59S and Texas 6 and drive west through multiple housing additions, golf courses, fresh water ponds, etc. New schools, strip malls and branch universities and hospitals from Houston were apparent and in various stages of completion. Sugar Land, in Fort Bend County, was growing in population at 10-15% per year. Houston offices and businesses were extending out along US 59S to swallow it like an amoeba or octopus extending a tentacle.

At Joy's request, Dirk stopped by an expensive home in the $350,000 and up range sitting next to a golf course with a pool in back surrounded by a privacy fence. There weren't any grass, flowerbeds, and trees yet, and only half the houses in that block were occupied. Dirk stayed in the SUV with attached trailer and boat while Joy eagerly rushed up with her key, went inside and inspected Austin's new house. He wasn't supposed to move in until after Christmas Holidays.

Joy had bid up Neva's house when he was trying to buy it. She had an office in the Medical Center Towers, but she needed enough space at home for a library and office for academic research and writing.

*   *   *

Dirk wasn't planning on any serious fishing. They'd drive down Hale's road to the river, put in at the public launch, hug the bank and fish against the current about a mile, motor back, load up, drive to the old house place, unhitch the trailer, take the SUV with 4-wheel drive and explore his newly purchased property which Dr. Hale was eager to unload for $3 million.

*   *   *

Dirk was aware that Joy had an inordinate curiosity about people and a scientifically trained and inquiring mind. She also was available and liked to "get out" and fish. Nowadays people were so busy that a "fishing buddy" was hard to find.

"Dirk, be honest. It's important to me. When you look at me, what do you see? Do you see your sister, daughter or mother, maybe some school teacher or mother figure? What do you see, be brutally honest?" asked Joy.

Dirk thought. She was playing mind games with him. Actually, she reminded him of the smiling young cuties in *Playboy*. "You won't get mad now?"

"No! What do you see when you look at me?"

Dirk blushed. "I'd just get you angry. Maybe I'd better not say."

Joy was adamant. "For goodness sake, just tell me. I don't bite. I'm a Psychiatrist for God's sake!"

"I see a good looking piece of ass, to put it frankly. You don't look like my daughter, mother, sister, nun or Virgin Mary, just a good looking sexually desirable woman. What would you expect?" Dirk was upset. Truth doesn't come easily.

Joy began to sniffle and cry. "That's the right answer. You told the truth. You're normal. You know why we have Psychiatrist? Just plain ordinary people lie 95% of the time. People and soldiers will fight and die to protect a lie."

"Why are you crying? Did I offend you some way?" asked Dirk.

"Happiness," replied Joy. "You are the first guy that ever told me. People lie all the time."

"I don't want to get slapped or sued for sexual harassment. You read about it every day in the newspaper. You tell a gal she looks like a great piece of ass, and they slap you with a lawsuit! They spend loads of time fixing themselves up to look attractive, and get mad if the wrong guy propositions them. I know the statistics on that one.

"If an ordinary guy stands on a street corner and asks every pretty girl that walks by to go to bed with him, you know how many accept? It's the same for selling Bibles, encyclopedias, and vacuum cleaners. You know what percent say yes?"

"I'll bite. How many?" replied Joy, drying her eyes.

"3%! He gets 97 slaps for 3 pieces of ass," replied Dirk, jokingly. It was an old joke among cops. He didn't know of any studies. Somebody would have called the cops before they could finish the study.

*   *   *

Back in antebellum days, the first Joshua Hale had a hundred slaves working on a sugar plantation. Pilings of a steamboat peer, warehouse, and ruins of a sugar mill and kettles were still about. Somewhere out there were brick kilns, slave cabins, and a Negro graveyard. All that stopped on June 16, 1865. It was grown up and swampy. He might look, if he had a Jon boat, push pole and mosquito net on a wide brim hat, but he wasn't in the mood today. There were old campfires and trash scattered along the bank, mostly recent.

If you could see Nutria rats sunning on a log, there weren't any alligators around. Nutria rats were stocked in the marshes by the Texas Fish and Game Commission for alligator food before Dirk's time. There were plenty of alligators now, and they had a hunting season.

There was a full moon, and the fish weren't biting which suggested to Dirk that the banks had been fished frequently or that the nuclear power plant was emitting toxic waste. Use of fish nets, telephones, and dynamite will deplete a fishery, but ordinary sport fishing would not. Most bass fishermen practiced catch and release.

On the way back, an eight point buck followed cautiously behind two does and a fawn and crossed the road. The rut was playing out. Dirk got out to unlock the gate, and Joy slid over and drove to the old house place. While Dirk unhitched the trailer and boat, Joy went back behind the house to tend to the needs of nature.

The steps and front porch were steady and no rotten planks. Dirk unlocked the door and let them in. He turned the light switch, and to their surprise the light came on and revealed an intact fireplace running up to a chimney in the roof and two rawhide bottom rocking chairs a hundred years old. There were two bedrooms, an old timey dining room with a wood table and attached benches. The kitchen was covered with linoleum and contained a wood stove with a stove pipe to the outside and a pantry with shelves. A calendar on the wall advertised hair tonic and was dated 1912. The guy parted his hair in the middle and wore knickers and a bowtie. The lights worked in the kitchen, and an old timey refrigerator was unplugged. Outside was a gallery that ran lengthwise to a closed off dog trot to the front. There was a washstand, broken mirror and a dried and cracked razor strap. A heavy wooden bench sat against the wall. A cistern contained water, but the faucet was frozen with rust. The back steps were rotten. The whole house sat on two feet blocks built on a rise.

Out back was a broken down picket fence, old garden place, small cow pen, hog pen, and a dilapidated barn that had collapsed on a rusted tractor. Further back was an "outhouse" toilet. There were no running water and indoor plumbing.

"How old is this place, Dirk?"

"Most got electricity in 1945. People didn't get indoor plumbing until they outlawed the outdoor toilet. Maybe 1952, after WWII. I can't remember. I was born in 1946," replied Dirk.

"Don't you think it would be fun to fix this place up. Vinyl is final! We could put in running water and indoor plumbing, paint everything, etc.," commented Joy enthusiastically.

"What for?" asked Dirk.

"To live in. It would make a lovely weekend retreat."

"Not really! I was raised in a place like this on the Trinity River in Liberty County. I'm addicted to indoor toilets and hot water for shaving."

*   *   *

Shadows were getting long when Dirk got the SUV stuck down to the axles. The tires spun but didn't get traction. Dirk didn't have chains and a wench. Neither cell phone got 911. They decided to leave the SUV and walk back to the old house. They'd build a fire in the fireplace and think what to do next.

CHAPTER 17

Bill chewed Opal's butt for missing a day of work and showing up late looking like *The Lost Weekend*. It wasn't lost yet. Austin's semen was still oozing down her leg. She sure as hell didn't want to get the "flu", so she'd contact Devine' only by telephone later.

She'd heard Tisha LaFemme was back from Onassis or Varanasi India, somewhere, after a Geology field trip with Bob Burrell whom she remembered very well from Brazoria two years ago when she prosecuted Austin Hale's brother, Jerry, for the murder of Joshua Hale Sr., their common father (*Murder on the Brazos*). After the trial she went back to the State Attorney's Office and paled around with Governor Ann Richards who gave her the yellow Ferrari. The whole world was a stage, and each played many parts. Snakeshit! Somebody gave Ann a silver plated motorcycle after she proclaimed on national TV that President George H. Bush was born with a silver foot in his mouth. Ann had a cutesy way of pushing the envelope and a big mouth. She was elected on President Clinton's coattail, and after the Monica thing, Opal wondered about Ann. Hook up was common among young girls, but not Ann's generation. To execute was one thing, really nothing, but to get caught was another. Semen tasted like sweet and sour sauce. She watched her mother go down on her dad, and when he got off, she just swallowed and swallowed and didn't gag one bit. They French kissed and shared the flavor. Both her parents were super educated Rocket Scientists. That's what the Astronauts did in orbit, she guessed. Semen just floated around in space. WOW!

*   *   *

So her competition, Bob Waller and Elizabeth Borden, were back from the grave and eager. Big deal! Houston was loaded with extraterrestrials and illegal aliens. Unless they broke some law the cops weren't allowed to ask for I.D. or question them about their nationality. She might get called back to Austin after the Shelby Fox case. She was still lead ADA on Shelby, James Fry Jr., and the crazy Arab, Abdullah Muhammad, who backed over the Jew over and over and flattened him like a pancake in mid day in front of twenty witnesses. The Feds wouldn't take him and said it was local. Try him like any other perpetrator. He wanted a mullah, shariah, and martyrdom. Percy was dropped because of justifiable homicide. She would have shot that mangy bastard too.

*   *   *

Many young women had a secret sorrow, the unpaid student loan. Debra Crawford was one of those. In addition to working for Wanda Townsend as a $5000 call girl and as an IRS paid informant, she was on Dr. Peter Rockford's Smithsonian Grant and awarded a Fellowship in Archeology and placed on an academic fast track for Ph.D., having achieved a BS and MBA from a state university in the Midwest. She was Sergeant Bobby Crawford's widow, knew the "real" Jésus Muhammad at the Shiite Baptist Mosque, and witnessed along with Reverend Jésus Muhammad, Lieutenant Shelby Fox's execution of Bobby Crawford out by the tracks behind the Shiite Baptist Mosque.

When Shelby and Ivry were caught in the act of loading 4 tons of recycled Colombian cocaine stamped with a red HPD, arrested and jailed, and Ivry with persuasion from Booker began to tell all, witnesses against Shelby came out of the woodwork.

Opal called Debra in advance to meet her for cigarettes in front of old Don Allergeri's statue to insure privacy. Very few adults smoked anymore, and the students smoked marijuana in the dormitories and avoided tobacco like the clap.

Debra's consuming passion was to be selected as Playmate of the Month and appear on the cover of *Playboy*. Debra charged women same as men and would show a prosperous professional woman a good weekend in Vegas for $10,000. More business women were preferring same sex, and Wanda was discreetly introducing them to Debra. Many ambitious young women were taking calls to pay for their education. They chose their same sex roommates in advance. At the Ivy colleges up north men were into same sex too. They were very discreet, and the incidences of STD and HIV were miniscule. Working in the State Attorney's Office, Opal had privy to the statistics kept on the sexual habits of teenagers and young adults. 25% of the girls started in the 7th grade, and a bunch had STD in the 12th. Dropouts for pregnancies among the blacks and browns were about 25%. A young girl enjoying unprotected sex on her first encounter ran a 20% chance of pregnancy. The obvious solutions were oral contraception and avoidance of casual sex.

CHAPTER 18

Barclay Theater
University of Saint Nicholas
12 Noon, Friday, December 13, 1993
Chilly, Temperature 50°F
Sunny, Wind 10 mph NE

Dr. Mambo Nigeria was at the lectern. "We may get some cold weather by Christmas. The Russians still use the old calendar and celebrate January 12.

"Before Christmas, the Romans celebrated December 25 as Sunday and made sacrifices to Apollo, the sun god, feasted, and gave gifts to family and friends.

"Today, Dr. Battenberg will continue her lecture on historic England. Dr. Winston Blood will discuss the battle of Borodino, the French retreat, and Leo Tolstoy's *War and Peace*. Dr. Peter Rockford will discuss pre-historic Europe, and Amy will finish with Chaos and complexity.

Dr. Levitra Battenberg wrote on the green board: **ANGLES, SAXONS, VIKINGS, NORMANS, CRUSADES, MAGNA CARTA, RICHARD III, WAR OF ROSES, HOUSE OF TUDOR, HENRY VII, BLACK DEATH, AND HORSE MANURE**.

"Aethelbert, Saxon King of Kent, built the first Saint Paul in 604 c.e. By 800 c.e. London was Christian. By 1200, there were 127 Christian churches in London alone.

"Enter the Vikings, Hagar the Horrible and his elk, who were after plunder and pretty maidens.

"The last Anglo-Saxon king, Edward the Confessor (r. 1042-1066), founded Westminster Abbey. He died on January 5, 1066 without a successor.

"William the Conqueror, Duke of Normandy, defeated Anglo-Saxon Harold II at the Battle of Hasting on October 14, 1066 and was crowned the King on December 25, 1066 in Westminster Abbey. It wasn't Christmas day back in those days until Pope Gregory changed the calendar. The Russians kept January 12 as Christmas.

"The Anglo-Saxons built earthen ramparts, and the Norman conquerors built castles. The castles you see around England, Wales, Normandy, Sicily, and the Holy Land were built by the Norman's. William built the historic tower of London where Mary, Queen of Scots, Sir Walter Riley, and many historic notables lost their head.

King Henry I granted London a charter to elect its own sheriff and magistrates. When Richard the Lion Hearted went on Crusade, his brother, King John, signed the Magna Carta and granted London the right to free market capitalism, the first of its kind anywhere.

"In 1399, Londoners deposed Richard II in favor of Henry, Duke of Lancaster. During the War of the Roses, Londoners supported the Duke of York and crowned him Edward IV. When Richard III died on Bosworth Field, they welcomed Henry Tudor as King Henry VII. There was no direct lineage from Henry I to Henry VIII. Bankers, merchants, and blacksmiths loved warrior kings.

"London was where it 'was at'. All roads led to London. In medieval times, London was a walled city containing a population of 50,000. It had a market and shopping mall named Cheapside. Cheap was the street name.

"The Thames became heavily polluted with human waste, and its cobblestone streets and narrow alleys piled high in horse manure. After the big London fire they installed modern sewage disposal, and Henry Ford in 1905 solved the horse manure problem. They shipped their poor to America and their criminals to Georgia and Australia.

"The Black Death (1348-1349) killed off a quarter of the population of England and half the population of London. Nobody knew its cause. There were no flea powder or antibiotics and it returned again and again littering the alleys and streets with dead, dying, filth and human excrement. Over the next century it was followed by tuberculosis, typhus, dysentery, diphtheria and measles. People died like flies all over Europe.

"Monday, I'll take up the Tudors and Henry VIII, everybody's favorite King. Thank you!

"Winston."

Dr. Winston Blood wrote on the green board. **GLORY OF WAR, NICHOLAS I, TSAR'S POLICE, CIVIL UNREST, CRIMEAN WAR, ALEXANDER II, GLASNOT, SELF RULE, STUDENT PROTESTS, ANARCHY, NILHIST, AND ASSASSINATION OF ALEXANDER II.**

"Later, I'm planning on devoting a lecture to the Napoleonic War. Leo Tolstoy actually fought in the Crimean War. The setting of *Anna Karenna* was during the Crimean War. *War and Peace* was set during the battle of Borodino, the capture of Moscow, and the disastrous French retreat.

"Remember, in Europe war was thought to be a good thing up until WWI where they killed off a whole generation of English, French, and German soldiers. War, unlike plagues and natural catastrophes, just kills men in their reproductive years. If you want to predict the population of a country, count the women in their child bearing ages.

"During the reign of Nicholas I (1825-1855) he quelled the Decembrist rebellion, witnessed the rising tide of Western Europe, formed his own secret police, repressed dissidents, intellectuals, and serf protests.

"Nicholas I was religious, moralistic, militaristic, and autocratic. He feared and refused to liberate the serfs.

"Russia was defeated in the Crimean War (1854-1856). Nicholas I died in 1855. Alexander II inherited the throne and conceded defeat.

"He abolished serfdom in 1861, freed the universities of state control, allowed self government of cities, legalized public jury trials, encouraged freedom of the press, and modernized the military allowing promotion through the ranks. WOW! Russia was a backward country runned by the nobles and the clergy.

"Discussions (glasnost) were encouraged and protected by the police. Village communes were established, serfs were given land, and the landlords retained a share of land.

"Alexander II learned what every parent knows. If you try to satisfy everybody, then nobody is happy and everybody complains. Peasants complained and radical groups formed. Alexander II was killed in 1881 by a bomb thrown by revolutionaries of the People's Will.

"Catherine the Great was right. Russia couldn't handle freedom. Some wanted anarchy. I'll stop. Monday I'll take up the 'Nihilist' revolution, and the students' rebellions. They antedated our 1960's hippies by 100 years. What they needed was 'hard rock'."

"Peter."

Dr. Peter Rockford wrote on the green board. **NEANDERTALS, CRO-MAGNONS, PALEOLITHS, MESOLITHS, NEOLITHS, WINDMILL, BEAKER, CELTS, ROMANS, ANGLES, SAXONS, VIKINGS, NORMANS, AND US**.

"During the great ice age which thawed 10,000 years ago, Paleolithic Homo sapiens migrated over all the continents. Land bridges extended across to England and Ireland, across Siberia to Alaska, across Korea to Japan, and from SEA to Indonesia and Australia, etc. As the glaciers melted the ocean rose, and those land bridges were covered. Over the last 8000 years continental shelves were covered. You can motor out from Galveston with a fish finder on your boat, and when it reads 300 feet expect a drop off at the continental shelf. The bottom of the ocean is not smooth. It comes off the continental shelf like rows and rows of deltas and canyons.

"The questions confronting archeologists are how the black tribes in southern India and the islands of the Indian Ocean, Bay of Bengal,

Indonesia, and Australia got there 50,000 years ago. Did they walk, eating seafood and hunting game as they went? Did they hug the shore and ride in reed boats and dugout canoes, or did they float in like coconuts?

"There are tribes of pygmies on the Andaman Islands in the Bay of Bengal that look identical to the pygmies living in the rainforests of Zaire. They're hostile to all strangers and are cannibals. The locals call them Negritos.

"Seismograph reports from around the Andaman Islands suggest rich deposits of gas and oil. There's a shooting war going on around the offshore gas fields of Myanmar Republic close by.

"There is an ongoing dispute between China and Japan over who owns the drilling rights offshore the Kuril Islands belonging to Japan in the East China Sea. Russia is claiming Japanese Islands north of Japan, and China is claiming sparsely inhabited islands in the South China Sea, also claimed by Vietnam, Philippines, and Taiwan. Other than the Negritos on Andaman the rest are not big enough to be inhabited. They are strategically located near the Straits of Malacca which are teeming with cutthroat pirates after your wallet, kidnap insurance, and women.

"What about the prehistoric tribes in Europe? The Celts were from Salzburg Austria and Bavaria and had iron, beer, and swords. They covered all of Europe and crossed over the Balkans where they were called Galatians' by the Romans. Their Druid priests did not allow writing. They arrived south of the Black Sea around 1000 b.c.e. about the same time the Indo-Iranians and Indo-Aryans migrated into Persia, Bactria, and the Indus Valley. They were warlike and hired out as professional mercenary soldiers to either side and would fight their own tribesmen if hired by an opposing side. They liked to fight.

"Celtic skeletons have been found near Snake River Montana dating back 20,000 y.a. and the Taklimakan Desert in western China dating back 5,000 y.a.

"Laplanders and Eskimos are Paleolithic Homo sapiens that wouldn't give up hunting and gathering. When the Vikings discovered

Newfoundland, the Eskimos were already there. Their blood wouldn't clot because of a steady diet of fish oil and blubber.

"Humans have a remarkable capacity to adapt. Thomas Malthus wrote populations outgrow resources, and Charles Darwin showed only the fittest survive. What's new? There has always been tribal warfare. Everything we eat was once alive.

"Life lives off life. Cannibalism still exists in remote cultures. Under desperate conditions you'll resort to cannibalism. If you trace back far enough, all primitive tribes practiced human sacrifice and cannibalism.

"Most of you know I have a Smithsonian grant to trace the origin of the Matigwa Indians a few survivors of which live on reservation two miles south of Groveton above Lake Livingston. There is an Indian mound out in northeast Houston where we dug up artifacts and traced them back to the caves of Guilin China during the Tang dynasty. We located an earlier cave near El Centro in Aguascalientes Mexico, and our next excavation will be in the abandoned jungle ruins in northern Costa Rico near the Nicaraguan border. It's about a day's walk through the rain forest from Fortuna and Aral Volcano which never stops rumbling and belching out lava and ash, day and night.

"Before the windmill people, beaker people, and Celts arrived in the British Isles, there were Mesoliths that lived on the banks and in the shallows in little grass huts on stilts around lakes found in northwest England and around Lake Zurich in Europe. Before them were the Neandertals and Cro-Magnons living in caves and rock shelters. Thank you. Amy!"

Dr. Amy Omikami wrote on the green board. **FISH AND CHIPS, PAY TOILETS, JOHN CRAPPER, CHAOS, COMPLEXITY, HEATHROW, ICE AGE, GREEN HOUSE, GLOBAL WARMING, SHIT HAPPENS, AND ALGORE**.

"We will keep these lectures going until Maria gets back with our Anthropology tour. Today they are flying from Zurich to London Heathrow where they will be put up in the Airport downtown Hilton. It's sandwiched between a professional Cricket Field and an Islamic

Mosque. Past the mosque is a Commons. There are usually ten checkered cabs out front, and a red double decker bus stops on the corner.

"The population of London is 9 million, and it's easy to get lost. It's best to take a cab if the driver is white and speaks English. If he's from India or Pakistan and drives his own car, he'll end up demanding about five times more than a white union cabbie. The same in Indian Restaurants. It's cheaper to walk or take a union cab to the nearest KFC or McDonalds. A Big Mac cost $7.00. Some of their convenience stores have outdoor tables where they serve Fish and Chips (fried cod and French fries). Water and ice cost extra all over Europe. Their pay toilets won't take American change. The inventor of the flush toilet was an Englishman named John Crapper.

"Major General Trudy Grits from the 44th Armored Infantry Division at Fort Hood will be here Monday and begin a lecture series on primitive combat, great battles, and the evolution of war. She is Professor of Military Science and Commander of R.O.T.C. here at the University.

"The abrupt change in climate we experienced August through October was chaotic. It began when an asteroid struck Jupiter and caused earth and all planets in the solar system to wobble and shift on their axis. Measuring tiny changes in gravity waves our scientists were able to predict its onset but not its severity or duration. It was deterministic, non linear, and predictable. We experienced a similar event last May of brief duration after an asteroid struck Saturn a thousand years ago. The so-called Little Ice Age was not a random event. It was chaotic, non linear, and deterministic.

"Global warming due to accumulation of greenhouse gases in our atmosphere, on the other hand, is an example of complexity and cannot be determined accurately or the outcome predicted.

"I'll stop here and take up global warming, photosynthesis, and alternate energies Monday. Everything on earth came from the stars, and all usable energy came from our sun. As we progress, I'll explain everything as linear or non linear, randomness, uncertainty and probability, and simple, complex, complexity, chaos, and bedlam which are what we can expect in the 21st century as our population approaches 12 billion, and we use up all fossil fuels and ground water, and we become like Christmas Island, Mars, and Venus."

CHAPTER 19

Kuala Lumpur Malaysia
1 A.M., Saturday, December 14, 1993
Hot and muggy
Temp 79°

Bob turned on the reading lamp and opened his briefcase. He tried to keep up with homework. Penny was snoring with her back to his bed. Maria knew Penny from before and recommended her to Don Tantalia because she was familiar with SEA and could talk the talk. For appearances, she was Bob's wife. They flipped and Elvis got head, and he got tail. He didn't know what kind of arrangement Don enjoyed with her. He who has the gold makes the rules.

They planned to fly by private jet to Haiphong, explore the Karsts caves just north which were obviously a geographic extension of similar terrain in Guilin China and the northeast coast of Vietnam. They'd fly to Saigon (Ho Chi Min City) and board a SROCO helicopter and explore the coastline of the Gulf of Thailand to Singapore at the tip of the Malaysian peninsula where they would board a SROCO yacht, explore the Spratly Islands and South China Sea, and motor through the Malacca straits to Andaman Islands off the coast of Myanmar in the Bay of Bengal where drilling was going.

The Chinese had a naval base at Fort Blair, standing guard over the vital shipping lanes through the Straits of Malacca and a hidden submarine base in the vicinity guarding the offshore oil wells drilled by Petronas, TOTAL, Daewoo, and others. In the South China Sea and the Bay of Bengal, they would dress in safari clothes and look for the last tribes of Negritos, little people, last seen in the dense rain forest of

Andaman Islands. They were 4 feet, went naked, had poison darts and arrows, and ate people alive, roasted, or boiled. They were descendents or cousins of the Pygmies in Zaire.

Africans migrated along the coasts of SEA 40,000 years ago, no question. When the Mongolians migrated across Siberia and Alaska to North and South America, black Africans migrated by foot and dugout canoes along the southern coasts of Africa, Arabia, India, Andaman Islands, Malaysian peninsula, Indonesia, Sumatra, Borneo, Australia and Tasmania. The Neandertals took the roads to Europe and Bulgaria, Homo erectus followed a million years later by Homo sapiens took the high road to Asia and the Indies, and the African blacks took the low roads and coastlines, and had to be Homo africanus the descendents of "Luey" the first Australopithicas africanus. They were a separate species from Homo erectus, neandertals, and sapiens. They were Homo africanus, black Africans. Negritos were little black men. They had a mutant gene for shortness.

Bob turned on the TV with the volume low and surfed the channels until he found CNN out of Hong Kong. It was 1 P.M. yesterday in Houston.

The English were dry and humorless, and their ladies didn't get braces growing up. If they cracked jokes, Bob wasn't smart enough to catch them. He only got a little news from Myanmar and combined with what little he found in the *US NEWS TODAY*, he'd guess that things had bogged down to a standoff, and a white knight, Russia, China, or India, was negotiating an agreement. The big threat, Than Shwe and the military Junta were blown apart, and everybody else had been taking orders.

Aung San Suu Kyi had formed a government. Generals Li Shan and He Wu had tamed Yangon and Mandalay, and the fractured Nationalist Army had stopped the Bangladeshis bogged down in the torrent rivers crossing the old Stillwell Road from India to Lashio. So far, the casualties were in the thousands and not millions which was light in that part of the world.

Actually, in India and Bangladesh you had to look at wars objectively from a survivor's perspective. Next to cyclones, typhoons, and floods, wars got rid of hotheads and troublemakers and left more for the non-combatants who stayed home.

There was no way to find out what was happening in the flaming waters of the Bay of Bengal. French Total lost a deep water driller and its crew, and a few gas wells caught fire and were extinguished, and except for a lot of maneuvering by China's hybrid Lithium-Biodiesel powered submarines, everything was back to near normal. In confusion, there was opportunity, and that's what Don Tantalia planned.

Vietnam was rapidly undergoing Americanization like Japan, South Korea, Taiwan, and the Philippines. With the backing of US Nuclear Aircraft carriers, Vietnam, was ready to confront China over the gas and oil off their coast in the South China Sea, mainly the Spratly Islands. In fact, Japan, Philippines, Taiwan, and Vietnam all claimed the Spratly as theirs by ancestral rights and were filing a class action suit in the World Court to make China stop bullying. It had become very apparent to all industrial nations that petroleum and petroleum products were necessary for prosperity and military preparedness in modern times.

> *U.S. Department of State*
> *Bureau of Consular Affairs*
> *Washington, DC 20520*
>
> *Consular Information Sheet:*
>
> *Malacca Straits*
> *South China Sea*
> *Borneo*
> *Spratly Islands*
> *Andaman Islands*
> *Bay of Bengal*

*   *   *

Bob went to sleep.

CHAPTER 20

Kuala Lumpur Malaysia
9 A.M., Saturday, December 14, 1993
Tropical, Hot and Muggy
Temperature 85°

Louiza Santos flew in from Bangkok and joined their little group as Donald Tantalia's consort and "wife." She could speak Mandarin Chinese, Spanish, several South American native tongues, and had a Ph.D. in Archeology. Bob not privy to Donald's and Maria's game plan thought correctly that everybody was there for a reason, *the magnificent five.*

Louiza was a young slender Sambo (Negro-American Indian) with a slight Spanish accent who looked like the locals, spoke Chinese with a Spanish accent, played a Spanish guitar and sang in Spanish and English. She and Donald knew each other from before and looked comfortable as a pair (hook up).

The skies were grey and sunless from ash rising high over Indonesia and Sumatra where several volcanoes were erupting and a tsunami warning was in effect. To Bob that was alarming, but to the locals it was a way of life. Malaysia, Indonesia, Borneo, Brunei, etc., etc. and on and on were located in the volcanic hot spot of Southeast Asia, and like Costa Rico, one was erupting somewhere every day. Rice paddies were everywhere, and like Costa Rico food grew on trees, and, if you lived like a monkey, you could get by on a dollar a day. First impressions were usually wrong, but at first glance, he thought not.

* * *

Don and Elvis went to the American Embassy to clear their scientific expedition, and the girls, Penny and Louiza, took a rickshaw to wherever, sightseeing and shopping. Bob bought copies of the *US NEWS TODAY* and the *ASIAN WALL STREET JOURNAL*, both fresh off the presses in Kuala Lumpur, and went back up to his room to watch TV and study. He knew why he was along, and in the world of politics, petroleum and risk, knowledge was golden and life saving too.

The climate was not big news in the South Sea tropics. It was hot and hotter and wet and wetter. Nobody prayed for rain.

Mount Merapi, near Yogyakarta City on Java erupted and spit ash and lava almost every day, but two big ones had occurred in the last week causing an earthquake and tsunami covering islands west of Sumatra. Merapi had set all kinds of records. It killed 1300 in 1930 and again in 1990 it caused a 9 Richter scale earthquake and drowned 250,000 people, the deadliest on record. Indonesia was made up of 17,000 islands, had 130 active volcanoes, and a total population of over 250 million. What they lost in natural disasters were a tiny fraction of their births which were second only to Mexico's 4% per year.

* * *

The Straits of Malacca was 200 miles wide and 1000 miles long and was the most important waterway of its kind in the world. When the USA blocked Japanese oil shipments through it, they bombed Pearl Harbor and started WWII on December 7, 1941 *a day in infamy*. Pirates made a living attacking unarmed ships like the Somali Pirates at the Straits of Hormuz. Anybody going through in an unarmed yacht, as Donald planned, did so at his own risk. Later, Bob found out that Don had the blessing and protection of the USA who cleared it with Malaysian authorities. When they crossed the Korean straits in the Sea of Japan, Bob realized that SROCO backed by the Chinese PLA would have to have official approval of all neighboring nations before seismography and drilling a test well.

At the beginning of the WWII, the Japanese crossed into Thailand, came down the Malaysia peninsula, and attacked the British from the rear. General Percival surrendered the whole allied Pacific command. Nobody knew at the time, but it was the largest surrender of healthy combat troops in history. To Japanese surrender was not an option. Japanese fought to the death for their Emperor, and, if defeated, their officers committed suicide. They looked down on the British, American, and French with distain and disgust and treated their prisoners accordingly, starvation and hard labor.

Very few Germans that surrendered en mass to the Russians on their eastern front made it back home after the war. Americans learned that lesson again and again in Korea and Vietnam. Those who do not study history are doomed to repeat it. In the East, it was better to fight until the last man than surrender. Genghis Kahn killed all the men, raped the women, and enslaved the children.

* * *

Bob scanned the U.S. Department of State Background Notes on Malaysia. The Communist takeover of Vietnam, Cambodia, Laos, and Myanmar did not include Thailand, Malaysia, and Indonesia. Anti personnel and anti tank mines still littered the jungles of Laos, Cambodia, and eastern Myanmar. There were no maps and records, and innocents who took shortcuts through the jungles and used the trails and poorly kept roads were at hazard of exploding them and losing life and limb. Both Khmer Rouge and Vietnamese mined northwest Cambodia. Millions of mines, booby traps, and unexploded shells were out there in the jungles.

* * *

Malaysia had 28 million people made up of 53% Malay, 26% Chinese, 8% Indians and the rest indigents. 60% were Muslims, 20%

were Buddhists, 10% were Christians and 10% were other. Each spoke his tribal tongue, and all understood a little pidgin English.

The country made up the lower half of the Malaysian peninsula along with Singapore and Sabah and Sarawak, across the South China Sea west of the wilds of Borneo. Through those waters passed the greatest volume of strategic shipping in the world. Singapore was the richest port. Malaysia had a Constitutional Monarchy and a Parliament like England and used the English court system and English common law. Shariah courts handled disputes and family matters for Muslims. GDP was 6% on average and 9-10% in good years.

Downtown Kuala Lumpur was ultramodern and high tech. Petronas Towers, owned by Petronas National Oil Company, was the tallest in the world. Malaysia was an exporter country to China, Japan, and the U.S.A.

*   *   *

Japan had amended its constitution and was building a new nuclear aircraft carrier and enlarging its Navy. Russia was claiming Japan's ancestral islands north of Hokkaido for offshore oil and gas exploration. China was claiming Japan's territorial waters in the East China Sea, and their patrol craft had been rammed by Chinese fishermen in the South China Sea. Vietnam, Taiwan, and the Philippines had complained to the UN because China was "bullying" them to get oil and gas drilling rights in their continental waters by claiming their ancestral islands. Not only was China trying to steal their minerals, but China would "muck up" their fishing waters. The same was going on around the Andaman Islands in the Bay of Bengal where a shooting war between Bangladesh and Myanmar was going on.

Neighbors get uptight when some company starts seismography and slant hole drilling. Everybody in Asia wanted "wheels." Their fossil fuels belonged to them for whatever reason they could conjure: god, ancestors, Kublai Kahn, and whomever or whatever gave them a claim.

Actually, the Pope divided the whole world in half and gave it to Spain and Portugal back in the 16th century when they both claimed Brazil. Portugal and subsequently Spain put cannons on galleons and invented the broadside which was quickly copied by the English, Dutch, and French. That began "gunboat diplomacy."

* * *

Both China and Russia were designing new fighter-bomber aircraft that would range the whole Pacific out to Wake Island. Their nuclear submarines could bomb Hawaii, Alaska, Canada, and the U.S. west coast. China had a submarine port in the Andaman Islands and were tailoring their ground-to-ground missiles to hit anything out to Wake Island and Southeast to Sri Lanka. Oil was the cause of all modern wars.

CHAPTER 21

Heathrow Airport
London England
Saturday, December 14, 1993
Rain, Temp 50°

The coach fare from London to New York was $300 and it took ten hours. If you rode the Concorde it cost $1200 and took three hours. If you heard a loud Zoom and rushed to a window to watch a Concorde take off, it was too late. By the time you heard, it it was gone.

They had delicious meals of eggs, bacon, and coffee with side orders of chocolates and cheeses on Swiss Air. It was a long sheltered tunnel from their plane to the concourse and baggage claim. They went to the toilet and used the John Crapper while waiting at the Baggage carousel and claim. After securing their baggage, they went as a group through Immigration and Customs, and then to the Currency Exchange window and exchanged dollars and all the miscellaneous excess currency they had forgotten to spend or convert in the visited countries for pounds, shilling, and pence. The British had long since quit minting the half pence popular in legends and poems for toll bridges and alms for the priests and poor, commonly called the "half pence bridge" and "give a half pence to Saint Peter," called the Peter tax for Saint Peter's in Rome. A Unisex was a barbershop in England, and the young Unisex wore their hair like the Beatles, and from behind they looked the same. Cocktail and smoking lounges were in all passenger waiting areas, and Sandra saw no "No Fumar and No Smoking signs". Diversity was everywhere. Planes from Heathrow flew to every point on the compass. Once England ruled the oceans; now it ruled the airways. With the U.S.A. military and money to back them, England probably still ruled the world.

*   *   *

Sandra read: **Tours from London**. Public or Private, large or small groups, pairs or singles. **Places to visit**: Salisbury, Stonehenge, and Avebury, **Close to Heathrow**: Winsor Castle and Eton College. **Outside of London**: Bath, Oxford, Stratford on Avon, Canterbury, The Cotswolds. Day trips to Paris France. 2 hours by train, leave early, shop and return late. SAVE MONEY. **Short Breaks to Scotland**: bullet train to Edinburg leaves every two hours. Golf at Saint Andrews by commuter. WOW! thought Sandra. Anybody with the time and money could schedule his own tour without joining a group. **Ferry to Dublin**: One hour over and one hour back, car extra. Explore Ireland by car. Can arrange tours, any size. Explore Ireland on a weekend.

Heathrow had five terminals and averaged 70 million international passengers a year, mostly to the Americas. It had two long runways greater than two miles running east to west, located in the western periphery of London 12 miles from central downtown. Today it was filled with college age passengers on standby. There were 60 hotels in a mile radius and their Hilton was five miles northeast toward downtown London in an area of dark skinned English speaking Islamic SEA Indians and Pakistanis, hence the Crickett field and mosque. Maria and Christy jewed them down to 50 pounds per night whereas those hotels next to Heathrow charged 100-200 per person per night and both included a buffet breakfast. The rest of the day you paid cash or ate out. To convert to cash equivalent you multiplied by 1.8 to 2.0.

*   *   *

Sandra read:

U.S. DEPARTMENT OF STATE
BACKGROUND NOTE: UNITED KINGDOM

HISTORY

The Roman invasion of Britain in 55 BC and most of Britain's subsequent incorporation into the Roman Empire stimulated development and brought more active contacts with the rest of Europe. As Rome's strength declined, the country again was exposed to invasion-including the pivotal incursions of the Angles, Saxons, and Jutes in the fifth and sixth centuries AD-up to the Norman conquest in 1066. Norman rule effectively ensured Britain's safety from further intrusions; certain institutions, which remain characteristic of Britain, could develop. Among these are a political, administrative, cultural, and economic center in London; a separate but established church; a system of common law, distinctive and distinguished university education; and representative government.

Union

Both Wales and Scotland were independent kingdoms that resisted English rule. The English conquest of Wales succeeded in 1282 under Edward I, and the Statute of Rhuddian established English rule 2 years later. To appease the Welsh, Edward's son (later Edward II), who had been born in Wales, was made Prince of Wales in 1301. The tradition of bestowing this title on the eldest son of the British Monarch continues today. An act of 1536 completed the political and administrative union of England and Wales.

While maintaining separate parliaments, England and Scotland were ruled under one crown beginning in 1603 when James VI of Scotland succeeded his cousin Elizabeth I as James I of England. In the ensuing 100 years, strong religious and political differences divided the kingdoms. Finally, in 1707, England and Scotland were unified as Great Britain, sharing a single Parliament at Westminster.

Ireland's invasion by the Anglo-Normans in 1170 led to centuries of strife. Successive English kings sought to conquer Ireland. In the early 17th century, large-scale settlement of the north from Scotland and England began. After its defeat, Ireland was subjected, with varying degrees of success, to control and regulation by Britain.

The legislative union of Great Britain and Ireland was completed on January 1, 1801, under the name of the United Kingdom. However, armed struggle for independence continued sporadically into the 20th century. The Anglo-Irish Treaty of 1921 established the Irish Free State, which subsequently left the Commonwealth and became a republic after World War II. Six northern, predominantly Protestant, Irish counties have remained part of the United Kingdom.

British Expansion and Empire

Begun initially to support William the Conqueror's (c. 1029-1087) holdings in France, Britain's policy of active involvement in continental European affairs endured for several hundred years. By the end of the 14th century, foreign trade, originally based on wool exports to Europe, had emerged as a cornerstone of national policy.

The foundations of sea power were gradually laid to protect English trade and open up new routes. Defeat of the Spanish Armada in 1588 firmly established England as a major sea power. Thereafter, its interests outside Europe grew steadily. Attracted by the spice trade, English mercantile interests spread first to the Far East. In search of an alternate route to the Spice Islands, John Cabot reached the North American continent in 1498. Sir Walter Raleigh organized the first, short-lived colony in Virginia in 1584, and permanent English settlement began in 1607 at Jamestown, Virginia. During the next two centuries, Britain extended its influence abroad and consolidated its political development at home.

Great Britain's industrial revolution greatly strengthened its ability to oppose Napoleonic France. By the end of the Napoleonic Wars in 1815, the United Kingdom was the foremost European power, and its navy ruled the seas. Peace in Europe allowed the British to focus their interests on more remote parts of the world, and, during this period, the British Empire reached its zenith. British colonial expansion reached its height largely during the reign of Queen Victoria (1837-1901). Queen Victoria's reign witnessed the spread of British technology, commerce, language, and government throughout the British Empire, which, at its greatest extend, encompassed roughly one-fifth to one-quarter of the world's area and population. British colonies contributed to the United Kingdom's extraordinary economic growth and strengthened its voice in world affairs. Even as the United Kingdom extended its imperial reach overseas, it continued to develop and broaden its democratic institutions at home.

20th Century

By the time of Queen Victoria's death in 1901, other nations, including the United States and Germany, had developed their own industries; the United Kingdom's comparative economic advantage had lessened, and the ambitions of its rivals had grown. The losses and destruction of World War I, the depression of the 1930's, and decades of relatively slow growth eroded the United Kingdom's preeminent international position of the previous century.

Britain's control over its empire loosened during the interwar period, Ireland, with the exception of six northern counties, gained independence from the United Kingdom in 1921. Nationalism became stronger in other parts of the empire, particularly in India and Egypt.

In 1926, the United Kingdom, completing a process begun a century earlier, granted Australia, Canada, and New Zealand complete autonomy within the empire. They became charter members of the British Commonwealth of Nations (now known as the Commonwealth), an informal but closely-knit association that succeeded the empire. Beginning with the independence of India and Pakistan in 1947, the remainder of the British Empire was almost completely dismantled. Today, most of Britain's former colonies belong to the Commonwealth, almost all of them as independent members. There are, however, 13 former British colonies-including Bermuda, Gibraltar, the Falkland Islands, and others-which have elected to continue their political links with London and are known as British Overseas Territories.

Although often marked by economic and political nationalism, the Commonwealth offers the United Kingdom a voice in matters concerning many developing countries. In addition, the Commonwealth helps preserve many institutions deriving from British experience and models, such as parliamentary democracy, in those countries.

GOVERNMENT

The United Kingdom does not have a written constitution. The equivalent body of law is based on statute, common law, and "traditional rights." Changes may come about formally through new acts of Parliament, informally through the acceptance of new practices and usage, or by judicial precedents. Although Parliament has the theoretical power to make or repeal any law, in actual practice the weight of 700 years of tradition restrains arbitrary actions.

Executive power rests nominally with the monarch but actually is exercised by a committee of ministers (cabinet) traditionally selected from among the members of the House of Commons and, to a lesser extent, the House of Lords. The prime minister is normally the leader of the largest party in the Commons, and the government is dependent on its support.

DEFENSE AND FOREIGN RELATIONS

The British Armed Forces are charged with protecting the United Kingdom and its overseas territories, promoting Britain's wider security interests, and supporting international peacekeeping efforts. The 37,000-member Royal Navy, which includes 6,000 Royal Marine commandos, is in charge of the United Kingdom's independent strategic nuclear arm, which consists of four Trident missile submarines. The British Army, consisting of approximately 99,200 personnel, the Royal Air Force, with 42,000 personnel, along with the Royal Navy and Royal Marines, are active and regular participants in NATO and other coalition operations. Approximately 9% of the British Armed forces is female, and 4% of British forces represent ethnic minorities.

U.S.-UNITED KINGDOM RELATIONS

The United Kingdom is one of the United States' closest allies, and British foreign policy emphasizes close coordination with the United States. Bilateral cooperation reflects the common language, ideals, and democratic practices of the two nations. Relations were strengthened by the United Kingdom's alliance with the United States during both World Wars, and its role as a founding member of NATO, in the Korean conflict. In the Persian Gulf War The United Kingdom and the United States continually consult on foreign policy issues and global problems and share major foreign and security policy objectives.

Trafalgar Square
London England
3 P.M., Saturday, December 14, 1993
Temp 45°, light drizzle

Admiral Nelson was killed in battle (1805) when the English bottled up and sank the French fleet at the battle of Trafalgar. From his statue you could see the London Bridge, Thames, Tower of London, Big Ben, Saint Paul's Cathedral, and Westminster Abbey. They shivered in plastic raincoats and under umbrellas from which they shelled parched peanuts and shared them with the pigeons. The Natural Museum of London held all the secrets of antiquity and was the largest of its kind anywhere. From the Parliament Building and the business district England had become the world's greatest superpower during the reign of Queen Victoria during which the sun never set on the British Empire, and the British Navy ruled the Seas.

CHAPTER 22

Joshua Hale's Old Place
Brazoria County Texas
8 A.M., Saturday, December 14, 1993
Sunny, clear, Temp 65°

A river never stays the same, and you cannot put your foot in the same water twice. It's like meeting an old girlfriend. Just because you liked her twenty years ago doesn't mean she stayed the same. It's better to meet a stranger, and leave ex-wives and old girlfriends alone.

Although Joy was married to her third husband who was half a world away working as a Geologist, Dirk screwed her several times during the night. He'd quit worrying about parentage since he divorced, and Jerry protected him, but Joy committed adultery. Maybe he did too. He'd confess to the new priest, Jésus Posadas, at Saint Colombo. Dirk wasn't Catholic, but to a man with a hammer (Jésus) everything looked like a tack.

His SUV sank to the axles in the bog, and their cell phones didn't work. Dirk decided to walk down the road from the doe decoy and ask his old buddy, the game warden, to call Angleton for a tow truck to wench him out. He figured about $100, but during deer season they upped the ante.

Jim, the game warden, was tall, skinny, and dark. When he laughed, he cackled like old Bezoar, the Karankawa Shaman, south of Dirk's property. Dirk began to wonder. They favored. He bribed Jim and asked him to call towing to wench him out of the mud.

"You know old Bezoar up the river about ten miles, back in the woods?" asked Dirk.

"That's my uncle," admitted Jim.

"Were your parents tall?" asked Dirk.

"My mother was average. I didn't have a father around the house. She put Wilt Chamberlain for the welfare and called Bezoar 'uncle'."

Dirk ran out of questions.

"You buy the Ben Milam property?" asked Warden James Tharp.

"Why yes!" replied Dirk, smiling.

"Did you find that crib full of bones back in the swamp? Ben butchered 4 wives, salted them down, and hung them in a smokehouse."

Dirk was shocked. "How did the law find out?"

"Relatives came looking and Ben fed them sliced on a platter with cornbread and cranberry sauce."

Jim Tharp smirked. He was dark and 6'8". "I was 'Little Black Sambo' in grade school. I look down from above on all those guys now. Old Bezoar could be my real uncle, not Wilt Chamberlain."

Dirk figured at least thirty minutes for the wench truck to arrive or maybe sixty if they got lost and had to call in. Nobody stopped and shot at Jim Tharp's decoy, and no buck came courting. Dirk asked, "There's a lot of Mexican and illegals that hang around during the day. Where do they go after dark?"

"Daytime, they get $5 and $6 dollar an hour jobs. Some Spanish speaking contractor will pick up a crew and pay them in cash. Most work construction and build houses in Sugar Land, where there are lots of new houses and shopping malls. A Mexican will work hard on Orange Crush and a Peanut patty," replied Jim, chuckling.

"Where do they sleep at night?"

"Up and down the river," replied Jim. "Their campsites are all along. They hear a boat coming and hide. There're no roads back in those swamps. Some take women in there."

"What about the shooting I hear up and down the river?" asked Dirk. "Who's doing it?"

"I don't know. There are no roads in there. Poachers shoot game wardens."

"Do you know Warden Farmer in Fort Bend? He's my game warden on Ben Milam's road." Dirk chuckled. "There's a private road and house place about a mile south of the Brazoria P&L Nuclear Plant. It belongs to a Dr. Mambo Nigero, Professor at USN. Who's the game warden?"

"Not me! Nobody goes down that road."

*　　*　　*

Dirk paid $100 cash in advance, and the tow truck driver winched him out, tipped his hat and drove off. December was their busy month. The only cap on their fees was competition. The truck cost $75,000, and you could depreciate it as a business expense over ten years and pay the truck off in five years. Then there were licenses, answering service, yellow pages, etc., not to mention your own valuable time and loss of opportunity if you went on vacation or took time off.

Loss of consortium and loss of opportunity were intangibles that lawyers loved to add on when suing some poor guy.

*　　*　　*

Dirk hooked up the trailer and boat, helped Joy put out the coals in the fireplace and sweep their living room. After all, they did have a good time. Sex was the number one adult recreation, and a strange piece was unquestionably the best. Dirk got to her before Dr. Austin Hale, but it was only a matter of three weeks when Austin came back from New Orleans and moved in the bottom floor of their new house in Sugar Land.

Since she was younger, Joy agreed to take the winding stairway and second floor, and they would share the kitchen, dining room, and library on the first floor. Nude swimming was okay if they didn't have guests. They were physicians and ignored nudity.

Joy had always heard that Pathologists did necrophilia. There was a specialty in medicine for every passion. Big deal!

*   *   *

Dirk worried about Jerry and wondered whether truth or lie was best. He'd tell the truth and leave out Dr. Joy Burrell. She'd feel sorry, but if she knew Joy was along, wow, she'd get angry. Women felt insecurity and didn't trust other women with their man of the moment. Except for drunk driving, love triangles accounted for the most traumatic deaths in modern societies. The two most dangerous calls a policeman would make were traffic stops and late night domestic quarrels between husband and wife. By nature, men had more extramarital affairs and were apt to be intoxicated. Rule Number One: never leave a loaded gun around the house where the wife could find it and never leave it in the bedroom.

Dirk left Joy off at the Braeswood LUX without making another date. She knew about Jerry and understood.

CHAPTER 23

Houston Heights, Texas
8 A.M., Saturday, December 14, 1993
Fair, no storm clouds
Temperature 75/44°

Captain Jerry Billings DPS had been married in the remote past and preferred separate apartments to living as a couple. Two couldn't live cheaper than one, if one was an impulse buyer. All men when they reached a magic age thought owning a $40,000 BASS RIG was a rite of passage to middle age, and it was so in East Texas. They watched professional football religiously and wouldn't go to church or spare a pence for Saint Peter.

Jerry was Catholic and divorced. If she got married again, it would be adultery in the eyes of the Catholic Church. The Pope, John Paul himself, would excommunicate her, forbid her the sacraments, and spoil her chance for Purgatory and Paradise in the hereafter. Paradise was Persian for walled garden.

When she was happy, she never thought about a hereafter, but when she was depressed or worried, she pictured herself shoveling coal in hell and a red devil with a forked tail and pitchfork standing behind her. She surmised every divorced Catholic felt the same. Protestants didn't believe in Purgatory, and Atheist didn't believe in hell. WOW! Every Italian (Sicilian) she knew was Catholic. Italy and Mexico were the two most Catholic nations in the world. At least the Mexican illegals selling us dope, crossing our borders, and taking our lower paid jobs were Catholics. You can't talk any sense with an Islamic Jihadist. Paradise was a walled off oasis with 70 virgins.

*   *   *

When Dirk didn't come home last evening, Jerry checked with his answering service, and his cell phone and beeper were out of range. The lady at the answering service unsolicitedly dropped a hint that Dr. Joy Burrell, Psychiatrist, was at the same place as Dirk, and she couldn't be reached either. Dirk's bass boat and SUV were gone from the garage. So she deducted that Dirk and Joy went bass fishing and decided to spend the night.

She called the county dispatcher in Brazoria County who gave her the home phone number of Warden James Tharp who didn't get in until 9 P.M. and told her that Dirk and some blond unhitched the boat and trailer and stuck his SUV in a marsh. He heard him racing his motor and spinning his wheels. He figured Dirk and the lady would spend the night in an old house place and call a tow truck the next morning. Jerry thanked Warden Tharp and explained she was inordinately concerned about their "daughter," but Dirk being a policeman and all could take care of himself. Actually, she did feel better that Dirk was all right, but of Dr. Joy Burrell, she was suspicious.

Jerry ate breakfast, put on denim, attached 0.32 cal. back and leg guns, brushed her hair and teeth, fixed her face, and drove her red Mitsubishi sports car over to Sandra's apartment to see Devine' about Sandra, the courthouse, and Dr. Joy Burrell, the Psychiatrist. Normally, she would drive her patrol car with siren and flasher on and show off, but she was concerned about how the world was turning.

Jerry had a U.S. Army Colt 45 given to her by her ex-husband just before he joined the U-2 pilots. It held a loaded clip with an empty chamber, so she would have to chamber a round before firing. Unlike the Glock and Beretta it had a thumb safety when it was fully loaded and ready to fire. You didn't have to chamber a round with a revolver, and a man good with a knife was faster than either at 20 feet. Dirk carried a balanced throwing knife strapped to his leg, but she didn't. She was on the Olympic pistol team in law school and DPS Lady Champion.

*   *   *

"Come in, it's unlocked," yelled Devine' before Jerry could go for her key. Only Deviné, Jerry, and Austin Hale had keys to Sandra's apartment.

Jerry found Devine' lying flat on her back with both legs up on three pillows reading *Mutiny on the Bounty*. Her briefcase and legal briefs lay nearby, and pop top cans of Diet Pepsi and Slim Fast were on the lamp stand by the head of her bed. A tennis ball can and rolled toilet tissue were under the foot of the bed.

"Deviné, did you hurt your back, for goodness sake?" asked Jerry.

Devine' embarrassed, smiled and whispered, "don't tell anybody. I'm trying to get pregnant."

Jerry, who had never enjoyed the pregnancy experience, laughed. "If you're not on the pill and ovulate and there are sperm swimming around, you'll get pregnant. Sperm swim upstream. Every male ejaculate has a million all fighting to get that little egg."

"I'm giving them a gravity advantage," replied Devine' proudly. She hadn't been out of bed for 24 hours.

"You can't feel when you ovulate? Boy! I can. If it's on the right, I think I have appendicitis."

"I've never felt ovulation, and it was too early to have a positive urine."

"Who's the lucky guy? You don't have black male friends."

"The guys weren't black, and I loved all three, but I had my favorite, and he died trying. He wanted a son badly to carry on his work."

Jerry didn't have to think. She went to Donald Tantalia's Rosary. Nobody mentioned he died in the saddle. Devine' was not present at his Rosary. She was *persona non grata*. "You might as well tell me the other two. Did Don lay you on the sea wall at Galveston?"

"They are secrets. Why did you ask about the Galveston Sea Wall? Misty said it was a joke," asked Deviné. As long as she didn't admit it, Jerry wouldn't know for sure. Any lawyer knew that. That was the Miranda warning.

Lie to your lawyer. Lie to the court. Lie to your fellow convicts and parole board. Texas had 20,000 recidivist prisoners in the State Penitentiary at Huntsville, and all lied. Just ordinary people in their daily conversations lie 95% of the time, and everybody lies under oath. It's okay for lawyers and preachers to lie. They get paid for lying.

Society would fall apart if people went around telling truth.

Jerry chuckled. Her grandfather, Sam Deagio Sr. down in Costa Rico was retired Mafia. Caesar, her father, and her Uncle Sam Jr. didn't want the hassle. They owned 21 Deagio liquor stores in Houston, and her Aunt Sophie looked after them. Sophie was a Tantalia sister. Jerry knew them all well, and she'd probably inherit the fruits of their labors, but she wanted nothing to do with that old country stuff.

Maria, Donald out of retirement, and Prince Kahli owned SROCO as a private oil company licensed in Saudi Arabia. Donald and Maria took her cousin Sherry Deagio out of a convent in Sicily and financed her through law school in Texas. She and Sherry were roommates where they were a pair and loved same sex. Ex-nuns were good lovers, they had a taste for cunnilingus. Devine' had shared the blanket with Sherry who lived two doors down from Sandra in the high-rise. All people thought about sex 80% of the time when they weren't eating.

Playboy was the greatest magazine for men ever created. When their wife had a headache, they could read *Playboy* and jack off. No matter how you got off it was the same. With a vibrator in her purse, a woman never had to be without sex on demand, just insert, push a little button, and WOW!

*   *   *

Jerry went to Sandra's windows and looked out over northwest Houston, the loop, and uptown Galleria shopping area with multiple high-rises and hotels, etc. She could see River Oaks and Buffalo Bayou.

Even though it was Saturday cars and shoppers were crowding up the place. She turned back to Deviné.

"You're not going anywhere at all?"

"That's right. I'm trying to get pregnant," replied Devine' adamantly.

"Deviné, tell me about Dr. Joy Burrell, the Psychiatrist, I really don't keep up with what's going on at the University," suggested Jerry.

"She's an expert in channeling thoughts and Cognitive Therapy. She's into taboos right now, and has a government grant to study incest. It's never been done on humans, only goats, sheep, and camels. They run out of women in those Arab countries, so they import sex slaves from east Africa. The Persians married their widowed mothers, sisters, and daughters. By legend and myth, incest was quite common among the Semites and Persians. Some still do. Joy said it was a Taboo not a sin. She has a grant to follow a hundred incestuous couples ten years."

Jerry thought about Caesar. "To be honest, I don't think my father has ten more good years. Sam Sr. might die in the saddle, and I don't have any brothers. So I guess I don't qualify. There's some prisoners in Huntsville that slept with their stepdaughters, but I can't remember a woman ever charging her husband for sleeping with his real daughter. There's a few school teachers in prison for having sexual affairs with under aged male students. That's pretty common. Band Directors and male soccer coaches get in trouble quite often if the parents catch them. I know of one case where a twelve year old came up pregnant by her 17 year old brother. He got a three year suspended sentence, and their mother kept the baby to get welfare. The baby was normal," replied Jerry, thinking.

"She wants doctors, lawyers, and ministers to enter with a daughter or young sister. It's a longitudinal study so she can study the offsprings. They have to practice unprotected sex. It's a taboo not a sin, and they must practice mental channeling. A woman can enter with her son, brother, or father if they pass the physical," explained Deviné. We didn't get that in Criminal Law at Harvard. Their big deal was same sex and overt homosexuality. Everybody was against, 'don't ask and don't tell'," said Deviné.

"Deviné, do you know where swearing on a stack of Bibles came from?" asked Jerry.

Devine' raised in Jamaica and *Magna cum laude* from Harvard answered, "Martin Luther King?"

"No, from the Bible! When Abraham's trusted servant took the family jewels to buy Isaac a wife, and Moses' wife stuck her hand up Moses's robe before he wrestled with God's angel, they had to swear allegiance on their Master's pecker," answered Jerry, laughing.

*   *   *

Jerry rang Sherry Deagio's door chimes.

"Hi Jerry, come in. I'm happy to see you. I hope you plan to spend the night. I'll fix us tuna on rye and open a can of pasta, like old times. You can take a girl out of a cloister, but not the cloister out of the girl. You have to be out by 7 A.M. Sunday is the only day my Rabbi has off," confessed Sherry, joyfully.

"Let me use your telephone. I want to call home and inform my live-in fiancée that I'm spending the night with you. He knows we do same sex," asked Jerry, determined.

Dirk was out hosing the mud off his SUV, and Jerry let it ring until he finally answered. Maybe he was beginning to get deaf. It happens at an early age in soldiers and policemen that don't wear earplugs on the shooting range. Firing Bazookas and 0.45 Cal. pistols without earmuffs were the worst. Later in life, when the high frequency ringing (tinnitus) stops, you are deaf.

Dirk knew it was Jerry checking on him. She wouldn't hang up.

"Derek Strong, private detective, **HAVE GUN WILL TRAVEL**," answered Dirk.

"Where have you been?" asked Jerry.

"I tried to call you, but my cell phone didn't work. I got stuck in the mud and spent the night in the woods. I had a game warden call this morning, and a tow truck winched me out. I'm washing the mud off my Suburban before it cakes. What do you want to do tonight?" asked Dirk.

"I need you to help me tomorrow. I'm spending the night with cousin Sherry. I'll eat here and be home at 7:30 A.M. dressed in denim, armed, and dangerous. Gas up that boat. I want you to take me up the river from Brazoria to San Felipe and look for illegals. They're camped all along and have a midget submarine with a periscope just like the Japanese in WWII."

"Jerry, that's crazy! There're so many curves, bends, horseshoe lakes, and cypress swamps it may be two hundred miles by river. We can't fight a submarine in a fiberglass boat. They'd rip out the bottom, and we'd sink. Adios!"

"You got life preservers and a fire extinguisher?"

"That's the law," replied Dirk, skeptical. She was punishing him. All she had to do was requisition a DPS helicopter and drop down on illegals from above. He didn't like the idea of shooting illegals. It was misuse of *maxim force*. The punishment didn't fit the crime. He wouldn't shoot a man over a little dope. They were fixing to legalize "pot" in California.

It was plain to Dirk that Jerry wasn't happy about his staying out all night, and if she found out about Dr. Burrell, he was in deep doo doo.

CHAPTER 24

Ho Chi Minh—Best Western
Hoa Lo Boulevard, Hanoi Vietnam
9 A.M. Sunday, December 15, 1993
Temp 34/20°, Light snow

Some times the best made plans of mice and men go awry, thought Bob Burrell, Geologist for SROCO oil. Mount Merapi, Indonesia's most dangerous volcano was erupting, blanketing the sun with ash, and causing earthquakes and tsunami in the Pacific Islands and South China Sea. Flights were cancelled, and they were lucky to get a standby to Hanoi. Asiana stewardesses were second only to Singapore Air.

After breakfast, they met in a private conference room where a map of Southeast Asia when raised revealed a black board, eraser, and chalk. Donald addressed the group. "Vietnamese authorities invited us. They were impressed with Bob's drilling Quanxi field. The oil reservoir extends to Vietnam's northern border.

"At the Vietnamese border are the Ka Long Caves and eroded mountains millions of years old which look similar to the Karst Mountains at Guilin China. We can't seismograph because of its proximity to China. I want an visual assessment. Texans know more about looking for oil than anybody. All great fields were discovered that way.

"China, Russia, and Southeast Asia remained intact when Pangaea broke up, and India banged into Eurasia forming the Himalayas. Oil goes back 65 million years. Anthracite goes back 300 million before break up occurred.

"Parcel and Spratly Islands in the South China Sea have long been claimed by Vietnam and only later by the Japanese and Chinese. Vietnam appealed to the UN. SROCO is independent. This time we are partnering with the Vietnamese. Their claim seems valid. We will honor our commitment to the Chinese PLA in Cambodia and Myanmar. Maria made no financial arrangement and asked for a year.

"Japan disputes Russian claim of the north Hokkaido Islands and China's claim of Senkaku in the East China Sea. The United States will avoid disputes and remain neutral. Japan is building a nuclear submarine. Russia will sell or lease anything nuclear. Countries will fight over gas and oil. In regional wars, atomic bombs cause too much collateral damage.

"It might surprise you to know that Vietnam has 86 million, a GDP of 8%, and the third largest national oil company in SEA after China and Malaysia. It will be the next 'Asian Tiger'."

* * *

Donald, Elvis, and Louiza took a taxi to the American Consulate. Penny and Bob rented a Suzuki. The famous Hanoi Hilton, a prison built by the French and occupied by downed American fliers from 1964-1974, was next door to their hotel and modernized to a museum for tourist. Senator John McCane's jumpsuit, flying boots, helmet, and parachute were on display. To Bob's surprise the Vietnamese didn't carry grudges. When the boat people came home for a visit, they were rich. Vietnamese weren't dumb and observed Japan and South Korea. Vietnam was the next Asian Tiger! Unemployment was down to 2%.

* * *

A $US bought 20,000 Dongs, the Vietnamese currency. A bottle of Tiger cost 10,000 Dongs. A massage cost 40,000, and a girl sent to your room was 100,000 Dongs. They knew all 68 ways and were insulted if you used a rubber. The prettiest got the most Dongs. Bob served during the Vietnam conflict, and the girls in Saigon charged what the traffic would bear. For all common soldiers since WWI and France, the going rate was $US 5 for a short time and $US 10 for an all night stay. Usually the black market exchange rate was $US 5 for a carton of cigarettes or a case of 3.5% beer. Bob heard about the German girls trading sex for three cigarettes, a chocolate bar, or a pair of nylons, but he took that on faith.

*　　*　　*

The Ganges, Red, Mekong, Irrawaddy, and Brahmaputra rivers all started in the Himalayas and ended in large deltas. Hanoi was on the Red River delta and was more densely populated than the Mekong delta below Saigon (Ho Chi Min City). Their only advertised tourist attractions were the Hanoi Hilton Museum next door, and the Delong Bay bordering on China, the Red River delta, and the Gulf of Tonkin.

Delong Bay was easily 300 million years old and had 2000 limestone islands eroded down to camel's humps and dragon's backs. A 19th century French soldier reported seeing a long snakelike dragon, and the name stuck. Even the locals admitted it was a tourist trap.

*　　*　　*

At Hanoi Vietnamese rushed more than Chinese and Japanese on bicycles, motorbikes, and cars like Houston, Texas. 50 years of war, bombed back to the Stone Age, lost millions, and were in a hurry. He did not see one fat or idle Vietnamese and only one fat man back in Hong Kong. WOW!

*　　*　　*

Donald and Louiza were a pair, and knew each other in another life. They visited a bar on the fourth floor where a Latin band with a vocalist performed and watched Donald and Louiza perform like professionals. They had been there and done that with the same band in Xian China.

*   *   *

Back in their room Bob studied. The Japanese Parliament had voted to increase its military budget and deploy troops in the East and South China Seas where large reserves of gas and oil were known to exist. All modern wars were about oil.

U.S. STATE DEPARTMENT
BUREAU OF CONSULAR AFFAIRS
BACKGROUND NOTES: VIETNAM

HISTORY

Vietnam had been inhabited since Paleolithic times and dated back 6000 thousand years. Civilization began late Neolithic and Early Bronze Age, from about 2000 to 1400 BCE.

By 1200 BCE wet-rice cultivation and bronze casting led to development of the Dong Son culture. Bronze weapons, tools, and drums of Dong-Sonian sites show a Southeast Asian influence.

Ancient copper mines were found in northern Vietnam, and boat-shaped coffins, burial jars, stilt dwellings, and betel-nut-chewing dated back to antiquity.

The Hong Bang Dynasty was the first Vietnamese state. In 257 BCE, the last Hong king lost to An Durong Vurong. In 207 BCE, a Chinese general defeated An Durong Vurong and consolidated Nanyue into the Chinese Han Dynasty.

For the next thousand years, Vietnam was under Chinese rule. By the early 10th century, Vietnam gained autonomy, but not independence.

Buddhism became the state religion.

Between the 11th and 18th centuries, Vietnam expanded southward in a process known as nam tiến (*southward expansion*) and conquered the kingdom of Champa and part of the Khmer Empire.

From the 16th century onwards, civil strife and frequent infighting engulfed much of Vietnam. First, the Chinese-supported Mac Dynasty challenged the Lê Dynasty's power. After the Mac Dynasty was defeated, the Lê Dynasty was reinstalled, but with no actual power. Power was divided between the Trinh Lords in the North and the Nguyễn Lords in the South, who engaged in a civil war for more than four decades before a truce was called in the 1670s. During this time, the Nguyễn expanded southern Vietnam into the Mekong Delta, annexing the Central Highlands and the Khmer land in the Mekong Delta.

Vietnam's independence was eroded by France-aided Catholic militias-in a series of military conquests from 1859 until 1885 when the entire country became part of French Indochina. The French administration imposed significant political and cultural changes on Vietnamese society. A Western-style system of modern education was developed, and Roman Catholicism was propagated widely in Vietnamese society. Most of the French settlers in Indochina were concentrated in Cochinchina (southern third of Vietnam whose principal city was Saigon).

Developing a plantation economy to promote the exports of tobacco, indigo, tea and coffee, the French ignored calls for self-government and civil rights. The French maintained control until World War II, when the Japanese war in the Pacific triggered the invasion of French Indochina in 1941.

With the defeat of France in Europe, the French Third Republic became the Vichy Regime. Vichy France was forced to surrender control of French Indochina to Japan. The natural resources of Vietnam were exploited for the purposes of the Japanese Empire's military campaigns into the British Indochinese colonies of Burma, Malay Peninsula, and India.

FIRST INDOCHINA WAR

In 1941, the Viet Minh—a communist and nationalist liberation movement—emerged under Ho Chi Minh to seek independence for Vietnam from France as well as to oppose the Japanese occupation. An estimated 2 million Vietnamese died during the Vietnamese famine of 1944-45. Following the military defeat of Japan in 1945, Viet Minh occupied Hanoi and proclaimed independence on 2 September.

French Republic sent their Far East Expeditionary Corps to restore French rule. On November 20, 1946 the First Indochina War between Viet Minh and the French began and lasted until July 1954.

The French and Vietnamese loyalists suffered a major loss at Dien Bien Phu. A million northerners, mainly Catholic, moved south, fearing persecution by the communists, and a line at the 17th separated north from south.

A partition of Vietnam, with Ho Chi Minh's Democratic Republic of Vietnam in North Vietnam, and Emperor Bảo Đại's State of Vietnam in South Vietnam, was not intended to be permanent. Geneva Accords forbade interference by third powers. The State of Vietnam's Prime

Minister Ngo Dinh Diem toppled Báo Đại and proclaimed himself president of the Republic of Vietnam. The Accords mandated nationwide elections by 1956.

Bob stopped reading. He already knew about the Vietnam War and the ending. Vietnam lost millions over 50 years and now were resurrecting. Hail Mary and Glory be!

He turned off the desk lamp and crawled in his own bed. Too tired for sex? He was maturing fast. The Brahmaputra and Ganges Delta, the Red River Delta, Kalong Bay, and Gulf of Tonkin were great fisheries, and the citizens would object to drilling and contaminating their grandfather's fishing waters.

The East and South China Sea were where "it was at" in that part of the world. The Andaman Islands, Brahmaputra and Irrawaddy deltas were where "it was at" in the Bay of Bengal. When drilling got deep in a mile of sea water, risks went up.

There would always be wars and rumors of wars. The whole time he surveyed the Sea of Japan he figured they'd never be able to drill off the coasts of South Korea, Japan, and China. Neighbors would fight over oil. The USA with its nuclear submarines and aircraft carriers were circling like a pack of wolves and a flock of buzzards. Maybe hawks sounded better.

Bob thought about the Deccan Traps in India. They were drilling for gas and oil off the western coast of Mumbai all way up to Karachi Pakistan. There were hundreds, maybe thousands of islands. Oil could be under the basalt overflow of the Deccan only 65 million years old. He'd suggest it to Donald after they finished China Sea and Bay of Bengal. It was easier to drill through basalt on dry land than two miles of sea water and four miles of sea floor and less risk.

*   *   *

Bob too tired to sleep, turned on the reading lamp, and picked up a history of Senator John McCain. He didn't see anything in the Hanoi Hilton or Hotel Book Store about Jane Fonda. Nobody remembered her. (Author spent two nights in the same hotel and visited the Hanoi Hilton War Museum where Senator McCain was a national hero.)

Bob read.

McCain followed his father and grandfather, both four-star admirals, into the United States Navy, graduating from the U.S. Naval Academy in 1958. He became a naval aviator, flying ground attack aircraft from aircraft carriers. During the Vietnam War, he nearly lost his life in the 1967 USS Forrestal fire. In October 1967, while on a bombing mission over Hanoi, he was shot down, seriously injured, and captured by the North Vietnamese. He was a prisoner of war until 1973. McCain experienced episodes of torture and refused an out-of-sequence early repatriation offer. His war wounds left him with lifelong physical limitations.

He retired from the Navy as a captain in 1981 and moved to Arizona, where he entered politics. Elected to the U.S. House of Representatives in 1982, he served two terms, and was then elected to the U.S. Senate in 1986, winning re-election.

Bob went to sleep.

CHAPTER 25

Edinburgh Scotland
Scottish Royal Castle
9 A.M., Sunday, December 15, 1993
Temp 50/30°, Light snow

The cobblestone carriage way which wound to the top of Edinburgh castle, the highest lookout, had eleven laminated foot thick steel doors which during siege had to be penetrated and breached to get to the top. On top were thick granite walls with medieval gun ports and 15th century cannons pointed out toward the Bay at entrance to the river named the Firth of Fourth. For tourist the incline was steep and slick when wet. According to the resident guide, the castle had never been breached or seriously damaged, and only surrendered once when they were starved out.

There was an active Regimental Guard assigned to the castle and Royal buildings with Headquarters on top. Their vehicles were allowed up. Ancient castles didn't have elevators or toilets. They used chamber pots and in the old days threw human waste out special slanted openings in the castle wall. The Scots were descendents of ancient Celts. Their religion was Presbyterian, and everybody attended Sunday services. The Scottish Royal Castle was the tallest and strongest in the world, and tourists never stopped visiting from daylight to dark.

The first Scottish King had 20 wives and 50 children, each of which started his own clan. Charlemagne had multiple wives but forbade polygamy after he was crowned Holy Roman Emperor. King Henry VIII invented serial monogamy when the Pope forbade Henry annulment from Catherine of Aragon.

The Edinburgh Castle was constructed on a basalt plug of a dormant volcano 300 million years old.

An outdoor bath house made of granite blocks was used by Mary Queen of Scots for wine baths. Cleopatra took milk baths. A royal lake out front was used by the King for trial of unfaithful wives. A priest was summoned to bless the water. If she sank, the holy water accepted her, and she was innocent. If she floated, she was guilty and beheaded.

*   *   *

"Hadrian's Wall was built in 130 c.e., housed 30,000 Roman troops, extended from York to Chester, and separated the Roman civilized Bretons from the wild Pics and Scots.

"Father Colombo, an Irish Monk, brought whiskey to Scotland and converted the fierce Pics to Christ. He was first to see the Loch Ness monster in 450 c.e.

"Rob Roy was a legendary bandit who robbed the poor and spent it. Robert Louis Stevenson wrote Dr. Jekyll and Mr. Hyde, retired to Tahiti, wrote Treasure Island, contracted syphilis, and died. His Island Mansion still stands and was named a world's UNESCO treasure.

"Sir William Wallace (1270-1305) and Robert Bruce (1274-1329) led the Scottish Clans against the British and won victories at Sterling Bridge in 1296 and Bannockburn in 1314.

"Wallace was hung, drawn and quartered in the London Towers in 1305.

"Bruce, after defeating the English, crowned himself King Robert I of Scotland in 1328. King Edward III of England granted Scotland independence the same year. King Robert lived 20 years longer than Sir Wallace, so it didn't occur overnight. Robert Bruce died fighting in Spain on Crusade against the Saracens (Muslims) in 1329, and his heart was shipped back to Scotland and buried in several Abbeys. He was quoted as praying in battle, 'lay me down to die awhile, raised to fight again'. Everybody knows about the spider."

*   *   *

They had to catch the afternoon commuter to Aberdeen the center of offshore North Sea Oil that Great Britain shared with Norway, Netherlands, ESSO (EXXON), and others. So they made a quick tour of the Royal Mile, Holyrood, Walter Scott's monument, and General Charles George Gordon on a horse. Saint George was the patron saint of Great Britain (England), and General Gordon's horse was on hind legs with both feet in the air. Chinese Gordon commanded the Chinese Army at the Emperor's request and won. He died at Khartoum as Pasha General of all Egyptian armed forces in Egypt. John Knox was buried under the parking lot of the First Presbyterian Church of Scotland (Slot 44), but his office was across the street passed the Royal mile. Mary Queen of Scots was Catholic and Queen Elizabeth, her cousin, had her beheaded in the Tower of London. Mary's son, James I of England and James VI of Scotland, had the King James Bible published and paid off the national debt. They used Erasmus' and Tindal's Bibles and William Shakespeare's plays. It set the pronunciation, punctuation, and grammar for the entire English speaking world like Vladimir I of Kiev's Bible established Russian vernacular and alphabet. Unfortunately, Vladimir's scribe had dyslexia and reversed letters producing the Russian we see today. Queen Mary Tudor (Bloody Mary), a Catholic, had Tindal exhumed and burned at the stake for translating a Bible into English.

When John Knox accused Catholic Mary of adultery, she had him decapitated, burned at the stake, and scattered his ashes on the church ground under the present day parking lot. After her first husband's funeral, she stopped off at Saint Andrews to play a round of golf after which she texted Lord Boswell on her cell phone.

CHAPTER 26

Aberdeen Scotland—Holiday Inn
8 P.M., Sunday, December 15, 1993
Temp 30°, Snowing

Aberdeen was just outside the Arctic Circle. It was also the main headquarters of North Sea Oil. The Pride of Aberdeen was their beautiful red roses.

The cheapest building blocks were granite for modern two bedroom one garage otherwise beautiful residential city homes which they built for the offshore oil workers all cost exactly the same, 50,000 pounds or US $100,000 cash. Everyone planted red roses.

Aberdeen had 10 month winters and 2 month summers of heavenly weather. The best beef cattle in Europe were named Aberdeen.

Aberdeen was the home of the famous Barclay Clan. There were 7 pages of Barclays in the phone book and over 30 George Barclays. Barclays were Berkeleys before William the Conqueror and the Doomsday book, but moved to Scotland and became Barclays. Those moving to Northern Ireland were Barklays and Dublin, Barkleys. As a rule of thumb in 1993, Barclays were Scots, Barklays were northern Irish, and Barkeleys were English. However, the two Barclays that owned Barclay's Bank with offices in London and New York and branches in every big city in the English speaking world, were Scots.

A Barclay donation earned a naming opportunity of Barclay Theater at the University of Saint Nicholas back home. For one billion, Maria promised to change Saint Nicholas to Saint George, the patron Saint of Great Britain, or better still Barclay University. There were plenty in East Texas and were the first to cross the Neches before Fort Teran and received Mexican Land Patents from Alcide John Bevil at Bevelsport on the Sabine River below Jasper, Texas. They brought the Alabama Indians now sharing a reservation with the Coushatta's between Woodville and Livingston in Polk County Texas. There are more Barclays in Canada than the lower 48 states, and they originated from and were kin to the Barclays in Aberdeen Scotland. Barclay University! Barclay Castle, Barclay Bank, Barclay Aberdeen Beef, and Barclay trucks! Everywhere you look in Aberdeen there were Barclay's Black Draught and Barclay's Old Mariner Pubs. General Barclay who led the Russian Army after the battle of Borodino was from Aberdeen, and his descendents remained in Russia. Reverend Berkeley of Trinity University, in all the Philosophy Texts and the Encyclopedia Britannica, was an Aberdeen Barclay. The great William Barclay, Theologian, father of the Quakers who broke away from the Anglican congregationists during Oliver Cromwell's reign, was from the Aberdeen Barclays.

The author of this book is a sixth generation Texan, and his ancestors were Quakers that arrived in Pennsylvania in 1740 before they migrated to North Carolina, Kentucky, Tennessee, Alabama, and finally Texas in 1828 and became plantation and slave owners along the way. On June 16, 1865, there was emancipation proclamation in Texas, and now there are more black Barclays (Barklays) than white. If you observe closely, they share many of the same characteristics. Before the automobile and TV, the white and black Barclay's had a barbeque and family reunion on the third Sunday in July every year to meet their new cousins and listen to the Light Crust Doughboys and any politician that happened by. (Author's note: the story of animosity between ex-slaves and owners were just not true, at least not in East Texas. We were all kin and still are. I've never known a rich cotton farmer, just poor and poorer.) Hickory smoked barbeque, potato salad, butter beans, banana pudding, and ice tea in a pint jar was the best eating that a five year old ever had until he ate his aunt Ruthel's cherry angel food cake. When the author dies, the memory of those days will be gone forever.

I visited Scotland and found the Scots to be unfriendly and cool in casual encounters. I didn't meet any women. My wife had the opposite experience in a bar in our hotel in Aberdeen when she and another lady went unescorted and were invited by Scotsmen in kilts to join their wedding party. I stayed up in the room, soaked my hurting feet, and read *Bonfires of the Vanities* and the Aberdeen phonebook where there were 7 pages of Barclays in 1992. There were 6 pages in the London phonebook, and only 3 Barclays in Dublin.

For the many Stewarts and Stuarts in the USA, they both go back to Mary Stewart, Queen of the Scots, who for a brief time was married to King Henry II of France. The French spelled it Stuart. Mary's son was James I of England and James Stewart VI of Scotland. Catherine de Medici was her mother-in-law in France. King James IV of Scotland married King Henry VIII of England's sister, Margaret, so Mary was first cousin once removed by birth to Queen Elizabeth I of England, next in succession, but that didn't happen. When they held up Mary's head after decapitation by her auburn hair, her head fell off and bounced across the floor. She was totally grey at 44 and wore a red wig and petticoat to execution.

Sandra could only remember half what the guides said, and, if you read the bare bones biography of Mary Queen of Scots, it would take a whole day. There were many around. She and her lover, Lord Boswell, murdered her husband, so she never made Saint.

Mary, a Catholic, got plenty of sex while her cousin Elizabeth, a Protestant, was the "virgin" Queen. English History is not required study in the USA, and there were a lot of cousin marriages and kin in Royal Families in the old countries and Russia. Who could keep up? The Scots and the English!

*   *   *

At the time of the dinosaurs, Pangaea was rotated on the equator, the temperature was 120° and there were no glaciers anywhere. Anthracite coal was formed from ferns and conifers in bogs 300 million years ago and made up 2/3 the land mass of Antarctica. Oil was made from tiny marine animals (zooplankton) deposited on sea beds 65 million years ago. There has been a lot of oil and gas drilled within the Arctic Circle all around the globe, namely Siberia, Alaska, and the North Sea. Russia sent a nuclear sub down to the ocean floor and planted their flag claiming mineral rights under the ice at the North Pole. The United States claimed the moon.

*   *   *

Aberdeen was an old but a modern, clean, and prosperous city. Everything was constructed with red shiny granite. There was a spacious City Centre and the boulevards were wide and clean. It was on the northeast shore of Scotland. They were prosperous on agriculture, beef cattle, and fishing before offshore drilling, but now they were rich. It was nicknamed

Granite City and the Oil Capital of Europe, all offshore. Population was 200,000 not counting transit oil workers and their families. Offshore oil was discovered in 1970 about the time the USA began its decline and just before the Mid-east oil embargo raised the price of oil, and gas lines formed at the pumps in the USA. The concept of underwater pipelines and floating production platforms were developed, and Aberdeen became a major oil exporter to Europe.

Since WWII, 30,000 shallow wells over and about the continental shelves of Texas, Louisiana, and Mississippi were drilled by American, British, and Dutch oil companies and 30 wells were in production out past the continental waters in deep waters 1 and 2 miles down where the great oil and gas reservoirs were. Canada was extracting bitumen (light crude) from tar sands, and American companies were drilling and producing oil and natural gas offshore of Alaska and California.

Land drilling in Texas, Oklahoma, and Louisiana is unattractive since the Saudis lowered the price of oil. Unknown to all the majors were the fantastic reservoirs of oil under the deep salt layers (evaporates) 100 miles offshore and under the salt domes of Texas and Louisiana. WOW! 80% of the gas and 60% of the oil was still down there in the "worn out" fields over and around salt domes along the coasts. Below the salt is where "it was at."

*   *   *

People had been living north of the rivers Don and Dee which traverse Aberdeen for 8000 years. It was classified a Royal Burgh by King Robert the Bruce in 1315, and the University dated back to 1495. Its seaport is the largest on the coast of northeast Scotland, and its Heliport is the busiest in the world. Further north, ruins of Stone Age dwellings date back to Paleolithic times. Aberdeen was sacked, burned, and razed by the Celts, Pics, Romans, Vikings and English and rebuilt many times. A quarter of its people were killed by the bubonic plague in 1647. It got City gas lighting in 1824 and an underground sewer system in 1865. Volcanic igneous metamorphic rock date back 500 million years and a granite rock quarry yielded stones for construction.

Daylight hours are 6-8 in the winter and 18 hours in summer. The temperature drops to 0°-30°F in winter, and rises to 55-15° in summer. They get 70-75 inches of rain per year. 2% are non whites. 40% are Presbyterians, 20% are Catholics, and 40% have no religion.

Aberdeen has an International Airport, and rail service to London, Edinburgh and Glasgow. Like the bullet train from Osaka to Tokyo, and the bullet from Barcelona to Madrid and Granada which traveled at 160 miles, they took the bullet train from London to Edinburgh, Aberdeen, and back. You could admire the purple heather, rolling hills, sheep, goats and mountains along the way.

CHAPTER 27

Houston Heights Texas
6 A.M., Sunday, December 15, 1993
Cloudy, 75°/48°
Chilly and fog

Fog meant clouds, no wind and sunny later. Dirk knew Jerry was punishing him by spending the night with her cousin, with whom she had shared an apartment in Austin during law school prior to Jerry's marriage to the U-2 pilot, Billings, who disappeared never to be heard of again (persona non grata). One of these days Billings would show up and sweep Jerry up into marital bliss, and he, Dirk, would be left with memories. A man could never understand a woman's mind, and all men thought the same, pussy. Dirk, brought up in Hardin on the banks of the Trinity River, was a keen observer of animals, fish, and foul, and all males were the same.

After cleaning up his SUV and boat, he disconnected the ground wire from the positive pole of the battery to the engine so the lights didn't shine and the engine went dead. Then he took the valve stem out of a tire on the boat trailer. He would act surprised when the truck wouldn't start, and he had a flat.

His common sense told him not to motor up the Brazos passed Richmond. Before all the dams were built above Waco, et al., the Brazos was navigated by steam boats, and although the docks were gone, the pilings were still there and usually covered by water. Then there were sandbars, submerged fallen trees, and snags. It was alright for canoes, rubber rafts, and rowboats, but a high speed fiber glass would tear a hole in the hull or crack the transom on a stump. Dirk didn't know what it was like from Richmond to San Felipe ten miles west of Katy on IH-10. Map distance and river distance were never the same, and rivers developed new twists and turns every flood. They formed horseshoe lakes and swamps. All the marshy grass estuaries were down below Freeport, but alligators and alligator gars went all the way up to College Station, hence cypress marshes.

In brief, Dirk wanted to look at Dr. Mambo Nigera's house and property for sale, and didn't want to boat up the Brazos looking for illegals and drug smugglers.

BRAZOS COUNTY, TEXAS
10 A.M., Sunny, no fog

"You can't see illegals camped out along the river banks from a helicopter. They hear you coming and hide. The midget submarines with periscopes are just rumors. Nobody's seen one. The Cuban submarine they bought from Russia surfaces a hundred miles out only at night. If they stay outside continental waters, we can't touch them. That's Coast Guard," explained Jerry. "Whom do you know that would know for sure?"

"I can ask Uzi Kalashnikov," answered Dirk.

"Why do you want to buy this woman's house and property on the Brazos?" asked Jerry. "You've got enough already. There're taxes you know. School and county taxes will eat you up. Where did you get all that money? When a cop spends more than his salary, he's either stealing or accepting bribes. How do you plan to pay for all that?"

"Credit! Misty extended me a line of credit at low interest. It's just a matter of time when they drill for the deep stuff."

"Do you think we'll live that long?" asked Jerry, giggling.

*   *   *

The tarmac to the river at Mambo Nigera's camp ran through unfenced pristine wilderness. It was swampy on both sides with moss covered great oaks. There were power and telephone lines alongside. Dirk had been there 14 months ago, and except it looked spookier nothing had changed. Palmettos and Muscadine grapes lived alongside the great oaks. Like the Black Forest in Germany, the ancient great oaks blocked sunlight below.

Mambo was in the process of moving. They had loaded a May Flower Van and were about to leave. Mambo recognized Dirk. He introduced Jerry, discussed her terms, $50,000 for the house, barn, and pier and $3,000 an acre for the land which was useless except for hunting and mineral rights. She had to leave with the van, but left the keys to the house and barn with Dirk and showed him where to hide them when they were through.

There was no dog trot, and the lumber was cedar on four feet blocks. A water line came up almost to the floor, and the house was on a rise above the river at least twenty feet. There was lots of space underneath for dogs and chickens, etc.

Inside was modern 2 bedroom house with all the conveniences and sliding doors leading to a back porch big enough for a bench and wash stand. The front porch ran all way across, and there was a swing she'd leave. Out to right on the north side was a barn and chicken yard with a place for Mambo to park her car and a four wheeler ATM which Mambo planned to leave with a new owner.

You had to walk down an incline to a pier which extended out about twenty feet over the water and was used by Mambo and Dr. Morton Salter for fishing and boating. Both were busy academics and really didn't use it as much as people with more leisure would. Everything fun cost money. They were on the land but didn't know its boundaries. Dirk would have to come back, trace the boundary, and locate the markers.

*   *   *

Driving back Dirk turned west along a well kept tarmac toward the Brazoria Power and Light nuclear power plant. It was about a mile upstream of Mambo's and maybe 5-10 miles downstream from his (Ben Milam's old place) and about 5-10 miles up from his newly purchased Joshua Hale's old place. Rivers turn and snake, and you never know without a recent aerial photograph, not one five years old or older.

They could see the steam rising from concrete towers on a rise about a mile from the Brazos River. The locals called it the willow bend plant. Two large concrete domes were surrounded by smaller buildings which Dirk surmised were the turbines and generators.

An administration building and control room were enclosed in a 12 feet chain length fence topped with concertina razor wire and were approachable only through a guard house and security gate. The woods were cleared a hundred yards and surrounded by a second fence which appeared to be wild animal proof. There were caution and no trespassing signs everywhere.

Dirk stopped for a moment. They saw it all, were satisfied, and drove back slowly, studying as they went. Dirk spotted a littered trail through the woods about a quarter mile from the plant. He stopped the Jeep, and they examined the trail finding discarded Frito and Dorito bags, stems from Jalapeño peppers, Corona beer bottles, etc., etc. It could have been made by illegal's walking along the river and detouring around the nuclear power plant.

"It's out of my jurisdiction, Dirk. I'm responsible for Montgomery, Harris, and Galveston Counties," remarked Jerry. "I can't stop what comes up the Brazos. I can suspect what's going on and report to my superior in Austin."

"What about the KNOCKERS? They live in Houston Heights and cross the border with contraband and Oriental beauties just about every weekend?" asked Dirk.

"We are working on that. I can't tell you my business. The powers in Austin want to catch them all when they cross the border," replied Jerry.

"Why don't you raid the warehouse in Heights?" asked Dirk.

"Booker has done that several times. Somebody in Headquarters tips them off, and they don't find anything."

"Sergeant Kelly Watts, Booker's loyal assistant," guessed Dirk, chuckling.

"Can you prove that?"

"Why, no! I was just guessing off the top of my head."

"You may be right. Why Kelly?" asked Jerry. "She's a great laboratory technician. DNA is art and science."

"She quit a good job in Baytown and commutes to Houston. Sergeant Armstrong at Baytown told me. They're a shady bunch down there. Nobody tells you why or what, but she left for some reason. Booker probably knows, but he's not about to lose a good laboratory technician just because of some minor something. She'd have to get caught robbing a bank in broad daylight with twenty witnesses."

*　　*　　*

Brigadier General JoAnn Johnson was at her desk at Ellington Field when a Colonel William W. Billings with bag and baggage, saluted, handed her his orders, and reported for duties as Deputy Commander, test pilot, and Astronaut trainee. He was 44, and his last duty was 1st Lieutenant, Ellington Field, flight instructor 1978 after which his duty record was blank. His orders were transcribed in the Pentagon and signed by the Chief of Staff, US Air Force, so they were official from the top.

JoAnn looked at Bill. He was 5'11", 160 lbs., and very fit. He looked young enough to run college huddles, and very virile. Although she was nearly white with mixed parentage, and he was lily white with an old fashioned GI crew cut, JoAnn lusted big time. She had been intimate with Dr. Charles Lanka a thousand times over the last three years, and they were no closer to marriage, and she couldn't get pregnant by Charles. Tamara Lewine, her gynecologist, said she was okay, and Charles had a low sperm count. She was 40 and not getting younger. She had been disqualified as Commander of the Mars Expedition when she reached 40 and assigned Commanding Officer of the Administration Headquarters at Ellington Field in the USAFR. It looked like Colonel Billings was going to join her.

"Stand at ease, Colonel Billings. You may be my new Deputy Commander. Where have you been the last 15 years?" asked JoAnn.

"I'm sorry, ma'am. I was on active duty with the Central Intelligence Agency. That's all I'm allowed to reveal," answered Colonel William Billings, standing at Parade Rest and looking straight ahead like a new cadet.

*　　*　　*

JoAnn went home in uniform that evening, knocked, and found Devine' in bed with her feet up.

"Deviné, what the hell? Did you hurt your back?"

"I'm trying to get pregnant. What do you think?" replied Deviné, giggling.

"I've come to get advice. Is it true a lawyer can't tell?"

"Only if you are a client," replied Deviné. "Otherwise, no promise! I've got my own problems."

"I'm in love," announced JoAnn.

"JoAnn, that's no secret. I heard when I moved in this high-rise you were the anticipated Commander of the U.S. Mars expedition and were engaged to Dr. Charles Lanka, the ER physician at West Mean M.A.S.H."

"Charles is okay, but we've been intimate three years, and nothing has happened. I met somebody new today, and it was love at first sight. I've got the hots bad. I want to let Charles down easily and not burn my bridge in case this new guy doesn't like me that way. He's lily white and my new Deputy Commander."

"Is he married?" asked Deviné. Marrieds were hornier than singles. If a man wasn't married by 40, chances were he wouldn't.

"I don't know. We have 'don't ask and don't tell.' All I can tell you is he graduated from Bellaire and Texas A&M. His parents are retired in Bellaire, and his father was Corporate Lawyer for Lockheed Martin," replied JoAnn, nervous with excitement, which was completely out of character for an Air Force General in uniform.

"Wear a chastity belt," advised Deviné. "Get Cealis to take Charles off your hands. Her engagement to Dr. Sanchez hit rock bottom when his wife came back from Colombia. She wasn't dead after all. They live over in University place, and she brought her mother with her so she could finish her residency in Radiology at Ben Taub. Her maiden name was Garza. She's Evita Garza's baby sister. I met the Garza's and General Emil Fernandez when I was on tour as Miss Jamaica. Emil was a fun guy, but Evita was jealous and threatened to slit my throat from ear-to-ear. She and Frieda Allegromande, both acquaintances of mine, live in 804 at the Granada."

"Where did you get a chastity belt? I've never seen one," asked JoAnn, chuckling.

"Toys R Us! They cost $8 for teenage girls, and you can adjust the waistband. You lock it and leave the key at home," replied Deviné. As an afterthought, "You can use the bathroom, and they don't show, but you can't wear hip huggers and a bikini. I have a couple in my dresser. They make vaginal penetration impossible, but everything else works. You can masturbate and everything, but penetration."

CHAPTER 28

Sugar Land Texas
2 P.M., Sunday, December 15, 1993
70°, Sunny

Dirk pulled up on the auxiliary ramp on the Brazos River Bridge between Sugar Land and Richmond on US 59S. The river down below was muddy brown and swift compared with others. The banks were 30-40 feet above the water level at the bridge but dropped down to reveal a heavily wooded area on the east side that extended a mile or more to his place, newly acquired. It flowed from the northwest in a very snake-like crooked pattern which curved and turned in a haphazard route where it flowed under I-10 at Historical San Felipe 3 miles east of Sealy on IH-10. Most of it was a wildlife refuge upstream and no roads on the map. That was easily 70 miles of river and plenty of covered hunting places. On his map it was the Atwater Wildlife Refuge, and the Brazos River passed under a bridge 15 miles west of Katy before it turned toward San Felipe, and there wasn't any road to San Felipe. Shit! He wasn't about to take his boat up through all that mess in a wildlife refuge during hunting season. He didn't care how many illegal aliens were camped in there. Out in California just ordinary American citizens were growing marijuana and shipping it on mail order by Fed Ex and UPS to the other 49 states.

*   *   *

They watched and saw the Loch Ness Monster submerge about a mile upstream of the Sugar Land bridge. It wasn't the Loch Ness Monster but a Mexican minisub with a periscope which dove out of sight until the periscope stuck up about a foot and moved slowly downstream under the bridge and out of site down river without turning on a motor or churning the water. Bubbles trailed it like a giant expelling human exhaust.

"That's it. We could have sunk it standing on this bridge," announced Captain Jerry Billings DPS.

"You can't drown a bunch of people just for hauling marijuana. The punishment is way out of proportion to the crime. You have to follow regular police procedures for arrest, search and seizure, and due process. You have to read them their Miranda Warning and let them request a lawyer. There's no law against operating a private midget submarine in Texas' rivers. It's a Coast Guard problem, or maybe the State's," replied Dirk, solemnly.

"I am the State," replied Jerry. "If you won't take me, I'll get a DPS helicopter. We can spot and follow a submarine in the middle of a river and bomb the hell out of it.

*   *   *

The City of Richmond was picturesque, and its Big Bend county courthouse was freshly painted and dated back to the 1890's. There was an old time gallows in back, and it had been in many movies, *Return to Lonesome Dove*. Across the River, Sugar Land had a Police Department with 500 police, 200 new modern patrol cars, and the lowest crime rate of any city in Texas. Texas was a big state, and the Brazos was the largest river in Texas and filled Possum Kingdom Lake upstream.

*   *   *

Anywhere along the Texas coast you could expect a major hurricane every 4 or 5 years. Tropical storm Allison flooded all Houston and surrounding counties. Sugar Land and Friendswood got 11 inches in

4 hours, roads were blocked and air flights were delayed at Hobby and HIA. Evacuation shelters were set up in Pearland. Floods caused more damage than wind or fire. Thanks to the Brazos River Water Authority, the Brazos remained in bank. Surprise!

*   *   *

Once the land of the Karankawa's, Fort Bend County was settled by the members of the Austin colony who received a Mexican land grant in 1824. Houston was growing west along the freeways, and Sugar Land, Pearland, and Katy were growing at 10% per year. Dirk could count the names of 50 industries, 4 hospitals, 5 university branches, and on and on.

"Did I tell you about old Bezoar, the Karankawa Shaman, who lives in a T-pee out in the woods below my place? Warden Farmer said he was a scout for the Union Army during the Buffalo war or some such."

Jerry thought, got sleepy, and yawned. "You did not. Could he speak English?"

"Not a bit, but he's into sign language. That could have been his tracks crossing the power plant road."

Dirk looked over and Jerry was leaning against the passenger door asleep. Brazos meant arms in Spanish. The first Spanish explorers named it *Rio de los Brazos de Dios*, river of the arms of God. It started on the Llano Estacado in the Pan Handle and ran 1300 miles to the Gulf below Freeport. Somewhere around Brazoria it was joined by the San Bernard which was clear most of the year, and the Brazos was muddy. All the Karankawas were gone by 1860. Old Bezoar might be the last one, unless Ben Milam, who sold him his land and was in the penitentiary for life at Livingston was part Karankawa. Ben ate his last four wives. Dirk remembered the crib back near the swamp in Ben Milam's old place where he saw skulls and bones. It was locked. He was distracted and hadn't investigated further. He hadn't been back.

Lawyer Freeman Jackson told him in confidence about Ben Milam's crime. Dirk hadn't planned on telling anybody. Like finding all that drug money in the log dog trot, Rico Carbello rising out of the slime like a zombie, and A. Fuller Bottle Jr. walking down and back up the stairs of a flying saucer carrying his head screwed on. He'd never tell anybody, not Jerry, his closest confidant and friend. They'd think he was off his rocker. Ben Milam stood up and was the first man killed at the first battle of the Alamo in Bexar County. He was in all the Texas History books.

There were blacks living in the woods in Brazoria County. They played basketball. Some were skinny and tall. Karankawa's were skinny and tall. It didn't take an Aristotelian logician to figure it out. Dirk was a sixth generation Texan. Lots of people had Indian blood in southeast Texas. Most didn't give it a second thought. Why should he, except the Karankawas were tall, skinny, black, and ate their captives alive. They had no Indian friends other than kin, and the Spaniards, pirates, and early white settlers tried to kill them all. Back in those days, Indian maidens were generous with their charms. Some scientist believed the Indians from the old south were half breed offspring of the Desoto's and LaSalle's that explored the south looking for the Fountain of Youth, El Dorado, and the Seven Cities of Gold and had a natural immunity to smallpox. That explained the blue eyed Indians in Mississippi who spoke Gaelic. Irish Monks beat Spain to the Americas by 500 years. A ship of Moors from the Spanish Armada in 1588 waded ashore and were the ancestors of the "Black Irish". Since the space program, human sperm floated around in space which was a deep freeze and preserved them forever. Dirk chuckled.

CHAPTER 29

Ho Chi Minh City Vietnam
10 A.M., Monday, December 16, 1993
79°/60°
Cloudy, showers

We didn't lose the Vietnam War thought Bob in Saigon. Everything was modern and the same people were hurrying around, fat, and happy. Of course, twenty years had passed, and everybody was into capitalism, under a Communist police state where everything was run by committees from top down. After Hanoi, he decided it was in Vietnamese character not to carry a grudge, and tourism put everybody back to work.

English replaced French as a second language, and Chinese characters disappeared. Just ordinary people smiled, nodded, spoke, and some saluted. The 'boat people' that escaped and came to America were returning on vacation and bringing the kids. Vietnam was destined to be the next SEA "tiger," and their GDP was 10% per year.

Vietnamese mechanics could fix anything, and America had a throwaway economy. The obsolete appliances and broken TV, etc. in garage sales in the USA were shipped by the boat people back to Vietnam for repair. Electronics sold by the Japanese and Chinese to Americans ended up being repaired and sold again by the Vietnamese. In the USA, poor people were fat. The only starving were those trying to diet. America was the only country where gastrectomy was recommended as a medical treatment for obesity.

*　　*　　*

Donald, Louiza, and Elvis were somewhere on business. Elvis was CIA, Donald had the gold, and Louiza was some sort of industrial spy. They were dealing with government and oil people about the Parcel and Spratly Islands in the South China Sea claimed by Vietnam, Japan, and, more recently, China. Chinese fishing boats were ramming Japanese gun boats, and China was trying to make the Spratly's a tourist attraction so they could establish squatter's rights. Not only were the Spratly's great fishing waters, they had prospects for oil and gas.

A seismography ship might start a war. China was adamant that anything in the East and South China Seas belonged to the Peoples Republic of China. SROCO had no problem drilling the You River basin and Quanxi field for the Chinese PLA, but they anticipated hostilities when in cooperation with the PLA and the Burmese's Shan they started drilling on the border of Laos in Cambodia near the Thailand border and the Bhamo Basin at old Batson Field in the Shawn State of Myanmar. Maria promised them a year and her share of the gold, and they promised military protection and a ready market.

Donald was more than retired co-owner of SROCO. He had Sicilian, Vatican, and Mafia connections. After observing Donald, Bob surmised that Don knew in advance about the atomic bomb released over Naypyidaw, and Louiza Santos was involved. If Elvis knew, which Bob doubted, he surely didn't let on.

Bob decided he was along because of his technical experience and expertise, and Penny was recommended by Maria because she was a journalist, knew the territory, and could communicate with the natives (Aborigines) hiding back in the rain forests and jungles of every inhabited island, some of which remained head hunters and cannibals dating back to Paleolithic times. There were thousands of islands in the South Pacific and hundreds of volcanoes making more. That's what volcanoes do.

*   *   *

Dark ash was rising over Mount Merapi causing suspension of regular flights out of Singapore and Malaysia. Tsunamis had drowned 500 people in the last week. Scientist predicted weeks not days of slow eruptions of hot lava and plumes of smoke which blanked out the sun, "like a marathon, not a sprint." Ana Krackatow, a hundred years ago, blew out the top, drowned 30,000 people on a nearby island, and caused winter in summer in southern United States half a world away. Earthquakes don't cause volcanoes to erupt, but volcanoes cause earthquakes which cause tsunamis that drown thousands.

Major Oils (Royal Dutch and Standard) had been drilling on land in Borneo and Sumatra for fifty years, and Standard built a refinery at Palembang Sumatra back in the 50's. More recently Petronas was formed to exploit the offshore fields around Malaysia. Petronas and French Total along with China were large investors in the offshore blocks leased by Myanmar in the Bay of Bengal.

Indonesia had 235 million people, thousands of islands, and hundreds of volcanoes on the "ring of fire" along the edge of the Pacific plate. Singapore had 63 islands and was the tip of the Malaysian peninsula.

When India broke off from Africa and moved up to join Eurasia to form the Himalayas, it passed over a ocean hotspot and formed the Deccan Traps which were step like layers of basalt over large spans of continental surface between Mumbai (Bombay) and Hyderabad India.

Ho Chi Min, formerly Saigon, sat on the Saigon River, north of the Mekong Delta, a densely populated rice growing area. North were the former French plantations and dense jungles under which the famous Viet Cong tunnels whose entrances were camouflaged and too small for the average GI to get through. You could go on bus tour from the hotel and visit the Royal Palace, inspect Army headquarters in the basement, and dance on the King's ballroom with dance floor and bar on top. The tour included a museum of natural history, and a pictorial review of ancient and recent wars of Vietnam including photographs of Americans torturing Viet Cong and North Vietnamese prisoners. Apologizing for the cowardly Americans, the guide explained ours was an army of conscripts whereas the Viet Cong and North Vietnam regulars were seasoned harden veterans who voluntarily fought the Japanese, French Foreign Legion, South Vietnamese, and United Nation forces from all over the world. He explained the Buddhist philosophy of returning to be "born again" in a better life and the loss of three million people in a crowded country was no great sacrifice for a Socialist Republic run by the people for the people, and not the French who plundered their country, and the Americans who wanted to destroy their Social Democratic ideas and Buddhist philosophy. They watched American TV and read their newspapers and knew that the Americans hated war not the Vietnamese, and it was just a matter of time until America would give up and go home. Body count meant nothing to the Vietnamese whereas the American public anguished over every soldier sacrificed in the rice paddies and jungles of Vietnam. Volunteer soldiers would always triumph over conscripts, and soldiers fought harder defending their own soil than those 10,000 miles from home. The talented and beautiful actress, Jane Fonda, gave them hope and boosted their morale to go on.

The French lost 30% at Dien Ben Pu and surrendered, and, if the American Congress had waited two more weeks, they were planning on an armistice like the Germans and Italians got, so they could get a Marshal plan and aid to rebuild like Japan and South Korea. What they really wanted was Social Security, Medicare, and a chance at industrialization like Taiwan, South Korea, and Japan. Two more weeks and they would have signed an armistice and proclaimed the end of the "Great Revolution" against France and its proxies.

Now, like China, they wanted to share in the "American Dream". Ultimately America would help protect them from the Great Dragon to the north with whom they had recently fought a war after ridding their neighboring Cambodia from Pol Pot and the Khmer Rouge radicals who were a holdover from Mao and the long march (kill all the land owners and intellectuals).

Bob decided that politics in Asia went back thousands of years, and Vietnam had a long standing disregard for the Chinese and hoped the United States and Russia would come to their aid when they stood up with Taiwan and Japan, et al. against China's claim of the islands in the East and South China Seas whose waters they had fished for thousands of years. China wanted to claim the mineral rights because some ancient map maker named it the China Sea. What we took for granted in the U.S.A., all SEA were after the American dream, a house, two kids, chicken in the pot, and a set of wheels.

Rockefeller was right. *The whole world runs on oil.* The Vietnamese NOC was third only to Malaysia and South Korea, not counting China and Japan.

Bob decided the real opportunity for development was in East Asia. America was protecting Israel and eastern Europe against the Arabs and Russians, but the real business opportunities were modernizing India, China, and SEA. At least, that was his opinion of the moment. Their little kids were all happy campers and smart in science and mathematics while the Europeans wanted a 32 hour work week, a month paid vacation, and social welfare. We had to save them from the Germans twice, protect them from the Russians for fifty years, and protect their oil supply from the Middle East. We were fighting their battles in Kosovo, Iraq, and Iran, after we fought France's battle in Vietnam. France and the rest of Western Europe except maybe England were idiot kin and lazy socialists.

*　　*　　*

After touring the South Vietnam headquarters, the Ho Chi Minh war museum, the Viet Cong tunnels in the jungles, and hearing the Vietnam side, Bob decided to read the current U.S. State Department history of the war. They edited it every time they changed administrations, whether Democrat or Republican. History was always written by the victor not the vanquished.

CHAPTER 30

Ho Chi Minh City
10 P.M., Monday, December 16, 1993
Smoky clouds

At dinner that evening Donald Tantalia announced they had reservations to Singapore in first class on Asiana Air the next morning, and it was a ten hour flight. No planes were flying at night because the Merapi ash clouds had blotted out the moon and stars, and only a few brave airlines would fly during daylight hours.

*   *   *

After everything was quiet and his bed partner, Penny, was asleep, Bob read. It was the Democrat's time to make history.

U.S. DEPARTMENT OF STATE
Background Note: Vietnam

PEOPLE

Originating in what is now southern China and northern Vietnam, the Vietnamese people pushed southward over 2 millennia to occupy the entire eastern seacoast of the Indochinese Peninsula. Vietnam has 54 ethnic groups; ethnic Vietnamese or Kinh constitute approximately 85% of Vietnam's population. The next largest groups are ethnic Tay and Thai, which account for 1.97% and 1.79% of Vietnam's population and are concentrated in the country's northern uplands.

With a population of more than 900,000, Vietnam's Chinese community has historically played an important role in the Vietnamese economy. Restrictions on economic activity following reunification of the north and south in 1975 and a general deterioration in Vietnamese-Chinese relations caused increasing anxiety within the Chinese-Vietnamese community. As tensions between Vietnam and China reached their peak in 1978-79, culminating in a brief but bloody war in February-March 1979, some 450,000 ethnic Chinese left Vietnam by boat as refugees (many officially encouraged and assisted) or were expelled across the land border with China.

Other significant ethnic minority groups include central highland peoples (formerly collectively termed Montagnards) such as the Gia Rai, Bana, Ede, Xo Dang, Gie Trieng, and the Khmer Krom (Cambodians), who are concentrated near the Cambodian border and at the mouth of the Mekong River. Taken collectively, these groups made up a majority of the population in much of Vietnam's central highlands until the 1960s and 1970s. They now compose a significant minority of 25% to 35% of the provinces in that region.

Vietnamese is the official language of the country. It is a tonal language with influences from Thai, Khmer, and Chinese. Since the early 20th century, the Vietnamese have used a Romanized script introduced by the French. Previously, Chinese characters and an indigenous phonetic script were both used.

HISTORY

Vietnam's identity has been shaped by long-running conflicts, both internally and with foreign forces. In 111 BC, China's Han dynasty conquered northern Vietnam's Red River Delta and the ancestors of today's Vietnamese. Chinese dynasties ruled Vietnam for the next 1,000 years, inculcating it with Confucian ideas and political culture, but also leaving a tradition of resistance to foreign occupation. In 939 AD, Vietnam achieved independence under a native dynasty. After 1471, when Vietnam conquered the Champa Kingdom in what is now central Vietnam, the Vietnamese moved gradually southward, finally reaching the agriculturally rich Mekong Delta, where they encountered previously settled communities of Cham and Cambodians. As Vietnam's Le dynasty declined, powerful northern and southern families, the Trinh and Nguyen, fought civil wars in the 17th and 18th centuries. A peasant revolt originating in the Tay Son region of central Vietnam defeated both the Nguyen and the Trinh and unified the country at the end of the 18th century, but was itself defeated by a surviving member of the Nguyen family, who founded the Nguyen dynasty as Emperor Gia Long in 1802.

French Rule and the Anti-Colonial Struggle

In 1858, the French began their conquest of Vietnam starting in the south. They annexed all of Vietnam in 1885, governing the territories of Annan, Tonkin, and Cochin China, together with Cambodia and Laos, as French Indochina. The French ruled Cochin China directly as a French colony; Annan and Tonkin were established as French "protectorates." Vietnam's emperors remained in place in Hue, but their authority was strictly limited as French officials assumed nearly all government functions. In the early 20th century, Vietnamese intellectuals, many of them French educated, organized nationalist and communist-nationalist anti-colonial movements.

Japan's military occupation of Vietnam during World War II further stirred nationalist sentiment, as well as antipathy toward the French Vichy colonial regime, which took its direction from the Japanese until the Japanese took direct control in March 1945. Vietnamese communists under Ho Chi Minh organized a coalition of anti-colonial groups, the Viet Minh, though many anti-communists refused to join. The Viet Minh took advantage of political uncertainty in the weeks following Japan's surrender to take control of Hanoi and much of northern Vietnam. Ho Chi Minh announced the independence of the Democratic Republic of Vietnam on September 2, 1945.

After 1954, North Vietnamese communist leaders consolidated their power and instituted a harsh agrarian reform and socialization program. During this period, some 450,000 Vietnamese, including a large number of Vietnamese Catholics, fled from the north to the south, while a much smaller number, mostly consisting of former Viet Minh fighters, relocated north. In the late 1950s, North Vietnamese leaders reactivated the network of communist guerrillas that had remained behind in the south. These forces—commonly known as the Viet cong—aided covertly by the north, started an armed campaign against officials and villagers who refused to support the communist reunification cause.

American Assistance to the South

In December 1961, at the request of south Vietnamese President Ngo Dinh Diem, President Kennedy sent U.S. military advisers to South Vietnam to help the government there deal with the Viet Cong campaign. In the wake of escalating political turmoil in the south after a November 1963 generals' coup against President Diem, which resulted in his death, the United States increased its military support for South Vietnam. In March 1965, President Johnson sent the first U.S. combat forces to Vietnam. The American military role peaked in 1969 with an in-country force of 534,000. The Viet Cong's surprise Tet Offensive in January 1968 weakened the Viet Cong infrastructure and damaged American and South Vietnamese morale. In January 1969, the United States, governments of South and North Vietnam, and the Viet Cong met for the first plenary session of peace talks in Paris, France. These talks, which began with much hope, moved slowly. They finally concluded with the signing of a peace agreement, the Paris Accords, on January 27, 1973. The Accords called for a ceasefire in place in which North Vietnamese forces were permitted to remain in areas they controlled. Following the Accords, the South Vietnamese Government and the political representatives of the communist forces in the South, the Provisional Revolutionary Government, vied for control over portions of South Vietnam. The United States withdrew its forces, although reduced levels of U.S. military assistance continued, administered by the Defense Attaché Office.

Reunification

In early 1975, North Vietnamese regular military forces began a major offensive in the south, inflicting great damage to the south's forces. The communists took Saigon on April 30, 1975, and announced their intention to reunify the country. The Democratic Republic of Vietnam (north) absorbed the former Republic of Vietnam (south) to form the socialist Republic of Vietnam on July 2, 1976.

The Republicans called it Kennedy and Johnson's war, and the Democrats called it American Assistance. Beauty is in the eyes of the beholder.

CHAPTER 32

York England—Best Western
8 P.M., Monday, December 16, 1993
Temp 65°/36°, Light rain

"The Vikings named it Jorvik. York was voted the number one tourist city in Europe. Everything in York is historic. With the bullet train it's only 30 minutes to London. I'll arrange for a local tour in the morning, and we'll sleep in our beds at the London Hilton tomorrow night. If I can't get standby tickets, we might take a bus to Wales and a ferry to Dublin, Ireland. It's only a couple of hours over and back.

"Please raise your hand, if you want to visit Blarney Castle, hang by your knees, and kiss the Blarney Stone," announced Maria.

No hands went up.

"We don't have any Irish on this tour?

"When the English traded the Spice Islands to the Dutch for New Amsterdam, they named it New York after the Duke of York. They named Virginia after Queen Elizabeth I, Jamestown after King James I, Pennsylvania after William Penn, and Georgia after King George. After the battle of Saint Louis, they named it Fort Pitt.

"The Puritans got to keep Plymouth, and so did Harvard and William and Mary which are two of the oldest universities in the original New England States. In the beginning Mexico was named New Spain. In Texas we call it Old Mexico.

"We've just finished a whirlwind tour of Scotland and are back in merry old England where you can hear grass growing. Some of you asked for what the paint colors are on the backs of the sheep. Some have more than one color. Each color represents a specific male (Ram) who bred with the female (Ewe) and mother-to-be. Those stone fences go back to Neolithic times. Each generation adds more stones.

"Tonight Dr. Eros Zenovenusetti will lecture on the Pics and the Druids. Dr. Christy Isaac will take the early Romans, York, and Hadrian's Wall. Dr. Aristotle Plotinus will discuss the Roman's, early Christianity, and civilization by which we mean Romanization. The English got civilized by the Romans. The Welch, Irish, and Scots did not. The Romans built a wall and kept them out. Saint Patrick brought Catholicism to Ireland, not the Romans."

"Eros," announced Maria.

Dr. Eros Zenovenusetti wrote on a green board. **WIND MILL AND BEAKER PEOPLE, AVEBURY, STONEHENGE, BRONZE, IRON, CELTS, BRETONS, PICS, SAINT COLOMBO, WHISKEY, AND THE LOCH NESS MONSTER**.

"Researching the Druids, Pics, and Celtics are a little like researching the life of Jesus outside the four Gospels. They didn't leave any literature, and the original authors were anonymous. You'll have to take a lot of what I say on faith.

"The British Isle separated from Continental Europe by the English Chanel around 8000 b.c.e. The glaciers melted, and the first Neolithic's arrived around 5000 b.c.e. Prehistoric stone and cave dwellings are abundant on the west coast of Ireland on up and are really abundant and in excellent condition on the islands of Orkney and Shetland. Males averaged 5 feet 3 inches, females 4 feet 11 inches, and they lived to be 35 and died of a tooth abscess or appendicitis.

"Around 5000 bce or earlier the Wind Mill people arrived in South-central England at Avebury in Wilshire County. Next were the Beaker people with their beer, domesticated animals, horses and wagons. The Wind Millers had long heads and the Beakers had square heads. Digs revealed a high incidence of Spina Bifida which occurs almost exclusively in the British and Irish today suggesting the propagation of a mutant gene originating within the Wind Millers. The square heads brought cattle.

"Stonehenge was started in 2600 b.c.e. A henge in a round embankment next to a deep ditch. The stones were arranged for religious rituals. Most of the stones at Avebury were destroyed by Puritan ministers during the witch craze.

"Megalith monuments are all over Ireland, Scotland, Ile of Levin in the outer Hebrides, Iceland, etc. on and on. The temperature was 4° hotter than now. The same was going on in Neolithic North America. It took rawhide ropes 65 feet long to drag the stones by 60 men for 60 yards. The megaliths at Stonehenge weighed 60 tons and were drug 18 miles back as early as 3000 b.c.e. The Beaker people arrived just as the Wind Mill people finished. Studies show Beakers had horses, wagons, and bronze technology.

"The Beakers and Wind Millers got together and became the Wessex culture in 1300 b.c.e. Stonehenge has 16 stones still standing with seven lintel stones.

"The Celts arrived with iron instruments, armor, and weapons around 1000-500 b.c.e. and began the Iron Age. The Druid priests kept no records and revealed no secrets, so the early Irish, Scots, and Pics couldn't read or write. Their songs and legends were handed down by word-of-mouth. In Scotland, the Scots lived in the Western Highlands, the Pics in the Eastern Highlands, and the Lowland Celts were called the Bretons who were defeated and tamed by the Romans around 25 c.e.

"The Druids in Great Britain have recently been recognized as a true religious organization right along with the Angleton and Catholic Churches. In the United States that means they don't have to pay taxes.

"The Pics painted their entire bodies and went into battle naked. Saint Colombo from Ireland showed the Druid priests how to distill whisky which means water of life and converted them all to Catholics. Around 500 c.e. Saint Colombo was first to report seeing the Loch Ness monster around 450 c.e.

"It occurred to me that the ancient Greeks erected stone phalluses in their front yards called Herms. The god Hermes' (Mercury in Roman and Gabriel in Hebrew) job beside carrying messages for Zeus was to guard the Herms. I think Stonehenge and Avebury were constructed for fertility rites. Thank you. I was brought up in Greece on Greek Mythology."

"Christy."

CHAPTER 33

York England—Best Western
9 P.M., December 16, 1993

Dr. Christy Isaac wrote on the green board. **YORK, HADRIAN'S WALL, ANTONINE'S WALL, PAX ROMANA, CIVILIZATION, 300 YEARS, FALL OF ROME, JUTES, ANGLES, SAXONS, WILLIAM THE CONQUEROR, AND BATTLE OF HASTINGS**.

"Hadrian had sex with both men and women. We saw a bust of his handsome male lover in Hadrian's Villa in Rome. The beginning of Hadrian's Wall is here at the entrance to ancient York. It was 20 feet tall and wide enough to walk on all the way to Colchester 70 miles away. Hadrian's Wall was fortified with stone and had a fort every mile with watch towers in between every half mile. They constructed ten feet deep moats front and back which were connected to rivers at both ends. The Romans signaled by torches. It was built in 120 c.e. and abandoned in 400 c.e. They built an earthen wall 37 miles wide about 60 miles north of Hadrian's Wall called Antonine's Wall.

"Raised and adopted by Emperor Trajan, Hadrian was one of Rome's great emperors. He invented a pony express that crossed the Alps and entire length of the Roman Empire in 7 days. He assembled and collected all Roman Civil Law later coded by Justinian I in 500 c.e.

"He finished the Giant Temple of All the gods (Pantheon) we saw in Rome, and the giant Temple of Zeus in Athens. He quashed the Jewish revolt in 130 c.e., ran all Jews out, made Jerusalem a Roman City, and forbade the Jews to return. He built a Temple to Aphrodite over Jesus' grave. Hadrian was born in 76 c.e., became Emperor in 117 and died in 138 and appointed Antoninus Pius his successor.

"As Emperor, he was Pontius Maximus (pope) of the Roman Church, very devout, and his tomb lies in the Castel Sant-Angelo in Rome.

"Fifteen generations civilized the Bretons. They got Roman law, bureaucracy, taxation, religion and the whole works. Constantine I was proclaimed Emperor in York, and they had a hundred years of Christianity.

"York as a home of humans has been here 8000 years. Paleolithic, Mesolithic, Neolithic, Wind Mills, Beakers, and Celts. The history of York is the history of England. After the Romans, were the Jutes, Angles, and Saxons followed by the Danes, Vikings, and lastly the Normans who defeated the Anglo-Saxon King Edward at the Battle of Hastings in 1099. The Normans wore armor, rode horses, used mechanical bows, and lances tipped with iron and had stirrups. The Normans built all the castles in England and most if not all the Gothic Cathedrals.

"Julius Caesar made the calendar used in those days, and an English legal yard was the distance from King Henry I nose to the tip of his thumb. In the western word, Julius Caesar standardized the length between wheels on axles and tracks on a train as the distances between the tails of two chariot horses. That's why you can drive on a train track on the rims of your car.

"Emperor Chin (Qui) did the same in China in 200 b.c.e. He also standardized the 75,000 Chinese characters, the Chinese Lunar Calendar, wrote the first Chinese laws, and had all Confucian scholars buried alive. The Han Dynasty restored Confucianism and the Civil Service examination. The Chinese called him Master Kong. Around 1600, the Jesuit missionaries named him Confucius, and it stuck.

"York was the principal city in northern England in the Middle Ages. York Minister was one of the first and finest cathedrals, and the Archbishop of York is second only to the Archbishop of Canterbury in the Church of England. I'll stop.

"Aristotle."

Dr. Aristotle Plotinus wrote on the green board**. JOHN KNOX, PROTESTANT, CATHOLIC, SAINT ANDREWS, GALLEY SLAVE, FRANCE, ENGLAND, BLOODY MARY, EXILE, JOHN CALVIN, SCOTLAND, PRESBYTERIANISM, MARY QUEEN OF SCOTS, JACOBITES, CLANS, AND BONNIE PRINCE CHARLEY**.

"John Knox (1515-1572) was born near Edinburg, attended Saint Andrews, and was made a Catholic priest in 1536 while King Henry VIII was gutting the Catholic Monasteries and seizing all Catholic lands in England. In 1540 Knox became a follower of Protestant reformer George Wishart who was burned at the stake on orders from the Bishop of Saint Andrews. The Protestants assassinated Bishop Beaton and seized the Castle of Saint Andrews. Knox was arrested and taken to France as a galley slave. People took their religion seriously in those days.

"In 1549, Knox returned to England as a Protestant minister and radical reformer. In 1953, Bloody Mary Tudor, a Catholic, became Queen of England and ordered all Protestants, alive or dead, burned at the stake. Knox fled to Europe and joined the Marian Exiles. He traveled to Geneva and studied under John Calvin. Eventually Mary died, and Elizabeth I, a Protestant, became Queen of England.

"Knox returned to Scotland in 1559 when Mary, a Catholic, was Queen of Scots. Under Knox leadership, the Scottish parliament voted Presbyterianism the state religion of Scotland.

"He disappeared from history in 1564.

"Jacobites were Highland Scots loyal to the House of Stuart. *Jacobus* was the Latin name of James Edward Stuart. In 1715 he led the Jacobites in a rebellion against English rule by German Kings and was crushed and fled to France.

"In 1745, James' son, Charles Edward Stuart, called Bonnie Prince Charlie returned and led the Highlanders against the English at Culloden Moor and were overwhelmed and defeated again.

"Bonnie Prince Charley fled to France, but the English destroyed the Clans by executing the Clan Chiefs, disarmed all Highlanders, and outlawed kilts and bagpipes.

"At that time, Scotland was the poorest country in Europe and most of the world. Those surviving the slaughter migrated to the Americas, Canada, South Africa, Australia, and New Zealand. There's only about 6 million in Scotland today, but about 40 million in the U.S.A. alone, plus another 40 million in the other English speaking countries. There're probably 50 million Irish, since they were Catholic. There are Scots all over the world, and Irish all over the United States. They were the original Celts.

"The Romans civilized the English, but built a wall to keep out the Scots and Pics to establish *Pax Romana* and Bretons."

*   *   *

After lectures Maria announced they would take a local tour of medieval York and York Minister if the weather permitted, and they could catch a night train to London. It was only an hour by bullet train, and they'd be back at the Heathrow Hilton for a late buffet dinner tomorrow evening. After the Romans left, London dwindled down to almost nothing, but York attracted immigrants from all over northern Europe. York was a great place to tour if the weather were pleasant.

Back in her room, Sandra slipped out of her clothes and shoes, donned an extra large HAIL MARY T-shirt, turned on the reading lamp, and read the tourist freebies about York England and Scotland. It was boring, but if you wanted to learn about North America you needed to study the Romans, England, Ireland, and Scotland. Houston and Southeast Texas were full of them and their descendents. Roman Catholics were Romans without legions, crosses, and bonfires to burn heretics and old ladies. Romans were crossing our borders now from Old Mexico (New Spain), and the Pope and priests were edging them on.

CHAPTER 34

York England
11:00 P.M., December 16, 1993

Early history

Archeological evidence suggests that Mesolithic people settled in the region of York between 8000 and 7000 BC, although it is not known whether these settlements were permanent or temporary. By the time of the Roman conquest of Britain, the area was occupied by a tribe known to the Romans as the Brigantes. The Brigantian tribal area initially became a Roman client state but later its leaders became more hostile to Rome. As a result the Roman Ninth Legion was sent north of the Humber into Brigantian territory.

The city itself was founded in 71 AD, when the Ninth Legion conquered the Brigantes and constructed a wooden military fortress on flat ground above the River Ouse close to its confluence with the River Foss. The fortress, which was later rebuilt in stone, covered an area of 50 acres (20 ha) and was inhabited by 6,000 soldiers. The site of the Roman fortress lies under the foundations of York Minster, and excavations in the Minster's undercroft have revealed some of the original walls.

The Emperors Hadrian, Septimius Severus and Constantius I all held court in York during their various campaigns. During his stay, the Emperor Severus proclaimed York capital of the province of Britannia Inferior, and it is likely that it was he who granted York the privileges of a colonia or city. Constantius I died in 306 AD during his stay in

York, and his son Constantine the Great was proclaimed Emperor by the troops based in the fortress.

In the 7th century York became the chief city of the Anglian King Edwin of Northumbria. The first Minster church was built in York for the baptism of Edwin in 627. Edwin ordered that this small wooden church should be rebuilt in stone, but he was killed in 633 and the task of completing the stone Minster fell to his successor Oswald. In the following century Alcuin of York came to the cathedral school of York. He had a long career as a teacher and scholar, first at the school at York now known as St. Peter's School, York, which was founded in 627 AD, and later as Charlemagne's leading advisor on ecclesiastical and educational affairs.

In 866, Northumbria was in the midst of internecine struggles when the Vikings raided and captured York. Under Viking rule the city became a major river port, part of the extensive Viking trading routes throughout northern Europe. The last ruler of an independent Jórvik, Eric Bloodaxe, was driven from the city in the year 954 by King Edred in his successful attempt to complete the unification of England.

Post conquest

In 1068, two years after the Norman Conquest of England, the people of York rebelled. Initially the rebellion was successful but upon the arrival of William the Conqueror the rebellion was put down. He at once built two wooden fortresses on motes, which are still visible, on either side of the river Ouse. York was ravaged by him as part of the harrying of the North.

The first stone Minster church was badly damaged by fire in the uprising, and the Normans later decided to build a new Minster on a new site. Around the year 1080 Archbishop Thomas started building a cathedral that in time became the current Minster. In the 12th century York started to prosper because of its position at the hub of an excellent communications network. It became a major trading centre and Hanseatic port. York merchants imported cloth, wax, canvas, and oats from the Low Countries, and exported grain to Gascony and grain and wool to the Low Countries. King Henry I granted the city's first charter, confirming trading rights in England and Europe.

In 1190, York was the site of an infamous pogrom of its Jewish inhabitants. The Jews sought sanctuary in Clifford's Tower, the fortification within the city belonging to the Crown. The mob besieged the trapped Jews for some days while preparations were made to storm the castle. Eventually a fire was started, whether by the Jews or their persecutors is uncertain. Several Jews perished in the flames but the majority (including Josce of York and the learned rabbi Yom Tov of Joigny) took their own lives rather than give themselves up to the mob. Those who did surrender were killed, despite being promised their lives. At least 150 Jews died in the massacre (although some authorities put the figure as high as 500).

Tudor and Stuart times

The city underwent a period of decline during Tudor times. Under Henry VIII, the Dissolution of the Monasteries saw the end of the many monastic houses of York, along with their hospitals. This led to the Pilgrimage of Grace, an uprising of northern Catholics in Yorkshire and Lincolnshire who were opposed to religious reform. Henry VIII eventually reinstated the Council of the North in York, and this increased in importance under Elizabeth I, leading to a revival in the city's influence. Guy Fawkes who was born and educated in York was a member of a group of Roman Catholic restorationists that planned the Gunpowder Plot. Its aim was to displace Protestant rule by blowing up the Houses of Parliament while King James I and the entire Protestant and even most of the Catholic aristocracy and nobility were inside.

In 1644, during the Civil War, the Parliamentarians besieged York, and many medieval houses outside the city walls were lost. The barbican at Walmgate Bar was undermined and explosives laid but the plot was discovered. On the arrival of Prince Rupert, with an army of 15,000 men, the siege was lifted. The Parliamentarians retreated some 6 miles (10 km) from York with Rupert in pursuit, before turning on his army and soundly defeating it at the Battle of Marston Moor. Of Rupert's 15,000 troops, no fewer than 4,000 were killed and 1,500 captured. The siege was renewed, but the city could not hold out for long, and on 15 July the city surrendered to Sir Thomas Fairfax.

Following the restoration of the monarchy in 1660, and the removal of the garrison from York in 1688, the city was dominated by the local gentry and merchants, although the clergy were still important. Competition from the nearby cities of Leeds and Hull, together with silting of the River Ouse, resulted in York losing its pre-eminent position as a trading centre, but the city's role as the social and cultural centre for wealthy northerners was on the rise.

CHAPTER 35

104ᵗʰ Criminal District Court
Judge Eva Petrarcelli
8 A.M., Monday, December 16, 1993
Temperature 75°, Clear, Sunny

Devine' had laid flat on her back four days and experienced dizziness early on when dressing for work. If she weren't pregnant by now, forget it. The little bastard had its chance.

Bill and Eva had arranged a preliminary hearing for Shelby Fox to set bail, establish charges, and schedule Grand Jury which would meet Wednesday for the last time this year. If the Grand Jury true billed, then arraignment would be early in January when Sandra got back.

After persuasion by Booker, Ivry Cost agreed to turn state's evidence on Shelby. She expected Everett Wilbur and Brice Redmon would do the same. Sandra's client, Dr. Raul Capistrano, was out on bail charged with conspiracy to commit murder, dealing in narcotics and money laundering. Raul and Shelby were brother-in-laws. Raul swam all way from Cuba, and Shelby grew up on the Matigwa reservation and made it to Lieutenant, Internal Affairs Division, HPD.

Bill decided to go for the gold. He was going to prosecute Shelby first, then charge Ivry, Brice, Everett, and Dr. Raul Capistrano after their testimonies at Shelby's trial.

Shelby had admitted nothing, not to Deviné, the cops, or anybody. He was waiting for Sandra. If he didn't confess, they didn't know for sure, and a well selected jury would not convict. Devine' thought Shelby wrong, but a jury could get hung up, and the judge would declare a mistrial. Governor Ann Richards had specifically appointed Sandra and

Devine' to defend Shelby. He had Grand Jury yet and if they true billed, arraignment.

All Devine' had to do was plead not guilty and argue bail. Shelby refused plea bargaining and was rolling the dice and bet Sandra would get him acquitted. *Impossible* thought Deviné. He was guilty as hell, but this was America, and it was better to let 10 guilty walk free than convict one innocent. Every prisoner on death row was "innocent."

*   *   *

"All rise"

"State of Texas vs. Shelby Bigbrave Fox"

"Charges: Murder in the First Degree, two counts.

Possession of Controlled Substance with intent to distribute.

Bill Riley DA approached the bench. "Your honor, former Lieutenant Shelby Fox, HPD, is well known to this court and the entire police force. At the time of his dismissal from the police force he was senior inspector of the Internal Affairs Division and had investigated charges brought against many of his former officers. Governor Richards has a personal interest that former Lieutenant Fox be given every opportunity to have a fair and impartial trial by a jury of his peers.

"Governor Richards has specifically recommended lawyer Sandra Lerner as lead attorney in his defense, and we seriously consider a change in venue to Liberty, Brazoria, or Fort Bend Counties where he is hardly known and very few prospective jurors watch TV or read a newspaper." Bill paused.

Everybody knew everybody except Deviné, Shelby's lawyer. Shelby clammed up and wouldn't speak to her.

Judge Petrarcelli, irritated, ordered, "Please present his case. We'll wait on the Grand Jury. Miss Lerner will be back. Why didn't Governor Richards recommend Polk County? They have an Indian Reservation."

"Your honor on June 8, 1993 Lieutenant Fox and two fellow police officers accompanied by eight black men in two Renta trucks were caught burglarizing a private home and hauling off 4 tons of illegally smuggled pure Colombian Cocaine in single kilo gram packages. They were arrested, and Sergeant Booker Washington turned in the cocaine to Evidence. We have in custody the driver of the lead vehicle who was under Lieutenant Fox's employ. He along with the two officers accompanying Lieutenant Fox will testify.

Later, the guards at the Waste Management Plant on the Brazos River in Fort Bend County were robbed by a masked man who drove off in a truck with the cocaine. Each kilo package was stamped with a red HPD by county Evidence before disposal. A Deputy Sergeant will testify.

One month later, a masked gunman wearing a County Deputy's uniform entered the County Jail at 2 A.M. and murdered the desk clerk and jailer, stole the keys, released two prisoners, and fatally wounded General Lupe Lopez of the Mexican Judicial Police. The drivers of the patrol car and getaway van will identify Lieutenant Fox as the shooter. The captured escaped prisoners identified Lieutenant Fox in a lineup.

3 months ago, the defendant, Lieutenant Fox, was witnessed deliberately murdering Sergeant Bobby Crawford, HPD. We have 4 eyewitnesses who will testify.

On the day of his present arrest and incarceration, he was arrested by Sergeants Sheila Mellons and Miguel Montalban who will testify."

Bill Riley DA sat down. Judge Petrarcelli looked at Lieutenant Fox glumly. "I take it the devil is in the details?"

"Yes, ma'am," replied Bill. "Waste Management is in Fort Bend County, and they dumped Bobby's body in a crack house on the Brazos River in Brazoria County."

Judge Petrarcelli looked at Deviné. "Has the defense prepared a defense, Miss Sparks?"

"Not guilty!" pleaded Deviné.

"Does the defense recommend change in venue?"

"Yes, ma'am. Fort Bend courthouse is closer and more convenient."

In Texas, a suspect in a capital murder case is not allowed bail. Devine' guessed Liberty County. It was the further of the three. The Grand Jury met for the last time Wednesday, and arraignment would be the first Monday or Tuesday in 1994. There were a lot of minorities in Liberty County, but few Native Americans.

Devine' followed Bill and Opal back to the elevator. She beckoned Opal aside when Bill got on.

"Try to get Bill to choose Big Bend County. Liberty is 70 miles off," pleaded Deviné.

"Forget it! I heard him tell somebody in the State Attorney's Office, Liberty County. He just wanted it to sound good. You know, run it up the flag pole, and see who salutes. Fort Bend and Brazoria are just next door. The per capita IQ in Liberty County is the lowest in Texas. They are 50% coonass," replied Opal, seriously. "Nobody reads a paper or watches TV. Believe me! It used to have oil fields and a port. Now all they have are stripper wells, cows, and manure. It's just a restroom stop on the way to the Big Thicket. Get Dirk to show you around. He graduated from Liberty High."

"What is a coonass?" asked Deviné, feeling stupid.

"It's a French African American. They call them French niggers," replied Opal. They go to Catholic Church. The whites go to the First Baptist Church across the main drag, across the railroad track, and three blocks north of McDonald's at the red light."

"I've eaten at McDonald's across from the light," commented Deviné.

"Then you've seen everything except Ames, Hardin, and the old oil fields plus the high school sitting back on the south side bordering on the Trinity River close to the docks," replied Opal, adamant. "The courtroom is old timey, big, and looks like the inside of church. They have a sheriff, 6 deputies, a bailiff and a 20 cell jailhouse. We're not talking about a big county since the oil fields went dry. When do you see Dirk again?" asked Opal.

"We have a date at the Red Lobster in Sugar Land. Our usual places, Park Shops and Luby's on Live Oak and Westheimer, are too crowded. You have to park six blocks away and eat standing up," replied Deviné, giggling.

"Hah! You have to call a day ahead for a reservation and stand in line at the Red Lobster. If it's seafood you want, try Long John Silver's. It's just as good and cost a third. There's a Wendy's about a block south in a new mall not on the map across from a new Best Western. While you are there, look at the new clinic being constructed on George Herbert Bush Drive. There will be a sign, The Joshua and Bernice Hale Clinic. That's Austin Hale's new clinic. Rich Berstein bought in as Chief of Gastroenterology. He'll keep a satellite office on Live Oak and keep up his teaching duties and Clinical Professorship at Ben Taub. Rich may be an asshole when it comes to women, but he's a good doctor. He's predictable. You have to make up your mind in advance or get a caller I.D."

"It wasn't many years ago that Bellaire, Heights, Pasadena, Humble, on and on, and River Oaks were outside City Limits, and now they're almost downtown. Houston keeps growing and growing," commented Deviné, thinking. She'd only lived there 7 months.

"In another 10 years we'll look like Guadalajara," commented Opal. "I'll see you at school. There'll be plenty of empty seats up back. As soon as they post the finals, they're out of there."

CHAPTER 36

Jerry stayed home from work and insisted Dirk take her fishing. She specifically wanted to see Bezoar, the Karankawa Shaman, and look for signs of illegal aliens from Mexico camping and living along the banks of the Brazos from the bridge at Richmond to the Brazoria County Willow Bend nuclear plant. Jerry brought some photographs of known smugglers thought to operate secretly along the river.

She hadn't given up on the idea of going up the Brazos from Richmond to San Felipe near Sweany. She really needed to get the DEA, ICE, and AFT interested, but it was just penny ante to them. They were at the border, and the Coast Guard was guarding our waters along Texas' 1000 miles shoreline. Who owned the river? The State! That could mean DPS. She had Montgomery, Harris, and Galveston Counties, and the Brazos River didn't run through any of those.

Dirk went to the morgue and would pick her up later. The motor wouldn't start on the SUV, and the bass boat trailer had a flat, minor obstacles to a real fisherman.

While waiting for Dirk, Jerry read. She didn't know where Dirk earned the money to buy Brazos River bottom land, but he got the certified checks from Misty Tantalia at the El Cyuga State Bank. He had to be buying up land for the bank and Misty. She read.

> *Sugar Land is a city located in Fort Bend County along the Gulf Coast region in the U.S. state of Texas within the Houston-Sugar Land-Baytown metropolitan area. It is one of the fastest-growing cities in Texas, having grown more than 158 percent in the last decade. The U.S. Census Bureau estimated that the city's population was 79,943.*

Founded as a sugar plantation in the early mid 1800s and incorporated in 1959, Sugar Land is the largest city and economic center of Fort Bend County. The city is the third-largest population and second-largest in economic activities of the Houston area.

Sugar Land is home to the headquarters of Imperial Sugar and the company's main refinery and distribution center was once located in this city. As a nod to this heritage, the Imperial Sugar crown logo can be seen in the city seal and logo. The city also holds the headquarters for Western Airways and a major manufacturing facility for Nalco Chemical Company. In addition, Sugar Land has a large number of international energy, software, engineering, and product firms.

Sugar Land has the most master-planned communities in Fort Bend County, which is home to the largest number of master-planned communities in the nation, including, First Colony, New Territory, Telfair, Greatwood, Chelsea Harbour and many others.

Sugar Land holds the title of "Fittest City in Texas" for the population 50,000—100,000 range, a title it has held for four consecutive years.

CNN/Money and Money magazine ranked Sugar Land third on its list of the 100 Best Cities to Live in the United States. Sugar Land's median family income is $105,905.

CQ Press has ranked Sugar Land fifth on its list of Safest Cities in the United States (14th annual "City Crime Rankings: Crime in Metropolitan American").

Forbes.com selected Sugar Land along with Bunker Hill Village and Hunters Creek Village as one of the three Houston-area "Top Suburbs To Live Well," noting its affluence despite its large population.

Sugar Land has a heritage tracing its roots back to the original Mexican land grant to Stephen F. Austin. One of the first settlers of the land, Samuel M. Williams, called this land "Oakland Plantation" because there were many different varieties of oaks on the land, such as Willow Oak, Post Oak, Water Oak, Southern red oak, and Live Oak. Williams' brother, Nathaniel, purchased the land in 1838. They operated the plantation by growing cotton, corn, and sugarcane. During these early years, the area that is now Sugar Land was the center of social life along the Brazos River. In 1853, Benjamin Terry and William J. Kyle purchased the Oakland Plantation from the S.M. Williams family. Terry is known for organizing Terry's Texas Rangers during the Civil War and for naming the town. Upon the deaths of Terry and Kyle, Colonel E. H. Cunningham bought the 12,500 acre (51 km²) plantation soon after the Civil War and developed the town around his sugar refining plant around 1879.

Sugar Land has two major water ways running through the city. The Brazos River runs through the southwestern and southern portion of the city and then into Brazoria County. Oyster Creek runs from the northwest to the eastern portion of the city limits and into Missouri City.

Sugar Land has many natural and man-made lakes connecting to Oyster Creek and one connecting to the Brazos River. The remainder of the lakes in Sugar

Land are man-made through the development of many master-planned communities.

Underpinning the area's land surface are unconsolidated clays, clay shales, and poorly-cemented sands extending to depths of several miles. The region's geology developed from stream deposits from the erosion of the Rocky Mountains. These sediments consist of a series of sands and clays deposited on decaying organic matter that, over time, was transformed into oil and natural gas. Beneath these tiers is a water-deposited layer of halite, a rock salt. The porous layers were compressed over time and forced upward. As it pushed upward, the salt dragged surrounding sediments into dome shapes, often trapping oil and gas that seeped from the surrounding porous sands.

The region is earthquake-free. While the neighboring city of Houston contains 86 mapped and historically active surface faults with an aggregate length of 149 miles, the clay below the surface precludes the buildup of friction that produces ground shaking in earthquakes. These faults move only very gradually in what is termed "fault creep."

Sugar Land's climate is classified as being humid subtropical. The city is located in the gulf coastal plains biome, and the vegetation is classified as a temperate grassland. The average yearly precipitation is 48 inches. Prevailing winds are from the south and southeast during most of the year, bringing heat and moisture from the Gulf of Mexico.

In the summer time, daily high temperatures are in the 95°F (35°C) range throughout much of July and August.

The air tends to feel still and the humidity (often 90 to 100 percent relative humidity) makes the air feel hotter than it really is. Summer thunderstorms sometimes bring tornadoes to the area. Afternoon rains are not uncommon, and most days Houston meteorologists predict at least some chance of rain. The highest temperature recorded in the area was 109°F.

*　　*　　*

I'd rather have a Catholic Mexican than a Muslim Arab, thought Dirk. In another 10 years Houston would look like Guadalajara.

He found Dr. Oh Nu hosing the place. No fresh bodies were visible.

"What did you do with A. Fuller Bottle?" asked Dirk.

"I released his body to SAVEMORE. The Rosary is Wednesday night. Afterward they will cremate him at the wife's request," replied Dr. Oh Nu.

"Who gave her the idea?"

"She did. I don't blame her. At least she can keep him in a bottle, no pun intended," replied Dr. Nu, chuckling.

"Well, what did you find?" asked Dirk, anxiously. He'd never seen Fuller alive, just screwing his head on walking up and down the stairway entrance to a flying saucer. He hadn't told. He didn't want to yell fire in a crowded theater. Houston had a lot of ET. Big deal! They weren't as bad as Islamic Jihadist.

Jésus was ET. He's masquerading as a Catholic priest at Saint Colombo. Big deal! When you start thinking you've seen everything, old age sets in. Maybe he was a new priest from Guadalajara. He found the right place. From above in the fourth dimension Houston and Guadalajara probably look the same.

Dr. Oh Nu thought. "Sandra Lerner put me on to it. When the tissue wouldn't stain with our usual laboratory stains, send it to

Biochemistry for polarized light refraction. Every plant and animal on earth refracts light to the left, no exception. If it reflects light to the right, then it came from an ET, no question.

"ET have a special enzyme in their gastric juices and O Rh negative blood. A. Fuller Bottle's tissue didn't stain, his proteins contained D-amino acids and, when isolated, his glucose refracted light to the left. He's our 10th case. I'm sure we'll find more. Drs. Austin Hale and Fatima Hussain had 5 cases in New Orleans and are moving to Sugar Land where, theoretically at least, more reside. Short answer, A. Fuller Bottle was ET.

"By-the-way, his Rosary is Wednesday night at 8 P.M. at SAVEMORE on South Main after which he will be cremated. She wanted him to look nice because he was such an asshole. All malpractice lawyers are assholes. They may be ET from a falling star," answered Dr. Oh Nu, laughing. "Like Satan!"

"What did you do with the two French Rabbis?" asked Dirk.

"Their bodies got lost in the vault. You want to help me look again?"

CHAPTER 37

Dirk motored down the Brazos well passed his property and Bezoars', and stopped before he reached the Brazoria Power Plant. Jerry jumped up on the back fishing platform with a black spinner bait rigged and started casting at stumps and cypress knees eager to catch the first bass. On the first cast she landed a 16 inch lunker that Dirk estimated 5 pounds. WOW!

He pulled up the troll motor and adjusted the handle against the 10 mph wind from the north. It was cloudy, overcast, and 50°. If it got colder, it might snow. Not counting the cosmological accidental freezes in April caused by asteroids striking Saturn and Jupiter in August, Dirk had only seen it snow three times this far south.

"Lip that bass and put him in the live well. We'll need him to give to Bezoar," instructed Dirk. "Don't forget to put in the plug." Dirk flipped on the aerator centrifugal pump to the live wells and put the expanding rubber plug in his up front. He rigged a black plastic worm Texas style and began to troll and cast. He was taught to use dark colors on a dark day and light flashy colors on a sunny day. Dirk felt a slow tug on his line and thinking it was hung gave it a little pull. His pole bent, and a big fish started pulling toward a log taking line. WOW! He lowered the tip of his pole and with both hands, stood up and set the hook expecting a big bass to break the water and fight the hook. Instead, the fish kept going and pulled harder. Dirk reeled him back to the boat and up to the surface. It was a big Grinnell (Carp) bony fish, slimy as hell that whites wouldn't eat. It was a lot easier to cut the line. They got slime all over in the boat. Dirk guessed 10-15 pounds and 30 inches long. He opened his live well, lifted the line, hook, and Grinnell out of the water, over the live well, and cut the line.

Two fish were enough. Dirk trolled closer to the bank, fought the wind and dodged the logs, cypress knees, and stumps. He could see a trail back in the woods about 5 yards from water's edge. It looked used. The only way somebody could get in there was by boat.

"Jerry, we have enough fish. Why don't we look along for campsites and signs of illegals."

*   *   *

When a river bends or curves, it's deep on the outside and deposits sand on the inside. Just before a sandbar, you'd see willow trees and cattails and small creeks running to shallow lakes back in the woods.

Perch and Grinnell spawned in there. Usually the lakes were full of turtles, nutria rats, alligators, deer, and whatever. They made good campsites when it wasn't raining, and the river wasn't over bank. Usually, they were too shallow to use the big motor and often a troller. You'd have to use a paddle and push pole. Occasionally, you'd have to get on bank, push off, and tow your boat to deep water and troll out. Bass spawned February through April. Perch spawned in May, and Grinnell spawned in August.

Squirrels mated in October and May, and does were in heat in November up until Thanksgiving. You could shoot a buck in December, but he'd quit chasing does, and by January the bucks were in Velvet and not interested in sex (growing new horns). An eight point buck was two years old, and a twenty point buck was eight years old. If you wanted a twenty pointer, go to west Texas or down to Big Bend. They didn't get that big in east Texas, only rarely, too many hunters, usually about ten points.

Dirk saw a sandbar where the river took a turn up ahead and a willow grove this side. The foot path slanted off into the woods before the willows. There was a campsite back there. He didn't see any smoke or hear any voices. He waved at Jerry, put this finger to his mouth and pointed at the trail. He eased down and got a paddle and push pole out of the bottom locker, handed Jerry the paddle, and took the push pole up front. He and Jerry both wore back holsters and leg guns. He kept a throwing knife on his left leg being right handed.

Dirk had always been told that if you saw Nutria Rats sunning on logs there weren't any alligators, and if you saw turtles on logs, the bass weren't biting. There were both. Nothing moved. A 200 pounds sow with eight pigs came down to drink and walked back through the woods rooting for grubs and whatever. When Dirk was growing up, there were plenty of armadillos and snakes. Now there were few, but the woods were full of Feral hogs, and they made great sausage. Pork had lost favor with the eating public. He wondered if the hogs had run the armadillos north and had eaten the snakes' eggs, could be. Cotton mouth moccasins were rarely seen now.

Across the lake was a clearing and vacant campsite and places where they had drug boats through the reeds and bushes. They watched and nothing moved. Dirk saw no buzzards circling. If they left any food, hogs or raccoons got it. The woods came alive with predators and scavengers at night. During Dirk's lifetime, the Texas Parks and Wildlife, stocked the thickets several times with brown bear (Grizzlies), but they'd wander up to houses with bacon frying and got shot.

Dirk gave the bass boat a push, and they glided in on a sandy beach and waited. There was no movement or sound. Dirk jumped out on shore and pulled the boat up a bit and tied it to a sapling. Under a couple of 200 year old Beech trees a sandy space had been cleared by humans and in the center were scattered remains of a campfire about three days old, since the last rain. The ground was worn where people sat in a circle. All tracks were barefeet, some large and some small, but no kids. Bare feet Indians from Mexico!

Whoever, weren't civilized. They didn't dig latrines or garbage dumps. Dirk figured Indians from Guatemala, and by chance he was nearly right. They were from Nicaragua, Mayans. They found Mexican labeled tins, Jalapeño, fried beans, Fritos, Doritos and wrappers from Taco Bell's.

Dirk figured he'd seen enough. The campers might come back. There were no evidence of a midget submarine, gasoline cans, roads into the place, and no helicopter pad. They either walked or paddled their own canoe, maybe two canoes and six people at most.

Dirk noticed when driving around Sugar Land that all the construction work was done by Latinos. There were white architects and bosses, but the houses were constructed by dark skinned laborers who spoke Spanish. Everywhere in Texas, it was the same. He hadn't seen a black pick up a board in years, and very few whites unless they worked in a lumber yard. The illegals had taken over construction by default.

*　　*　　*

When they neared Bezoar's, Dirk noticed smoke and guessed Bezoar was cooking. Remembering Warden Farmer's advice, they brought him fresh fish as a gift. Bezoar spoke in "tongues", and didn't know English. There were eight Jon boats turned over instead of six. A full grown yellow Curr was chained to a tree, the tree bark was worn, and a circle of sandy dirt surrounded the tree at chain length. He barked, growled, and showed his fangs. Jerry took some Hershey's out of her jacket, unwrapped one, and tossed it to him. Curr caught it in midair, shook it, broke its neck, put it between his front paws, licked, and then gulped it down.

A complete transformation was miraculously visible. Curr lost his hostility, started whining, and wagged his tail. Jerry unwrapped another, and he ate it out of her hand after which he licked her hand and face.

"You're going to give that dog the shits," warned Dirk, knowingly.

Jerry left Curr wagging his tail and whining, and followed Dirk up the trail. She was shocked. Dirk had been there and seen that. There were deer horns, buffalo skulls and horns, cougar, bear, and hog skulls nailed to trees. Some skulls looked human. After the skulls were the dolls, gutted, hanging by nooses, staked, and hanging from trees. Jerry, who thought she had seen everything, cringed in fright and horror.

Bezoar put them up long ago to frighten off evil spirits and any human that might wander by.

"He doesn't know a word of English," whispered Dirk. "Let me have your fish and stand behind me. He'll think you are my squaw."

Dirk knocked. A cackle of laughter and a garbled greeting came from inside. They waited, and the plywood door on rawhide hinges was opened by an Indian squaw, about 22, 5'2", and 140 pounds wearing a one piece homespun dress and no shoes. She had to be a Mayan from Nicaragua. She smiled and opened the door. They walked in and found Bezoar squatting next to a boiling pot, laughing, and waving a spoon.

Dirk handed Bezoar the fish. Bezoar laughed and pointed to his squaw who took the fish, gutted them alive, wrapped them in palmetto leaves, and stuck them in the hot coals under the pot. Fish taste delicious if you eat them fresh. She turned and probed them with a stick.

Beside horns and skulls lining the walls, Dirk and Jerry noticed scalps hanging on pegs.

Bezoar, raised the lid and showed them a brown human foot he was boiling for dinner. He laughed, garbled, and by sign language invited them to eat. Dirk, answered with sign language explaining he just dropped in to introduce his squaw and meet Bezoar's new squaw. Bezoar cackled, pushed his squaw on the shoulder, and pointed to a blanket in the corner.

Dirk was afraid that Bezoar wanted to trade wives. That was not Dirk's idea of being neighborly, in this case.

The squaw pulled an object wrapped in a woven pine needle basket, opened it, and held up a scalp attached to a shrunken head. Dirk had seen that before. It wasn't local. She was from Copper Canyon at El Fuerta Mexico. They weren't Mayas, but they were cannibals. The pine needle basket was made in Copper Canyon. Small world!

*   *   *

Dirk had an appointment to meet Devine' at 6 P.M. at the Red Lobster in Sugar Land. Jerry was silent in thought driving back.

"Did you find out why the former owner wanted to sell you Ben Milam's place so inexpensively? They don't make land anymore, and you got the mineral rights and land for $2000 an acre. Someday Houston will expand to include all of Fort Bend and Brazoria Counties. $2000 an acre was a steal," commented Jerry.

"Just Ben Milam's in the pen for life, and decided to sell," replied Dirk.

"Why is Ben Milam in for life? You only get that for first degree murder. I would have read about it in the paper. Murder gets front page pictures and headlines."

"All I know is what Mr. Freeman Jackson, my lawyer, told me. You can't tell or I'll never be able to sell it if I need the money. Promise?" asked Dirk.

"I never make a promise like that. I testify under oath in court quite often. A judge will find you in contempt," said Jerry.

"Good! That takes care of that question," replied Dirk, smiling.

Later, "you rat! Now you have me curious. I promise to lie in court and never tell."

CHAPTER 38

Barclay Theater
University of Saint Nicholas
Houston, Texas
12 noon, Monday, December 16, 1993
Temperature 70°, cloudy

Dr. Amy Omikami was at the lectern. Printed on the green board in big letters were: **HOLIDAYS, NASA, CONCORDSKY, MOSCOW, ICE CUTTER, SAINT PETERSBURG, FREE, BRANIFF, HEATHROW, HILTON, COMMONS, MLK'S BIRTHDAY, AIR CONTROLLERS, PROSTITUTES, AND POOPER SCOOPERS**.

"Dr. Peter Rockford went deer hunting today. Dr. Fatima Hussain will discuss terrorism and Islam, Dr. Battenberg will fast forward to Glasnost, Perestroika, and democracy Russian style, and General Trudy Grits will begin a series on a Volunteer Army, Information Technology, and Modern Warfare. Lectures will end Wednesday and begin again on the first work day after New Years'. I don't have my 1994 calendar.

"For you that haven't gotten a notice or read the bulletin board, school lets out Friday after final exams. Registration is January 11 and 12 and first classes begin on January 13.

"We will not take a day off on MLK's birthday, such nonsense! This is a private university. Those so inclined may observe 5 minutes of silent prayer outside of class, somewhere.

"Maria didn't ask you to come, but she may ask you to leave. She who has the gold, rules, and that includes us, the faculty.

"For those of you that miss Dr. Winston Blood. He and his former wife Kay Berkeley, Maria's photographer, flew to London. It's easy to fly into Heathrow. You can't fly out. The Weather Man said snow tomorrow in London.

"I've got some exciting news. Because of our close proximity to NASA, we were put on the short list to furnish a student group to fly on the maiden voyage of the new and improved Concordsky supersonic commercial passenger jet to Moscow, take a luxury nuclear ice breaker round trip cruise to Saint Petersburg and return to Heathrow in London. They furnish an overnight stay in Best Western, and it's **FREE** to the university accepting. It's frozen in Moscow and supposed to start snowing in London. I'll pass the world on to Maria. Heathrow has four terminal hotels and 100 nearby hotels plus downtown. They're staying in a downtown Hilton between a Professional Cricket Stadium and an Islamic Mosque next to a Commons (Park) where you can rent dogs to walk as conversation pieces. They're in an immigrant community where McDonald's serve Halal burgers and French fries.

"In Paris, there are two French Poodles for every tree, and 6000 Pooper Scoopers ride around on bicycles and spend a lifetime scooping up dog poo poo.

"Dog lovers know that canines commonly eat dog poop and dirt due to some deficiency in commercially prepared dog food, and it doesn't hurt them one bit. The French are esthetic that way. In 1900, an advisor to the King of England predicted that London would be 6 feet deep in horse manure by 1910. Henry Ford solved their problem by inventing the assembly line to make cars. The Pooper Scoopers have a well organized union and next to air traffic controllers are some of the highest paid government employees. Like the Air Traffic controllers and garbage collectors they are forbidden to go on strike. A good pooper scooper makes more than an open heart surgeon in socialized medicine. The only capitalist in Paris are the prostitutes, and they get free medical care and Sundays off. Germany legalized prostitution after the Berlin Wall came down. Those girls get everything including free medical care, one month's vacation, retirement benefits, and equal social status.

"Braniff was the only American company that leased 10 Concordes, and they declared bankruptcy. You can fly around the world in one in 3.6 hours at 60,000 feet and 1400 miles per hour not counting 5 fuel stops. For those of you interested, Trafalgar offers a World Tour in 7 days for only $100,000 a person. You can go up and spend time on the Russian Space Laboratory for $US 25 million. Considering what it cost the Russian space program, that's real value. I couldn't get on one of ours for love or money at NASA.

"I'll get serious about supersonic air travel tomorrow. I just learned about the Concordsky deal 30 minutes ago. Levitra!"

Dr. Levitra Battenberg erased the green board and printed, **STALIN, TERROR, UTOPIA, GULAGS, IRON CURTAIN, COLD WAR, COMPAC PRESARIO, GORBECHEV, BERLIN WALL, RONALD REAGAN, AND ERROL FLYNN**.

"Amy asked me to talk about modern Russia today, since our Anthropology group may be taking the Corcordsky to Moscow. After the Holidays, I'll go back to Nicholas I and the Crimean conflict. Leo Tolstoy wrote *Anna Karenina* just after the Crimean War, and *War and Peace* was a historical novel. They change history all the time, and you have to read fiction to find out what really happened. There have been fiction writers as long as storytellers. Now we have TV and the Internet.

"Beauty is in the eyes of the beholder. Most Russians loved Stalin and Communism. Enemies of the state were given a trial before execution. The Russians were victorious at Stalingrad and won WWII. They got their act together. Hitler and Germans were evil. After WWII, they dropped an iron curtain, and the Cold War began. Stalin died on March 15, 1953 and was followed by Krushev (1953-1964), Brezhnev (1964-1982), Andropov (1982-1984), Chernenko (1982-1984), and finally Mikhail Gorbachev, our hero of today. Ronald Reagan compared Gorbachev with Errol Flynn.

"Now, Errol Flynn in his early years was the most exciting leading man in Hollywood. Men cheered his daring, and women swooned. He took Douglas Fairbanks' roles and remade some of Fairbanks' pictures. He played George Custer in *They Died With Their Boots On* and a swash buckling *Captain Blood* in the days of the Spanish Main. He volunteered to fight with the loyalist in Spain against Franco in the Spanish Civil War. He was wounded in battle by shrapnel and returned to Hollywood a celebrated national hero.

"Does anybody in this audience remember the saying 'In like Flynn'? No hands went up.

"Look it up on the Internet, and I'll ask again tomorrow. By-the-way, I have an old IBM computer with DOS. I'm buying me a new Compact Presario with Windows for Christmas. They got them down to $3500, loaded, and you can find anything and get up to the minute weather, stock quotations, and sport scores just by clicking on Search or Enter. Fantastic! The students will get one for Christmas, so you'd better get yours. If computers get any smarter, students will quit buying books. I said it first.

"Gorbachev, unlike all the rest, except maybe Vladimir Lenin, was a thinker. He observed that the upper 3% of Communists were rich oligarchy, got all the fancy perks and lived high on the hog like before in Czarist Russia.

"The crème-de-crème always rose to the top even in the ultimate welfare state. There was zero unemployment, but nobody worked, and the space and weapons race was bankrupting the country. People were lined up to get free condoms and cheap Vodka. The black market flourished.

"Toilet paper disappeared, except on the black market. Ordinary Russians were looking back at the Czars as the good old days.

"To mimic President Jimmie Carter, there was a 'malaise' of the people. They were looking for a Messiah, but they wouldn't get off their butt except in glamorous occupations. They wanted plenty of sex, but no babies.

"Their kids dressed like Elvis, and spent their time drinking and dancing in discos. They focused on sports and ignored politics. They put graffiti on the walls and joined counter-culture gangs. It was not suppose to happen under Communism. Something was wrong.

"Pulling out of Afghanistan and losing a slam dunk war was unprecedented in Russian history. Mothers demonstrated in Kremlin Square. Disgraceful, like America in Vietnam! Islam was rebelling, and nobody gave a Ruble. The price of oil and gas went to zilch, and no country would loan them money. Russian bonds were worthless. They couldn't pay the army. The black market kept them afloat. U.S.A. President Reagan demanded, 'Mr. Gorbachev, tear down this wall'. Reagan, who never won an Oscar, gave the best performance in his acting career. Boris Yeltsin, sobered up and seized the moment.

"The U.S.A., CIA, and everybody, were caught completely by surprise. Unbelievable!

"I'm going to stop here and study. I'm winging it from memory. Dr. Omikami caught me by surprise. I thought the Concordsky blew up in test flight twenty years ago, killed everybody on board, and destroyed a Russian city about the time Chernobyl blew up and contaminated half of U.S.S.R. It's important to know how events unfolded chronologically to understand how the Soviets went belly up."

"Fatima."

Dr. Fatima Hussain wrote on the green board. **KISS ASS AMERICANS, LYING RUSSIANS, AL-QAEDA, SABER-RATTLING JEWS, JIHAD, PARADISE, VIRGINS, AYATOLLAHS, AND THE GREAT SATAN**.

"Let me put some minds to rest. I'm an atheist, no discussion. I was in Saudi Arabia, my home, when the **WTC** and **PENTAGON** were bombed. Operating room surgeons broke scrub, opened up champagne, and cheered for the home boys, all Saudis, while they watched the **WTC** crumble. Everybody in Islam cheered.

"The U.S.A. should explore and drill their own reserves and quit kissing the Saudi's ass. Pardon the New Orleans' French!

"When a woman gets married in Islam, and if she's not a virgin on her wedding night, she's exposed by her husband publicly, and stoned to death by her brothers and family to restore family honor. That's Shariah. Loss of virginity before marriage is same as adultery. Stoning is a terrible way to die. The sword is merciful compared with stoning. In Saudi Arabia, a guilty man is allowed to run, and they ride up behind him and measure how far he can run after his head is cut off with a sword.

"<u>Whahabi</u> is the state religion of the Saudi's. Osma bin Laden is Whahabi, and Al-Qaeda is financed by the Whahabies. One plus one equals two. It's as simple as that. Americans should wake up. Islam is at war with America and all Christendom, like it or not.

"Terrorism is the war of the present and future. You can kill all you want in conventional western warfare going by the Geneva Convention. The Islamic Jihadists don't care how many they lose. Martyrs go to Paradise and 70 virgins. By blowing themselves up and killing innocent women and children, they will break your will.

"Only the Mongols knew how to fight the Muslims and win. They killed all the men, raped the women, burned their cities to the ground, and took their children as slaves. You're not going to do it by heavy tanks, carpet bombing, and nuclear weapons. It will take courage, soldiers with rifles, and ruthless blood thirsty officers. You have to fight them like the Mongols, steal their wealth, and leave ashes in your wake. You have to kill all the Sheiks, Caliphs, Emirs, Mullahs and Ayatollahs.

"Having bared my soul, I'd like to get on today's subject. I'm a Forensic Pathologist and Molecular Biologist. I moved to Houston at the request of Dr. Austin Hale, my mentor at New Orleans. We think that we'll find more ET in Sugar Land than anywhere else. Dr. Amy Omikami caught me by surprise when she asked me to lecture on terrorism and Jihad. I see General Trudy Grits is to follow. Maybe she will cover what I miss. I'm lecturing off the cuff today. Tomorrow, I'll be more organized.

"First, you have to take out Saddam Hussein. He didn't learn anything from Desert Storm. He has nuclear weapons. You can bet. He thinks he's Nebuchadnezzar. I think he's Pol Pot, only worse. President

George H. Bush should have taken out Saddam like a rabid dog, a mad dog, which he is, no question.

"He and his two sons looted Iraq's treasury, bribed the crooks running the U.N., cheated on his oil quota, and let the babies starve. That's going on right now. Even the Ayatollahs want him dead. When Saddam suggested Iraq, Iran, and Syria combine forces and quash Israel, Ayatollah replied, 'the way to Jerusalem is through Karbala'. Meaning? He wanted Saddam dead before he made a land attack on Israel through Syria and Lebanon. Before you control terrorism, you have to take out Saddam and the Ayatollahs. You say, 'that'll start WWIII.' You are already in WWIII. What do you think Jihad is? The Israelis know. They are sitting over there armed to the teeth, waiting to pull the atomic trigger.

"That's all today. Tomorrow I'll have an outline."

"General Trudy Grits."

General Grits in uniform sporting two stars wrote on the green board. **DESERT STORM, GENGHIS KAHN, STALINGRAD, BATAN, COACH TOM LANDRY, ANDREW JACKSON, SUICIDE BOMBER, OASIS, AND 70 VIRGINS**.

"140,000 Iraqis threw down their arms and gave up in Desert Storm while the rest hightailed it out of Kuwait and littered the road all way back to Bagdad.

"They did put up a token resistance. The English surprised the Japanese by surrendering 150,000 able bodied armed troops trained for combat in Singapore during WWII. If we fought like Genghis Kahn, we'd gunned down 140,000 prisoners, chased the Republican Guard all way back to Bagdad, flattened the city, and hung Saddam Hussein. Nobody gave the order. It would have saved a lot of trouble later on. Troops just take orders.

"Very few of the Germans that surrendered to the Russians on the Eastern Front in WWII made it back to Germany alive. Many of our troops that surrendered on Batan and Corregidor did not survive.

We had very few surrender in Korea, and in Vietnam it was shot down pilots, like Senator John McCain. It's better to fight to the last man than surrender. There's always hope that help's on the way. When you're ambushed, you charge the ambush don't turn your back or you're dead.

"Now that I've fought the last wars, I'll discuss the present and future. All generals fight the last war, but it's never the same. Up at Fort Hood, we're training for the next war. In the end it's always boots on the ground and rifles that take and hold ground. For you that saw *No Time For Sergeants*, it's the infantry where the real fighting is.

"Duane Thomas was the best broken field runner the Cowboys ever had. When Dallas won the Super Bowl with Thomas, every coach in the NFL adjusted their defense to stop Duane Thomas and the Cowboys. Coach Tom Landry changed to a straight ahead running game, shotgun, and pocket passer. Duane Thomas called Coach Landry a 'plastic man'. Thomas became obsolete! Football changes every Sunday, and eventually Coach Landry became obsolete, the only Coach Dallas ever had. Coach Jimmy Johnson brought in Aikman, Smith and Irving and won two Super Bowls in a row. Coach Jimmy Johnson had to go. You can't stick with the same game plan. The other side thinks up new ways to beat you.

"We watch war on our tube every Sunday. War is football. When the enemy changes, you change. The Germans at Stalingrad, and the British at Singapore didn't study their enemy and anticipate the climate. The Russians loved snow, and the Japs loved the jungle. We had to use the atomic bomb which has become obsolete. Naypyidaw was an obsolete atomic bomb that the French bought at a Russian army surplus. Modern warfare has changed. You have to get a new coach or a new team, maybe both. WWII stuff didn't work but once in Iraq. Arab Jihadist aren't gentlemen that walk six paces, turn on count, and shoot. Dueling went out with Andrew Jackson.

"Suicide bombing is the cheapest form of warfare. Homemade vehicle bombs and road bombs exploded by handheld cell phone are next cheapest if somebody is furnishing the explosives. In Jihad, religion provides courage and disregard for life. Martyrs go to paradise with 70 virgins. The terrorists disappear in a crowd or house of innocents who are controlled by fear.

"Modern warfare against terrorism causes collateral damage, death of civilians, and social protests. So they get away to bomb another day. In Islam there is no shortage of mad bombers and suicide candidates.

"How do you fight them? Genghis Kahn! When the paddy wagon comes, it takes the good girls with the bad. Each kid is a potential bomber. Flatten the whole town, village, and city, whatever.

"Today, I came prepared to discuss Napoleon's great victory at Borodino. That was a gentlemen's war, totally structured on a chosen battlefield like a game of Chess. Tomorrow, I'll discuss non-classified wars of the future. Thanks!"

CHAPTER 39

The Red Lobster and Long John Silver's were packed with late Christmas shoppers. Red Lobster was inside the new Sugar Land Town Square while Long John Silver was on Texas Drive, and Wendy's was across from Wal-Mart in a mall under construction across from a new Best Western up the new boulevard from a new Shell station with a Wendy's attached to its convenience store. Exxon's Jiffy Mart had Subway's, Mexican food, and foot long hot dog stands. Most of the shoppers were strolling, shopping and dining at the new Sugar Land Town Square (mall).

Dirk noticed that Devine' didn't have any signs of coryza or 'flu'.

"Elizabeth Borden and Bob Waller are back," announced Deviné, like ho hum.

Dirk, not surprised, asked, "How do they look?" ET were common now.

"Just the same. Elizabeth moved back in her old apartment at the LUX, and Cathy Reyes moved in with Tina Mazon in 802 at the Granada. Louiza Santos left for parts unknown. She was from Colombia."

Dirk thought, *nothing surprised him anymore*. "Where did Bob move? The Shady Methodists got a new minister out in Shady Oaks?

"I didn't ask, but heard somebody say Bob moved in with Vaca de Vaca who was his former church secretary at Shady Methodist and now a prime suspect in her former husband's shooting death, Cabez de Vaca President of the North Park State. You remember! They acquitted Jotte' Jalopena when the maid showed up from Old Mexico, pregnant, and admitted she saw Vaca shoot Cabez. Vaca's prints were on the door handle and steering wheel, and it was his pistol she used. Vaca has an alibi. She was in a beauty salon at the Galleria, and the beautician backed her story. Bob obviously doesn't know, since he was dead at the time," replied Devine' smiling.

The waitress brought them their orders. Devine' had the special: beef burger, chocolate milkshake and fries. Dirk had a fish burger and Diet Pepsi trying to stay on a cardiac diet.

"Where's Bob's wife and kids?" asked Dirk.

"She got married again after the funeral. May I change the subject? You may already know," asked Deviné.

"Surely! You can't shock me. Wait until I tell you what I saw today. Our last Karankawa has taken a squaw from Copper Canyon. The Nehuahua are cannibals, and the Karankawas were cannibals."

"Big deal! My ancestors were cannibals. You go back far enough everybody were cannibals. It's ET I'm worried about. You ever heard of William Wallace Billings?"

"No, why should I?" replied Dirk without making a connection with Jerry.

"JoAnn Johnson came in today all gaga about some Colonel out at NASA named William Wallace Billings. She wants me to get Cealis a date with Dr. Charles Lanka, so she can flush Charles and hook up with William Wallace. The first thing somebody told me when I moved into the Olympia high-rise that JoAnn was moving out with Charles to get married, no less," said Deviné.

"You think Dr. Lanka is ET?" asked Dirk.

"I know he is! He's got magical powers. I saw him in action out at Blue Bird Hospital. They are a mile from NASA. They have all kind of waves that make particles, and particles that make waves and give off energy out there, $E=mc^2$. It's all coming together. From where do you think ET are coming?"

"Fourth dimension," replied Dirk, chuckling. "You can't see it."

*   *   *

Dirk bought a couple of chicken salad on rye Subways and a six pack of Miller's and went home to see Jerry who was watching the news and waiting. She was the only Italian Dirk knew that didn't know how to cook. Some anchor on Channel 30, Houston, was discussing Mexican drug cartels hooking up with drug gangs in Houston. *That wasn't news* thought Dirk. They ought to drive up Tex 35 under US 610 Loop to the Convention Center and Enron Field. It looked like Matamoras under there. He wouldn't drive under at night. They'd cut your throat and drink your blood.

Jerry turned off the TV, took a Sub and beer, and Dirk put the rest in the refrigerator for later. He'd just eaten. Jerry could talk and eat at the same time. Cops got that way. They inhaled fast like a bass does a plastic worm. *Bass drink fresh water and inhale oxygen through their skin. Salt water fish don't drink water and inhale oxygen through their gills. It took fish 500 million years to learn to survive in fresh water, and they could drown just like humans in fresh water, but not salt water*, thought Dirk. *It took one billion years to make a worm.*

"Dirk, before we get off on some hair brain tangent, let me tell you about the real world while it's on my mind." Jerry took another swallow of Miller's Lite. "I've got to explore up the Brazos from Richmond to San Felipe. That's at where they are hiding."

"Who?" She got Dirk's attention. "ET?"

*   *   *

"Jerry, I'm going to buy Dr. Nigera's camp house and 100 acres on the Brazos. It's never been drilled."

"That's dead money! No major oil company's going to drill it. If there were any oil, they'd gotten it long ago. You can make diesel fuel out of palmetto berries and wine out of wild grapes. What about alligators, Feral hogs, Nutria, and gar fish. You can sell them to the blacks," teased Jerry, smirking.

"Slant hole drilling and fracking! There's oil under those salt domes at 14,000 feet. It's safer than drilling in the Gulf. 60% of the oil and 80% of the gas are still down there. We could use it as a vacation home. I could rent it to Dr. Joy Burrell, the Psychiatrist."

Jerry stopped smiling. "I try not to be a jealous nag. Joy comes on too strong. I know 'fishing buddies' are few and far between. She'll get too busy. That's a blue collar sport. I'll tolerate Joy as your 'fishing buddy', but I'll not tolerate a love nest. I'm not your wife," declared Jerry, adamantly. "When we stop having sex, I'm walking out and get my half of what you've got before you spend it all on worthless bottom land that just grows Feral hogs and alligators."

*   *   *

"Does the name William Wallace ring a bell?" asked Dirk.

"Yeah, he was the first King of Scotland," replied Jerry. She bet she was the only person in Houston that knew that. That was her former husband's name. Once, she was Mrs. William Wallace Billings. Wally was the only Air Force Cadet at Texas A&M named William Wallace. He was in her high school yearbook and her sophomore heartthrob.

"Be serious," replied Dirk. "His name came up today."

Jerry turned serious. "In what way?"

"Devine' gossiped! JoAnn Johnson across the hall from her at the high-rise has the 'hots' for a Colonel William Wallace out at NASA and wanted Devine' to fix up Cealis with a grown up date with Charles Lanka."

"JoAnn Johnson! She's been engaged to Charles Lanka ever since his wife was murdered. She's been shacking up with Charles as long as I've known her, ever since Sandra moved into the high-rise."

"What about William Wallace?" asked Dirk again.

"Never heard of him," lied Jerry who turned her back to Dirk, switched off the bedside lamp, fluffed her pillow and went to sleep.

Even cows fart natural gas thought Dirk. It's so cheap, we have been flaring it in Texas for a hundred years. If people up north would just burn natural gas and quit heating their houses with coal, they could clean up the air, get rid of acid rain on Europe, and global warming, whatever. Women didn't think the same as men. Every time a man gets a good idea, they threaten to walk out and take half his money. No wonder Thomas Edison was a bachelor, and Isaac Newton never had a date. Julius Caesar, Alexander, and Jesus Christ were all bachelors. When Muhammad's fat wife died, he got rid of his milk goat and camels and married nine wives. You could do that if you were boss.

*   *   *

Dirk couldn't sleep. Jerry was snoring and turned away. He went to the refrigerator, got half a Sub, and can of Miller's and turned on the TV.

"This morning in Myanmar Chinese infantry and artillery have beaten back Bangladeshi and Burmese Loyalist troops on two fronts. The Bangladeshi are in hasty retreat, and who could blame them? The Chinese completely disregard hostile fire and outnumber their enemy 10 to 1. No matter how many Chinese are killed, they keep coming in wave after wave like locust destroying everything in their path."

Dirk switched channels.

"Today, police shot eight homeless children to death on the streets of Rio de Janeiro—."

He tried CNN and watched ten commercials. Afterward, they showed President Bill Clinton strolling with Russian President Boris Yeltsin, same height and dressed like twins, along a gravel road with a split rail fence and budding spring-like forest in the background.

They were smiling and discussing the weather in lock step all the way. Obviously it was a photo-opportunity. Which twin was the phony?

Dirk turned off the TV and went to bed. *Like Hee! Haw! If he didn't get bad news, he wouldn't get any news at all.*

CHAPTER 40

Singapore Novatel
6 A.M., Tuesday, December 17, 1993
Dense smoke, volcanic ash
80°, Tropical

They were lucky to catch Singapore Air on standby from Ho Chi Min City. Singapore Air had tall statuesque oriental beauties for stewardesses who wore form fitting traditional high collar Chinese dresses and were walking Chinese dolls. With the exceptions of a high class geisha Bob saw on the elevator at Osaka and a young street walker in Hong Kong, they were almost the sexiest women in the East. Any man would lust. Singapore stewardesses were Chinese, Malay, and Indian mix and selected for height and beauty. WOW!

Caucasian women had small waists and broad hips. Orientals had smaller bones and their waists tapered down to smaller butts. There were few, if any, fat young women in SEA. If they had big boobs, they were nursing a baby somewhere. It was difficult to guess their ages up to 40.

Judges ordered juveniles paddled (caned) in Singapore, and if a man made a pass, he'd end up in jail.

Penny was asleep, and it was too early to go down for breakfast. Bob read.

Singapore looked like the Mississippi Delta at the mouth of the Singapore River at the tip of the Malaysian peninsula. Classified as a peninsula made up of 63 islands, the Japs rode bicycles from Thailand down the Malaysian peninsula and crossed the bay by wading and rubber boats to attack during the cover of darkness and completely surprised General Percival and 150,000 British Commonwealth troops with their guns pointed seaward at the Singapore Straits. The Brits gave up, and most died of fever and exhaustion in Japanese work camps. *THE BRIDGE OVER THE RIVER KWAI* was filmed in Sri Lanka (Ceylon), and the actual steel bridge is still in use on the Kwai Noi (Little Kwai) River at Tha MaKham Thailand. The author was Pierre Boulle a French POW. Bob chuckled. The POWs called it the "Death Railroad" where 13,000 POWs and 100,000 civilians died constructing a railway from Bangkok to Rangoon Burma (258 miles). It was a tourist attraction now.

Singapore was the fourth busiest port in the world strategically sitting on the banks of the Straits of Malacca and the Straits of Singapore. It had a population of 5 million, made up of 70% Chinese, 13% Malays, 10% Indians, and 7% others. They had a 99% literacy, per capita income of US $45,000, and a 10% GDP. Cargo containers were stacked for miles and miles. They worked in shifts and cargo ships came and went at all hours.

Bob read: Following WWII, Singapore held its first general election in 1955 and joined the British Commonwealth. Singapore declared independence from Britain in 1963 and joined the Federation of Malaysia along with Sabah and Sarawak. It was expelled because of heated ideological conflicts between Islamic Kuala Lumpur and Buddhist Singapore. The Peoples Action Party declared independence in 1965 and voted to allow alcoholic beverages, open gambling, and kickboxing to attract tourism. There were 60,000 kick boxers, and prostitution was not a crime.

They retained British common law, but abolished trial by jury because of ethnic diversity. Judicial corporal punishment (caning) was enforced for rape, violence, resisting, graffiti, drug use, vandalism, and illegal immigration.

There was a mandatory death sentence for first degree murder, drug trafficking and firearms. Observed offenses were presumption of guilt. Singapore has the highest execution rate of any city of its size in the world. In 1992 alone, there were 101 Singapore citizens and 40 foreigners executed for drugs. Pirates received no amnesty.

Singapore claimed its sovereign right to have its own laws and impose punishment. Confucius was first to say, "Be good for goodness sake."

Donald was planning on sailing around Indonesia, the Straits of Malacca and Andaman Islands. He and Elvis were negotiating through diplomatic channels to buy a private yacht that traveled at 30 knots and carried a crew of Chinese mercenaries. Modern day pirates, Somali and Oriental, roamed the Indian Ocean from the Straits of Hormuz to the Straits of Malacca.

Bob read.

U.S. DEPARTMENT OF STATE
Background Note: Singapore

HISTORY

Although Singapore's history dates from the 11th century, the island was little known to the West until the 19th century, when in 1819, Sir Thomas Stamford Raffles arrived as an agent of the British East India Company. In 1824, the British purchased Singapore Island, and by 1825, the city of Singapore had become a major port, with trade exceeding that of Malay's Malacca and Penang combined. In 1826, Singapore, Penang, and Malacca were combined as the Straits Settlements to form an outlying residency of the British East India Company; in 1867, the Straits Settlements were made a British Crown Colony, an arrangement that continued until 1946.

The opening of the Suez Canal in 1869 and the advent of steamships launched an era of prosperity for Singapore as transit trade expanded throughout Southeast Asia. In the 20th century, the automobile industry's demand for rubber from Southeast Asia and the packaging industry's need for tin helped make Singapore one of the world's major ports.

In 1921, the British constructed a naval base, which was soon supplemented by an air base. But the Japanese captured the island in February 1942, and it remained under their control until September 1945, when the British returned.

In 1945, the Straits Settlements was dissolved; Penang and Malacca became part of the Malayan Union, and Singapore became a separate British Crown Colony. In 1959, Singapore became self-governing, and, in 1963, it joined the newly independent Federation of Malaya, Sabah, and Sarawak—the latter two former British Borneo territories—to form Malaysia.

Indonesia adopted a policy of "confrontation" against the new federation, charging that it was a "British colonial creation," and severed trade with Malaysia. The move particularly affected Singapore, since Indonesia had been the island's second-largest trading partner. The political dispute was resolved in 1966, and Indonesia resumed trade with Singapore.

After a period of friction between Singapore and the central government in Kuala Lumpur, Singapore separated from Malaysia on August 9, 1965, and became an independent republic.

GOVERNMENT

According to the constitution, as amended in 1965, Singapore is a republic with a parliamentary system of government. Political authority rests with the prime minister and the cabinet. The prime minister is the leader of the political party or coalition of parties having the majority of seats in Parliament. The president, who is chief of state, previously exercised only ceremonial duties. As a result of 1991 constitutional changes, the president is now supposed to be elected and exercises expanded powers over legislative appointments, government budgetary affairs, and internal security matters.

PEOPLE

Singapore is one of the most densely populated countries in the world. The annual population growth rate is 1.8%, including resident foreigners. Singapore has a varied linguistic, cultural, and religious heritage. Malay is the national language, but Chinese, English, and Tamil also are official languages. English is the language of administration and also is widely used in the professions, businesses, and schools.

The government has mandated that English be the primary language used at all levels of the school systems, and it aims to provide at least 10 years of education for every child. Primary and secondary school students total 489,484, or 9.6% of the entire population. Enrollment at public universities is 72,710 (full-time/part-time) with another 80,635 at the polytechnics. The institute of Technical Education for basic technical and commerce skills has 24,846 students. The country's literacy rate is 96.3%.

POLITICAL CONDITIONS

The ruling political party in Singapore, reelected continuously since 1959, is the People's Action Party (PAP), headed by Prime Minister Lee Hsien Loong. The PAP has held the overwhelming majority of seats in Parliament since 1966, when the opposition Barisan Socialis Party (Socialist Front), a left-wing group that split off from the PAP in 1961, resigned from Parliament, leaving the PAP as the sole representative party. In the general elections of 1968, 1972, 1976, and 1980, the PAP won all the seats in an expanding Parliament.

ECONOMY

Singapore's largely corruption-free government, skilled work force, and advanced and efficient infrastructure have attracted investments from more than 7,000 multinational corporations from the United States, Japan, and Europe. Also present are 1,500 companies from China and another 1,500 from India. Foreign firms are found in almost all sectors of the economy. Multinational corporations account for more than two-thirds of manufacturing output and direct export sales, although certain service sectors remain dominated by government-linked companies.

Trade, Investment, and Aid

Singapore continued to attract investment funds on a large scale despite its relatively high-cost operating environment.

The United States leads in foreign investment, accounting for 11.2% of new actual investment in the manufacturing sector. The stock investment by U.S. companies in the manufacturing and services sectors in Singapore is $76.86 billion (total assets). The bulk of U.S. investment is in electronics manufacturing, oil refining and storage, and the chemical industry. About 1,500 U.S. firms operate in Singapore.

Transportation and Communications

Situated at the crossroads of international shipping and air routes, Singapore is a center for transportation and communication in Southeast Asia. Singapore's Changi International Airport is a regional aviation hub served by 80 airlines. A third terminal is dedicated to low-cost budget airlines. The Port of Singapore is the world's busiest for containerized transshipment traffic. Singapore is linked by road and rail to Malaysia and Thailand.

DEFENSE

Singapore relies primarily on its own defense forces, which are continuously being modernized. The defense budget accounts for approximately 33% of government operating expenditures (or 4.3% of GDP). A career military force of 55,000 is supplemented by 300,000 persons, either on active National Service, which is compulsory for able-bodied young men, or on Reserve. The Singapore Armed Forces engage in joint training with Association of Southeast Asian Nations (ASEAN) countries and with the United States, Australia, New Zealand, and India. Singapore also conducts military training on Taiwan.

Singapore is a member of the Five-Power Defense Arrangement together with the United Kingdom, Australia, New Zealand, and Malaysia. The arrangement obligates members to consult in the event of external threat and provides for stationing Commonwealth forces in Singapore.

Singapore has consistently supported a strong U.S. military presence in the Asia-Pacific region. In 1990, the United States and Singapore signed a memorandum of understanding (MOU) which allows United States access to Singapore facilities at Paya Lebar Airbase and the Sembawang wharves. Under the MOU, a U.S. Navy logistics unit was established in Singapore in 1992; U.S. fighter aircraft deploy periodically to Singapore for exercises, and a number of U.S. military vessels visit Singapore. The MOU was amended to permit U.S. naval vessels to berth at the Changi Naval Base.

U.S.-SINGAPORE RELATIONS

The United States has maintained formal diplomatic relations with Singapore since it became independent in 1965. Singapore's efforts to maintain economic growth and political stability and its support for regional cooperation harmonize with U.S. policy in the region and form a solid basis for amicable relations between the two countries. The United States and Singapore signed a bilateral free trade agreement. The growth of U.S. investment in Singapore and the large number of Americans living there enhance opportunities for contact between Singapore and the United States. Many Singaporeans visit and study in the United States. Singapore is a Visa Waiver Program country.

TRAVEL AND BUSINESS INFORMATION

The U.S. Department of State's Consular Information Program advises Americans traveling and residing abroad through Country Specific information, Travel Alerts, and Travel Warnings. Country Specific Information exists for all countries and includes information on entry and exit requirements, currency regulations, health conditions, safety and security, crime, political disturbances, and the addresses of the U.S. embassies and consulates abroad. Travel Alerts are issued to disseminate information quickly about terrorist threats and other relatively short-term conditions overseas that pose significant risks to the security of American travelers. Travel Warnings are issued when the State Department recommends that Americans avoid travel to a certain country because the situation is dangerous or unstable.

CHAPTER 41

Singapore
10 A.M., Tuesday, November 17, 1993
Billowing clouds in the south over Indonesia
Temperature 80°, Tropical

It was "Ash Tuesday", dark clouds, and umbrella day in Singapore. Singapore in Malay is Singapura which means Lion City named after a Bengal tiger once seen but no longer, except in the zoo. It was established as a British trading post by Sir Thomas Stamford Raffles for the British East India Company in 1819. By 1869 it had 100,000 inhabitants. Today it had 5 million and was the most organized, densely populated, and prosperous port city in the world. Close to the equator, its days remain the same hours year around. They attracted 10 million tourists a year.

Singapore introduced Medical Tourism before India. You could get your kidneys and heart replaced and save enough from your insurance to tour Singapore, Malaysia, and Thailand. Like England and Europe, Singapore and the United States had a visa free agreement. Their judicial system was rated number one in SEA while Vietnam and Indonesia were tied for number ten, the lowest. Burma was not rated.

*   *   *

Don addressed the group: Bob, Elvis, Penny and Louiza.

"I'm going to let Bob tell us what he knows about drilling the Bay of Bengal, and what you saw on your helicopter flight over the Brahmaputra-Ganges Delta. Then I'm going to discuss what I know, and you'll ask me questions, okay? Thesis, antithesis, and synthesis! The buck stops here!" he exclaimed, pointing to himself. "No matter how many lectures I listened to at the University, I'm not Bob and Louiza, who've been trained in Geology and jungle work. Louiza has spent time digging in Xian China, is an Amazon guide, and field Geologist.

Hence forward we are National Geographic explorers looking for the last Negritos who previously lived in the jungles of Borneo and Andaman Islands. In reality, there may be a tribe left in the Andaman's, but the Japanese destroyed whole villages and killed 200,000 when they occupied Borneo in WWII. They are cannibals and the men are only 5 feet and the women are 4 feet 10 inches at most. There are Aborigines on all these islands, and if they are over 5 feet they are not Negritos. They use poison darts and arrows, spend most of their time gathering caterpillars off plants and dead animals, and hunt small game. They are close cousins to the African pygmies and probably some of the same bunch. The Belgians tamed those in the Congo (Zaire).

"Bob, whatcha got?"

Bob cleared his throat. "If the volcano keeps up, and the shooting war in the Gulf of Bengal doesn't abate, we might fly over to India or Sri Lanka and take a look at Deccan Traps. Drilling through a mile of basalt is easier than drilling at the bottom of two miles of ocean. It dates back 65 million and probably sits on oil and gas. The Deccan Traps step down from Bombay to Hyderabad, similar to the Llano Estacada in West Texas Permian Basin. Deccan Traps has never been drilled. Some Geologist in Sweden wrote that if you drill deep enough you can find oil anywhere even through granite.

"While the monks were protesting in Rangoon, 9 companies were exploring 29 blocks leased from the Military Junta in Myanmar. That money went to private offshore bank accounts of Than Shwe, and others.

"The companies involved were Total (TOT), Petronas, PTTEP, Dae woo Int. Corp, CNOOC, and Sinopec. CITIC did not bid since they are involved in onshore drilling and fully controlled by the PLA with whom we're partnered in our three land deals, Quanxi Basin, North West Cambodia, and Bama Basin at Batson field in Shan State Myanmar.

"After Naypyidaw, China has remained neutral, however, if Bangladesh appears to be conquering Myanmar, the Chinese will support Myanmar to stop Islam.

"There are no gentlemen in the oil business. The Chinese will cut your throat and drink your blood. You really have to know with whom you are dealing. Nothing would make them happier than to do away with Than Shwee and his thieving sons-of-bitches. Until the ignorant masses in Myanmar rise up in armed rebellion can anybody help them get rid of the ruling military junta who are stealing them blind.

"We have Generals Li Shan and He Wu backing us. We are right, and they are wrong. Land drilling is best. Deep water drilling will contaminate the fisheries. That's true whether it's the Brahmaputra-Ganges Delta, Andaman Islands, Spratly and Parcel Islands in the South China Sea and the Japanese Islands in the East China Sea. There are two islands in the south Indonesia Archipelago that have not been explored. They are Thot and Banda. EXXON has Sumatra and Dutch Royal has Sarawak in East Malaysia on the western third of Borneo. Both go back more than fifty years." Bob stopped and looked at Louiza.

Louiza took over. "It's obvious to me that the Chinese released the atomic bomb over Naypyidaw. Total (TOT) and Petronas are after oil, the deep stuff in the Bay of Bengal.

"Andaman is off the west coast of Myanmar along the Malaysian Peninsula extension of Myanmar. The Continental Waters off the Andaman Islands and the Irrawaddy Delta provide Myanmar a gunboat claim to all the Bay of Bengal except off the southern coast of East Bengal (Bangladesh) and the BPG Delta.

"In the distant past, India claimed the southern half of the Andaman, but they have their own offshore oil fields to protect around Sri Lanka and the continental waters from Mumbai (Bombay) to Karachi Pakistan.

I think you can count Pakistan out. They have internal problems and a divided government.

"For Petronas and Total it is greed and avaris. For China, Sinopec and CNOOC and the Oligarche in Beijing it's gas and a pipeline to Kunming. For Daewoo, it's a chance to make money. They'll lease them drillers. Japan is not interested in the Andaman's or the Bay of Bengal. They'll defend the Spratlys, Parcels, and the hundreds of fishing islands in the East China Sea which China has no claim except the U.S.A. defeated Japan in WWII.

"Gentlemen, The Great American Civil War General Bedford Forrest said, 'Success in battle goes to the one who gets there first with the most'. I'm for land drilling and let the hogs fight over the offshore stuff. After we get in the jungles, I'll be happy to guide you to the oil," said Louiza and stopped.

"Any questions or arguments? This is antithesis time," asked Don.

"What do you want me to do?" asked Penny.

"Look sexy! Play decoy! We will be looking for Negritos. Don't worry! Your time will come. There are pirates and coastal patrols."

"And me? I helped you get around in the Embassy and paid for the big stuff, like the armored yacht and quad fifties. I'll just be dead weight at sea," asked Elvis.

"When we're boarded by Indonesian gun boats and pirates, don your Elvis costume and guitar and sing You Ain't Nothin But a Hound Dog. You're a decoy," replied Don, laughing.

"Okay, tomorrow we'll go on a maiden voyage in our armored yacht, Chinese mercenaries, and quad fifties and motor through the Straits of Malacca to Madden Sumatra. Bring all your stuff and don't forget your Passport. We'll ship out as soon as we can see. I have a Chinese Captain and Pilot, and they refuse to sail in the dark with all the volcanic ash," announced Don, smiling.

"How far is Madden?" asked Elvis, meekly.

"300 nautical miles. If we don't get stopped by pirates, we should make it about dark."

"What about tsunami's?"

"Don't worry! Tsunami means harbor wave. You're okay at sea. Just the people on bank have to worry. You'll get side arms and AK-47's when we go aboard," replied Don.

"Why AK-47's?" asked Bob. He'd never used one although they were ubiquitous in Asia.

"That's the only kind of ammo out here," replied Donald Tantalia. "I got the quad 50's and 0.50 cal. ammo from surplus at the U.S. Embassy.

CHAPTER 42

Downtown Hilton-Heathrow
London England
8 A.M., Tuesday, November 17, 1993
Temperature 50°, Light drizzle

"We've got a couple of hours before our bus takes us to Wales where we catch a ferry to Dublin and Trinity College. We'll walk across the halfpence bridge and visit the Guinness Brewery, the largest brewery in the world named after the *Guinness Book of Records*. Trinity got its name from the Catholic Rosary, Father, Son, and Holy Ghost," announced Maria, giggling. "If you want to go to Blarney Castle and hang down from your knees and kiss the Blarney Stone in this rain and cold, speak now or forever miss the chance of a lifetime."

No hands went up. They were "castled and churched out."

Maria was handed a brown looking envelope by the hotel clerk. She opened, read, sighed, and announced. "This is special delivery from NASA. We've been selected by President Clinton to represent the U.S.A. to ride on the maiden voyage of the supersonic Concordsky to Moscow, take a voyage on a nuclear ice breaker to Saint Petersburg, and be back in three days. We'd spend two nights in Moscow and one night in Saint Petersburg where everything is frozen, and the trains aren't running. That sounds like more fun than kissing the Blarney Stone, and the Russians are picking up the tab."

"This morning I've arranged for Eros to tell us about Guy Fawkes' Day. Aristotle will discuss Westminster Abbey, Saint Paul's, and Henry VIII, and Christy will lecture on the Grand Revolution, William, and Mary, and the Baptists, Shakers, and Quakers. There's a church out there for everybody. Down in Mexico City they have a shrine and Saint for Sinners, Banditos, and prostitutes, not to mention the Virgin of Guadalupe (Devine sky) which had spread to Central America and the Vatican. The Virgin of Guadalupe is right up there with the mother of Jesus in Rome since they're getting 10% of the drug money collected in Mexico. They didn't turn down Mafia money either. Jihad means war without taking loot, like Joshua in the Bible, kill everybody and his dog but don't take booty.

"Then we'll take a break and load up for Wales and the Dublin Ferry.

"Don't forget your money belt and Passport. From here on everything will be Irish potatoes, mutton, and Guinness Stout. You'll have plenty of time later to see the changing of the Royal Guard at Buckingham Palace, Scotland Yard, Big Ben, London Bridge, the Tower of London, the Beefeaters, Harrods's, and My Fair Lady with an aging Julie Andrews and what's-his-name. Audrey Hepburn played Eliza in the movie back in the 60's before I was born."

"Eros."

Dr. Eros Zenovenusetti wrote: **GUY FAWKES, MUERTA DIA, HALLOWEEN, ALL SAINTS DAY, SCAPEGOAT, DRUID PRIEST, MOSH PIT, MUD WRESTLING AND WET T-SHIRT CONTEST**.

"In America all celebrate Halloween as our harvest festival, but in England everybody celebrates Guy Fawkes Day by building bonfires and shooting firecrackers. In antiquity they had a scapegoat replace the King, and everybody threw rotten eggs and complained, like a mosh pit and mud wrestling in wet T-shirts with your best friend. Everybody works off their anger at the Queen or King. Guy Fawkes is a folk hero. History might have been different if he succeeded.

"Mexicans call it Muerta Dea (Dea de los Muerta), the day of the dead, the Mexican's National Holiday honoring their ancestors and death that antedated the Spanish. We celebrate Halloween the last day in October like the Druids, while the Mexicans celebrate November. In

Houston it's 50%-50%. I don't see why they don't combine and celebrate the same day. That's called economy of size. Everybody could wear their skeletons, spooky costumes, have a feast and shoot firecrackers like the English on Guy Fawkes's Day.

"The English celebrate November 5 as Guy Fawkes Day. It was a Catholic plot organized in 1605 to blow up King James I and both houses of Parliament at state opening on November 5, 1605 by exploding barrels of gunpowder stored in the basement of the House of Lords. Guy Fawkes was caught with the explosives before they were detonated, and he and the other conspirators were executed. We saw Fawkes' house in York."

"Aristotle."

Dr. Aristotle Plotinus wrote on the black board. **ELIZABETH, JAMES I, HENRY VIII, ANNE BOLEYN, SIX FINGERS, MARY QUEEN OF SCOTS, TUDORS, STUARTS, QUEEN VICTORIA AND GERMANS**.

"When Queen Elizabeth I had Mary Queen of Scots beheaded in the Tower of London, Mary's son, James I, was next in succession to Elizabeth who died in office in 1603. Elizabeth was daughter of Henry VIII by Anne Boleyn who had six fingers on both hands and was beheaded by Henry VIII in the Tower of London for adultery. Sound complicated? Mary Queen of Scots was daughter of Henry's sister, Margaret, who married King James V of Scotland. The Scots were Stewarts, and the English were Tudors. Mary Queen of Scots changed Stewart to Stuart when she was married to the King of France.

"Henry VII was Earl of Richmond who defeated King Richard III at the battle of Bosworth Field in 1445, and was King of England until his death in 1509.

"Henry VIII, his son, was King of England from 1509 to 1547. Henry was a sportsman and lover. When he failed to get a divorce from his first wife, Catherine of Aragon, he forced Parliament to pass acts making him Supreme Head of the Church of England and renounced the Catholic Church thus establishing the English Reformation and marrying Ann Boleyn who was pregnant with Elizabeth. Henry VIII sister married the King of Scotland, and that's how Mary Queen of Scots' son inherited the throne of England after Elizabeth died.

"Now, I whizzed through all this. If I went into details, we'd be here all day. Hopefully, Christy, will tell you how England got rid of the Stuarts and invited the Germans over here. In fact, the German's are still here. Queen Victoria was German.

"Christy."

Dr. Christy Isaac wrote on the black board. **JAMES II, WILLIAM AND MARY, ANNE, HOUSE OF HANOVER, GEORGE I, JACOBITES AND CULLODEN MOOR**

"Anybody that says they know the details of all English monarchs, wars, and religious disputes and doesn't have a Ph.D. from Oxford or Cambridge is probably fibbing. King Charles II had a brother named James, Duke of York, who became King James II. They ran James II off and invited Mary, daughter of James II and married to William of Orange in the Netherlands, to become Queen Mary II and King William III of England. They weren't strangers. William was the son of Mary, daughter of Charles I of England and William II, Prince of Orange. They didn't produce issue (kids) and next in line was Anne (1702-1714) the second daughter of James II.

"The English Parliament passed the Act of Settlement in 1701 that the English crown would go to the Protestant House of Hanover in Germany. Anne was the last Stuart, and Elizabeth I was the last Tudor. Anne's cousin, George, Elector of Hanover, became George I of England.

"I've been told that the Kings and Queens of Great Britain don't get the Roman numeral after their name until after they die.

"Actually, George I was great grandson of James I, so the Germans that rule England have a tad of Stuart kin.

"Jacobites were followers of James Edward Stuart. Jocobus is Latin for James. In 1746 the English defeated the Jacobites at the battle of Culloden Moor. They killed the clan chiefs and forbade the Scottish Highlanders kilts, bagpipes, and firearms. Bonnie Price Charley fled to France (James' son).

CHAPTER 43

Houston, Texas
8 A.M., Tuesday, November 17, 1993
Temperature 68°/45°
Sunny with few clouds

"May I sit in back and listen when you present to the Grand Jury tomorrow?" asked Deviné, smiling. Defense counsels were barred from Grand Jury hearings. Grand juries either true or no billed. In Houston, true billed went to arraignment where bail and trial date were set usually the Tuesday after the first Monday. Shelby would be arraigned the first Tuesday after New Year's.

Lois Morrison, who had Grand Jury Wednesday, shook her head. Eva chirped in, "Ann Richards and Lois e-mail. Ain't science wonderful? Obviously, we have to get Compac Presario with Windows. I never learned DOS. I took Latin instead of typing in high school," commented Judge Petrarcelli.

Bill Riley rose and went to the black board. "An unidentified homemade miniature submarine was reported crossing under the Brazos River Bridge at Sugar Land yesterday by Captain Jerry Billings. The Brazos doesn't cross into Harris County except when Oyster Creek floods. They have their own municipal police force, very modern, 500 police and 200 new reinforced Fords with computers and cameras. Sugar Land has the lowest crime rate in Texas cities.

"Just because they have low crime, doesn't mean that illegals aren't crossing through Sugar Land or anywhere along the game reserve that borders the Brazos all way up to San Felipe. That's a State Game Reserve.

"During the August to October freeze we lost a lot of undesirable and many illegals went home. They have returned. It looks like Matamoras in southeast Houston and under our overpasses on Texas 35. They have signs saying NO GRINGOS AND BLACKS over their Cantinas. The Vietnamese and SEA are allowed visitation only to enter fighting cocks and dogs. You can drive up and buy marijuana and coke, and select the girl of your dreams for dollars or Pesos. As far as I know, there's been no increase in AIDS, but most of the street girls have herpes and penicillin resistant gonorrhea. Mexicans are macho and won't use condoms. I haven't heard of male prostitution, but they have a Gay Bar.

"Their fighting cocks wear razor blades, and pit bulls kill. They chain them in their back yards.

"We are getting more indigents (Indians) and fewer semi-skilled Mestizos.

"The indigents don't speak English and very little Spanish. They practice animism. They sacrifice animals and drink their blood. Everybody takes a swallow, and they pass it around usually at marriages and funerals. They sit around communal fires and smoke Peyote, see animals, have hallucinations, convulse and in extreme cases go berserk, and run wild with any weapon they can get their hands on, usually a machete or gun.

"Family feuds at formal weddings are typical. The men get drunk and kill their prospective in-laws. Nothing is planned. It's spontaneous. We have a little Rio de Janeiro inside the loop. Actually, the Federal Housing Project is tame, and most Mexican Americans will cooperate. They don't want the indigents here either.

"Around Sugar Land, Katy, Friendswood, and Pearland they can get construction work when sober.

"Look for a surge of illegals after Christmas. Up the Brazos!

* * *

"Are you going to A. Fuller Bottle's Rosary? Afterward, his wife, Mellita, will have him cremated," asked Deviné of Opal.

"Rich may be with me. A. Fuller sued him for $100,000,000," replied Opal.

"You all quit looking for A. Fuller's killer? Who amputated his head in Sandra's office?" asked Deviné, confused.

"Rene' Descarte Gilbert said he was ET and quit looking. Autopsy was confirmatory. It's a closed case. Rene' stopped looking. 25% of unsolved murders in Canada are performed by ET, and they close the case. 100% of big explosions of unknown cause are due to ET. Spontaneous Combustion in humans are due to gamma rays from the 4th dimension, like the Buck Roger's comics."

* * *

Unknown to Opal and Deviné, Dr. Richard Bernstein represented Israel in Sword Fighting in the Seoul Olympics. He was on Student Visa.

* * *

Captain Jerry Billings read the historical marker.

> *Saint Nicholas University is the second oldest fully accredited university in Houston. It is private, financed by an endowment started by Don Allergeri Tantalia in 1934. Don Allergeri entered this country in 1905 at the age of fifteen and never learned to read and write English, but by 1934 he was the richest man in Houston. A devout Catholic, his idea was to build a Catholic college for immigrant and underprivileged boys.*

His son, Donald Tantalia, took over at his death in 1940. Donald enlarged the college to meet the demands of the three military services in

WWII, and after the war made it coed and expanded the facilities to meet the requirements of a complete university with all liberal arts and sciences represented. The College of Science was further expanded to meet the needs of the National Space Agency and the ever expanding petrochemical industry in southeast Texas. It receives large grants from the government and private industry for research in the biological and physical sciences.

Despite its rich endowment and rapid expansion, SNU kept Don Allergeri's dream of a school for immigrants and the underprivileged by offering five hundred full scholarships a year to those who meet his benevolent wishes. Now SNU has an enrollment of 10,000 students of which 2,000 live on campus. English, a foreign language, is required of every student and is required as a minor by every graduating student expecting to enter the professions or private industry.

CHAPTER 44

Barclay Theater
University of Saint Nicholas
Houston, Texas
12 noon, Tuesday, December 17, 1993

Dr. Amy Omikami was at the lectern. Her predictions for the 21ˢᵗ Century was pulled down over the green board.

PREDICTIONS FOR THE 21ˢᵀ CENTURY

1. *Jesus was an extraterrestrial.*
2. *Extraterrestrials are here from the fourth dimension to steal our bodies for cloning experiments.*
3. *Gene action is through networks of genes that have activation, stimulatory and inhibitory feedback loops.*
4. *Nanotechnology will construct enzymes, anti enzymes and proteins that will replace all chemically synthesized pharmaceuticals.*
5. *Sleep and consciousness will be demonstrated on PET and MRI as a neuro-physiological phenomena and will explain objectively Freud's clinical observations.*
6. *Cognitive research will establish conclusively that homosexuality occurs subconsciously only in men. Same sex in females is mutually voluntary masturbation on a conscious level (free will).*
7. *Nanotechnology will change every aspect of our lives.*

8. *Quantum Physics, General Relativity and the Theory of Everything (TOE) will be taught in the 8ᵗʰ grade. The scientific origins of life and molecular biology will be taught in the 9ᵗʰ grade.*

9. *Earth sciences will be taught in the 3ʳᵈ grade.*

10. *Our gravity telescopes will make natural disasters, gravitons, and gravity waves easily detectible and replace satellite weather forecasts.*

11. *Bosons and Higgs field will explain weak nuclear force.*

12. *Dark force that is pushing our universe out faster and faster will be determined to be negative energy which occurs naturally in a complete vacuum at zero absolute temperature.*

13. *Religion will merge with science, philosophy, and metaphysics as a cultural unification, and they will be taught as one discipline on the post graduate level at our best universities, making doctrinal seminaries obsolete, absurd, and boring.*

"Has everybody read this? If not, stop by, and I'll give you a copy." She raised "Predictions," and wrote on the green board. **WORLD TERRORISM, PARADIGM SHIFT IN HOUSTON CRIME, AND WAR IN THE TWENTY FIRST CENTURY**.

"This morning Dr. Levitra Battenberg will discuss international terrorism. At the time Maria rescued Levitra she was the British attaché to our American Embassy in New Delhi and consultant to Interpol on Terrorism and Islam.

"I invited a guest speaker, Captain Jerry Billings DPS. Jerry is graduate of the University of Texas Law School with a Doctor in Laws degree. She has a gubernatorial powers of Texas Ranger, and judicial powers of State District Judge for Search and Seizure, and is a member of Governor Ann Richard's Committees on Narcotics. Jerry answers directly to the Governor and Commander of the Texas Department of Public Safety. Her office is in Conroe, Texas, and her immediate territorial assignments are Montgomery, Harris, and Galveston Counties.

"Jerry is a home grown graduate from Bellaire High, Texas University and TU Law School where she was recruited by Governor Clements to join the Governor's Task Force on Drugs. Captain Billings will discuss a paradigm shift in intercity crime.

"Finally, General Trudy Grits will discuss war in the 21st Century.

"President Clinton has nominated our fellow classmates to be guest of the Russians to ride round trip from London to Moscow on their new and improved Concordsky and take a nuclear powered ice breaker to Saint Petersburg for a one night stay. It only takes 2 hours to fly to Moscow on a Concordsky and about 3 hours to go by ice breaker to Saint Petersburg. So we're not talking about a long travel time, and it's free.

"The Weather Man says ice and snow all up and down the North American east coast, northern Europe, Russia, and anywhere else in the Northern Latitudes. The Concordsky flies at 60,000 feet way above the snow clouds. Actually the Russians rented the Concordsky from the French. Theirs blew up on test flight at an European Air Show in 1973 with a full complement of flight crew and passengers aboard. They'll have a Russian flight crew and plenty of Vodka. You have to wear an oxygen mask at greater than 40,000 feet, so you can't smoke.

"The nose of the Concorde turns down so the pilot can see the runway when landing and taxing to and from the runway.

"Briefly, the Aerospatiale-BAC Concorde is a supersonic jumbo jet passenger airplane designed by the English and French governments which was first flown experimentally in 1969, entered routine flight service in 1976, and has satisfactorily flown commercially for 17 years. It is twice as fast as other airplanes if you are in a hurry. To be honest I think teleconferences, telephoning, and riding coach on a Boeing 747-400 is a lot more relaxing and a lot cheaper.

"The Concorde gets 14 miles per passenger per gallon. The Gulf Stream Business Jet that carries 7 and cruises at 50,000 feet gets 16 passenger miles per gallon, and the Boeing 747-400 gets 91. The Concorde costs 4 times coach air fare, uses up 5 times as much gasoline, and only gets there twice as fast as a Boeing 747 where you can smoke in first class, drink whiskey, go to the bathroom, and take a nap."

"Levitra."

Dr. Levitra Battenberg wrote on the green board. **TERROR, POLITICS, FANATICISM, RELIGION, JIHADIST, SUICIDE BOMBING, ANARCHIST, ASSASSINS, WWI, VERDON, TRENCH WARFARE, ARMENIANS, GENOCIDE, BOLSHEVIKS, LENIN, RED OCTOBER, STALIN, AND THE GREAT PURGES**.

"Terror is planned violence to cause fear, panic, and transformation for political gains. It's used against civilians, non combatants and innocents. An idea legitimizes the acts for a better world or future. It requires fanaticism, sacrifice, commitment, and justification in the beliefs of the perpetrators.

"I don't have to get deep into definitions or examples. Our newspapers and TV are replete with suicide bombings, North Korea threatening to 'nuke' us, Islamic Jihadist, Al-Qaeda, IRA and Spanish Basques. Captain Billings will tell us about local gangs. There are certain hotspots and countries you don't want to visit. The U.S. State Department puts out a list and warnings which are available at any Consulate or Embassy and on the Internet. Costa Rica is the only nation in South America not on that list. The rest are too dangerous.

"Anarchist try to stir the masses to revolution. Assassins seek personal glory and infamy.

"In the Battle of Vernon in WWI, 700,000 French and German soldiers were killed. Millions were killed. Half the dead were never recovered or identified. The Ottomans massacred a million Armenians in deliberate genocide.

"The Bolsheviks took power in 'Red October' of 1917. They executed Tsar Nicholas II and his family on July 16, 1918.

"WWI killed 10 million and wounded twice that number, called the 'lost generation.' There were 20 million displaced refugees. Civil War in Russia 1918-1922 killed another 10 million. Lenin died in 1924, and by 1927 Stalin was in charge after having Trotsky assassinated and opponents purged. 10 million Russians died in the famine of 1932-1933. In subsequent terrors and purges several millions died. In 1937, 9 of 10 generals were executed along with half the officer corps. The Gulag held 2 million and forced labor accounted for 15% of the economy.

"Mussolini introduced a new paradigm in government by combining nationalism and revolution. He organized black shirt gangs, murdered political opponents, and marched on Rome. By 1929, Mussolini was 'Il Duce', dictator of Rome. He defined fascism as 'action', and his regime as totalitarian.

"Many countries followed suit and by 1939 60% of European countries had authoritarian governments, and four in South America, Peru, Bolivia, Brazil, and Venezuela. They got that way by force and terrorism. Tomorrow I'll take up Japanese Imperialism, the Spanish Civil War, Ethiopia, and Nazi Germany.

"Captain Billings."

Captain Billings wrote on the green board. **URBAN SPRAWL, GANGS, OUTSIDE THE LOOP, MEXICAN CARTELS, TEXAS SYNDICATE, BROTHERHOOD OF LATIN GUNMEN, CRIPS, BLOODS, AND THE SOUTH WEST CHOLOS**.

"As I speak, there are 230 documented organized criminal gangs in the Houston Metropolitan Area. Gang recruitment is at an all-time high, and they are getting younger, more violent and ruthless. Boys and girls! They are spreading to the suburbs. Why? New found connections with Mexico's well financed and organized crime syndicates. Plain and simple! This is not California. Texas' traffickers and dealers have to import their narcotics from Mexico across our 1000 mile border.

"A gang named Houstonas has 2500 members confirmed by police.

"Our gangs are involved in such criminal acts as burglary, robbery, kidnapping, extortion, money laundering, drug trafficking, and street dealing. Some perform murder for hire.

"According to DEA and National Gang Assessment reports, Houston has more, by far, than any city in Texas. They have more active members than our city has police officers. They claim to have the names of at least 10,000 documented by arrests who admitted to be gang members.

"There is no part of Houston or the surrounding area that does not have a gang presence. That includes our most exclusive neighborhoods and businesses. You can probably buy Meth, crack, marijuana, and Ecstasy at the airport or in the Galleria. Sugar Land has the lowest crime rate in Texas, but it's out there. You might be able to buy drugs in NASA.

"The general movement is from inner city to suburbs to rural areas. Most are into trafficking and wholesale, not street selling. They carry cash and weapons including grenades and grenade launchers.

"The second largest gang are 52 Hoover Crips, Treetop Bloods, Bounty Hunters, Southwest Cholos, and Texas Syndicate.

"The Texas Syndicate extends from Houston to the Mexican Border, and, so far, 10 have been imprisoned for murders and robberies. Another Latin gang is the Brotherhood of Latin Gunmen.

"The Houstones wear Astro caps and emblems. Conflicts between gangs are not good for business. They try not to draw attention. Drugs travel north and money and guns go south to below the border.

"In summary, there're more gangs now than before. They are outside the loop. I don't think we need more cops or more money. They are smarter. Before we can arrest somebody or stop and search, we must have probable cause. We need to get smarter. Demand exceeds supply. Thank you."

"General Trudy Grits."

General Grits wrote on the green board. **GUY FAWKES, OVERPOPULATION, CULTURE, ASYMMETRICAL WARFARE,**

JIHADISTS, SUICIDE BOMBERS, OASIS WITH 40 VIRGINS, FANATICAL FUNDAMENTALISTS, OIL, NUCLEAR THREATS, STOCK MARKET, AND FLASH CRASHES.

"Who was the first modern terrorist conspirator? Guy Fawkes! He and his conspirators were English Catholics whose 'gun powder' plot tried to blow up King James and the Protestant English Parliament on November 5, 1605. In England, they celebrate Guy Fawkes Day like we celebrate April Fool's Day and Halloween. They dress up, feast, and shoot firecrackers like the Chinese New Year. Instead of Dragons, they have dummies of Guy Fawkes.

"If unchecked, a one cell bacteria divides every twenty minutes and would cover the entire earth a foot deep in twenty-four hours. Elephants would eat up the foliage, and cover the entire earth in 100 years. Wars, natural disasters, famine, diseases, and death, the four horsemen of the Apocalypse, are terrible to those experiencing them but are necessary to keep the population in check. The population of humans doubles every 40 years. By 2040, there will be 12 billion mouths to feed. People are making little kids much faster than modern old folks are dying off. China is the only country that restricts births.

"If you want to estimate the future population of any country, count the women in child bearing age and multiply times the average number of births per female.

"Back 500 years ago, conquering Armies would kill off the men, rape the women, and take off the kids to sell or use as slaves. Terrible! Now we have the Geneva Convention and the rules of modern warfare, and wars are more civilized.

"Terrorist wage war on civilians, innocents, and the unsuspecting. They are sneaky, like blowing up the World Trade Center during the busiest time of day. Like a pregnant woman in a bourqa blowing up a market place or the mad bomber sending it in the U.S. Mail. Like North Korea and Iran threatening to 'nuke' everybody. During the Cold War, the United States and the Soviet Union built enough nuclear warheads to blow up the world. It was called mutual deterrence. Castro and

Khrushchev were planning on putting nuclear warhead guided missiles in Cuba. I hope you saw the movie. Bobby Kennedy saved the world from mutual destruction. That was 1962, three years before I was born. It would be like an asteroid striking planet earth and knocking off the moon.

"Warfare is an expression of culture. There will always be wars, have and have nots, rich and poor. The race does not always go to the biggest and fastest, but that is the way to bet.

"The U.S. Army has become an ultramodern high tech fighting machine. We must stay prepared to fight China and Russia in their homeland on a large scale. Unfortunately, we've been fighting poorly equipped armies in jungles and deserts. Deserts are preferable to mountains and jungle. In the end, it's boots on the ground and the assault rifle that wins and holds ground.

"Asymmetrical wars are where two opposing sides use different types of warfare. We use so-called WWII Geneva Conventional warfare, and the other side uses terrorism. Most of world conflicts are carried out against poorly equipped armies, militias, and gangs. Insurgents stage a surprise attack and disappear into civilian population or use civilians for shields. The AK-47 is light and inexpensive, and child soldiers have increased. Half of Pol Pot's soldiers were juveniles. Boys 10 years old and up are made soldiers in Africa.

"The computer Internet is used by insurgents and terrorists. Cell phones can remotely detonate bombs.

"The local gangs of which Captain Billings spoke are using cell phones to avoid detection and militarize crime. In Mexico soldiers desert and join the drug cartels where the pay is better and it's safer. The 50 caliber sniper rifle is popular in Mexico. One bullet can tear a human half in two. Piracy has emerged along the coasts of East Africa and Southeast Asia. So far, our Navy has not intervened. They are busy protecting South Korea, Japan, and Taiwan from the Chinese and North Koreans. India and Bangladesh play war games with our Navy, but buy their fighter aircraft from Russia. The Chinese have a submarine tender in the Andaman Islands protecting their gas and oil interest in the Bay of Bengal and the South China Sea.

"Stock market reactions may deter war. No country wants its stocks to go down, too much civic unrest. Every time the price of oil goes down Iran threatens to 'nuke' somebody, usually Israel. Russia is helping Iran with their nuclear program and selling them long range ballistic missile.

"Our biggest problem is Supernatural. What to do about Islamic fundamentalism? Modern Islam is not violent. Wahabism, Taliban, Al-Qaeda, and Shiaism are fundamentalist and Jihadist. Jihad means war without taking loot, like Joshua at Jericho.

"Volunteer forces are certainly more effective than conscripts. We learned that in Vietnam. Educated officers and enlisted men and women make better soldiers.

"Tomorrow, I'll discuss the economics of war. You'll be surprised. Capitalist countries make money, modernize their economy, and drive technological innovations. The economy booms, the GDP rises, and the costs of war make up less and less of the GDP. It's like the survivors of the Bubonic Plague, there's more of everything.

"In Vietnam we lost 50,000 in 10 years, and they lost 3 million. In Desert Storm, we lost 12 soldiers, and they lost hundreds of thousands and hightailed it back to Bagdad and left most of their equipment.

CHAPTER 45

Dirk not wanting to get lost in the river bottom of Fort Bend and Austin Counties west of Katy consulted his Reader's Digest *TRAVEL GUIDE USA*. He didn't trust Texas maps when it came to rivers and forests.

There were two towns, Simonton and Wallis, bordering the Brazos River that ran through Sugar Land and Katy. Just north of IH-10 on the bank of the Brazos was San Felipe de Austin, now a historical marker, the first Capital of Texas.

About 3 miles west on IH-10 was Sealy, Texas which bordered on the northwest of Fort Bend County. Simonton was in Fort Bend County and San Felipe and Wallis were across the Brazos in Austin County. There were two Parks and Wildlife Refuges, San Felipe and Brazos Bend.

Dirk refused to motor up the Brazos in his bass boat for obvious reasons. There were 70 miles of meandering river with sandbars, stumps, horseshoe lakes, steamboat dock pilings, downed trees, sunk steamboats, etc., etc. and on and on, that could rip out his bottom and break the transom, and he would lose his $6000 Black Max Mercury sunk to the bottom.

During his lifetime, Dirk had made every possible mistake a bass fisherman with a $30,000 (plus) fiberglass boat bass rig could make. The easiest way to kill yourself was to hit an invisible piling going 60 mph.

Dirk dialed Sheila Mellons (Sergeant HPD, Vice) and woke her.

"Whatcha doing?" asked Dirk.

"You bastard! I'm pole dancing and waiting tables at the Foxy Woman. You woke me. Time and tide wait for no man. That's from the *Holy Bible*," answered Sheila, waking.

Dirk was tempted, but sex was the last thing on his mind. Dirk had to watch it with Sheila. He found out indirectly from her partner, Miguel Montalban, that he, Dirk, was her only guy. When he was 38, okay, but he was nearer 46. Sheila was still a young chick. "Didn't you grow up in Needmore?"

"Needville! For goodness sake! You woke me for that? Come on, I'll wait."

*   *   *

Dirk carried two cards, OSHA MAN and HAVE GUN WILL TRAVEL. He needed to go by Black's Appliances on South Main and see if they remembered him when he, Frieda, and Evita stole Jésus $5 million out of Cecile's husband's warehouse and find out from Carmaleta what she did with it.

While Sheila slipped into denim and high top shoes plus her usual police belt, flashlight, and concealed weapons, Dirk stepped across the hall and was met at the door by Carmaleta Posadas.

"You heard Jésus is back. I saw him at our house on Dewberry," announced Carmaleta.

Dirk smiled. "What did you do with the $5 million of Jésus' we recovered from the warehouse at Black's Appliances?"

"I spent some buying Juan Baptista's house, fixing up our place on Dewberry, and taking flying lessons from Hernan Costello, my brother. Jésus owned a third of that plane."

Dirk sighed, "I need to know where the money is."

"Nothing to worry about. Misty at the El Cyuga State Bank deposited all $US 5 million in the Yokohama-Kyoto Bank and extended me a line of credit at the El Cyuga at 5% interest."

*   *   *

"Dirk, where did you meet Carmaleta?" asked Sheila, en route.

Dirk decided on his Jeep Grand Wagoneer because it had an extra low power gear and new mud tires. There would be marsh, and he didn't want to get bogged down if possible.

"I met her in the family waiting rooms and coffee shop at Del Arroyo the night Juan Baptista was shot. She was a widow then. I believe Jésus was assassinated by Lupe Lopez in April. Carmaleta returned from her home in Matamoras to attend Jésus' funeral. I specifically remember she would not identify his body in the morgue," replied Dirk.

Katy was once an oilfield town. Before the Civil War it was a sugar plantation and afterwards they grew rice using flooding irrigation from the Brazos. The railroad came through, put up a station, and they named it Katy after the telegraph operator.

Now it had 12,000 middle class with 75% whites and 25% Mexicans inside the city limits, and 200,000 upper middle class and almost rich whites, Hindus, SEA and Muslims living outside the city limits of Katy, but inside the tax jurisdiction of Greater Houston. It was part of the Baytown-Houston-Clear Lake-Humble and Sugar Land Metropolitan area. All up and down IH-10 west from Houston to the crossover lights at Katy were ultra modern shopping malls and housing developments which from the back and mostly hidden by privacy fences were luxury homes in the $150,000 to $300,000 range with backyard swimming pools, lighted tennis courts, and jogging paths. People walked their dogs and carried a plastic bag and poo poo scooper. They had 60,000 pooper scoopers riding bicycles and drawing city pay in Paris France. After you got on IH-10, it was a ten minute drive to downtown Houston.

Dirk turned at the sign to Stephen F. Austin State Park and drove a quarter mile on a two lane asphalt hardtop to a historical marker and a hewed square log two room dog trot house that had all shutters closed and was locked. There was no one around, so he and Sheila parked, got out and inspected a fancy new replica of Stephen Austin's office and home.

It was built without nails just using an axe. However, the ladders running up to the lofts on both sides were painted iron. They had moved it back from the river, and it was sitting on two feet blocks with enough space underneath for dogs, potatoes and watermelons. The original was built in 1824 and was the capital of Anglo-Mexico. They drove to the wood line and found a rusty barbed wire fence with a NO TRESPASSING sign.

The ground was dusty, the grass was low protein costal, and the trees were scrubby, nothing like his place. There were no giant oaks, vines, Spanish Moss, and Cypress trees. Nothing on which you could hang a full grown man, no cottonwoods.

More important, he didn't see any recent or old campfires, food wrappers, discarded cigarettes, or bottles suggesting illegals had camped there. When he got to the bridge, he was surprised to see the Brazos low with sandbars on either side, clear not muddy, and with very slow current. There were places he could walk across. They weren't opening the locks at Possum Kingdom, and there hadn't been any rain or runoff. The tide was out! The Brazos was tidal to IH-10. The Trinity was the same. All rivers run to the sea. When the tide comes in at the beach, the river rises. Lakes do the same. A midget submarine could only come up so far or it would get stuck when the tide went out. *Time and tide wait for no man* thought Dirk.

"You ever use moon tables to go fishing?" asked Sheila, smiling.

"I don't believe in Astrology," replied Dirk, chuckling. They bite best when the tide comes in at the beach and best when the tide starts going out in a river. It took millions of years for salt water fish to learn to swim in fresh water. Actually, moving water brings bait fish to the bass either way. They hide in wait, and face upstream.

*   *   *

Sealy was across the river in Austin County. It was an easy 30 minute commute to Houston on IH-10 west on the west bank of the Brazos. It was the home of football All-American Eric Dickerson, NFL Hall of Famer. Houston was growing out the major Interstates like a giant amoeba incorporating every community in its pathway. Actually main street of Sealy was 50 miles west downtown Houston and located just across the Brazos. It was home of the Sealy Mattress Company created in 1881. They got a railroad in 1879. Population was 5000 with whites 75%, blacks and Asians 13%, and Mexicans 30% which was seasonal. 15% were below the poverty line. Sealy was the home of Blinn Junior College whose football program was haven to senior college athletes of exceptional aptitude who could not read or otherwise pass. Unfortunately, Texas' high schools graduated some great athletes that couldn't read. They were enrolled in Blinn for remedial work and football. It was legal to sign your name with an X in Texas, like *Will Penny*.

Austin County had a total population of 25,000 not counting migrants. Bellville was its seat. In the whole county 60% of couples living together were married. 12% were below poverty line. Obviously, prosperity stopped at the east bank of the Brazos.

Dirk turned south at the red light in Sealy and sped to Wallis, population 1200, only 5 miles south on Tex 36. Its racial composition was 70% white, 25% Mexican and 14% black and SEA. 58% of couples were married. 12% of households were below poverty line.

At the light in Wallis, Dirk turned east on a two lane hardtop where a sign read Brazos River 1, Simonton 4, Rosenberg 12, and Richmond 15.

A concrete and steel bridge crossed over the Brazos River one mile east of Wallis. Next to it was an old rusted iron railway bridge, now abandoned and in pieces. The River was low and barely moving. Dirk estimated 30-40 yards across with Sandbars on either side on inside of curves as far as he could see. Again, no willows, large oaks, Spanish Moss or Cypress. The soil was sandy, dry, dusty and would barely grow low nutrient grass, and scrub oaks.

Dirk drove off the road, and back under the bridge up to the bank where huge concrete pilings supporting the bridge had big stacks of driftwood from previous floods. They hadn't been cleared, ever. There was no place to drive under the bridge or along the east bank.

Under the bridge he found a few coals of an ancient campfire, a couple of empty sardine cans back in the brush, and that was all. He and Sheila walked up and down the bank and found nothing to suggest campsites, illegal aliens, hunters or anybody had been there, not even a used condom or beer can.

"Don't couples park and neck anymore?" asked Dirk, chuckling.

"You're telling your age. They neck on a couch and watch TV," replied Sheila, giggling.

*   *   *

"Did you know Jésus before he was gunned down by Lupe at Little Mexico Mall? Carmaleta couldn't identify him in the morgue, but she did yesterday. You think she was imagining things?" asked Dirk.

"I don't remember him. Miguel and I were working southwest Houston. I guess I heard about him. In Houston, Jésus is very common name. Posadas is Spanish for hotel," replied Sheila. "She seemed sincere to me. I believe her."

Dirk hadn't told anybody, but he definitely saw a ghost in June on the bank of Buffalo Bayou. It was the real thing. Something he'd never forget. The ghost left his footprints in the mud after he vanished.

*   *   *

"What can you tell me about Needmore?" asked Dirk.

"Needville! Needmore is like Bear Creek and Coonskin. The Post Office changed it to Needville because there were too many Needmores.

"I was born in Bandera. My dad was a DPS trooper. My mother was a music and dance teacher, and we moved to Needville when I was three. I went to K through 12 at Needville High and Lamar University in Beaumont where I got a B.S. in Criminal Justice and Fine Arts.

"I found immediate employment with Houston HPD, and after my obligatory 3 years as a patrolwoman, I was assigned to VICE, promoted to Sergeant Undercover, and here I am. Miguel Montalban and I have been together as a team. Don't ask me my age or personal questions. You don't get experience by reading books. Knowledge yes, but you get experience by doing.

"Dirk, I'll never forget the day you gave me a five dollar tip and bought me a beer when I was dancing topless at the Charisma Lounge. It was love at first sight. Please don't tell anybody I said this, but having sex with you is like fuckin' my own Dad. I loved it."

Dirk had difficulty concentrating on detecting with Sheila along, or anybody else for that matter. Real detective work required systematic thought.

"I'm looking for places illegal aliens and Mexicans can come up from the coast and follow our rivers and infiltrate the greater Houston Metropolitan area. They are 25% in most of these towns and 50% inside loop 610 in Houston. They're 70% in Heights and 100% up Texas 35, and SE Houston is beginning to look like Matamoras, for goodness sake."

Sheila thought and was silent which was a relief.

"About halfway between West Columbia and Needville, there's an old road through the wilds that's been closed off by the forest rangers as too dangerous. I went with my Dad when I was about seven, 1967 or 1968. There's an old filling station and country store that sold live bait and groceries to campers. They closed it off because the alligators got too bad. If you follow that road down to the river, you can launch and motor up the river two miles until you come to 10 MILE BAYOU which meanders north parallel to the river for ten miles to 10 MILE ISLAND.

"The Island is on a rise and has uncut pine. 10 MILE BAYOU was once called PINE ISLAND BAYOU. That was an old Karankawa village. It was sacred ground where they buried their dead. It's haunted. Nobody goes there.

"That's all I remember. It's way south of Needville which is headquarters of the Brazos Bend State Park. That has alligators and lots of feral hogs and deer. It's run by Texas Parks and Wildlife and is mostly a tourist trap, but nice. They sell campsites and hookups for trailers. They open it for hunting on certain days to keep the game down," answered Sheila.

"Why don't we go back and look?" asked Dirk.

"I'm not crazy," replied Sheila. "We'd probably bog down and have to walk out. Get Miguel Montalban. This Jeep wouldn't help in that muck. You need a power winch and a long cable with a hook on the end."

CHAPTER 46

The Raffles Hotel
Singapore
8 A.M., Wednesday, December 18, 1993
79°, billowing black clouds over Indonesia and rocks falling from sky

There were 18,000 islands in Indonesia and 129 active volcanoes. Mount Merapi, the most active, had been rumbling and grumbling for weeks belching hot ash and rocks high in the air. The locals paid no mind and went about their business, like "ho hum." Volcanologists were predicting a hundred year eruption, and energy was building up. Big eruptions caused earthquakes which caused tsunamis which drowned people and swept away coastal villages all way to Sri Lanka and India.

The islands had an estimated population of 250,000,000 which were increasing at an alarming rate. 40,000 lived on and around Mount Merapi most of whom were farmers and herders and refused to leave their crops and livestock. Disasters were commonplace, and there were new mouths to feed. Most were headhunters and cannibals before Islam and Christianity. There were no shortages of little kids.

Mercenaries were available for hire, and land drilling was cheaper and less risky. Any gunboat or hostile plane could destroy an offshore drilling rig.

The Philippines had announced they were enlarging their Navy. The USA was protecting Japan, South Korea, Taiwan, and the Philippines from Chinese encroachment. The US Navy was playing war games with South Korea, Bangladesh and India. They would keep open the Straits of Malacca through which all shipping supplying oil to those countries had to pass.

India was the world's largest democracy, and Indonesia was the world's largest Islamic nation and presumably a democracy. Undemocratic China, now going capitalistic, was a bully. Nobody ever made any money dealing with the Chinese. China was making unrealistic claims in the East and South China Seas and was no doubt responsible for the atomic bomb blast over Naypyidaw which precipitated the invasion of Bangladesh across their common border and declared war on Myanmar who had drilled for gas in their disputed territorial waters.

China would not stand by and let Bangladesh overrun resource rich Myanmar. Washington was demanding "human rights." Russia had plenty of gas and oil and other than selling arms to favorites, had no real interest in SEA and South China Seas. North Vietnam, once a Soviet protégé, was counting on the US Navy to protect their islands in the South China Sea.

Sumatra, Java, thousands of islands and most of Indonesia lay to the south and southeast of Singapore. 300 miles east of Singapore across the straits of Singapore and the South China Sea was Borneo, the third largest island in the world.

Politically and by force of arms, Borneo was divided by three countries: Malaysia (26%), Indonesia (73%) and Brunei (1%). Brunei was a sultanate protected by Great Britain and owned 99% of the wealth thanks to Royal Dutch Shell who had exclusive rights to drill its rich offshore oil reserves. Sarawak and Sabah making up the rest of the east coast were part of Malaysia. The rest of the islands made up of mountains and jungles containing the last Orangutans and the wild men of Borneo belonged to Indonesia.

The Orangutan females were sexy and would come on to a human male. The Japanese Army occupied Borneo during WWII, killed off many natives and used Orangutans as 'comfort girls.' Bob knew of no missing links. Before white men came all natives were headhunters and cannibals and practiced animism where drinking blood from a communal cup was a universal practice, same as South America when the Spanish arrived.

Drinking human and animal blood from a communal cup was a sacrament by all primitive tribes if you went back far enough. It was practiced in Africa, Indonesia, and the Americas. The Romans knew that when they invented the Eucharist. By speaking Latin over red wine and wafer, they changed it to Jesus' body and blood. Just like the primitives still think they incorporate the spirit and courage of their slain enemy when they drink his blood and eat his flesh. The heart was the seat of his soul. The Aztecs were sacrificing a 1000 live humans a day when Cortez arrived. The natives of Indonesia and Borneo out in the jungles were headhunters and cannibals and still practiced animism.

*   *   *

Don Tantalia and Elvis Presley were elsewhere tending to business and left Penny and Bob to entertain themselves in the ultra modern new Raffles Hotel in the middle of downtown Singapore. The Chinese crew and British captain refused to navigate the Malaccan Straits with ash blotting out the sun and rocks falling from the sky bigger than baseballs. Helicopters wouldn't fly and commercial aircraft were grounded. The peat bogs in Borneo were burning and smoking up the place.

When Don called it off, they had a couple of drinks at the Raffles' bar and came back up to their room where they promptly had sex and Penny went to sleep. He had her trained. He could tap on her on shoulder, and she would roll on her back, spread her legs, and hold out her arms like a female Orangutan.

Bob chuckled. Deer Cave in Borneo was 300 feet deep in bat shit (guano) and housed four million bats. Mount Kinabalu was 15,000 feet above sea level and surrounded by dense jungle. During their occupation of Borneo in WWII, the Japanese sent 10,000 British and Australian prisoners to Borneo and only 6 survived.

Reading about Borneo was better than going there. Drilling offshore would be profitable. Australia and Borneo were like pussy on a fat woman. Everybody knew it was there but nobody cared.

CHAPTER 47

After three drinks, Penny asleep, and nothing to do, Bob lay across his bed and took a nap. He dreamed in Technicolor.

Jack flew over the drilling rig which looked huge from above and circled the production platform a mile off where a reddish white hot flame sprang from the waves and shot high into the sky. The blazing column was visible for miles. It would die out a few seconds only to erupt again and shoot flames skyward.

The production platform was about two hundred yards from the sky blaze which put itself out for about 15 to 30 seconds then re-ignite and send roaring flames 1,000 feet into the air. It was frightening!

The tethered production platform looked unscathed. Service boats had towed it aside, and they could see workers in fireproof suits on deck. A dark stain of oil spread from the blaze, but it was gas that bubbled up, flared and re-flared, out of control.

Jack flew back to the drilling rig and circled above a helicopter pad that stuck out over the waves off the main deck. Beside the rig it looked small and hazardous.

The semi submersible bobbled on the waves like a cork with a fish on the line. It was half a football field wide and a football field long. A three decker, on top was a drilling rig from which drill pipe ran down through 1500 feet of water and 10,000 feet of sea floor. Two cranes stuck out over the water, and stacks of drill stem, casing, and drilling mud were nearby. Pumps, tanks, motors, blowers, cables, and busy men in orange coveralls and blue hardhats added noise and excitement.

The semi submersible rode on hollow concrete columns that could be adjusted in depth or height by pumping in or out water. They had raised the bottom deck up above the waves, and there was no way all the air would go out. It would just float, if they lost their moorings.

They slowly descended to the helicopter pad and two men ran out with cables to secure the helicopter. They took off their earmuffs. They had learned not to yell above the noise of the chopper blades.

Jack stayed and helped tie down the helicopter, and Bob led them down to the second deck and unlatched the door to a big room. Everything was built to withstand big waves and rough weather. He led them into a cozy lounge for recreation and relaxation which had a walk through cafeteria line and kitchen. The dining tables and booths were bolted to the floor. A cook stood behind a counter and served breakfast to workers just coming in or going out, whatever. There were women in orange coveralls and hardhats and segregated facilities on board. Not quite a college dorm, however.

Bob led them to coffee. They drew up a cup and sat down at an empty table.

"At least we found the drilling rig this time. I'm going to drink this coffee, tell you what's here, and give you a quick tour of the rig. Then I'm going to motor over to the production platform and see if I can help Keats and Beets fix the leak and put out the fire.

"People on a drilling rig in the Gulf get good pay, work 12 hours a day, sleep, eat, and watch TV. Most are seasoned workers. You can have steak and ice cream every meal if you want. SROCO believes in feeding employees well."

Sherry smiled. "If you think this drilling rig is expensive and this is dangerous work, you ain't seen nothing yet. Our biggest, cheapest fields are out here in the Gulf under a mile of water, and we have to drill down two miles."

"This drilling rig cost a billion. That production platform costs millions, plus expensive pipelines, and you add it all up, and you're talking real money." Bob got up, left, and returned with four hardhats and handed one to each.

"We're down only 1500 feet of water, but semi-submersibles can drill in over 5000 feet of water if needed."

He led them out on the deck where the wind whistled, waves splashed below, and the ever present noise of the rotary and clanging pipes made casual conversation impossible and Bob yelled.

"Except for the driller's shack, all the control rooms are down here." Bob helped them put on life jackets and adjust their hardhats. He walked to a closed door and stopped. There was CRO painted on the door. Bob yelled, "This is the Control Room Operator's shack. He's a Master Seaman and is responsible for stability of the rig."

They followed him to the next door on which was painted MIC. "This is the Tool Pusher's shack. He runs the deck and rig and is 'boss' of the rig crew. He came up through the ranks and is our most experienced driller. He works closely with the drilling engineer who is usually a college trained Mechanical or Petroleum Engineer. They decide drilling strategy and have responsibility for everything on the rig. MIC means man in charge." Bob turned and walked upstairs to the drilling floor. He stopped. "We have an 80 man crew, and they work in two twelve hour shifts. They rotate every ten days with another crew on shore leave.

"The driller runs the traveling block and is floor boss. We have six qualified derrick men, eight roughnecks, twelve roustabouts, two assistant drillers, two pump men, four crane operators, and two maintenance foremen. We contract out catering service, tug and supply, production platform crews, firefighting, and anything else we can outsource. Everybody gets high pay, and the lowest paid man on a drilling rig is the cook's helper, and he makes $50,000 a year before overtime. The tool pusher makes $120,000 and the engineer gets $160,000 a year before overtime. All the big companies pay the same to discourage job hopping." Bob walked over to some large engines or motors, whatever.

"This rig runs on diesel fuel brought in by barge. Newer models in construction will run off wellhead gas. These diesel engines supply the power that run the electric generator that supplies the energy that runs the hoisting drum, the rotary table motor, the mud pump and everything else you see moving on this rig plus the electricity that run the lights, hot water heaters, refrigerators and on and on.

"The driller controls the hoisting cable that raises and lowers the traveling block that lifts or lowers the drill pipe out or in the hole down below on the ocean floor. At the end of the drill pipe is a bit that bores the hole and finds the gas and oil." He walked over and pointed to an open mud pit.

"The mud pump motor runs the pump that pumps the mud to the top of the drill pipe where it flows all the way down to clean the drill pipe and bit and back up inside the outer casing to the top where the drill cuttings are filtered out, and the mud is recycled back to the mud pit to be used again."

There were two derrick men above and three roughnecks around the rotary table. One was a lady with a red face and long blond hair. They watched for a few minutes.

"Why don't you three put on some coveralls and hard toe shoes and make yourself at home. I'm going to motor over to the production platform and see if we can put out the fire and fix the leak before the storm gets here."

*   *   *

At 10 P.M. the Yucatan tropical storm blew in with gales and sheets of rain at 70 mph and waves twenty feet high. The drilling rig held steady. Water splashed across the decks, the driller closed down the rig, and everybody got inside and battened down the hatches.

At 4 A.M. the wind blew out the gas flame and Beets and Keats lowered their divers to 1500 feet, closed off the manifold, fixed the Christmas tree and leak and didn't see a shark.

At 6 A.M. the wind died down, and the rain slacked to a drizzle.

At 8 A.M. the tugs pushed the displaced production platform back in place and hooked up the conduits from below. They turned on the valves, filled the separators, started the pumps, and no leaks occurred.

Beets and Keats hightailed it back to Houston, and Bob motored back to the drilling rig anxious to fly to Houston and catch a commuter flight to Tulsa.

*   *   *

Dr. Li Pwe, a lady Petroleum Engineer with CITIC, was waiting for Bob with a

Helicopter standing by. All Bob had was his backpack in the overhead, so he bypassed Passport, the metal detector etc., and met her halfway.

"Jim McNutt got burned up when the dynamite went off," announced Dr. Pwe when Bob was in hearing distance.

Bob was shocked. He had no idea. Jim McNutt had twenty years experience and was an

Aggie just like him. Bob guessed they had a fire. Jim was his replacement. Bob had no excuse.

"The fire won't go out, and we're waiting for you. General He Wu called Beets and Keats, and they said you were the best in the East."

"What happened? Which well? How did it start?" asked Bob, perplexed.

"Accident! We got leak in top valve of Christmas tree. Worker went in to turn off blowout valve, caused explosion, killed worker and fire started. Now 7 days. General He Wu look for you. Everybody look for you.

"We close off other two wells. We try water hoses, asbestos suits, throw dirt on it, carbon dioxide, long poles, two men run into wellhead, we spray with hoses. They wear asbestos suits, get burned and go to hospital.

"We need to put out gas fire, cool manifold with water, close off valves and fix leak. I will try next if you will talk me through earphones on headset. We got big bulldozer with blade (up front), fireproof windshield, asbestos suits, gloves, boots, dynamite satchel, dynamite,

dynamite caps and detonators, fire trucks, pressure hoses, chemical foam,—"

Bob stopped her. "How much chemical foam?"

"It's liquid nitrogen. About five tanks. I can get carbon dioxide if you want it," replied Dr. Pwe.

"Can we get a high pressure hose with jet nozzle to spray the fire and freeze it?"

"We'll use the ones for the carbon dioxide tanks. They look the same. You think it will work?" asked Dr. Pwe, giggling. "I never heard of using nitrogen gas. We spray that on the rice paddies for fertilizers. Carbon dioxide foams and nitrogen freezes up close. Like taking off warts.

"How did the fire start?"

"He Chu ran in to turn off the blowout valve smoking a cigarette. It blew him to bits and pieces. Jim got mad as hell. He got careless, rushed in with the dynamite and bulldozer, and blew himself up too. His head came off at shoulders."

"How many men you got left?"

"There're six just standing around smoking. It's not dangerous unless the fire goes out. As long as it is burning it's safe to smoke," replied Li Pwe.

"Where's General He Wu?"

"He flew back to Wuhan. He's got 20,000 men working on the dam, and they smoke. Those pile drivers hit natural gas pockets. Gas pockets are an industrial hazard. So far, they've had only 200 fatal accidents. They lost a half million building Great Wall of China. Nobody knows for sure. They buried them in the wall."

*   *   *

Bob boarded the CITIC helicopter with Dr. Li Pwe. The Chinese crew didn't understand English, but Li Pwe did. It was two hundred miles away. The overhead blades made conversation impossible. Bob, already getting deaf, put on the earmuffs. Li Pwe was the best engineer at CITIC and bilingual.

Kuwait was about the size of Connecticut, and there were 700 wells ablaze when the Iraqis pulled out of north Kuwait near the end of Desert Storm. Bob was one of many that answered the call, and all totaled it took them almost a year to extinguish all 700 (February to November 6, 1991) just 20 miles from Kuwait City and US Army Field HQ. Sadam Hussein made military history by introducing oil fire ignition as a military tactic.

In the oil business, extinguishing oil well fires was a very hazardous occupation. The job was best left to experts. Everybody knew that. Bob knew it. Some of his best Aggie buddies had died trying to put out oil well fires. Extreme caution was absolutely essential. Spraying with water and chemicals seldom worked, and you put the dynamite next to the blaze not in the fire. The tiniest spark could start it again. They had already lost one American field engineer and four Chinamen.

Only four things were needed to start an oil well fire: a leak, oxygen, fuel, and a spark. You could cut off the oxygen, stop the fire, cap the well, and fix the leak. Simple! The professionals charged $250,000 a phone call and $1,000,000 a day to put out a well. Only a crazy person would do it for a living.

Bob thought dynamite was the most effective. If he used nitrogen at flame temperatures, it might combine with oxygen and form nitrates with potentially disastrous results. He didn't know. The valves might freeze.

Fire itself was a great oxygenator of toxic gases which if inhaled were poisonous. In Kuwait they had sand storms and changing winds to contend with along with carbon monoxide, sulfur dioxide, hydrogen sulfide, acidic aerosols, soot from heavy oils and tar and non-toxic carbon dioxide which made up 95% of burning crude oil smoke. If hot liquid oil escaped, pooled, and ignited, then a surface fire had to be extinguished before the well fire.

In Kuwait after the well fires burned up 6 million barrels of oil a day for eight months, they had 300 oil leaks contaminating 40 million tons of earth and sand that had to be cleaned up to prevent further contamination of precious underground water that yet had to be tested for safe human use.

In SEA, if one country wanted to sabotage another and destroy their source of wealth and income, all they had to do was send a flight over and fire bomb their oil fields. Vietnam had sent a fighter reconnaissance jet over every morning at daylight just like clockwork since they had started drilling only one hundred miles from their border. China was unhappy with Vietnam because of their unseating Pol Pot. Russia backed Vietnam in their invasion of Cambodia in 1978 and their two week border war with China in 1979. Thailand was continuously at war on their border with Myanmar because of the refugee and immigrant problems that got worse not better.

Such misguided courage enhancing phrases as, "eyeballing won't move a board, faint heart never seduced the babysitter, and do something even if it is wrong," made Bob chuckle as he prepared himself mentally in route to the well fire. After blowing out the flame with the dynamite, they had to wash everything down to cool the wellhead and prevent re-ignition before they went in, closed off the valves, and fixed the leak. Even the tiniest spark could re-ignite the fire.

Dr. Li Pwe had her **ESSO FIELD MANUAL** along for referral. Bob borrowed it, looked up oil fires, and read.

> *To cap a well, specialists must remove all the damaged equipment around the exploded wellhead, using bulldozers and special vehicles called Athey wagons to clear the area. Removing the debris allows the oil flow and fire to shoot straight up in the air as opposed to spraying in different directions. This allows firefighters to inspect the well closely and determine the best course of action.*

Normally the flow is left burning to minimize ground pollution and burn off any poisonous gases. Meanwhile, the firefighters begin to cap the well. If the wellhead is damaged, a special cutter is used to remove part of it. Then a long tube called a flow tube is placed over the wellhead to direct the flames high enough into the air to allow specialists to more closely inspect the remaining wellhead. Using a wagon, firefighters then place a capping assembly consisting of several valves connected to a long tube on the salvaged wellhead. At this point the valves can be closed to stop the oil flow and extinguish the fire. Once the fire is extinguished, the surrounding area is quickly flushed with water to prevent the hot sand from re-igniting the lingering vapors. Then firefighters move on to the next well.

There are several techniques used to put out oil well fires, which vary by resources available and the characteristics of the fire itself.

Dousing with huge amounts of water

Raising the plume—Inserting one metal casing 30 to 40 feet high over the wellhead (thus raising the flame above the ground). Liquid nitrogen or water is then forced in at the bottom to reduce the oxygen supply and put out the fire.

Drill relief wells to redirect the oil and make the fire smaller (and easier to extinguish with water).

Using a jet to direct high pressure water and air over the well.

Using dynamite to 'blow out' the fire by blasting fuel and oxygen from the flame and consuming oxygen in the combustion.

Dry Chemical (mainly Purple K) can be used on small well fires such as those in refineries.

Special vehicles called "Athey wagons" as well as the typical bulldozer protected by corrugated steel sheeting are normally used in the process.

Oil well fires can cause the loss of millions of barrels of crude oil per day. Combined with the ecological problems caused by the large amounts of smoke and unburnt petroleum falling back to earth, oil well fires such as those seen in Kuwait can cause enormous economical losses.

Smoke from burnt crude oil contains many chemicals, including sulfur dioxide, carbon monoxide, soot, benzopyrene, Poly aromatic hydrocarbons, and dioxins. Exposure to oil well fires is commonly cited as a cause of the Gulf War Syndrome, however, studies have indicated that the firefighters who capped the wells did not report any of the symptoms suffered by the soldiers.

About halfway to Kwangxi Field dark storm clouds in the west over the Shan and Himalaya mountains formed and blotted out the afternoon sun causing near darkness. The helicopter vibrated and turned with the wind as the pilot struggled to stay on course. *Shit* thought Bob. *We're about to have a real gully washer.* He thought about the You River and a flash flood, but was confident they'd drilled outside the flood plain.

A Vietnamese MIG broke the sound barrier, climbed high, and performed a couple of rolls to aggravate the Chinese MIG pilots on standby at CPRAFB in Wuhan. As expected, 3 Chinese MIGs rose up in formation, and the Vietnamese turned and headed south toward the Vietnamese border leaving a long vapor trail.

The helicopter motor began to miss and started slowing. It would speed up and lift, then slow and drop. The pilot announced it was a change in the humidity, but Bob suspected he was running out of gas. It kept coughing.

Dr. Li Pwe picked up her overnight bag and visited the tiny one hole toilet in which you couldn't stand erect in to pee. It was a unisex and latched from the inside. It took her at least five minutes, but she came out smiling at Bob. "Forgive me, but I'm starting my menses. You can go in if you like."

The helicopter was low on gas so the pilot put down at a farming village of 30,000 at the base of a mountain surrounded by rice paddies 50 miles north of the You River and Kwangxi field.

The You River was knee deep and clear during the dry season. Its bottom and banks followed a serpentine path through the valley and was lined by pebbles, cobblestones, and boulders previously washed down from the Himalayas.

Education is expensive. We learned early in Korea, by experience, that you don't put your Headquarters near a bend in a river under chestnut trees. A heavy downpour would cause a wall of water ten feet high traveling a hundred mph.

The sky was filled with storm clouds which blocked out the sun and caused near darkness at midday. They located a petrol station and convenience store. They had diesel or leaded.

It rained solid sheets and takeoff was impossible. The pilot shook his head, went inside the store and bought a bowl of hot rice with boiled cabbage sprinkled with red pepper, Mexico's gift to the world.

Bob followed Dr. Pwe to a table with fresh chopstick settings, condiment bowls and a menu in Chinese characters with prices in YMB (Yuan). She ordered for the two of them. The waiter who was also the gasoline pump attendant and cook brought them two large bowls of steaming rice, a platter of baked canine, and a bowl of live eels. Bob asked for ketchup and got sliced tomatoes.

The Chinese would eat any kind of animal or insect. They ate humans during the ice age. In good times they ate rice, vegetables, fruits, fish, chickens, hogs, and dogs.

Eels were popular with the Romans, and they fattened them by letting eels suck blood out of human slaves. Saint Thomas Aquinas died of food poisoning at the age of 58 after eating live eels at a church dinner.

*   *   *

The rain didn't stop. It rained all night. The pilot slept in the helicopter, and Bob and Li Pwe slept in the attic of the town's commune leader. In a Chinese Village they elected the biggest man, year after year.

They didn't have "medicine men" or university trained physicians. They had barefeet doctors who diagnosed by reading your palm and prescribing herbs, roots, and tea. All you had to do was point to where you hurt, and they had a different tea leaf for every ailment. Life threatening illnesses were referred to the nearest specialist in Acupuncture.

Dr. Li Pwe bought condoms, lubricant, and Tampax at the store before they went to their attic for the night. She read Bob's mind and commented. "I'd rather be safe than sorry!"

*   *   *

During the night a flashflood swept away everything that wasn't secured at Kwangxi Basin oilfield. The steel derrick embedded in a concrete base survived. The three manifolds connected at the tops of 8000 feet of drill pipe and casing were intact. The fire extinguished, but the leak persisted, and it could restart at any time. The six Chinamen, the tools and sheds, and Bob's Jeep were swept away never to be seen again. Only the bulldozer remained, and its gas tank was full of water.

*   *   *

The rains stopped around 5 A.M. and at 9 A.M. they landed at the well sights. The You was almost back in bank, but it left uprooted trees, huge boulders, and countless cobblestones out to a mile on either side.

263

"Put down about a quarter mile from the first well, let it idle, and don't smoke or make any sparks."

Bob got out and walked the quarter mile (440 yards) to the first well. It was hissing and smelled of rotten eggs. There was frost around the leak of the "L" joint coming off an 18" pipe screwed into the top manifold valve which was open to discharge. All they had to do to fix the leak was to unscrew the discharge line, apply sealant on the threads, reseat the "L" and put it on tight with a 48" wrench and long cheater. Then they'd reconnect the discharge line and no leak. Ole!

All he had to do was shut off the blowout valve, the safety valve, and the discharge valve without making a spark and blowing things up, himself included. If you worried about such things, it would drive you insane.

Although not Catholic, he made the sign of the cross, muttered "Hail Mary and Glory be to the Father, and to the Son, and to the Holy Spirit" and walked up on the platform and turned off the blowout valve, the safety valve, and the discharge valve. The hissing stopped, the rotten eggs floated away, and the pressure gauge dropped from 200 to 0 psi on top the Christmas tree. Bob relaxed and waved.

The helicopter picked up Bob, and they flew down and inspected the other two wells which were correctly shut down. The derrick and derrick platform collected trash, but was otherwise intact.

Natural catastrophes could cause more damage in minutes than standing armies in months and years. Wildfires and mudslides could devastate Santa Barbara, Los Angeles, and San Diego and do more damage than an army or a nuclear bomb, and only the homeowners and insurance companies got upset. Let terrorist set off one bomb in New York City or bomb Pearl Harbor on Sunday, and the whole nation rises up to go to war. Caligula led a Roman Legion into the sea to fight the Greek god Poseidon. Caligula stood and hacked the waves with his sword until he killed Poseidon and returned to Rome in triumph.

They'd drilled three wells and had three more to go before he turned the field over to Dr. Li Pwe, the new field Superintendent from CITIC.

So far, it had only cost SROCO poor Jim McNutt and Bob's time and expertise plus their capital investment.

*　　*　　*

A surface to surface 110mm percussion shell exploded over their heads, shook the ground and rained down fragments. Somebody fired a warning shot. Bob borrowed the helicopter pilot's field glasses, climbed on the well platform and looked across the rice paddies to the south. A formation of Russian T-72 heavy tanks with 110mm canons and 50 cal machineguns aimed at them were racing across the rice paddies followed by armored troop carriers in hot pursuit.

"Let's get out of here," yelled Bob, and they jumped in the helicopter and started to rise. Ten streams of 50 cal. tracers popped overhead, and the pilot sat the helicopter down, turned off the motor, and they scrambled for places to hide.

In modern tanks equipped with stereoscopic rangefinders a mile is an easy shot. The gunner places the crosshairs on the target, pushes a little button, and he can watch his missile all the way to the target. Boomb! Adios! Whoever it was wanted a neighborly talk, or they would have killed them with the first shot.

From the north in direction of Wuhan a dozen Chinese MIGs rose to the challenge and would be over their position in 5 minutes. A battalion of Chinese helicopter gunships accompanied by troop carriers rose up from Guilin and would be there in one hour. At the rate the hostiles were traveling across the rice paddies, unless they slowed, they'd be there in ten minutes.

Dr. Li Pwe offered Bob a cigarette. He usually didn't smoke, but in time of war he never left without a couple of packs of Camels, his pocket Gideon Bible, a "C" ration can opener, his dog tags, a big spoon, his canteen with chlorine tablets, a prophylactic kit, his rifle, and steel helmet which GIs called a "piss pot."

*   *   *

"The weather is great for flying. I can't get the drilling rig on the radio. Nobody's had contact with them since last night. Galveston got a big wave around midnight, and there's an oil slick on the coastline all the way from Sabine Pass to Freeport."

Sherry was apprehensive. "Maybe it's not safe to go."

"I have to go," replied Bob. He looked at Austin, who smiled and nodded. Then Sherry and Sandra nodded.

Bob handed them a thermos and a sack of Danish pastry. Then he introduced their pilot, Jack Daniels, who turned and spoke, switched on the ignition, started the motor, let it warm up, and then rose high above the SROCO building and downtown Houston. He headed south along IH-45, over Hobby Airport, Johnson Space Center, Clear Lake, and Galveston Island. They strained to see along the seawall and beach. Cars were moving, but they really didn't see much oil.

Bob scanned the horizon with field glasses. Sandra looked down and saw an occasional whitecap. The water was choppy, and she saw several drilling rigs at a distance. After five minutes from Galveston, she saw nothing but water. The noise of the motor and blades made conversation below a shout impossible, so they drank coffee, ate Danish, and closed their eyes for a nap.

An hour later the pilot slowed and started circling. They were about three hundred feet above an oil slick which looked a quarter mile across. Everybody looked down as the pilot slowly circled. Something terrible had happened! Finally Bob turned and announced to the three, "SROCO SIX and eighty workers are gone. They've vanished, and nothing is here but an oil spill."

At a distance they saw a submarine taking on passengers from life rafts. The pilot tried radio contact with no success. The men on the deck were scrambling for the coning tower, riflemen started shooting, and the pilot veered away. The helicopter took hits and began to sputter while the pilot fought to maintain control.

Frightened and speechless, they suddenly realized the helicopter was losing altitude fast, and they were going to crash. The pilot steadied the falling aircraft. They opened the escape door about thirty feet above the waves, dropped a rope, and the inflated life raft. Sandra, Sherry, Austin, Bob, and finally Jack jumped from the helicopter which flew another hundred feet, lost power, fell into the Gulf and sank within seconds.

Bob woke up. He was having nightmares. His pecker was standing up, and he had to pee.

*　　*　　*

CHAPTER 48

Dublin Ireland
Wednesday, December 18, 1993
Temperature 29°, snow

Pembroke Castle, the ruins of which were the pride of Pembroke Wales where they boarded the ferry, was the birthplace of Henry VII, the father of Henry VIII. The Chapel was used by John Wesley when they forbade him to preach in London. It was the birthplace of Methodism. Sandra was Methodist, and she didn't know that John Wesley was ex-communicated from the Angleton Church for "tongues". The American Pentecostals were an offshoot of the Methodist Church which was an offshoot of the English Anglican Church. Interesting!

The temperature dropped, and a blizzard blew in from the north Tuesday afternoon causing the pedestrians to seek shelter, and the traffic to slide to a halt. There were plenty of rooms at the Dublin Best Western which boasted its buffet served Irish potatoes prepared six ways, if you liked them raw mixed with a salad along with baked, boiled, broiled, fried, and stewed. They were long on mutton, and fish was not counted as meat on Fridays.

First cousin marriages were allowed in Ireland, and, like the Chinese, Irish looked alike.

Mesolithic Homo sapiens, Celts, Vikings and Normans in that order settled Ireland over 5000 years ago. English and Gaelic were their national languages, and some spoke both. Dublin was settled by the Vikings who made it their capital. Before its independence as the Republic of Ireland, it was ruled by the British for a hundred years.

After the potato famine in 1845, hundreds of thousands immigrated to America and Canada where about 30 to 40 million of their descendents prosper today. 4 million still live in Ireland where they practice the old traditions in genteel poverty. The whole country of Ireland was less than 1% the size of the United States.

Whiskey, made from barley, was invented by Saint Patrick who called it the water of life (whiskey in Gaelic). Saint Colombo, an Irish monk was first to carry whiskey to the war-like Pics in Scotland and convert their Druid Priests to Christianity. Saint Colombo was first to report seeing the Loch Ness monster in 450 c.e.

Stout, a brownish black beer, is very popular in Ireland and tastes like spent crank case oil.

The Liffey River runs through the middle of Dublin into Dublin Bay which joins the Irish Sea. The first toll foot bridge ever joins north from south Dublin and cost a Half Pence. Rock fences seen over most of Ireland were present since Neolithic times. Peat bogs cover 10% of central and south western islands, are popular for fuel and really smoke up the house. Peat was used as fuel in electrical power plants. There was no EPA in Ireland. They had no coal, gas, or wood. Oliver Cromwell complained there was no tree to hang a man when he crossed the channel with a Protestant Army, burned Drogheda to the ground, and massacred every Catholic they could find.

What every tourist saw when they visited Dublin was "Ha Pence Bridge, Dublin Castle, Trinity University, and Guinness Brewery, the largest in the world, where they mass produced Guinness Stout to be drunk warm in mugs from a tap. Before TV, pubs were the favorite meeting places in Ireland.

CHAPTER 49

Dublin Ireland
8 P.M., Wednesday, December 18, 1993
Snow storm across Europe
Heathrow, Paris, and Madrid Airports closed to Commercial Flights

Maria Tantalia was at the lectern.

"Ireland is green all over, gets lots of rain, has mild winters, and it never snows. That's what the tour packages say. Of course it's long been known that Irish monks in little reed boats visited the shores of Iceland and North America 500 years before the Vikings. The blue eyed American Indians of the Mississippi Valley spoke Gaelic. The moors of Spain shipwrecked off the shores of Ireland after the defeat of the Spanish Armada were ancestors of the 'Black Irish'. And, the ten lost tribes of Israel built the pyramids in Mexico and South America. Jesus visited India, Japan, and South America before he ascended to heaven.

"I think you'll notice a difference in the Celts of Ireland and the Celts of Scotland. The Irish are friendly and easy to meet. They think they invented whiskey and beer, the bagpipe, and harp, and that kissing the Blarney Stone will bestow on you an eloquent voice and the gift of gab. Presidents John Kennedy and Ronald Reagan were Irish and probably President Clinton too.

"More snow is forecast for London and all northern Europe. Ole! I really need to be home by New Year's to prepare for graduation and the spring semester. Most of you girls have finished your work except for this trip, so don't worry. Our colleagues back home know what's going on. The Weather people in London say it's the worst in twenty years, and it's supposed to hit New York and the whole east coast of U.S. in the next 24 hours. Heathrow ran out of de-icing fluid. They handle 1200 flights a day, normally. The air terminals are filled with stranded people sleeping on their bags.

"Eurostar, which operates the high-speed trains between London and Paris are still operating but suffering a lag jam by stranded airline passengers. If our Hilton Hotel in London fills, we'll just spend the night here tomorrow.

"I'd like to welcome back Dr. Winston Blood, who will share a room with Dr. Plotinus. He's our only English History expert. Dr. Eros Zenovenusetti will discuss Leprechauns, Saint Patrick, and John Wesley. Dr. Plotinus has Oliver Cromwell and the English Reformation and Dr. Blood will discuss Irish History. It's quite complicated and may require several lectures. Lastly, Dr. Christy Isaac will discuss the construction and aerodynamics of the Concordsky in case they don't cancel our flight.

Dr. Winston C. Blood, Ph.D., Professor in English History wrote on the black board. **ROMANS, SAINT PATRICK, WHISKEY, SAINT COLOMBO, HENRY II, PETER PEN CE, HENRY VIII, KING OF IRELAND, BLOODY MARY, ELIZABETH I, JAMES I, OLIVER CROMWELL, JAMES II, WILLIAM III, AND BOYNE.**

"Ireland and Scotland were not civilized by the Romans. In fact, Romans built walls to keep them out. Saint Patrick tamed Ireland, and Saint Colombo tamed the fierce Pics of Scotland. The *Book of Kell* preserved here in Dublin antedated *Canterbury Tales*. Ireland was once known as the Land of Saints and Scholars before Guinness Stout, Irish Pubs, horse racing, and the Irish sweepstakes.

Henry II of England was named by the Roman Catholic Pope in Rome as the first Lord of Ireland and demanded Henry collect one pence taxation from every Catholic in Ireland for Saint Peter's in Rome. The Irish named it the "Peter-pence."

"Dr. Christy Isaac has agreed to discuss pre history of Ireland, and I'll start with Henry II, and take it down to the Grand Revolution, James II, and William and Mary of Orange. Elizabeth I and Oliver Cromwell, Lord Protector of England, did the most damage to Ireland short of the

Potato Famine in 1845-1848. Before the potato famine there were 8 million, and today they're about 500,000 in Dublin, 300,000 in Ulster, and 200,000 in Cork, with a total population of less than 4 million in all Ireland.

"After Bonny Prince Charlie and execution of the chiefs of all the Scottish clans, you can say the same about Scotland. If you add up all the Canadians and Americans with Irish, Scot, and Scots-Irish ancestry, it's at least a hundred million. Then there's South Africa, Australia, and New Zealand. WOW! The Celts really got around. They make up a majority of the white English speaking people in the world. The Scots-Irish pioneered America, and the Irish fought the Civil War." Dr. Blood smiled. "All history is rumor and gossip, and the victor writes the history.

"Henry Tudor, Earl of Richmond, defeated King Richard III at the Battle of Bosworth Field in 1485 and was crowned Henry VII whose major accomplishments were enlarging Westminster Abbey and fathering Henry VIII and Margaret, a daughter, who was married off to King James Stewart of Scotland.

"Henry VIII was England's most famous King. He declared himself King of Ireland in 1541 and encouraged colonization of northern Ireland by English Protestants, established English laws, and outlawed Catholicism. Bloody Mary Tudor, Henry's daughter by Catherine of Aragon, went further. Mary established plantations in Ireland and gave them to English settlers. Queen Elizabeth I, daughter of Anne Boleyn, outlawed Roman Catholic Services and executed Bishops and priests. Catholic protests led by Shane O'Neill in Ulster was quashed by Elizabeth. James I, Mary of Scots son and a Protestant, sent Scottish and English Protestants to colonize Ulster. King James I, author of the King James' Bible, created Northern Ireland of today and was originator of Scots-Irish culture which made America what it is today. The Angletons and Presbyterians just wanted their land, but the Puritans wanted their body and soul (dead).

"The Irish Catholics revolted and Oliver Cromwell, Lord Protector of England, invaded Ireland with a large Army and massacred all inhabitants of Drogheda when they refused to surrender and bragged about it. He rewarded his soldiers with Irish lands in Ulster.

"In the Glorious Revolution in England against James II in 1688, the Irish Catholics supported James II, who fled to Ireland and raised an army to fight the English. William III invaded Ireland and with the help of Ulster Protestants defeated James in the Battle of Boyne in 1690. As a result Catholics were left with only 15% of Irish land and were forbidden to practice Catholicism, and own, rent, inherit and purchase land. They were refused the right to serve in Parliament or military and the right to bear arms. For the next 100 years Ireland had a Protestant Parliament, but the Catholics were oppressed to new serfdom, *persona non grata* until 1798 when Parliament restored their rights to own land and practice Catholicism. In 1801, English and Irish Parliaments voted for the Act of Union, and Ireland became part of the United Kingdom of Great Britain and Ireland.

"Wellington who defeated Napoleon at the Battle of Waterloo was of Irish birth, and Barclay, a Scotsman, led the Russian Army against Napoleon in his retreat from Moscow (family tradition). Thank you. Nothing really exciting happened next until the great potato famine in 1845 after which the great exodus to America occurred."

"Christy."

Dr. Christy Isaac wrote on the green board. **PREHISTORY, 8000 B.C.E., GARDEN OF EDEN, CAIN AND ABLE, CELTS, ROMANS, PATRICK, VIKINGS, NORMANS AND ASSIMILATION**.

"If you travel or walk along the Atlantic side of Ireland and Scotland and especially out into the Orkney and Swetland Islands north of Scotland, you will be overwhelmed in awe over the ruins of early prehistoric humans. Many of those manmade caves and houses look livable today. Burial vaults contain skeletons that date back to 8000 b.c. when the glaciers melted and the seas began to rise in Europe. They first migrated up from Spain and France and could walk across. After the water rose and they could not walk across, they made boats out of reeds and paddled across the shallow Celtic Sea where they were guided by the coastline. It really depended on where the glaciers melted first. The Gulf Stream has always kept the British Isle temperate, and there were plenty of rain, runoff, and rivers. All of Ireland was forested, and there were deer, nesting birds, and fish. I'm making it sound like the Garden of Eden. The first explorers were either naked or wore animal skins to keep warm.

"The first were hunter-gathers. The next were pastoralist and farmers, like Cain and Able. The same was happening all over the world. Archeologist had shown that Homo sapiens are 200,000 years and all came from the same "Eve." They migrated out of Africa 125,000 years ago and were all over the earth by 30-40,000 years ago. Paintings on walls and in caves date back 35,000 years ago. Thatched houses built out over stilts around lakes have been found in Switzerland and Northwest England. The Windmill People, Beaker people, and Celts of England in Stonehenge and Avebury Plane were relatively late comers compared with the Paleo, Meso, and Neoliths of Ireland and Scotland.

"Around 400b.c.e. the Celts from Europe and Britain invaded Ireland. They had iron tools and weapons, wheels and carts. They controlled the whole island, split it up into smaller kingdoms and made one king of all. Saint Patrick was a Breton who was a slave in Ireland around 400 c.e. He escaped to France, joined a monastery and studied to be a Saint. He returned to Ireland as a Christian missionary in 432, established monasteries, taught the Roman Alphabet, Latin, and converted the Druid Priests and everybody to Roman Catholicism. Due to Patrick, Ireland's monasteries became a center of learning, an island of scholars and saints.

"Then the Vikings came and raided the east and south coast along the Irish Sea. Dublin was built at the mouth of the Liffey River. They also established ports at Cork, Limerick, and Waterford. An Irish hero, Brian Bork, King of the Irish, defeated the Vikings and instead of killing them like Oliver Cromwell, made them a deal that they couldn't refuse.

They could keep their ships and ports, if they would become Catholics and marry their daughters and sisters. The same thing happened when Americans settled in Texas. They found them a young senorita, became Catholics, and divorced their wives back in the states.

"Next came the Normans building castles everywhere. They were tamed Vikings who were already Catholic and spoke French. The Normans took Irish brides, learned the language and customs and became Irish too. That's called cross cultural breeding. Thank you."

"Aristotle."

Dr. Aristotle Plotinus wrote on the blackboard. **NEW SPAIN, AUSTIN, CATHOLICS, KARANKAWAS, COMANCHES, APACHES, PIRATES, SCOTS-IRISH, BOND SERVANTS, EAST TEXAS, SLAVES, TOBACCO, COTTON, SUGARCANE, AND HOUSTON**.

"Moses Austin contracted with the Mexican government to settle 3000 Catholic families in Texas along the Brazos River, the home of the Karankawa Indians who were known cannibals. The Spanish had established a colony from the Canary Islands in Bexar on the San Antonio River where they maintained several missions. They had missions at El Paso and Santa Fe. Everything west of San Antonio was uninhabitable because of the fierce Apache and Comanche Indians. Most of the early Anglo-American (white) adventurers and settlers in Tejas were Scots by ancestry who had come from Protestant Ireland. They were commissioned in the Mexican Army and commanded Mestizos troops in Mexico's war of independence from Spain. Mexico passed laws forbidding slavery and limited immigrants only to Roman Catholics.

"All of Austin's 300 families and the early settlers who came through Nacogdoches and up the Coushatta trace from New Orleans to Fort Teran on the Neches and Bevil's Port on the Angelina had to be baptized Catholics and take on the name of a Catholic Saint.

Sam Houston was baptized Sam Pablo Houston. Each man was awarded a league (4000 acres) and a labor (200 acres). As an incentive, if a Anglo settler married a Mexican wife performed by a Catholic priest, they were granted a patent for 2 leagues and 2 labors.

"I didn't intend this to be a Texas history course, but I thought it would explain how Scots-Irish, who were passionately anti-Catholic and slave owners were first to settle Texas. The first law passed after Texas became a Republic was to divorce those Texans that had married Mexican wives from their American wives back in the states.

"It all started with King James I and Oliver Cromwell back in England, allowing the Protestant Scots to establish plantations in Ireland and using Irish as slaves. That's how so many Scots-Irish ended up in Houston and southeast Texas. When the slaves were freed in Texas in 1865, they took their owner's name. Understand? The Scots-Irish sailed out of Dublin.

"You've heard the expression beyond the Pale? Well, Pale was a little strip just north of Dublin.

"Henry II was the first Lord of Catholic Ireland and ran all the Jews out of the British Isles and seized their lands and wealth.

"Oliver Cromwell was a Puritan Protestant and hated Catholics. He let the Jews return to Britain and allowed the modern Baptist, Quakers, and Shakers to form their own churches. Some Baptists came with the Puritans that landed at Plymouth Massachusetts and erected the First Baptist Church nearby in Rhode Island. The Quakers went to Pennsylvania, and somehow the Catholics got in New Jersey. The Shakers are still around, but they forbade sexual intercourse in marriage and have to recruit new members who are celibate.

"Many rural folks in Tennessee, Alabama, and East Texas can live all their lives without meeting a Catholic unless it's a Mexican or a French African American from Louisiana."

"Eros."

Dr. Eros Zenovenusetti wrote on the blackboard. **WINTER SOLSTICE, DECEMBER 25, SUNDAY, CHRIST'S MASS, RICE, POTATO SOUP, BREAD, BEER, BABY JESUS, AND THREE WISE MEN**.

Eros sang sweetly, "*I'm dreaming of a white Christmas. Just like the one I used to know. Where the tree tops glisten and children listen for sleigh bells in the show.*"

"Just 7 more days until Christ's Mass. Where I was raised we celebrated January 12 as Christmas. I was raised Greek Orthodox. A Roman Pope Gregory changed the calendar. Well, here we are spinning our wheels at the most celebrated time of the year stuck in the snow at Heathrow. At least we have a lovely new Best Western in picturesque Dublin, rather than that stodgy old Hilton in downtown London. The five things to see are the Castle of Dublin, Halfpence Bridge over the Liffey River, Guinness Stout Warehouse, The Book of Kell and Trinity University a.k.a. the University of Dublin.

"In China, they serve rice last because it is the cheapest. In Ireland, you get a potato soup appetizer, before your main course of mutton along with baked, boiled, or fried potato.

"In Russia, they make bread beer out of stale bread soaked in water and fermented with yeast, and after the bubbles stop, they strain it through a porous cloth and serve it as beer along with fast food. It's very inexpensive and tastes good. If you distill it you can get 180 proof bread whiskey which is clear and looks like Vodka.

"The Christmas story in Mathew and Luke were just made up. The Q book never existed. You're never going to find proof positive that Jesus existed, performed all those miracles and was resurrected. You are more likely to find Jesus back home in Sunday School than on one of those Holy Land tours. All religions are faiths.

"The Christmas shopping rush is the greatest commercial gimmick ever invented. The merchants will never give it up. All the other religions combined cannot match it. The Hajj to Mecca doesn't come close. Wall Street depends on Christmas. Christian churches depend on it for support.

"Mexico, China, and India plus other toy and gift manufacturing countries. China makes all our Christmas decorations. In the U.S.A., Jewish merchants make the most profits at Christmas. What difference does it make if it's not true. It's the thought, camaraderie, and cheer that counts. It's a guilt trip home to visit their family for the kids, and an opportunity for grandparents to see their grandchildren.

"Did Jesus resurrect from the grave like the Bible implied? There was not one eyewitness. If it were true, then it would be history. Pen and papyrus had been commonly used for six hundred years, and there were plenty of scribes around.

"Paul wrote he saw a bright light and heard Jesus' voice, and that's your proof. Everything else was hearsay or fabrication. According to Paul, to receive grace and achieve salvation you must believe Jesus was resurrected from the dead and be baptized.

"Belief is through faith because no one knows for sure!" Dr. Zenovenusetti smiled.

"Yesterday, we passed by Pembroke Castle in Wales where John Wesley once preached Methodism. Methodists and Episcopals are a spinoff of the Church of England (Anglicans) started by Henry VIII.

"What is the difference in Truth based on faith, and truth based on facts? You write Truth based on faith with a capital T. You cannot use the Bible to prove the Bible is true, nor can you use passages taken from the Bible as evidence in a court of law. If you compare Biblical Creation with Scientific Creation, then either pastors or scientist are wrong. If they know they are wrong, and continue to preach belief by faith, then they are professional liars, and only dummies and people with an agenda will follow. An atheist, except Thomas Jefferson, has never been elected President. I don't think George Washington belonged to any church.

"The Bible says, 'Act as you have faith, and you will have faith.' There are no truths only opinions even in science, and the Bible is 95% fiction. Which part is truth? I don't know.

"Epistemology is that part of Philosophy that begs the question, 'How do you know what you know?'

"As an afterthought, George Washington would never tell a lie. He believed in Deism which was popular in Europe at the time. What is a Deitist? George Washington wore false teeth."

CHAPTER 50

Houston, Texas
8 A.M., Wednesday, December 18, 1993
69°, cloudy, fog
No wind

When no wind is blowing the clouds drop down and cause fog. When the earth rotates toward the sun, the fog rises and becomes clouds, and you have a windless sunny day.

Houston was expanding like a big octopus sending out its tentacles along every major thoroughfare and engulfing adjacent counties. Sealy, across the Brazos in Austin County was part of the Sugar Land-Houston-Baytown Metropolitan area. Austin, Fort Bend, Brazoria, Galveston, Chambers, Liberty, San Jacinto, and Montgomery Counties all housed workers that commuted to Harris County and Houston.

Houston was only 150 years old, and the first Anglos arrived in Texas 170 years ago, 6 generations for most whose ancestors arrived early on. Mexicans were crossing the Rio Grande like roaches bringing their culture. To sneak up the Brazos River, they had to evade our Coast Guard or cross the border. The easiest way for a Mexican to get into Texas would be with a legal Passport or Visa. Then he could walk through, or ride in an automobile, bus, train or commercial airliner. No problem! Some said there were twenty million illegal Mexican immigrants, and half were in Texas, Arizona, and California. Houston led Texas in race related crimes, and, next to California, Texas was the biggest supplier of marijuana to the upper 48 and Canada. To the best of Dirk's knowledge Florida was still number one distributor of cocaine.

Dirk had lost track. When he was with the Dallas PD, they bragged they were number Uno.

Parts of Houston looked like Matamoras, and in another 20 years Houston would look like Guadalajara. Mexicans were up to 41%, and, if all were legal, they could team up with the blacks and win every general election in town. Dirk considered himself a typical normal male, and every race raised a finite percent of beautiful young maidens. He liked those, but it was the men, old ladies, and little kids that made him a racist.

Pretty young women were all over the world, even Eskimos and far off Africa. He wasn't too old to have nocturnal erections and "wet dreams." Pretty young women were a country's treasure. They dressed in bathing suits and had beauty contests. Genghis Kahn and Tamerlane knew that. Their armies were volunteers. They'd kill the men and old folks, rape the young women, and sell the kids off as slaves. It was fun, and they'd loot. That was cross culture breeding and population control. Economists voted Genghis Kahn the greatest, and Historians voted Muhammad.

Dirk got off the loop on US 288 south to Angleton and drove cautiously in the fog and pulled up to the light in forty minutes. He turned right at the light on Tex 35 and drove to the intersection at Bailey's Prairie where there was an Exxon Station and convenience store. He filled his tank, walked in, gave the lady his credit card, and looked for the rest rooms.

"Pardon me, but could you tell me where are your rest rooms?" asked Dirk.

She turned and took the key wired to a paddle and pulled a roll of toilet tissue from under the counter and handed them to Dirk. "Go round back and follow the trail. Lock the door from the inside. It's a two holed unisex."

Dirk had never experienced an Exxon filling station with a two holed toilet. That was the kind they had at Hardin where he grew up.

*   *   *

He passed over a rusty iron bridge and the Brazos River which he estimated as 75 yards wide. The current was rapid and the color was a dirty reddish brown, much faster than his place and much much faster than Sealy and Wallis. There were no sandbars at the curves, and the waters were eroding the banks and exposing the roots of pines and oaks. Tree branches covered with vines were hanging out over the water and every 30-40 yards a large tree had been uprooted and fallen into the water. After the Brazos passed under the bridge it curved to the west and parallel the road albeit in a snakelike fashion.

Dirk passed over Varner Creek and noticed a sign: East Columbia 1 mile. Dirk turned left (south) on a two lane hardtop and drove to the main street of East Columbia. There were a few vinyl covered frame houses with garages, pickup, ATM, and kid's toys out front.

A sign pointing to a historical marker pointed toward the river so Dirk made a left on a rock road toward the river. He passed a neat brick church with freshly painted door and shutters with a sign painted out front, First Presbyterian Church of Texas 1844. He continued up to the water's edge where on a rise he saw a sign, Bell's Landing, 1824. There were no sandbars. The water was swift and laden with silt which gave it a deep red-brown color. He was told that the San Bernard over in Wharton County was not nearly as long as the Brazos, and they came closest two miles west of West Columbia and overflowed in a flood and ran side by side until they merged into one muddy red river.

The Brazos flowed to Freeport, and the San Bernard ran into a wildlife refuge before emptying into the Gulf. Dirk was re-learning a lesson he should have remembered. A river never runs in a straight line, and the Brazos was crooked as a barrel of snakes and probably just as dangerous as it got closer to the Gulf. Also, all major rivers were tidal. They rose and fell with the tide. Some wise man of antiquity, probably Socrates or Plato, said you never put your foot in same river twice, meaning it changed all the time every day.

Dirk drove into West Columbia and resisted the temptation to see the Varner Hogg plantation. The old West Columbia Oil Field began back there. To Dirk's knowledge there weren't any wells being drilled in Brazoria County at the moment, but like most counties along the Gulf there were plenty of old stripper wells that would produce 10 or 15 barrels a day if the price got up to make a profit. That was true of most counties in Texas. The majors only got out the easy stuff, 60% of the oil and 80% of the gas was still down there. Along the Gulf, oil was mixed with salt water which had to be separated, and they always flared the natural gas.

Sinkholes weren't uncommon around salt domes, and at Conroe they had a whole drilling rig sink out of sight. No company had tried slant hole drilling under the salt or river, and hydraulic fracking was still in the experimental stage. Dirk had confidence that these old oil fields would some day be revived like Jesus rising up from the grave.

West Columbia had a population of 4000 on the last census. There were 60% white, 21% black and 19% Mexicans. 20% were below poverty level and on food stamps. Dirk looked around and didn't see any industries that would provide high paying jobs, except maybe dope dealing. You could say that about any rural town in southeast Texas where they didn't have an oil refinery or petrochemical plant. Most weren't feeding cows for beef anymore. He hadn't seen a milk cow, vegetable garden, chicken house, or hog pen since WWII because of food stamps and supermarkets.

He did notice more small churches built by independent fundamentalist denominations. They got together and swapped food stamps. Where two or more were gathered together in his name, somebody passed the plate. The social welfare net had put subsistence farming out of business, and cheap foreign oil had closed down the oil business.

At the west end of town was a Super Wal-Mart, McDonald's, and a new Best Western Hotel. Somebody had faith in the future. He made a right at the intersection of Tex 35 and Tex 36 north toward Sealy. At a mile on the left were a country club, swimming pool and golf course. There were about six cars in the parking lot and two carts on the course. Dirk slowed and read the monument, Brazoria County Country Club 1950. Further were signs on the left where overgrown roads, rusted iron gates, and multiple oil wells were all abandoned. He didn't see any cows or goats.

On his right as far as he could see were dense forests and no side roads. It hadn't been cut. Why? There was little underbrush and no pines. The oaks were giants, 200-300 years old, and were draped with Spanish Moss that hung to the ground. Obvious to Dirk it was the flood plane of the Brazos River which meant swamps, alligators, horseshoe lakes, and bayous, etc. The Brazos' course was as crooked as a barrel of snakes. Land distance was not the same as map distance, and river length was impossible to measure due to crooks and curves. It was much greater than map distance. He estimated 150 miles of river from Richmond to East Columbia and another 50 tortuous miles from East Columbia to Freeport. Nobody knew, and it was useless to ask. It changed after every flood. There were many square miles of marshy woods and swamps.

The swamp would hide an army, hundreds of illegal aliens, and several tribes of Karankawa Indians. In fact, the Karankawa might be still out there. Old Bezoar could be the tip of the iceberg, a decoy. The Jones Creek massacre was just down the road. Dirk tried to calculate it (30 x 7). WOW! That was 200 square miles of swamp below Richmond, and (24 x 3) if you added the marsh land, 72 square miles, from Sealy to Richmond you got 272 square miles. If 3/8 of a square mile equals 247 acres, then one square mile has 660 acres.

Dirk didn't know anything about surveying. The Spanish used hectares which was 2.5 acres. Then one square mile was 264 hectares or 660 acres.

Every Anglo-American that got a land grant from Mexico got 4200 acres (4000 + 200) which was 1680 hectares or 6 square miles. The square root of 6 was, oh shit! 2 x 3 was equal to 6. They walked off 2 miles one way and 3 miles the other and measured the length of their step. They didn't have pedometers or cars back in those days. A good pair of mules could haul a load of cotton at 10 miles per hour.

Only rich people had pocket watches, and nobody had a compass, and most could not read or write and counted on their fingers. They used the sunrise and sunset for east and west, and it changed in winter and summer. Allowing an average 5'8" man's stride was 3 feet, one mile equaled 1800 steps in a straight line. Then they drove a stake at each corner and fired their gun four times and yelled "this is my land," each time. Everybody used the honor system.

When Texas got lawyers, surveyors, and courthouses, they had it surveyed and filed in the courthouse. Nobody paid for any land in Texas. Austin and Zavalla took land as their pay. Dirk chuckled. If any lawyer or judge he knew, could read a surveyor's map, he'd kiss his ass in front of the courthouse and give him all day to draw a crowd. Surveyors went all way back to the ancient Egyptians who built the pyramids.

Below West Columbia if you counted all the land around Jones Creek between the Brazos and San Bernard rivers, you could add another (12 x 6) 72 square miles or 50,000 acres of marshlands. That made 240,000 acres of marshlands just up to Sealy. If each acre supported one alligator family, and a mother alligator hatched 100 eggs every year, that made 24 million alligators hatching out a year. If unchecked, alligators would cover the entire earth in 10 years.

Between the Colorado River at Matagorda and the Sabine River at Orange and Port Arthur from west to east there were the San Bernard, Brazos, Oyster Creek, Clear Creek, Buffalo Bayou, San Jacinto, No Name River, Trinity, Neches, Angelina, and Sabine River all empty into the continental shelf in the shallow part of the Gulf of Mexico. All of them had estuaries, marshes, and flood planes plus the landscape was relatively flat and tapered. They meandered over time and left shallow lakes and horseshoe bends heavily wooded and silted. Each big river had one or more dams upstream in Central Texas for power generation and water conservation to supply cities and irrigate crops.

Dams collected silt, which robbed the lower coastal areas of alluvial soil and land mass from overflow and flooding. The coastal cities like Houston, Baytown, Port Arthur, and Beaumont were sinking and some day the cities of Galveston, Baytown, and Port Arthur would be ankle deep in salt water. They could build dykes like Holland. Parts of New Orleans were built on the Mississippi Delta, and it was sinking and so was Houston, albeit slowly.

30,000 wells had been drilled offshore of Texas and Louisiana, and many thousands of wells had been drilled around salt domes along both coasts. The majors got the easy stuff, but 60% was still there. They had not drilled for the really deep stuff below the salt.

CHAPTER 51

Needville, Texas
11 A.M., Wednesday, December 18, 1993
74°, Sunny, no wind

Dirk drove north on Texas 36 and entered the limits of Needville, population 2000, which he estimated was at least 12 or more miles west across the Brazos River from his Old Ben Milam's place on the east bank of the Brazos. He figured the hunters he heard shooting on his place didn't come across from Needville. They'd need a swamp buggy with wheels or a helicopter. They could walk across from Pearland or come up the river in a boat which was the easiest way. He'd never known Mexicans or blacks to hunt deer.

Rednecks hunted deer for sport. Horns and trophy bucks! Rednecks thought about deer hunting all the time and put out corn feeders off season. There were lots of deer on Old Ben Milam's place. It was a natural sanctuary. He could sell deer leases to Rednecks. There were deer on the Hale's old ranch too! Rednecks would sit for hours and days in deer blinds and watch their corn feeders. They could die on a deer stand and nobody knew until the buzzards started circling. It was crazy! He could raise Loblolly pines and sell deer leases. There were deer and Feral hogs all over Southeast Texas, and alligators. It was Redneck heaven!

*　*　*

Needville appeared to be a quiet prosperous small town with a population of 2500 with 25% Mexicans, 15% blacks, and 60% whites that thrived on agriculture, goat herding, hunting, fishing and tourism.

They had a farmer's market, Wal-Mart, McDonald's and only 12% were on welfare and food stamps. It was on the west periphery of the great Brazos swamp and was gateway to the Brazos Bend State Park. Somewhere off the map was the Brazos Valley Energy Plant which no doubt fired natural gas and re-circulated water to the Brazos River.

Dirk turned down the road to the Headquarters of the Brazos Bend Park which was run by the Texas Parks and Wildlife for the benefit of nature lovers, bird watchers, campers, and hookups for motor homes, etc., but it was closed during gun season for obvious safety reasons. There was a replica of an old timey log cabin where a happy camper could buy tickets for an overnight stay or maybe a week sold in advance. Game Wardens carried side arms and checked MV registration and driver's license just like cops. You couldn't smoke marijuana or crack in there. There were outdoor toilets for both sexes, and indecent exposure was strictly prohibited.

They had a sign out front with the nature trails, campsites, and boat ramps shown. They were too far across the swamp from the Brazos, but they allowed fishing on natural lakes close by which no doubt they kept stocked. Dirk was familiar with those kind of camps. Texas had hundreds, probably thousands. Big Bend National Park 800 miles to the west was the biggest and best. It was part of the Chihuahua Desert that started in Mexico City and went all way up into Arizona. The Rio Grande River separated the U.S. from Mexico won by the force of arms.

The worse thing about Brazos Bend were mosquitoes, alligators, and wild hogs. Dirk hadn't heard of alligators eating little kids or pet dogs, lately, but those things happened.

*　　*　　*

Texas Highway 36 passed under US 59S into the City of Rosenberg, population 25,000 with 60% whites, 8% blacks and 55% Mexicans. Most of the Mexicans were "green card" carrying natives of Old Mexico and their population was seasonal. The best way to cross into Texas was carrying a green card and a Texas Driver's license. Neither your employer nor the cops would bother you, and your kids could enroll in school. Dirk had a rule of thumb. If they smiled and spoke good English, they were born here. If they worked hard and long, accepted substandard pay, and spoke and understood some English, they were on "green card" and legal. If they looked at the ground, mumbled, couldn't understand or speak English, then they were illegals and waded across the Rio Grande. He decided that most, if not all, the illegals in Texas waded or swam across the Rio Grande.

Rosenberg was begun in 1843, and was just 2 miles west of Richmond, the county seat, on the Old Spanish Trail from Nacogdoches to San Antonio in Bexar. The Brazos River meandered around and crossed between the two. It crossed again under US 59 in Sugar Land.

*   *   *

Richmond, population 14,000 with 26% whites, 15% blacks, and 60% Mexicans, was the County Seat of Fort Bend County. It was on the west side of a meandering Brazos River, and if it weren't for bridges and the river, Richmond and Rosenberg would be stuck together like Siamese twins. Both had more than their share of Mexicans, apparently attracted by all the construction in Sugar Land across the river where "it was at."

Richmond was founded in 1837 as a blockhouse called Fort Bend. While the white flight to Sugar Land was occurring their spaces were replaced by Mexicans coming up from south of the border. The population of Fort Bend County was 350,000, mostly whites across the river in Sugar Land which was doubling in population every 10 years. Somebody predicted Fort Bend County would have 500,000 by 2000 only six years away. Sugar Land was founded in 1837 the same year as Richmond. Anyway, Richmond and Rosenberg were attracting

Mexicans, and Sugar Land was the fasted growing city in the U.S.A. and the world, for that matter.

Richmond had an old timey courthouse, three story yellow brick, dome on top, and four white pillars out front. It had a three story red brick jail with bars on the windows and a gallows out back for public hangings. The kind of windows from which Blue Duck jumped in *Lonesome Dove.*

Dirk stopped at the Fort Bend County Library and was directed to the History section. At one time Mexicans were counted as whites, but now they were counted as Latinos since they were brown and spoke mostly Spanish. Dirk didn't take either Latin or Spanish in school.

In 1850 the census was 974 whites and 1,554 blacks in all Fort Bend County. All work was done by blacks. In 1870 they counted a total of 7,114. In 1880, 9,380 total with 7,508 negroes reported, and in 1900 there were a total of 16,528 of which 10,814 were black. The greatest industries were stock raising, rice cultivation, cotton, and sugarcane. The population of Rosenberg in 1900 was 519 with no breakdown of races, but the name was German Jewish.

Dirk read from Historical Review of South-East Texas, dated 1910.

"Said Commissioner, the Baron de Bastrop, and the Empresario Estevan F. Austin, the witnesses John Vince, Robert Vince, John Keller, the surveyor, John Cooke, and the party interested, John Austin, we all repaired to the said land which by the foregoing deed we have granted to the latter, situated on the Bayou, called Buffalo Bayou, and from a place where the land mark was placed on the southern bank of the said Bayou 1,000 varas below the junction point of the two branches of said Bayou, the surveyor began the surveys of the said two leagues, measuring thence 1,000 varas south, where another land mark was placed, thence west 7,080 varas where it was placed, thence north 7,080 varas crossing the western branch of said Bayou to another land mark near its northern branch, thence east 7,080 varas, where another land mark was placed, thence south 6,080 varas, crossing the said Bayou 1,000 varas below the junction of its two branches to the place of beginning, containing inside of these lines two leagues of land in superficie in a square, including the junction of the two branches aforesaid and all the place where the settler, George Harrison, first located, bounded on all sides by vacant lands, we gave to said John Austin possession of said land, taking him by the hand over it, telling him in a loud and audible voice that by virtue of the commission and powers granted to us in the name of the government of the Mexican Nation we give him possession of said land, together with all appurtenances, rights and belongings, for himself, his heirs and assigns, and the said John Austin, on being given the real and personal possession of said land, without objection from anyone, shouted loudly, pulled grasses, threw stones, planted stakes and performed the other necessary ceremonies, being notified that he is under the obligation to cultivate it inside of two years as being the term prescribed by law."

*   *   *

Dirk bet they used a set form and didn't get off their butts at San Felipe. It was mostly marsh, alligators, mosquitoes, and fierce Karankawas. It was part of the original patent for a Mexican land grant to Stephen F. Austin's family. It was later sold to the developers of Houston after the glorious victory by Sam Houston at San Jacinto where Santa Anna et al. were trapped between the flood waters of Buffalo Bayou and the San Jacinto River.

Nobody paid any money to Mexico. Cortez surely didn't pay the Aztecs for Mexico, and Spain didn't pay any guilt money either. We were sure as hell paying Arabs for Jerusalem.

Dirk read.

. . . . After he saw the town in ashes, according to his promise to Commodore Patterson, Lafitte set sail from Galveston on the 12th of May, 1820."

A few weeks later Gen. Long returned to Bolivar, and then took possession of the site of Lafitte's town, rebuilding the fort with a temporary structure. In February, 1821, occurred the battle of "the Three Trees," on the island, in which Long's forces met and defeated a large party of Carankaway Indians. A little later Long set out on his expedition into Texas, ending with his imprisonment and death in Mexico. In the meantime his wife remained at Bolivar until informed of the death of her husband. After this for many years Galveston island was practically uninhabited, and a consecutive narrative of events does not begin until the time of the Texas revolution.

The last 7 Karankawas were massacred in their sleep by members of Austin's colony at Jones Creek near Lake Jackson.

CHAPTER 52

Sugar Land, Texas
12 noon, Wednesday, December 18, 1993
70°, Sunny, no wind
Few cumulus clouds

Sugar Land, the Texas land of dreams, was in two parts, the new and newer both growing toward each other on the east bank of a tortuous meandering Brazos River and the equally tortuous Oyster Creek which came off the Brazos somewhere between Rosenberg and Sealy in the swamps. Oyster Creek cut across the northeast of Fort Bend County, coursed south in Brazoria County and emptied in the West Bay of Galveston somewhere between Danberry and Clute. A more descriptive term as it neared the coast was Chocolate Bayou. It had its own little overflow swamps, alligators and mosquitoes, etc.

When tropical storm Alecia dumped on Fort Bend and Clear Lake, it rained 11" in two hours and Sugar Land, Pearland, Friendswood, and League City all went under water, and it soaked the downstairs carpets in a lot of new homes, stopped traffic on US 59 which went under, and empty tankers on 18-wheelers were floating around dragging the cabs. Some of those white people pulled up stakes and moved to Kerrville sixty miles northeast of San Antonio where the Guadalupe River ran right through the middle of town. In West Texas, you don't have marshes, alligators, feral hogs, and mosquitoes in your back yard. You have Mexicans to do the work! In Brazoria, Galveston, and Fort Bend Counties you get all that plus snakes, poisonous and non-poisonous. They seek out the high ground and climb trees, etc. When the Brazos overflows everything wild heads for high ground. You can figure in a

Class IV-V hurricane every four years and one or two tropical storms every year plus an average rainfall of 50" in the Greater Houston Metropolitan area bordered by Sealy on the west, Conroe on the north, Baytown, Liberty and Anahuac on the east, and the Gulf of Mexico on the south. The Indians named it Atascocita meaning mud hole, the land of the man eating Karankawas.

*   *   *

Dirk chuckled. The settlers in Texas, men, denied knowing their American wives in favor of their Mexican wives when the American wife showed up in Texas. Dirk read.

"The infernal brute, her husband, cut off her ears and maltreated her until she signed before an Alcide that she was an imposter and lied about him being her husband back in the States."

*   *   *

Sugar Land was named after Imperial Sugar. Their refinery shut down, but their home office and Icon were still there. It was the hot bed of expansion and economic activity in Houston Metropolitan area. It was the biggest city in Fort Bend, and the average home cost $300,000.

Sugar Land led the nation in master planned communities. All the Houston universities and big hospitals had branches there, and their public schools, police, and fire departments were outstanding. Why not? They were Republicans and the upper 3% that the Democrats were always wanting to tax.

Sugar Land was rated number one in everything by organizations who rate such things. It was a place where everybody wanted to live, but few could afford it (the upper 3%). However, you could eat out and shop there and share in its elegance.

Just like Elvis and the Beatles captured the world's imagination, Sugar Land attracted wealth and professionals like fly on flypaper. It

293

had more swimming pools, manmade lakes, and exquisitely manicured golf courses than Lake Land Florida. Both Oyster Creek and the Brazos flowed through. It reminded Dirk of Osaka Japan without the Japanese. Dirk couldn't think of enough adjectives and superlatives. If you had a Ph.D. in Physics or Engineering, made a salary of six figures, and had a loving wife and two lovely kids, then Sugar Land wanted you. There were few blacks, Mexicans or welfare recipients, if any, in Sugar Land. The economically challenged who worked in the franchise businesses, utility companies, hospitals, churches, schools, and various city employees could eat and shop in Sugar Land, but they couldn't afford to live there. They lived in Friendswood, Pearland, Alvin, and League City, etc. The Mexican construction workers mostly lived across the Brazos in Richmond and Rosenberg plus others which weren't bad.

*   *   *

To get to the heart of downtown Sugar Land from Richmond you go northeast toward Houston on the Old Spanish Trail (90A) and turn right on Tex 6 which will take you to its intersection with US 59S where YOU ARE HERE. On the east side of the intersection are the City Hall and Town Square. If you can see P.F. Chang's all lit up YOU ARE HERE. Every possible luxury and convenience you could ever dream up was YOU ARE HERE. If you were shopping and sightseeing, you really didn't need to go anywhere else. It had everything.

If you drove southwest on US 59S a couple of miles you came to River Park Shopping Center which was the newest of the new, and you could cross over the Brazos River twice, once on 59S and once on Grand Parkway which intersected US 59S running east and west. It was from the bridge on Grand Parkway that Jerry and he saw what they thought was a periscope of a miniature submarine.

Dirk parked on the side ramp of the bridge overlooking the Brazos on Grand Parkway and decided it was easy to get turned around. Previously he figured it was a mile or two downstream to the boat launch next to his property, but could easily be 5 or 6 miles. That's why they called it the Big Bend. Things looked close together and easily found on maps drawn to scale, but, when you got out and looked, they weren't really close and easily identified at all. The Brazos meandered back and around and there were swamps and maybe bogs. Nobody really knew where the county lines were down there. It was a guess, a sign on the highway, and dots on a map, somebody's map. He'd question the surveys. They were whatever was filed at the county courthouse, Fort Bend and Brazoria. People could move the property markers. In Texas, people sold surface rights, and heirs kept the mineral rights. You could cut timber off land, and somebody else got the oil royalties. It happened all the time.

Cortez claimed Texas in the name of God, the Pope, and the King and Queen of Spain. They probably saved maps in Mexico City and Madrid. God only knew for sure. The Pope had the final say.

In the U.S.A. it had to be settled in court with lawyers arguing on both sides in front of a judge and jury. WOW! That cost money. Anybody could sneak out and change a property line. He needed to go to Hardin and check the lines on the property he inherited. His dad showed him the markers, but he couldn't remember. The old courthouse burned down (Menard).

It was a good thing that oil companies, lawyers, and judges were honest. Heirs couldn't keep up with all that. There were absentee land owners scattered all over, and most died. The county judges and commissioners were honest and elected by the citizens, and the oil companies wouldn't drill unless all the heirs signed. Drilling offshore and in foreign countries where there weren't any lawyers made sense. God only knew who owned the land! There was such a thing as squatter's rights.

CHAPTER 53

Barclay Theater
University of Saint Nicholas
Houston, Texas
12 noon, Wednesday, December 18, 1993
Temperature 80°, no wind
Cumulus clouds

Dr. Amy Omikami was at the lectern.

"Our Anthropology tour group is stuck in Dublin Ireland by the worst snow experienced in northern Europe in the last century. London Heathrow and International Airports all over Europe have been closed to all but limited local traffic. The Eastern Seaboard in the U.S. and Canada are suffering the same fate. LaGuardia and Kennedy in New York, Dulles in Washington, and James E. Carter International in Atlanta have all been temporarily closed to International traffic. Since Paris has shut down, the Concordsky flight to Moscow will be delayed or cancelled, whatever.

"I really don't accept the concept of global warming. Garbage in and garbage out! A lot of NASA's work was using Russian temperature data extrapolations which fooled our computers. Figures don't lie, but liars figure. Computers do what you tell them.

"Our Geologists and Geophysicists have studied glacier core samples, petrified tree rings, and evidence of climate changes over hundreds, thousands, and millions of years. The earth undergoes a severe Ice Age every 10,000 years. At present, according to scientists, our earth is cooling 0.5°C every 100 years, and we are due for a new Ice at any time. The latter scientists are in a minority, and have remained less vocal. There are some declaring we are back in the Ice Age now. There're always contrarians on both sides of a political issue, and global warming is more political than scientific. It depends on whether you want corn whiskey and molasses in your tank or a Bengal tiger. I'll take the tiger, please.

"Back in the 19th century a German named Diesel proved you could run an internal combustion engine on peanut oil without needing a spark plug. It was hard to start and run in cold weather. Gasoline made from petroleum is cheaper and easier to get than vegetable oil and will start and run easier in all kinds of weather, but you need a spark plug and starting battery. You need lubricating oil and grease made for moving parts for both gasoline and diesel, and they are distilled out of petroleum, not peanut oil.

"The GDP and prosperity of a country is a straight time correlation with petroleum consumption. The U.S.A. uses up 25% of the world oil and has only 5% of earth's people. Easy petroleum will run out by 2020, and we will pay $200 a barrel for oil and $5 a gallon for gasoline at the pump, some say much sooner, like 2010.

"The Chinese and SEA Indians will want prosperity just like we, and their demand will determine the price. The whole Russian economy depends on natural gas, and they have more than anybody.

"If you burn fossil fuels, like natural gas, you produce CO_2 and H_2O. Big deal! Combustion provides heat and energy. H_2O stays in the atmosphere one week and falls out as rain. CO_2 stays up five years. Humans started burning coal in 1700 c.e. Our atmosphere is a closed system, only H_2 gas gets out. Everything else just orbits and eventually burns or falls because of earth's gravity.

"Venus has a CO_2 atmosphere, and its temperature is 660. Mars doesn't have an atmosphere and gets down to—150° every night. It doesn't have any fossil fuels, O_2, and water either. I think the manned space station on Mars is our most stupid idea, ever.

"Over the last 200 years since we started burning coal, the Russians calculated our earth's surface has increased 0.6C. Big deal! NASA agreed to get along. It was 120° when all the continents were at the equator, and the dinosaurs roamed the entire earth and farted natural gas. The odor must have been terrible. The hydrogen sulfide smells bad in natural gas is dinosaurs' fart.

"Alarmists say a big piece of ice will break off Antarctica and cause the Gulf Stream to change and freeze Great Britain, Ireland, and northern Europe for a 1000 years. Bullshit!

"Fossil fuels furnish 90% of human's requirement for fuel and energy. Bio fuels are not economical. It takes energy to make energy. It's a political football at best. You don't put corn, sugar, and peanut oil in your gas tank. You want a Bengal Tiger in your tank!

"You can't convince anybody in Europe and on our East Coast this morning that we are having global warming.

"The obvious solution to global warming, if any, and have our atmosphere clean and carbon free is to switch to burning natural gas. We've been flaring it for a hundred years. You can't drill in Texas without finding plenty of gas. Thank you!

"Joy."

Dr. Joy Burrell MD PhD, Psychiatrist wrote on the green board. **THE FIRST PICTURE SHOW, SEEING IS BELIEVING, MIND'S EYE, LANGUAGE, READING, MEMORY, LEARNING, DECISIONS, EMOTIONS, EXECUTION, SLEEP, AROUSAL, CONSCIOUSNESS, ATTENTION, FIGHT, AND FLIGHT**.

"Our eyes detect electromagnetic waves but our brain sees color and a picture. Our ears are sensitive to pressure waves, but our brain tells us what. Our senses send our brain electrical signals, and our brain makes a picture. We read words on a page, and our brain forms a picture. Our mind's eye makes pictures while we are awake or in dreams when we are asleep (unconscious). It's all in the mind. No two people are exactly alike, and nobody sees exactly the same picture or hears the same sound.

"Our brain tells us how something taste, and whether sensations are pleasant or painful. You can't feel somebody else's pain or pleasure.

Augustine discovered silent reading and thought God was talking to him. Up until that time everybody read aloud. He described mind's eye as communications with God.

"From a few nerve cells, a human brain will regulate all the other organs of the body. It will solve complicated mathematics, create new theories, and compose great music. WOW! Did evolution do all that? We are a lot smarter than monkeys! Everything evolved from pond scum.

"The adult human brain contains 100 billion neurons. Half of them are in the cerebellum which keeps everything coordinated. Each of the neurons make thousands of synapses. There are about a quadrillion synapses in the adult human brain. From limited information the brain constructs the world we experience in all of its complexity. Our brain accomplishes both thought and action.

"Language is an inexpensive and effective way we engage the world. Spoken language communicates facts and organizes sensory experience. It allows us to communicate our innermost feelings and thoughts to others. Written language is a record.

"The Limbic system is a complex structure of interconnected neurons which together allow learning, memory, emotion, and execution. You could not make a single decision without your limbic system. In cognitive research, it lights up well on MRI, PET, and EEG.

"The Limbic system is interconnected with the reticular formation which plays a critical role in sleep, arousal, attention and consciousness.

"You say, Dr. Burrell all that is complicated, and you are correct, but we haven't gotten to neurohumeral transmitters, receptors, cell membranes, electromotive potentials and on and on and on. Eventually we'll get down to subatomic particles where everything is a crap shoot, and you can't see it on a microscope. At that level we will need a leap of faith. The brain acts like a computer that evolved over 4 billion years. You get an impulse, and it gives you a picture and tells you what to do.

"Tomorrow, we'll take up neurotransmitters at the synaptic junctions. Thank you.

"Mambo."

Dr. Mambo Nigeria, Professor of Anthropology and Comparative Religions, wrote on the green board. **ABORIGINES, NATIVES, KARANKAWAS, MISSIONS, FORTS, LAFITTE, CANNONS, SOLDIERS, AUSTIN COLONY, ANGLOS, MASSACRE, AND EXTINCTION**.

"I've been asked to speak about the Native Americans and specifically the Karankawas who inhabited the Gulf Coast in this area before the Spanish. The Karankawa were extinct by 1860, before the Civil War. Any existing today would be a miracle or an accident of birth, like finding a valley of dinosaurs shut off from the real world, like King Kong or Tarzan the Ape Man, like *Jurassic Park*.

"I found an old *History of South East Texas* dated 1910 in the library that reads like this. Mambo read.

> *"The Indians existed, but the day circumscribed all their acts and purposes. Institutions they had not, the fabric of organized society showed the most primitive patterns. They were in the various stages of barbarism. These creatures of the forest and plain had not reached the state of mental and social development which had been attained by races of Mesopotamia and the Nile Valley three thousand years ago. The Indian in early American history had a status not unlike a wild animal not a fellow human being. The Indians could not mix or form a part of a new world civilization, and even now accommodate themselves imperfectly to citizenship."*

"The Indians were at continuous war with each other. The Tonkawa's and Apaches wanted the Spanish to aid them fighting the Comanche's that were driving the plainsmen from their hunting grounds. The Spanish brought diseases responsible for thousands of deaths across Texas. Whole tribes died of smallpox, chickenpox, measles and other European diseases to which they had no immunity. The white men killed off the buffalo, their main source of food.

"The Spanish fought north from Mexico City, killing off whole tribes, and bypassing others. They established Presidios, forts, and missions, but stopped at Texas. Why?

"The primitive but fierce and independent Karankawas along the Gulf coast failed to assimilate and remained faithful to their native ways of life. The Spanish sent soldiers to track them down. The Karankawas attacked settlers and forts. Out west it was the Apaches and Comanche's. That was 200 years ago, only 10 generations. The Spanish had been here 200 years and western Europeans were in North America 100 years after the Spanish. They were fighting the Reformation of the Catholic Church in Europe and millions died. Until the English sank the Spanish Armada, Spain was the greatest empire in the Western Hemisphere.

"Nobody kept up with what was going on in Russia, India, and China. They heard about Napoleon and the French. In Texas they were fighting the Indians. In fact, people were fighting all over the world.

"General Cornwallis surrendered to George Washington, gave us our independence, and was rewarded by being appointed the Viceroy and Commander of all British Forces in India. Napoleon marched into Portugal and Spain. The King of Portugal moved his capital to Brazil, and all the Spanish colonies in the Americas started revolt for Independence.

"All that was going on while the Karankawas were fighting for their lands and lives at Sugar Land, Texas. They were holding their own until Jean Lafitte and his pirates built a fort on Galveston Island. That was the beginning of the end for the Karankawas. The last bunch were massacred in their sleep by the Stephen Austin Colony at Jones's Creek near Brazoria. There's a historical marker down there. The Karankawas were 7 feet tall, had bad breath and B.O., and ate their captives alive. I'll stop and take up Jean Lafitte and the Karankawas tomorrow. Thank you!

"Peter."

Dr. Peter Rockford wrote on the green board. NAYPYIDAW, CHAOS, MALACCA, WELL EXPLOSION, BANGLADESH INVADES MYANMAR, CUR'AN, PORK, JIHAD, SPINDLETOP GUSHER, GOOSE CREEK, SINKHOLE, HOUSTON, AND NEW ORLEANS.

"Reports of the atomic destruction last week of Naypyidaw Myanmar included Than Shwe and the general command, 150,000 elite guard, and 4,000 domestic elephants housed within the compound wall. There remains 11 field combat battalions under the command of field grade general officers, Senior Colonels and Brigadiers, and several Major and Lieutenant Generals. Insurgent forces made up of Shan tribesmen have occupied Mandalay while border Chinese and Burmese Hmong forces under command of a rogue Chinese General have seized Rangoon (Yangon).

"China has declared strict neutrality, denied knowledge who detonated the atomic bomb, and issued a warning that they would use military force to protect their oil properties in the Bay of Bengal. There is a permanent Chinese submarine base in the Andaman Islands. The Chinese Navy patrols the Bay of Bengal routinely protecting its gas leases and guarding the shipping route of the Straits of Malacca, between Malaysia and Sumatra, which oil tankers from the Persian Gulf and Arab countries must take en route to China, North Korea, Japan, South Korea, etc., etc.

"They are twelve hours ahead of us. At midnight tomorrow, 12 noon today our time, Bangladesh declared war on Myanmar, blew up a French TOTAL deep well driller which is on fire 40 miles south of the Irrawaddy Delta and spilling 200,000 gallons of crude per day. Efforts are being made under fire to repair the damage while a Naval battle between gun boats of Bangladesh and Myanmar is in progress. Bangladesh troops in force have crossed the border into the northern Kachin state and are progressing along the old India to Lashio Burma Road.

"Now, why did Bangladesh sink TOTAL's deep well? The fish! Everybody in Bangladesh eats fish. They all eat fish in India, Bangladesh, and SEA. The military junta dictators in Myanmar didn't care. They eat pork which is strictly against Islamic laws. That's how Myanmar got the whole Bay of Bengal to lease out to foreign oil companies. The Bangladeshi are fighting mad because the Myanmar drink wine and eat pork. All old Monks drink wine and eat pork. They get fat. The Bangladeshis declared Jihad, holy war. The common people just eat rice. If all you eat are rice, lentils, and vegetables, you stay thin. There's not a fat person in Bangladesh. They don't eat pork or drink alcoholic beverages.

"They are going to kill every fat person in Myanmar. The Curan strictly forbids pork and alcoholic beverages. Buddhist are idolaters, heretics, don't accept Muhammad, eat pork and drink wine. Hindus drink alcohol and eat pork, but don't eat beef. Brahmans are sacred in India. Bangladesh is greatly overpopulated and short of land. Once Bangladesh establishes a military front in Northern Myanmar, land hungry Bangladeshi peasants will come across their porous borders in waves, by the thousands and millions. The Shan and Hmong's can't stop them. All they can do is guard Mandalay and Yangon and control the two lane tarmac between the two major cities. It divides the country in half. Bhamo Basin is in the eastern half close to China.

"We want to land drill in Burma and not mess up their fishing waters. You can't keep from spilling deep water oil. The pressure is too high. When you drill deep, you tap into high pressure oil and blowouts occur. Ask any deep water drillers. It costs more and more to go deep. Oil collects under salt evaporates.

"The oil well that blew in last night in Houston Heights was over a salt dome. It's started another oil boom. No major oil company ever drilled in a graveyard. Seismography would jar the graves open, and you'd get caskets and skeletons all over. The cemetery is sinking because they let out the gas, oil, and salt water. The same as the Astrodome sink hole. Houston is sitting on a salt dome. Drive over there and look at Saint Colombo. Caskets, skeletons, and bodies are everywhere. It's Chaos! The earth is yielding up its dead.

"Every country in the world is blaming Bangladesh for nuking Naypyidaw. In retrospect, it's obvious they had to eliminate the Military Junta and Myanmar's strike force before they sank TOTAL's deep well and invaded Burma. Suicide bombing is a unique Islamic device because they offer martyrdom, paradise, and 70 virgins to young people gullible enough to believe it.

"I'm going to digress from our usual scientific lectures on petroleum Geology and talk about the world's first big gusher, Spindletop Gusher in Beaumont, and the problems they had. Get a video or DVD of *BOOM TOWN* with Clark Gable and Spencer Tracy filmed in 1940 about the early oil days in Texas. Your parents might remember *GIANT* with James Dean, Elizabeth Taylor, and Rock Hudson. They changed all the names and put it in West Texas, but the real life story occurred in Chamber's County, next door. James Dean played Glenn McCarthy. The hotel that the Dean character built was the Shamrock across from the Texas Medical Center, and Elizabeth Taylor in real life married Nicki Hilton, son of billionaire Conrad Hilton, her first wedding in white, at the opening of the Shamrock. In the end, Rock Hudson beat up James Dean who won the heart of Elizabeth Taylor. They didn't put raw sex in movies back in 1950. It got 5 Academy Awards and was best film of 1950. James Dean star of *East of Eden* was killed in single car accident. Rock Hudson died of AIDS, and his estate was sued for Palimony. Elizabeth is still alive after seven husbands, bilateral hip replacements, and a live-in boyfriend. They'll probably make a movie of her life. She was Cleopatra, like George C. Scott was Patton. You can get them all on DVD on the Internet at Amazon.com secondhand and inexpensive. All the old "great movies" have been copied, and they don't make "great movies" anymore. They went out with the dinosaurs. Today's movies target teenagers. After they went up in the price of popcorn, adults quit going. Why? They remember when popcorn was a nickel, and the movie cost ten cents. Before WWII you could buy a two door Chevy or Ford sedan for $700. Now they are $20,000. Up until 1974, gas was 21 cents at the pump. Now it's only $2.00. When oil goes up to $60 a barrel, you should pay $5.00 a gallon at the pump just to keep up with inflation. That's why you're filling your own car and airing your own tires and pay with a validated credit card. Inflation! By 2020 you'll pay $5 at the pump. It's simple economics. We could 'go broke' running a car on corn liquor

"The Lucas Gusher at Spindletop in 1901 was brought in on LouAnn Salt evaporate of Jurassic age (208-144 million years ago) laid down during the age of the dinosaurs. However, many fields have been found in the Tertiary Age sediments supporting marine planktons as the early precursor of petroleum. Spindletop blew out to 150 feet for nine days before they capped it at 100,000 barrels per day. Oil was 3 cents a barrel. In one year 500 oil companies were formed and 285 active wells were flowing. It continued until 1936, after which they mined it for sulfur until 1975.

"The Goose Creek Oil Field in Baytown, Texas blew in several similar gushers in 1918. The field sank and was covered with Gulf and became Texas' first offshore field. It's still pumping and over 75 years has produced 150 million barrels of oil. If you take the LaPorte Bridge, it's about a 30 minute drive out Texas 146. It was the first to produce oil under a deep salt dome from porous sands and clays. The whole southeast county has sunk 3 feet. Geologic oil survey revealed that Houston and New Orleans are sinking.

"I'll stop and pick up on this tomorrow. Amy!"

Dr. Amy Omikami wrote on the green board. RANDOMNESS, PROBABILITY, UNCERTAINTY, COMPLEXITY, NON LINEAR, DETERMINISTIC, FRACTALS, AND CHAOS.

"Shooting craps and playing roulette are randomness. We live with uncertainty from conception to death. It occurs on all levels down to quantum. Heisenberg was a Nazi scientist who invented the uncertainty principle. He was in jail awaiting trial when he heard about the atomic bomb exploding (Chaos) over Hiroshima. He got out his slide rule, repeated his calculations, and found one tiny misplaced decimal point in calculating the critical mass. He told Hitler to put his money on rockets, because an atomic bomb was too big to fit in an airplane.

"In small particles traveling near the speed of light you can measure the speed but not the position or, if you measure the position, you can't the speed. On a subatomic level the momentum or position of an electron can only be calculated by probability within a limit of uncertainty. On an atomic level it's a crap shoot. We live in a relative world flowing temporarily in the stream of space and time in which there are no absolutes. Time and change govern everything, and nothing escapes uncertainty.

"Complexity, an abstract term, has always been with us. Every generation back to the Great Ice Age and cavemen days has been complex. The world population of humans double every 40 years. Wars and natural disasters may cause temporary misery, but populations will expand, invasions will occur, and boundaries change. As fossil fuels and groundwater diminish, countries will invade other countries to gain strategic and valuable resources no matter what the pretences are. When populations outgrow natural resources, survival of the fittest naturally occur. Religion and threat of weapons of mass destruction provide a morally acceptable reason to invade your enemy, but you will seize his valuable land, rivers, and natural resources.

"All modern societies operate at a maximum complexity bordering on CHAOS. Your brain is complex when you sleep. Chaos wakes you. Society stays at maximum complexity, and shit happens. That's chaos! Conquering armies in the past have killed the men, raped the women, and taken their children into captivity. That's Chaos!

"Modern computers, properly programmed will allow visualization of probability, complexity, and Chaos which I will cover tomorrow. Thanks!

"President Clinton's embrace of Monica Lewinski and the atomic bomb exploding over Naypyidaw were a perfect example of Chaos.

At least, that's what Chaologist are proving by high speed complex computers.

"It's too early to tell whether Bangladesh's invasion of Burma was complex or chaotic. I favor complexity. It was predicted several years back when Myanmar started leasing drilling rights in the Bay of Bengal. There was an overlap of ancestral territorial waters and a gentlemen's agreement to drill shallow and extract only natural gas. TOTAL of France cheated. What China, India, and USA will do, is anybody's guess. I think they will think chaotically. Stay tuned. Tomorrow, computer math and science of the 21st century.

"By-the-way, in afterthought, the 400 point market drop that somebody caused when they hit the wrong decimal place selling P&G is a perfect example of complexity turning to Chaos in a blink of the eye. The more complex the market, the more volatility and Chaos you can anticipate. Computers do what you tell them.

"The same occurred when that high pressure oil well blew out, caught fire, and sank to the bottom. When dealing with high pressure a mile deep, you have to use more cement in the wellhead casing and have an automatic blowout preventer. That's CHAOS! Hasta La Vista!"

CHAPTER 54

Savemore Mortuary
South Main Street
Houston, Texas
8 P.M., Wednesday, December 18, 1993
Nice weather, stars and satellites out

After a nice Rosary, Melita was going to have A. Fuller Bottle Jr. cremated and keep his ashes at home in a vase (urn) on the mantle in her living room fireplace. There was a black undertaker in Georgia that dumped the bodies in a swamp and sent their loved ones sand in a crematory urn. He believed in excarnation. He sold all their jewelry, watches, and false teeth which led to his discovery. The price of gold and false teeth went up. He offered to give the bodies back, but the State revoked his license.

In Singapore, it's law that every dead body gets cremated unless you donate your body for medical research. Singapore was the first to introduce Medical Tourism before Calcutta was the "place to go" to have your body parts replaced all paid for by insurance and Medicare.

*   *   *

Devine' and Opal, in black, attended as a same sex couple and sat on the nun's side where they could see A. Fuller Jr. and Father Jésus Posadas. They had never seen either in life.

The nuns from Del Arroyo attended services at Saint Colombo Cathedral where Jésus was the new Parish priest assigned Father Villa's place. The old priests in residence, Father Eusebuis and Archbishop

Galbreaux, were retired. It was a lot less expensive and more convenient to have services in Savemore than at Saint Colombo. Savemore had a concealed bar and would serve cocktails where the friends and kin could get together and meet after formal services. It was win-win.

Rene' Descarte, Bill Riley DA, and Booker Washington were there in official capacity. The killer often attended the funeral and mourned the loudest. Olinda Starr liked to kiss dead men. General JoAnn Johnson was escorted down by Colonel William Wallace Billings. William's grandmother was a Fuller, and he was distant cousin to the Fuller Bottles. Fuller Bottle Sr. sat on the front row with his wife, Lolita, secretary and former wife of Fuller Bottle Jr. Two rows were taken up by Fuller Bottles, Fullers, and Bottles. Wanda Townsend sat behind the mourners escorted by Dr. Richard Bernstein, Sandra's Gastroenterologist, who had tears down his cheeks and was smiling bravely. That was odd. Devine' had never seen a Jew at a Catholic Rosary.

Unknown to Devine', Sandra, Rene' Descarte, and everybody, A. Fuller Bottle Jr. had sued Rich for $100,000,000, and Richard followed Fuller Jr. to Sandra's office on the afternoon after the first snow in August and sliced his head off on Sandra's couch with the two handed broadsword he used representing Israel in the Seoul Olympics. He and A. Fuller Jr. were ardent bikers, charter members of the **KNOCKER**, roommates at the University and frequent clients of Wanda Townsend's Escort Service. Conspicuously absent were Devine's Private Investigator Wallace Derek Strong and his fiancé Captain Jerry Billings, Dirk's steady live in. Devine' had no idea or notice that Dirk and Jerry were bogged down to the axles in his Jeep Wagoneer near his home place on the bank of the Trinity River near Hardin, Texas in Liberty County.

*   *   *

Father Posados raised his arms, and the nuns and choir stood. On signal, Father Posados led them in the Alleluia chorus, all stanzas, a cappella, and heavenly. They remained standing. Father Posados raised his arms. Everyone stood and Father Posados bowed his head and prayed.

> **"Our father, who art in heaven, hallowed be Thy name; Thy kingdom come; Thy will be done on earth as it is in heaven. Give us this day our daily bread; and forgive us our trespasses as we forgive those who trespass against us; and lead us not into temptation, but deliver us from evil. Amen."**

The nuns chanted.

> *"Hail Mary, full of grace! The Lord is with Thee; blessed art Thou among women, and blessed is the fruit of thy womb, Jesus."*

> *"Holy Mary, Mother of God, pray for us sinners, now and at the hour of our death. Amen."*

> *"Glory be to the Father, and to the Son, and to the Holy Ghost. As it was in the beginning, is now and ever shall be, world without end. Amen."*

> **"I believe in God, the Father Almighty, Creator of heaven and earth; and in Jesus Christ, His only Son, our Lord; who was conceived by the Holy Ghost, born of the virgin Mary, suffered under Pontius Pilate, was crucified, died, and was buried. He descended into hell; the third day He arose again from the dead; He ascended into heaven, sitteth at the right hand of God, the Father Almighty; from thence He shall come to judge the living and the dead. I believe in the Holy Ghost, the Holy Roman Catholic Church, the communion of saints, the**

forgiveness of sins, the resurrection of the body, and life everlasting. Amen.

The congregation and choir sat down. The nuns and Father Jésus remained standing.

"After the Last Supper our Lord led the disciples out of Jerusalem to Gethsemane, the olive grove where He had spent so many nights in prayer. Agonized by the thought of what He was to suffer for the sins of men, He prostrated Himself and prayed for strength to face the coming ordeal."

"Hail Mary, full of grace! The Lord is with Thee; blessed art Thou among women, and blessed is the fruit of thy womb, Jesus."

"Holy Mary, Mother of God, pray for us sinners, now and at the hour of our death. Amen."

"Glory be to the Father, and to the Son, and to the Holy Ghost. As it was in the beginning, is now and ever shall be, world without end. Amen."

"Thinking to placate the blood lust of the mob, Pilate ordered his soldiers to scourge Jesus. They stripped our Lord to the waist, chained Him to the low whipping post, and then set to mangling His body, lashing His naked back with leather thongs weighted with metal."

"Hail Mary, full of grace! The Lord is with Thee; blessed art Thou among women, and blessed is the fruit of thy womb, Jesus."

"Holy Mary, Mother of God, pray for us sinners, now and at the hour of our death. Amen."

"Glory be to the Father, and to the Son, and to the Holy Ghost. As it was in the beginning, is now and ever shall be, world without end. Amen."

"After the soldiers had scourged Jesus, they placed on His head a crown of thorns twigs, clothed him in a purple mantle, and put a reed in His hand as a scepter. Then, crying, 'Hail, King of the Jews,' they struck Him and spat upon Him."

"Hail Mary, full of grace! The Lord is with Thee; blessed art Thou among women, and blessed is the fruit of thy womb, Jesus."

"Holy Mary, Mother of God, pray for us sinners, now and at the hour of our death. Amen."

"Glory be to the Father, and to the Son, and to the Holy Ghost. As it was in the beginning, is now and ever shall be, world without end. Amen."

"Condemned to be crucified, Jesus is presented with the Cross, which He is to carry to the place of execution. Meekly He shoulders the cruel burden and begins the journey to the little hill outside the west gate where He is to die. The great cross cuts into His shoulder; the mob jeers and derides. Each of the thousand steps to Golgotha is a separate agony."

"*Hail Mary, full of grace! The Lord is with Thee; blessed art Thou among women, and blessed is the fruit of thy womb, Jesus.*"

"*Holy Mary, Mother of God, pray for us sinners, now and at the hour of our death. Amen.*"

"*Glory be to the Father, and to the Son, and to the Holy Ghost. As it was in the beginning, is now and ever shall be, world without end. Amen.*"

"The executioners have stripped Him, nailed His hands and feet to the planks, and hoisted the heavy cross into position. As the soldiers begin their terrible vigil, every fiber of Christ's body cries out for rest and relief. For three long hours His agony continues. Then spirit and flesh are parted; the price of redemption has been paid."

"*Hail Mary, full of grace! The Lord is with Thee; blessed art Thou among women, and blessed is the fruit of thy womb, Jesus.*"

"*Holy Mary, Mother of God, pray for us sinners, now and at the hour of our death. Amen.*"

"*Glory be to the Father, and to the Son, and to the Holy Ghost. As it was in the beginning, is now and ever shall be, world without end. Amen.*"

"It is the dawn of the third day, and the body of Christ lies silent and lifeless within the tomb. Suddenly the sepulcher is filled with light; the shrouded figure stirs, casts off the winding sheet, strides forth radiant and

omnipotent. The great stone blocking the entrance is hurled aside by an Angel and the Roman guards lie stunned and terrified. 'He is risen as He said'. Alleluia."

The choir stood and Father Jésus Posados led them again in the Alleluia Chorus. The choir sat down and the nuns chanted.

"Hail Mary, full of grace! The Lord is with Thee; blessed art Thou among women, and blessed is the fruit of thy womb, Jesus."

"Holy Mary, Mother of God, pray for us sinners, now and at the hour of our death. Amen."

"Glory be to the Father, and to the Son, and to the Holy Ghost. As it was in the beginning, is now and ever shall be, world without end. Amen."

"On the fortieth day after the Resurrection our Lord supped with his disciples in the Cenacle. Jesus spake: I am the truth, the way and the life. Thou shall not behold the Father except through the Son. Then He led them out of Jerusalem to Mount Olivet, and after bidding them farewell He 'was lifted up before their eyes, and a cloud took him out of their sight.'

"Hail Mary, full of grace! The Lord is with Thee; blessed art Thou among women, and blessed is the fruit of thy womb, Jesus."

"Holy Mary, Mother of God, pray for us sinners, now and at the hour of our death. Amen."

"Glory be to the Father, and to the Son, and to the Holy Ghost. As it was in the beginning, is now and ever shall be, world without end. Amen."

"After the Ascension the disciples returned to the Cenacle to await the Paraclete promised by Christ. On the morning of the tenth day a sound like a great wind filled the room and tongues of flame appeared over the heads of all present. Filled with the Holy Spirit, the disciples went out and preached boldly, converting some three thousand souls that very day."

"Hail Mary, full of grace! The Lord is with Thee; blessed art Thou among women, and blessed is the fruit of thy womb, Jesus."

"Holy Mary, Mother of God, pray for us sinners, now and at the hour of our death. Amen."

"Glory be to the Father, and to the Son, and to the Holy Ghost. As it was in the beginning, is now and ever shall be, world without end. Amen."

"Upon the death of the Blessed Virgin her body was miraculously preserved from corruption and, after being united to her immaculate soul, was carried by Angels into heaven. It was most fitting that our Lord should exempt from corruption the body of His holy Mother, that virginal body in which He assumed human flesh."

"Hail Mary, full of grace! The Lord is with Thee; blessed art Thou among women, and blessed is the fruit of thy womb, Jesus."

"Holy Mary, Mother of God, pray for us sinners, now and at the hour of our death. Amen."

"Glory be to the Father, and to the Son, and to the Holy Ghost. As it was in the beginning, is now and ever shall be, world without end. Amen."

"Upon her assumption into heaven our Blessed Mother was received by her Son and crowned as Queen of Heaven in the presence of the angelic choirs and all the saints."

"Hail Mary, full of grace! The Lord is with Thee; blessed art Thou among women, and blessed is the fruit of thy womb, Jesus."

"Holy Mary, Mother of God, pray for us sinners, now and at the hour of our death. Amen."

"Glory be to the Father, and to the Son, and to the Holy Ghost. As it was in the beginning, is now and ever shall be, world without end. Amen."

Hail, Holy Queen, Mother of Mercy, hail our life, our sweetness, and our hope! To Thee do we cry, poor banished children of Eve! To Thee do we send up our sighs, mourning and weeping in this vale of tears! Turn then, most gracious advocate, thine eyes of mercy towards us; and after this, our exite, show unto us the blessed fruit of thy womb, Jesus! O clement, O loving, O sweet Virgin Mary.

"Hail Mary, full of grace! The Lord is with Thee; blessed art Thou among women, and blessed is the fruit of thy womb, Jesus."

"Holy Mary, Mother of God, pray for us sinners, now and at the hour of our death. Amen."

"Glory be to the Father, and to the Son, and to the Holy Ghost. As it was in the beginning, is now and ever shall be, world without end. Amen."

After the resurrection, the eleven disciples went into Galilee, to the mountain where Jesus had directed them to go. And when they saw him they worshipped him. And Jesus drew near and spoke to them saying, 'All the power in heaven and on earth has been given me. Go, therefore, and make disciples of all nations, baptizing them in the name of the Father, and of the Son, and of the Holy Ghost. Amen."

"Hail Mary, full of grace! The Lord is with Thee; blessed art Thou among women, and blessed is the fruit of thy womb, Jesus."

"Holy Mary, Mother of God, pray for us sinners, now and at the hour of our death. Amen."

"Glory be to the Father, and to the Son, and to the Holy Ghost. As it was in the beginning, is now and ever shall be, world without end. Amen."

"In the name of the Father and of the Son and of the Holy Ghost, may all the power of the devil against you be

at end, through the imposition of our hands and through the invocation of the holy and glorious Virgin Mary, Her most worthy spouse Joseph, and of all the holy angels, archangels, patriarchs, prophets, apostles, martyrs, confessors, virgins, and all other saints. Amen."

"Hail Mary, full of grace! The Lord is with Thee; blessed art Thou among women, and blessed is the fruit of thy womb, Jesus."

"Holy Mary, Mother of God, pray for us sinners, now and at the hour of our death. Amen."

"Glory be to the Father, and to the Son, and to the Holy Ghost. As it was in the beginning, is now and ever shall be, world without end. Amen."

"In the name of the Father, and of the Son, and of the Holy Ghost. Amen."

CHAPTER 55

Hardin, Texas

8 P.M., Wednesday, December 18, 1993

Dark, Hoot Owl

"You mean we'll have to sleep in this Jeep and fight the mosquitoes all night?" asked Jerry. She was mainly mad at herself for letting Dirk talk her into coming along.

"I can't leave this Jeep. Somebody will strip it. The Tow Truck lady said she'd be out after daylight in the morning. I wanted you to see what's left of my old home place, and where I grew up. I broke a cardinal rule in driving on unimproved roads."

"What's that?" asked Jerry.

"When you're driving down a steep hill, never turn around on the grass and head back up. You'll get stuck and sink to the axles every time. A tow truck costs $50 to wench you out. It's a gold mine for them," replied Dirk.

"Fuck you, Dirk! I'm calling a Smokey to take me home. Nobody's going to strip this Jeep. We're miles from civilization."

* * *

Dirk knew he was where an oil field once existed, and there were shelled roads and stripper wells out there somewhere. His home place was an eye sore, and the county demolished it, probably. If he hadn't let Jerry talk him in to finding an indoor toilet (McDonald's) he wouldn't have U-turned out on the soft boggy grass and started back uphill. He'd driven 4 x 4 Jeeps most of his life, and never had one stuck before. When they bog down to the axles and and the wheels just spin, you have to wench them out. He stuck the SUV the same way at Hale's old place. He and Joy spent the night in the ancient farmhouse which now belonged to him. Ole!

Dirk figured they stuck a quarter mile from the river two miles west of Hardin which was five miles north of Liberty Texas. He'd walked it to Hardin once and left Jerry in the Jeep.

"Fuck her! Fuck me!" said Dirk. What difference did it make where he slept? Jerry took their only flashlight. "Fuck Jerry!" Without a flashlight, he couldn't lower the back seats and make a bed. There was no way a grown man could lay down in a Jeep Grand Waggoner and get comfortable. If he used his field jacket for a pillow, he'd get shaking cold. It had to be 45-50 degrees out there. If he turned on the motor to run the heater, he'd use up the rest of the gas. "Fuck me," mumbled Dirk. It was just moments like this that he wanted a cigarette which he'd quit after bypass. Thank goodness!

He'd left the key on! He tried the ignition, and all he heard was click, click, click. He tried the lights, and they didn't come on. The horn wouldn't blow. *Shit! The battery was dead*, thought Dirk, correctly. People run down the battery trying to get out of a mud hole. It happens to everybody. The tow truck driver would have a jumper cable, and he'd get a charge or new battery and a wash job at WalMart's.

Dirk pushed the seat back and leaned back behind the wheel and went to sleep and dreamed about Brazil and Maria Tantalia. Why Maria? He didn't know. You don't choose your dreams. They just happen.

*   *   *

Aeroporta, Sao Paula Brazil
7 P.M., Friday, November 16, 1993
Not safe outside after dark
Nobody understands or speaks English

"We can't leave this airport, and I think Louiza Santos may be in Rio. They only fly to Manaus when the plane fills. It's 1,000 miles up the Amazon, and they have a rat problem. I talked with a German who could speak English. He said the best thing to do was fly PAM to Rio, stay at the Pink Tulip on Copacabana beach, and have them call us when a plane is scheduled to fly to Manaus. He never heard of Louiza Santos.

"All the white people have left Manaus except the zoo keepers and Academics studying Botany and rats. The rats are eating up the palm trees and bamboo and will make it to Manaus in about a week. If you like to eat rat barbequed on a stick, it's a good time to go. They are breeding like flies, multiplying exponentially, and destroying everything in their paths," explained Maria.

She had left Dirk guarding their bags and luggage while she chatted with passengers waiting for flights at the tables of the bars and food outlets. Dirk hadn't seen a McDonalds or an American fast food window anywhere. No native could speak English, and the natives treated you like untouchables in India. He hadn't figured out why yet. Maybe it was Texas on their luggage tags. He probably had halitosis and B.O., but he and Maria traveled symbiotically and didn't notice such things about each other.

"I think that's a great idea," replied Dirk standing and grabbing the handles on his bag and baggage. Maria carried her own, because of security and customs, etc. She rolled both hers, and he hand carried his bag and rolled his baggage. He followed her to the PAM main ticket counter where they presented their passports, and Maria asked for two tickets to Rio de Janeiro on the next available flight. Three women, each a little older shook their heads, but Maria insisted and finally threatened to call the U.S. Embassy. The last lady, about 50, disappeared in back, and a bald headed man of about 60 came out and spoke a little pidgin. He listened to Maria and made out two tickets and boarding passes leaving at Gate 3 in the basement in one hour, 9 P.M. to Rio.

*　　*　　*

They picked out their bags and headed for the exit of the aeroporta in Rio de Janeiro, the home of perpetual carnival and naked women, all with 38 inch busts from puberty to seventy. It was like National Geographic *déjávu*, the most striking example of natural selection Dirk had ever seen. Those Portuguese sailors in Africa picked out the gals with the biggest boobs. At first he thought of silicon, but decided they were the real thing. You could play telephone. *Stick one in your ear and the other in your mouth.* In high school they had a joke. Falsies taste like rubber, but these gals looked like Guernsey in Holland.

After the shock of big boobs, Dirk was able to find a porter who would find a cab to the Pink Tulip, a tourist hotel, located on International Boulevard just across from Copacabana Beach made famous by the movie, *Blame it on Rio*, with several big name actors whose names he couldn't remember and two teenage girls who delighted in running up and down the beach topless. Needless to say, they were selected for their big boobs. It was a comedy, otherwise the movie would have been a flop except for the young girls and their boobs.

Maria paid the cabbie one hundred bucks for a thirty minute drive through the residential and business sections of downtown Rio. Occasionally Dirk noticed ghettos with naked black kids and graffiti. The driver sped through those areas to avoid thrown rocks and one fingered iconic gestures.

They pissed on the sidewalk and gave them the finger as they drove by. Dirk decided they were racists and were welcoming Maria and him in the Brazilian custom.

Dirk had heard that the real ghettos were on a mountainside on the north part of Copacabana and the rich people lived on the south side. He also heard that Rio de Janeiro was the most corrupt city in the world and was run by four families. He didn't know what family was in Portuguese, but in Sicily it was Mafia. They had moved their capital way interior to Brasília to get away from the blacks. Brazil was the largest organized Black African nation in the world, and they confessed to be Catholic.

* * *

Dirk was awakened when a rattling pickup with a covered bed drove by headed for the river. By moonlight, he saw three Mexicans up front and about a dozen huddled together in back. They were laughing and chatting in Spanish and no doubt tipping the bottle. They didn't look his way.

CHAPTER 56

At 6 A.M. the next morning the Mexicans drove back from the river and toward Hardin. Everyone was asleep except a woman driver. They woke Dirk. He didn't remember a woman driver last night, but the driver was on the other side. Maybe they had a camp on the bank of the Trinity and worked elsewhere. There was plenty of work in Houston. He went back to sleep and dreamed about Argentina.

Louiza Santos was not in Buenos Aires. The plan was her showing Maria known oil reserves. Brazil had nationalized their oil companies and drilled offshore. They would outsource at day rates, but not split the profit. In Argentina they agreed to split the profit with England near the Falklands.

Maria called Sherry Deagio in Houston, told her the situation and asked her to find Louiza Santos, call the Dutch Royal in London, and if Louiza Santos didn't show up by tomorrow, she was sending Dirk back to Houston and fly to Cairo. She'd gotten word it was 130° at Luxor and the Valley of the Kings. Camels refused to get out of the shade, vehicle tires were melting, and terrorists were shooting, robbing, and raping Christians in the name of AL-LAH.

The students were off until January 15, 1994. They would go to Llasa or someplace holier than Egypt.

*　　*　　*

By chance Maria chose the Elevage Hotel about 3 blocks from San Martin' Plasa and 4 blocks from Florida Street. Around the corner was the second floor Almacen Tango show. The Elevage, a tourist favorite, had a one price buffet with anything and every you wanted eat and drink. Their room was ten floors up with windows on two sides, two double beds, large TV with CNN, and every modern convenience.

"Dirk, I've about given up on Louiza Santos. Do you know how to Tango?" asked Maria, giggling. There were Tango advertisements all over.

"Yes, ma'am. I was married to a dancer. She taught me everything I know. I saw at least six second-floor ballrooms within blocks from here advertising Tango. I don't know how you live in Argentina without knowing Tango. Tango is a dance of passion.

"Let's clean up, take a siesta, dress, buffet dinner, attend a Tango show, walk up and down Florida Street, watch TV, go to bed early, get up early, and go to the airport. You catch the next back to Houston, and I'll catch the next plane to Cairo."

Dirk was caught by surprise. "What's in Cairo? That's a dangerous place! More dangerous than Rio! Are you going alone?"

"Ilysa will meet me. She'll have CIA credentials, hail the taxi, pick the hotel, and taste the food so I won't get poisoned," replied Maria, smiling.

* * *

Maria was a beautiful and desirable woman, but the thought of intimacy never entered Dirk's mind. He did not allow himself consider it. Pussy and the bodyguard business were not compatible. He would get careless. He was to anticipate trouble and remain alert at all times. Maria was all business most of the time, but occasionally she would tease him like the guard outside Buckingham Palace. But he remained at attention and never looked down. *Cannons to the right. Cannons to the left. Ours is not to wonder why. Ours is but to do or die.*

* * *

There were no English speaking TV stations in Buenos Aires. Argentineans had not forgotten the Falkland's debacle. They were ruled by a military dictator, and all their cops were military police. Dirk read from a bulletin provided for American visitors and tourists by the local US Embassy located in the Palermo barrio near the Plaza Italia stop on the "D" subway. The locals were half Sicilian and half Spanish with a few Nazis and Jews scattered around.

US Embassy Bulletin for tourist.

Argentina is a geographically diverse country with mountains, forests, expansive deserts, and glaciers, making it a popular destination for outdoor and adventure sports. Despite the best efforts of local authorities, assisting visitors lost or injured in such remote areas can be problematic. American citizens have been killed in recent years while mountain climbing, skiing, trekking, and hunting.

TRAFFIC SAFETY AND ROAD CONDITIONS: Driving in Argentina is generally more dangerous than driving in the United States. By comparison, drivers in Argentina tend to be very aggressive, especially in the capital city of Buenos Aires, and frequently ignore traffic regulations. U.S. driver's licenses are valid in the capital and the province of Buenos Aires, but Argentine or international licenses are required to drive in the rest of the country.

CRIME: Few American citizens visit Argentina without incident. Street crime in the larger cities, especially greater Buenos Aires and Mendoza, is a problem for residents and visitors alike. Visitors to Buenos Aires and popular tourist destinations should be alert to muggers, pickpockets, scam artists and purse-snatchers on the street, in hotel lobbies, at bus and train stations, and in cruise ship ports. Criminals usually work in groups and travelers should assume they are armed. Criminals employ a variety of ruses to distract and victimize unsuspecting visitors.

A common scam is to spray mustard or a similar substance on the tourist from a distance. A pickpocket will then approach the tourist offering to help clean the stain, and while doing so, he or an accomplice robs the victim. Thieves regularly nab unattended purses, backpacks, laptops and luggage and criminals will often distract visitors for a few seconds to steal valuables. While most American victims are not physically injured when robbed, criminals typically do not hesitate to use force when they encounter resistance.

Your passport is a valuable document and should be guarded. Passports and other valuables should be locked in a hotel safe, and a photocopy of your passport should be carried for identification purposes. The U.S. Embassy has observed a notable rise in reports of stolen passports in the past year. Some travelers have received counterfeit currency in Argentina. Unscrupulous vendors and taxi drivers sometimes pretend to help tourists review their pesos, then trade bad bills for good ones. Characteristics of good currency can be reviewed at the Argentine Central Bank.

Along with conventional muggings, so-called express kidnappings continue to occur. Victims are grabbed off the street based on their appearance and vulnerability. They are made to withdraw as much money as possible from ATM machines, and then their family or co-workers are contacted and told to deliver all the cash that they have on hand or can gather in a couple of hours. Once the ransom is paid, the victim is usually quickly released unharmed. There have been some foreign victims, and visitors are particularly advised not to let children and adolescents travel alone.

Travelers worldwide are advised to avoid packing valuables in their checked baggage. In Argentina, officials have publicly acknowledged the systematic theft of valuables and money from checked baggage at Buenos Aires airports. Authorities are working to resolve the problem and have made a number of arrests, but travelers should exercise continued care and caution.

Counterfeit and pirated goods are widely available. Transactions involving such products may be illegal under local law. In addition, bringing them back to the United States may result in forfeitures and/or fines.

On a scale of 0-10, Dirk rated Buenos Aires a 5 compared with USA and Western Europe. After dark, it wasn't safe to get out of a well lighted public area. Argentina had an inflation and prices were about twice that of the USA.

Argentina's maintained boulevards were the widest in the world, maybe 10-12 lanes across. There were pedestrian islands halfway across. Florida Street was closed to traffic and covered with tile for six blocks. After dark, anything and everything could be bought.

Nobody knew how or where the Tango started, but it required a certain type of rhythm and music peculiar to Argentina where it originated. In the USA it was called a dance of passion, but in Argentina it was foreplay for sex.

*   *   *

The shower had stopped, and from sounds Dirk imagined Maria somewhere between drying and beautifying her face. He surfed the channels and found BBC. If he concentrated he could understand. The difference between the girls on British TV and American were teeth. The American female talking heads had sparkling perfect teeth and dimples. They got braces when they were young.

No Wolf Brister or Christiane Amanpour! Some English reporter was standing in front of the Sphinx near Cairo.

"Today, masked bandits in south Egypt kidnapped a camel caravan of European tourists from Holland, Belgium, Denmark, and Finland.

"Nobody was killed or injured. The tourist thought it a practical joke and went freely into the Sudanese Highlands north of Darfur where they are being held.

"29 hostages are held including camel drivers and tour guides. The kidnappers are demanding 30 million Franks (US $25 million) for their return unharmed."

Maria alarmed, opened the door abruptly in bathrobe and watched.

"Tourism minister ZaZa Renter said negotiations were underway by her company, Exotic Tours, but the kidnappers didn't have a negotiator that could speak Egyptian or English. She thought they were "freelance" amateurs and not militant terrorists. Militants usually came in with suicide bombers, grenades, and Ak-47's. They were most likely Sudanese nationals seeking relief for the starving in Darfur.

"Al Qaeda leader, al-Zawari, refused to take responsibility, said it wasn't religious zeal, and consider Sudanese nationals, Chad rebels, or Egyptian outlaws. It reminded him of Butch Cassidy and the Sundance Kid. He suggested they hire Pinkertons and use bloodhounds."

Maria pulled off her bathrobe, threw the towel on the floor, walked naked over to Dirk, and said, "Fuck me, Dirk."

Dirk didn't hesitate. He pulled Maria over his lap and began to spank her bare butt with his open palm. He didn't stop, because the harder he spanked the more she laughed. He tried to get his belt off while holding her with his left arm. He pulled out his belt, and she pulled down his pants. He pushed her down with his elbow.

*   *   *

Dirk caught his plane to Houston at 7 A.M. and would arrive in Houston 9 P.M. same day (Wednesday). There was a thirty minute stopover in Lima Peru. He bought a *USA Today*, put it in the pocket before him, pushed back, closed his eyes and went to sleep. He was on the window side, and a very attractive young woman of color about five nine and one hundred twenty pounds sat in the isle seat beside him. She was trim, slim, well mannered and smelled good.

"Would you like to buy me a drink?" She smiled and showed nice teeth.

"Yes ma'am, two or three if you like," replied Dirk. She had nice looking knees too.

"Are you going all the way?" she asked.

Dirk decided she liked to chat. It was okay, as long as he didn't have to talk too much. He'd like a nap. He put the little pillow against the seat and window, leaned into it, and closed his eyes. She reached over and got his *USA Today*. She studied every picture. The beverage cart rolled up. She ordered two bourbons on ice and waited on Dirk who handed the stewardess $US 10 and ordered coffee, black, no sugar. They pulled down their trays and the stewardess handed them their drinks.

"What do you do?" asked Dirk.

"Oh, I'm an entertainer. I have a job waiting in Houston, Texas. Are you flying to Houston?"

Dirk sipped his coffee. It was too hot. "May I have a piece of your ice?"

She started to pour in a piece of ice and hesitated. "Are you going to Houston?"

Dirk smiled and pressed his cheek against the pillow and closed his eyes. It was a six hour flight to Lima. She retrieved a business card from her pocketbook.

"Have you heard of the Blue Goose Nightclub?"

Dirk opened his eyes. It was Maria Tantalia's business card with Maria's signature on back. WOW! Dirk hadn't left Maria's side.

"Pardon me, may I ask where Maria gave you this card?"

"You may not. I always tell the truth, and nobody believes me. You'll call me a liar. What is your name?"

Dirk whipped out his billfold with PI license and badge. "My name is Derek. My friends call me Dirk."

"My name is Louiza Santos, and I am a female impersonator."

Louiza Santos returned Dirk's *USA Today*, so he opened it and began to scan at random. His eyes caught an article from AP.

SUDANESE BANDITS SEIZE EGYPTIAN CARAVAN. AP.

Yesterday, masked bandits, armed with handguns and riding French Jeeps, attacked a camel train of tourists in Southern Egypt near the borders of Sudan and Chad. The tourists were from European and Scandinavian countries and went willingly without resistance.

The number of tourists and identities have not been released by Christian Tours, Inc. according to ZaZa Reuter, Egyptian Tourism minister.

Molly Ecles, spokeswoman for Christian Tours, in Lakeland Florida, refused to release names or notify families. Christian Tours sold routine medical insurance. In twenty years, this was their first experience. It was her impression that the kidnappers made a mistake. "Ministers and wives don't have any money."

George W. Barclay Jr., M.D.
gwbarcl@sbcglobal.net
1/16/2011